Lucky 8

Other Books by Rae D. Magdon

Amendyr Series
The Second Sister - Book 1
Wolf's Eyes - Book 2
The Witch's Daughter - Book 3
Wolf Eyes – Book 4

Devil Wears Yellow Garters

Fur and Fangs

Lucky 7

Tengoku

And with Michelle Magly

All the Pretty Things

Dark Horizons Series
Dark Horizons – Book 1
Starless Night – Book 2
Eclipse – Book 3

Lucky 8

Rae D. Magdon

Desert Palm Press

Lucky 8
By Rae D. Magdon

ISBN (book): 9781954213098
ISBN (epub): 9781954213104
ISBN (pdf): 9781954213111

Desert Palm Press
1961 Main Street, Suite 220
Watsonville, California 95076
www.desertpalmpress.com

Editor: Cal Faolin; Kellie Doherty
Cover Design: Rachel George

Printed in the United States of America
First Edition March 2021

Acknowledgement

Special thanks to Cal, my editor, and Lee, my patient publisher. Also to Hazel, Kristen, Natalia, Rey, and Tory for their work as sensitivity readers and translators.

Dedication

This book is dedicated to everyone who deliberately chooses hope in the face of despair.

part one

Rae D. Magdon

Chapter 01

I STARE AT THE blinding billboards of SLKC, familiarity weighing heavily on my shoulders. The products featured in the ad rings surrounding the skylanes have changed over the past decade, but the lights look the same. Bright neon beams bounce off each other, merging into a muddy brown shadow. The Gateway Arch stands in the distance, a silver half-oval illuminated by constant ad cycles.

Below our shuttle, the nighttime crowd trickles along climate controlled walkways, following their tributaries like the sluggish waters of the Missouri. There are more walkways since my last visit, with new ones under construction. When I was growing up, they were a luxury. They're a necessity these days, thanks to rising temperatures and superstorms.

The Eagle soars high above the ground, but I don't need to hear the city to remember how it sounds. Beneath the roar of air traffic and the rumble of the transit tunnels is the persistent hum of the power grid. When older sections of the grid overload, everything pauses, eerily reminiscent of a stuttering heartbeat. Of course, that never happens at the poles, where we are now. The east and west business districts have backup generators for their backup generators.

"You good, Sasha?" A warm hand covers mine on the shared armrest. Elena glances at me from the seat to my left, her brown eyes worried. Usually, just looking at her makes me happier than I've been in a long time, but even that heart shaped face and those soft, full lips aren't enough to make me forget why I'm upset. Or maybe nervous is a better description. We're here to awaken a piece of my past that I would much rather keep dormant.

"I'm fine," I tell Elena. She's nosy, but even she must sense this isn't the time to pry.

"We've got bad memories buried here, me and Sasha," says Cherry, our wrench. Rami and Doc, our cloak and our medic, have occupied the forward facing pilot seats, leaving Cherry and me directly across from

1

each other in the back. Unfortunately, that makes ignoring her all the more difficult.

Rock, our grunt, is buckled in beside Cherry. He tilts his head, but as usual, the big guy doesn't say anything. Meanwhile, Cherry continues staring at me, her heavily made-up green eyes full of expectation beneath her bright red bangs.

I press my lips together, refusing to take the bait.

Elena speaks up, though, because of course she does. "This is where you and Sasha met. Right, Cherry?"

"*Claro, chaparrita*. After Sasha made her break from AukPrep. I'd already, uh, *left* KC-Tek a few months earlier."

I stifle a groan. I have no interest in rehashing that particular period of my life, but ordering Cherry to shut up will only stoke Elena's curiosity. She's seen flashes of the memories stored in my brainbox, but according to her, they're disparate fragments, more emotion than story. That's probably a good thing. The details even make me uncomfortable sometimes, and I'm the one who lived them.

Elena arches an eyebrow at Cherry. "*¿Qué pedo?*"

Cherry shrugs. "Why did I leave KC-Tek? There might've been a teensy explosion when I dropped out. Wasn't nearly as dramatic as Sasha's exit from boarding school, though."

"Drop it." I glare at Cherry and remove my hand from beneath Elena's. "That was over seventeen years ago."

Annoyance flickers in Elena's eyes, but behind that is a kicked puppy look she can't quite hide. Damn her for being cute. I reclaim her hand, squeezing to show I'm not pissed at her, just on edge.

"Rami, what's our ETA?" I ask, hoping to change the subject.

Rami peers around the edge of their seat to meet my eyes. They're dressed fairly femme today, with a hairless face and crisp, purple cat's eye liner. Their sleek black hair is pulled into a perfect French braid. "Impatient, are we? It'll be at least another five minutes, my lovelies."

They bring the Eagle out of the skylanes, merging into a ground level lane that runs alongside the walkways. Pedestrians scurry along like too many hamsters squished into a single tube, not bothering to glance up at passing traffic.

"Which entrance are we using, Boss Lady?" Rami asks.

So far, there are no signs that Axys Generations is following us, but it's in my nature to be cautious. Of all our boltholes around the globe, the ones in SLKC and Siberia are the ones we can least afford to reveal to the corps. Siberia is where our crewmate Val, the only fully realized artificial intelligence in existence, keeps her primary servers. SLKC houses Val's backup servers, as well as the person we've come to pick up.

"South entrance," I tell Rami. "Traffic's thinner there."

Rami changes course without further comment.

"I don't get why you're so freaked out," Doc says, craning her neck to look back at me from the copilot's chair. "It's just another mission, right?" Her blue eyes are worried behind her VIS-R, and I can tell she isn't ribbing me because she's thirteen, and that's what teenagers do. She's fishing for information. Trying to figure out whether I'm being cautious, or if I'm actually afraid.

I am afraid, but not of AxysGen. They aren't the first triple diamond corporation to try and kill me, and I'm still alive (in a sense). I'm afraid for more existential reasons. Afraid the person we're meeting won't be happy to see me. Afraid I won't be happy to see her either, even though coming here was my decision. I've been itching to do this since the worst of the heat from AxysGen died down. It's probably still too soon, but I've been gnawing on it like a dog with a bone. Both missing sleep and dreaming about it.

Doc watches me, probably waiting for some kind of reassurance. "SLKC wasn't always good to me," I offer, an admittedly pitiful response. "Just got some skeletons buried here, is all." Elena always says dragging words out of me is like pulling teeth, which is a pretty accurate description of my conversational skills.

"Back at it again with the cryptic shit, huh?" Doc flops back in her chair. "Don't worry. I'll break you eventually."

"Sure you will, kid."

The steady drum of rain fades as we pull through the mouth of a tunnel beneath the Gateway Arch. Traffic slows to a standstill. More ad projections flicker above us, casting a shifting pattern of light onto the checkpoint leading down to the tunnels. Walkways and skyways converge on the same spot, adding to the clog.

Except for corps executives, everyone uses the tunnels, cogs and undesirables alike. The top level is for private vehicles. Second level is a series of overcrowded trains nicknamed 'the web' because they resemble a sprawling spider web. Beneath the web is the power grid, but the public isn't allowed.

Of course, 'not allowed' doesn't mean uninhabited. Plenty of jobless people seek shelter in the grid's tunnels because they're climate controlled. Most corps provide their cogs shitty, one-room cubes to live in, but those are still better than the streets, as I know from personal experience. People without jobs usually don't have homes, forcing them to survive wherever and however they can.

As Rami brings the Eagle to an idle, Rock makes a concerned noise. He never speaks, but I can read his face, which looks a lot like his sister, Doc's. He's an eight-foot-tall cyborg and she's a skinny-ass teenager, but they have the same dirty blonde hair and sharp features. Rock knows I don't want to be here, so neither does he.

"I'm fine," I tell him, trying to convince myself too.

"Request for entry submitted," Val says through the Eagle's speakers. She's fully sentient, one of a kind, and the main reason Axys Generations has it in for us, although breaking into multiple secure facilities and blowing up their CEO's house probably didn't help. If any other corps knew our crew included the very first FRAI, they'd be gunning for us too. We barely managed to stop my ex-girlfriend, Megan, from unleashing a much more malevolent version with Val as the template.

"Thanks," I say. "You read my mind."

"My programming was partially modeled on your personality, Sasha. Currently, I can predict your desires with 96.3 percent accuracy."

Elena laughs. "You and I gotta talk more, girl."

"Your friendly overture is noted. My algorithms also tell me that during the past three months, your negative comments about fully realized artificial intelligences have decreased 62.7 percent. Your negative comments about me as an individual have decreased 96.5 percent. Your positive comments about me have increased—"

"Yeah," Elena grumbles. *"Somos camarades."*

We all go silent as our shuttle arrives at the gateway checkpoint, a circle of shining light waiting to approve our passage. The Eagle has a fake vehicle history tied to false credentials for this trip, but any checkpoint or scanner is an opportunity to get flagged. I hold my breath until the circle flashes from red to green.

"We may proceed," Val says.

Rami pulls forward, weaving to the right side of the tunnel where various exits branch off. Signstrips scroll around us, a distracting blend of directions and more advertisements. Paragon Solutions VIS-Rs. The latest Chevy-Ford Cougar, with all the bells and whistles. Sea Queen Yachts. I roll my eyes at that one. The coasts have encroached on the Midwest, but we're not *that* close to the ocean. I rub my face, but the neon lights still burn under my eyelids.

"ETA two minutes," Rami says. I open my eyes in time to see them activate the Eagle's cloak and fly straight through an unassuming billboard for NutraBrand flavor paste. Rami and Megan cooked up the camouflage together a few years back.

Megan. My stomach sinks. Memories of my ex crop up far more often than I'd like. She betrayed us to AxysGen and forced us to kill her and Dragon, the new FRAI she created when Val proved too willful. Even three months on, I still haven't worked through all my feelings of anger, guilt, and loss. In fact, I've been avoiding it as much as possible. Megan might have betrayed our crew, but that didn't mean I wanted to be the one to kill her.

Darkness closes in as we descend into the tunnels. The sounds of traffic fade and the power grid's hum swells around us. Above, the ceiling rattles and shakes. We're directly beneath the web, flying along a maintenance shaft. Soon, Rami brings the Eagle to a stop. The floor opens, and we touch down in our SLKC hideout's garage.

My hand twitches beneath Elena's and she grasps it tighter, offering silent reassurance. I squeeze back, then let go to unfasten my safety harness.

Val's avatar appears in the middle of the Eagle. She's dressed for business, wearing her preferred purple blouse and pencil skirt, her dark skin slightly translucent. "All external and internal defense grids are active. No unidentified organics detected."

I nod. That's something, at least.

The SLKC garage isn't as cold as the Hole in Siberia, but it isn't warm either. A shiver runs down my spine as I hop out the Eagle's rear doors, the soles of my boots hitting concrete. I'm glad we soundproofed the base. Otherwise, the goddamn hum would drive me crazy.

"What now?" Doc asks, exiting through the passenger's side door. "You wanna wake her up right away, or..."

I shoot Doc a warning look, and she averts her eyes.

"Shit, just asking."

It's a fair question. Part of me wants to get it over with. Needs to, before the anxiety of unfinished business eats me alive. But I'm also terrified. I've spent the last seventeen years running major ops from London to Taiwan, outsmarting the most dangerous corps crews and freelance mercs in the world. Died six times doing it. But in no way, shape, or form am I prepared for this.

Heavy footsteps approach as a broad chest in a faded green shirt takes up my entire field of vision. When I look up at Rock's face, I notice a wrinkle of concern on his blocky brow.

"I'm okay," I tell him, but my voice isn't convincing.

Rock opens his arms, and I step into them, resting my cheek against his shoulder. Despite his powerful muscles, he gives the gentlest hugs. We embrace for what, under other circumstances, might be an embarrassingly long time. Eventually, Rock lets me go and pats my head with his enormous hand. Only he can get away with doing that.

The others are waiting for the elevator on the other side of the garage, pretending they aren't watching. When we join them, I notice Elena failing to hide a grin. "Get over yourself," I grumble, but she smirks until the elevator arrives.

"Hey, I'm not judging you. It's cute. Even wolves need hugs."

I roll my eyes. "Can't we give the nickname a rest for one fucking day?" 'The Wolf' is actually a pretty cool nickname in my opinion, but I'd never admit it aloud. Bitching about it like the grumpy asshole I usually am is one of the ways I bond with my crew.

"Fine," Elena says. "But you'll have to extract separate promises from Cherry and Doc, and they'll be harder to convince. They love pushing your buttons."

Cherry winks. "Trust me, I'd push a lot more of *Jefa's* buttons if I could. But I'm married, and Rami's the jealous type."

Doc pulls a disgusted face while Rock offers Cherry a fist bump. Rami shakes their head in affectionate exasperation. Honestly, I have no idea how they deal with being married to a sex-obsessed pyromaniac, but I'm not one to talk, considering my past relationships.

I breathe a little easier in the relative safety of the bunker. It has a clean, sterile smell thanks to the air filters, but the old, ratty furniture throughout the living room and kitchen gives the space an aura of casual reassurance. Cherry flops on the couch, taking up all three cushions. Rami heads for the fridge, and Rock joins them, a silent shadow over twice their size.

"Gotta pee," Doc blurts out, rushing for the bathroom with an incredible lack of subtlety.

"Think they wanna give you privacy or something?" Elena mutters to me.

I glance at Cherry in time to catch her eyes darting away from mine. She and the rest of my team know me. If I ask them to come to the med bay with me, they'll be there in a heartbeat, but I don't want an audience for this. Managing my own emotions will be hard enough without worrying about theirs.

"Val? Come with me."

Val's avatar reappears beside me via one of the room's many mounted projectors. "Of course, Sasha."

The knot in my chest loosens. Maybe this won't be so bad? I have to admit, part of me is curious. At the very least, I'll get answers to the questions floating through my head. What will she be like, aside from the obvious? Will she learn to like, or maybe even love me? What if she wants nothing to do with me? I've run through countless scenarios, but I won't know until I take the plunge.

Before I leave the kitchen, Elena touches my arm. I hesitate, watching her lick her lips, obviously struggling to find the right words. Eventually, she says, "I'm glad you're you, *Jefecita.* Even if you're a pain in my ass. You know that, yeah?"

My smile is small but genuine. "I know."

Elena lets me go, and I head for the hallway with Val by my side.

The walk to the med bay is too short. Only five doors—bunk, bathroom, stockroom, armory, backup servers—and we're there. My finger slips as I punch in the access code. The door beeps a rejection, and I grit my teeth.

"This process may be difficult," Val says in a soothing voice. "If you need more time to mentally prepare, everyone will understand."

I look away, jaw working. "I had three months in Barbados."

"You are recovering from multiple physical and mental traumas. Compared to the average human lifespan, three months is a short time."

"My lifespans so far haven't exactly been average."

I punch in the code correctly this time. The doors hiss open. When I step inside, my eyes lock on the med bay's most prominent feature, an eight-foot tube full of blue liquid. Suspended within the tube is a body: tall, broad-shouldered, with smooth, unscarred brown skin. Her tight black curls cling to her head, and her eyes are closed.

"Sasha?"

Val's voice makes me realize I'm staring intently at the woman's face. She looks peaceful, like she's sleeping, despite the electrodes pasted onto her body. "She looks different than I expected."

"You are accustomed to seeing your own face in reverse. A mirror's reflection flips the image."

"No, I mean..." *I don't know what I mean.* There's a lump in my throat I can't swallow, and it feels almost like jealousy. The person in the tube can sleep without nightmares. She doesn't have a single bad memory in her head. Her entire existence is full of potential.

I take a page from Rami's book, going against my instincts and trying to put a positive spin on the situation. All that potential is exciting, in a way. My stomach flutters as I realize I'm about to witness the 'birth' of a brand new person. A person created with my DNA. A person who, if I have anything to say about it, will have a way better life than I did. A life with me and the family I built, if that's what she chooses.

I turn away from my eighth clone and give Val a nod.

"Wake her up."

Chapter 02

A HIGH-PITCHED WHIR comes from inside the tube. Bubbles stream through the viscous blue liquid, causing the electrode wires to sway. Despite the disturbance, the clone stays still. Only her eyes move, darting behind their closed lids.

I turn to Val. "What's happening?" I have vague recollections of my own awakening, but I've never observed the process before. Cloning is rare these days since the ultra-rich prefer to grow replacement organs *a la carte*. Only a few complete clones are grown as body doubles or corporate heirs.

"I am awakening her autonomic nervous system and downloading several educational programs," Val informs me. "In the interest of full disclosure, some of these programs were originally created by Axys Generations, and others by Megan."

I frown. When it comes to creating sentient beings who aren't terrifying forces of destruction, Megan only has a fifty percent success rate, Val herself being the success. Megan's other attempt, Dragon, almost killed us.

"You sure that's a good idea?"

"I have implemented numerous quality and safety modifications. Additionally, I have written several programs myself, designed to teach muscle coordination and speech, a basic overview of humanity's history, and the ability to empathize with other sentient beings."

"You can teach her empathy?"

"Since you strenuously objected to the installation of your own personal memories, as was the process in the past, I have created unique formative experiences for this purpose." Val offers the clone a look that's almost tender. "One of these involves a birthday party."

Jealousy eats at my stomach. *How come she gets to start off with good memories about birthday cake and toys?* My resentment feels almost childish, but there's nothing to do except bury those issues. This clone is my responsibility. I won't undo Val's hard work by fucking the clone up with my baggage on the first day of her life.

Inside the tube, the clone kicks her right foot.

"Testing muscle response via primary motor cortex stimulation," Val announces.

The clone moves her legs, followed by her arms and shoulders, as much as the person-sized tube will allow. Suddenly, her eyes snap open. I take an involuntary step back. The clone's irises are almost as black as her pupils, and even though they're identical to mine, something about them sends a chill straight through me.

Air hisses into the tube and fluid drains from the bottom. The clone's brown skin gleams, tinted blue by the glowing lights around her. Once her mouth is free, she takes her first breath. As her chest jerks outward, I flash back to the pain of my own awakenings. The forced expansion of my lungs burned like hell every time.

I don't realize I'm touching the tube's plexiglass until I feel its smooth surface beneath my palm. The gesture is instinctive. I want to be closer to this person who looks so much like me. To meet her. Jealousy aside, she was created with my DNA. That makes her family, in a weird way. Not the most important kind of family, the kind forged in the crucible of life, but family nonetheless. I don't like the idea of her experiencing pain.

The clone watches me with wide eyes. The fluid has drained to her chest, and she drags her hand through it. With some effort, she presses her palm against the glass, directly over mine.

"Can she hear me?" I wonder aloud. It took a while for my hearing to kick in during my awakenings.

"No," Val says. "The enclosure is soundproof."

I step closer and exhale against the glass. My breath makes a cloud of condensation, which I draw on with my fingertip: a circle, two eyes, and a mouth. A smiley face. The clone's lips spread in a matching smile. She wiggles her right hand. I wave back. It's like seeing a little kid wave at you on the street. Returning the gesture is just something you do.

The fluid finishes draining. More air whooshes through the tube, blowing across the clone's wet body, and the glass walls sink into the floor. The clone tries to step forward, but the tube hasn't finished lowering. Her shin bumps the edge of the glass and she falls.

I rush to catch her. She trips into my arms, clutching my shirt with damp hands until I help her straighten. "Careful."

"Ahnoo."

I glance at Val. "Uh...?"

"Give her a chance to practice. At the moment, her understanding of speech is only theoretical."

The clone's face screws up in concentration, and her lips move awkwardly. "Tank...eeou..."

"Welcome." I release her and open one of the supply cabinets, withdrawing a towel. "Here."

The clone reaches for the towel but misses by several inches. She pulls another face, then tries again, catching the towel and drying her head. As she wipes the remnants of fluid from her limbs, her movements become noticeably more confident. Apparently, a little practice goes a long way.

My smile becomes more genuine. It's kind of cute, like watching a toddler learn to walk, even if said 'toddler' is six feet tall and fully developed.

Once she's slightly less sticky, the clone tries to return the used towel, thrusting it toward me.

"Why don't you keep that 'til we get to the showers? You taught her how to do that, right Val?"

"She should be capable of maintaining personal hygiene without assistance. However—"

A loud, metallic crash fills the medbay, causing my adrenaline mods to kick in. I take a deep breath and relax when I see that the clone has only knocked over one of the IV poles next to Doc's exam table. She steps back, holding her hands up with a sheepish grin. "Sorry!" she says, dropping the towel onto the floor.

"However," Val continues, with a hint of dryness, "there will be a learning curve."

I straighten the IV pole and retrieve the towel. "Wait, Val, did you give her a name?"

"Currently, she is nameless."

Fuck. That's a problem. While I do feel a sense of obligation and protectiveness toward this new person, naming her will make me feel like her parent. That's a scary thought, although not entirely inaccurate. I woke my clone intending for her to be her own person. I'll guide her until she can start making decisions for herself, but this ends the cycle of downloading myself into a new body every time I die. Megan encouraged that cycle for her own selfish reasons, and it's one I refuse to continue. Even with a new body waiting for me, dying is traumatic, let alone dying six separate times while remembering every detail.

I help the clone wrap the towel around her body again. "She needs a name, and she can't have mine."

"Hi, Sasha," the clone says, forming the words slowly.

"You know who I am already?"

"She knows the names of the Lucky Seven," Val says. "In addition to a few basic facts about your personal histories."

"How basic?" It's bad enough that Elena got to see a montage of my entire messy life via my brainbox. I don't need this clone knowing everything there is to know about me, too. She's already got my DNA. I don't want her to have my memories.

"Birthplaces, technical specialties, combat abilities. A few trivial facts such as favorite foods."

That doesn't sound so bad. Certainly not the invasion of privacy I was initially worried about. "Okay." I focus on the clone. "You can pick your name later. First, you should shower. You're kind of gross."

The med bay doors whoosh open. Doc enters, her body language all business. For someone so young and short, she projects an undeniably commanding presence as she strides to the exam table. "Hold it. She can shower after I run my tests."

I arch an eyebrow. "How long have you been waiting outside?"

"Long enough for you to have your moment of angst or whatever." Doc lowers her VIS-R from atop her messy blonde hair to her nose, scanning the clone with intense interest. "What's up, Sasha Eight? How you feeling?"

The clone tilts her head, studying Doc with unabashed curiosity. "Cold. Wet. Fast heart. Sasha Eight?"

I glare at Doc. "Don't call her that."

"Then what should I call her?"

"Whatever you want, except Sasha. She can pick a name later."

Doc shrugs. "Fine. You, Not-Sasha, get on the exam table."

"Seriously?" I grumble. "That still has 'Sasha' in it."

"You want me to stop, give me an alternative. Now, you. Table."

The clone looks confused, but when Doc points, she hops onto the exam table. Much to my relief, she doesn't end up falling and hurting herself. Once she's situated, Doc bustles about, scanning the clone with her VIS-R, checking vitals, and muttering.

"Organic parts are functioning. Let's check the mods. Not-Sasha, activate your eye mods."

The clone blinks. Her eyes glow yellow.

"Adrenaline boosters."

The clone's breathing speeds up. Although I don't see any other visible reactions, I know what that mod feels like. Her lungs are opening, her muscles are tingling, and her heart has started pounding twice as fast.

Doc removes a handlebar-shaped grip from a drawer underneath the table and gives it to the clone. "Squeeze as hard as you can." The clone squeezes. The grip beeps loudly. "Strength mods are working."

The clone looks to me as if searching for a reaction. Approval maybe? I smile. "Good job."

The clone returns the smile brilliantly, and I have to look away. I'm feeling more like a parent by the moment, and a very emotionally unprepared one. I've always thought of myself as something like a parent to Doc what with the age difference, but raising my own clone feels different. Weird. Maybe I should think of the clone more like a younger sibling. That type of relationship has less of an inherent power dynamic.

"One last thing." Doc pulls out a tray of surgical instruments from the side of the exam table. "Sit up straight and hold still. I'm gonna implant your jack." She pops the cap off a tube of anesthetic cream and smears it behind the clone's left ear, then picks up a black instrument that looks like a slim staple gun. "This'll only take a second and it won't hurt. I numbed you."

"Okay," the clone whispers. She stares at me with wide eyes, and I realize she's scared. I wonder if Val gave her some painful formative memories after all. It would have been cruel to deprive her of all physical and emotional pain before dropping her into the world which is full of both.

I take the clone's hand in mine. "Go ahead, Doc."

Doc pulls the trigger on the jack installer. There's a hissing pop, and when Doc withdraws, a small port gleams behind the clone's left ear. "There. Told you it wouldn't hurt."

The clone heaves a sigh of relief but doesn't let go of my hand. That confirms it in my mind. Val definitely gave her a small taste of pain, or she wouldn't have been afraid of the jack implant, or relieved afterward.

"Did you give her Dendryte Bronze?" I ask Doc.

"Silver, actually," Doc says. "Which reminds me, we need to upgrade your jack."

Ugh. Last thing I need is my clone being more cutting-edge than me. Jacks are important to the job, although not everyone uses them.

Those who don't want or can't afford a direct connection to their brain rely on VIS-Rs instead, but in our line of work, every millisecond matters.

"I know, I know. Elena hasn't shut up about it since you upgraded her to Platinum. One nag on this crew is enough." I disentangle my hand from the clone's grip. "If Doc's done, let's clean you up and get you some clothes."

"She can use the emergency shower." Doc jabs her thumb over her shoulder toward a basic shower stall tucked in the corner of the med bay.

"That would be prudent," Val says. "The clear walls will allow you to observe her."

Doc wrinkles her nose. "Why do we need to observe her? You downloaded the coordination training programs, right?"

The clone hops down from the exam table...clumsily. She stumbles, her towel coming loose again.

I snort. "That's theory. This is practice."

"You okay?" Doc asks the clone, stepping over to steady her by the elbow.

The clone nods and smiles. "Yeah."

My stomach gives a guilty churn. I should've been the one to steady her. *I'm usually better than this. What happened to those protective family instincts?* "She'll be okay, right, Val?"

"Yes. You were given the opportunity to process significantly more cognitive material before your own activation," Val says. "The prior Sashas' memories stored on your brainbox translated directly into lived experience. This new clone is still learning, albeit at an enhanced rate. Currently, her rate of absorption and retention is equivalent to that of a two-year-old, although her cognitive abilities have already surpassed that age range."

The clone regains her footing, removing her elbow from Doc's hold. "I can shower by myself," she says, like she's annoyed we would question her abilities. Doc and I watch carefully, ready to intervene, but she makes it to the shower without incident. She manages to open the stall, turn on the water, and test its temperature with her hand before stepping under the flow.

"See?" Doc says, giving my hip a nudge with her elbow. "She's already doing stuff. Soon, she'll be one of us."

One of us. I stare at my boots. That's exactly what I intended when I woke her up, but it's also terrifying. The biggest reason is selfish and illogical, but no matter how hard I try, I can't dismiss it. *She's me without the damage. What if that makes her better than me? What if my crew ends up loving her more?*

I shake it off by remembering Elena's words. *'I'm glad you're you,* Jefecita. *Even if you're a pain in my ass.'* I have to believe she means it, and the rest of my family feels the same.

Rae D. Magdon

Chapter 03

ONCE THE CLONE IS clean and dry, she has a much better handle on her coordination. Her speech, too. By the time she's ready to leave the med bay, she's become a regular chatterbox. "Where are the others?" she asks while I pull a white tank over her outstretched arms.

I frown. "Others?"

She pokes her head out through the top. "Elena. Cherry. Rami. Rock."

"Stuffing themselves in the kitchen," Doc says. She's perched on the edge of the exam table, feet swinging through the air as she observes us without offering to help. Now that the clone has passed her tests, Doc's professional attitude has softened a bit.

The clone's face lights up. "Food? What kind?"

"It's a surprise," Doc says. "Wanna try some?"

"Yes!"

The clone's enthusiasm is kind of adorable, but also a punch to the gut. I can't remember the last time something as simple as food got me so damn excited. I'm not sure I ever beamed the way she's doing, with a smile that stretches from ear to ear.

Stop being a baby. Maybe you should take a fucking lesson on appreciating the small things instead of being so goddamn depressed. I force myself to return the clone's smile. "If Doc and Val say you're good to go, we'll get you something to eat."

"Cloney here's in great physical condition," Doc says.

I wince. That nickname better not stick.

"I agree with Doc's assessment," Val adds. "I also recommend extended periods of social interaction to encourage healthy psychological development."

"Got it. Keep her company." With one last look at the clone, who appears positively delighted, I open the med bay door.

I'm not at all surprised to find Elena waiting outside. Judging by her startled expression, she was eavesdropping from the hall. *"¿Qué onda, Jefecita?"* It's painfully awkward, the way she tries to resist peering past me into the room.

"Just get it all out now," I mumble, stepping aside.

Elena's eyes get huge when she sees the clone. "Holy fuck, she looks exactly like you."

"No shit, Nevares. You know what a clone is, right?"

The clone's greeting is much friendlier than mine. "Hi, Elena!" she says, far too loudly. Seems she hasn't gotten the hang of modulating her volume yet.

Elena looks even more surprised. "You know my name already?"

Val's avatar materializes in the hallway. "As I have already explained to Sasha, I provided the clone with basic information about the members of the Lucky Seven."

"Then it's time for some official introductions." Elena takes my hand in hers, a gesture I appreciate despite my grumpiness. "Come on. The crew has a surprise for Ocho in the kitchen."

"Ocho?" I ask.

"We had to call her something. I know you don't want us calling her Sasha."

"Isn't Ocho kind of on the nose, though?"

Elena smirks. "Not everything's about you, *Jefecita*. We were thinking Ocho because she's the eighth member of the fam."

I consider it. 'Ocho' is still a number, but it's better than a number with my name tacked in front. There's some shallow justification besides her being the eighth clone. Plus, if she doesn't like it, she can change it. "Guess it's up to you," I tell the clone.

"Oh-cho," she says, testing the name out. "Ocho. Ocho... Okay!"

Elena shoots her a wink. "Come on, Ocho. Your surprise awaits."

Ocho's surprise turns out to be a steak dinner, with a mushroom steak and lentils for Rami. The table's set, and the rest of the crew is waiting with big smiles. My mouth waters as the smell wafts toward me. This might be Ocho's party, but I'll never turn down steak.

Rami gets up from their chair, coming over to give Ocho a hug. "Hey there. Welcome to the world."

Ocho freezes, as though she's too overwhelmed to respond. Then her brain seems to kick in. Her eyes light up and she squeezes Rami extra tight. "Hi!"

Rami coughs, allowing the embrace for a bit before wiggling free to catch their breath. "Whoa. Those strength mods are definitely working, huh?"

Ocho looks at Cherry and Rock, who are waiting their turn to say hello. Cherry offers Ocho a fist bump, which she hits on the second try. Rock picks her up, spinning her around several times before setting her gently on her feet.

"Hi, Cherry! Hi, Rock!"

I heave a sigh. Ocho's enthusiasm already has me exhausted, and she's been conscious less than an hour.

"What's up?" Cherry leans in to kiss both her cheeks. "We're going with Ocho, right?" She leans back, looking Ocho up and down before her eyes flick toward me. Apparently, everyone needs to play spot the difference. I resign myself to the fact that this is how it'll be for a while.

"Yeah," Elena says.

Doc groans with impatience, hopping into one of the empty chairs. "C'mon, I'm starving."

I realize I'm starving, too. I grab one of the free chairs, while Ocho and Elena do the same on either side of me. My eyes widen as I examine my plate. "Holy shit. Is this actual cow?"

Val examines the food with an unwavering stare that tells me she's scanning it. "Yes."

"That isn't a problem, right?" Rami asks, reclaiming their seat. "I thought you were practically an obligate carnivore."

"If it is a problem," Cherry adds, "we can always throw a cricket burger on for you."

I roll my eyes. Cricket protein powder is healthy and all, but I grew up in SLKC, right in the middle of cow country. Even a poor kid like me got to try cow once or twice, though usually in stolen scraps from restaurant trash cans. You can fake decent burgers with bugs, or even lab-grown beef, but I've never tasted an imitation steak that passed muster.

"Fuck you, Cherry."

"Believe me, I've thought about it," Cherry says with an exaggerated pout. "But my heart belongs to another, and they say my hoeing days are done. You'll have to settle for *chapparita*."

I grab my knife and fork, practically drooling. "For now, I'm good with this steak."

Elena scoffs. "You'll regret saying that later."

'Oohs' echo around the table. Even Rock lets out a rumbling chuckle.

"Forgive them," Rami tells Ocho. "They act like children sometimes."

Ocho tilts her head, her smile turning inquisitive while Doc makes a gagging noise. "I'm the resident child here, and you're ruining my innocence."

"Ocho might not be a kid, technically speaking, but if anyone has innocence that needs ruining…" Cherry stands up, heading for the liquor cabinet where I keep the good stuff. She selects a bottle of peach schnapps, holding it by the neck and wagging it back and forth.

I grin through my confusing mix of emotions. Fear, uncertainty, even some excitement. Leave it to Cherry to come up with a good idea. A little alcohol will probably help me cope with all this, even though it isn't the best stuff we have. "Some for me too, Cherry. Thanks."

"You got it, *Jefa*. Drinks all around!"

Cherry grabs some more bottles—vodka, lime, and cranberry juice, which tells me exactly what she's making—then lines up five glasses from a nearby cabinet. After shaking it all together, she brings the end result to the table in a skillful balancing act.

"Here we go, everyone. My patented Smooth, uh…" She gives Doc a sidelong look. "… Kitten."

Doc blows her stringy blonde hair away from her forehead. "Seriously, Cherry?"

Ocho beams. "I love kittens! I've never met one, but I know I love them from the sims."

"Of course you do," Rami says, patting her on the shoulder. "We'll show you a kitten sometime soon."

"She could be allergic," I point out. "I am."

Rami just clicks their tongue. "And has that ever stopped you from petting a cat before, sweetie?"

The answer, of course, is no. Even I can't resist the temptation of cats.

"That is not how allergies work," Val adds. "While genetics contribute to the development of immunosensitivities, environmental factors also play a significant role."

Cherry waves her hand. "Val, I love you, but we're doing shots, not a science lesson. I propose a toast: to Ocho! Welcome to the world, *gatita*. Be curious about everything and get into as much trouble as possible."

"Please," Rami says. "Don't do the trouble part."

"And," Cherry continues. "To our fearless leader! Sasha, we love you. We wouldn't be us without you."

I look at Ocho. She's smiling at me so sincerely that the knot in my chest loosens. It unravels even more when a warm hand touches my knee. Elena smushes her cheek against the side of my arm, and her warm breath washes across my shoulder.

I lift my glass. "Hear, hear. Drink up, so I can dig into this steak."

We clink glasses in the middle of the table, Rami and Doc with their water, Val with a glass made of projected light, which clips partway through Rock's. I throw my drink back, savoring the burn. Cherry's Smooth Pussy has more of a kick than I expected.

Beside me, Ocho wheezes. She's managed to down her drink, but her eyes are bugging out of her head, and she can't catch her breath. I pat her on the back while Rami holds a glass of water to her lips. "Are you all right?" they ask, full of concern.

Ocho gives us both a look of utter betrayal. "Why would you drink that?"

Cherry bursts out laughing. "You'll figure it out in about thirty seconds."

"I'll finish it," Doc offers, craning her neck hopefully.

Elena takes Ocho's glass and gulps the rest. "Not a chance, *chiquita.* I know you've got brain cells to spare, but you're sticking to water." She rests her head on my shoulder again, squirming close and stretching so her lips can reach my ear. *"Puedes probar una pussy más dulce luego."*

The words send a stab of want straight between my legs. I glance around the table, and from the sparkle in Cherry's eye, I can tell she's overheard.

"I thought Sasha was in the doghouse for prioritizing that steak over you?"

Torn between two primal desires, one of which is conveniently right in front of me, I grab my knife and fork. I have to restrain myself from swallowing the first chunk too fast. A moan escapes my mouth before I can stop it.

"Yeah, well," Elena says. "You better show that same enthusiasm later."

I slide my left hand over to squeeze her thigh. Later, I'll thank her for how supportive she's been lately. Fuck knows I'm not always easy to deal with, especially recently.

For now, though, things are all right. Ocho seems to be enjoying her steak (although I wish she'd chew with her mouth closed). My crew is happy. We aren't in any immediate danger. *Maybe things will be okay after all.*

Chapter 04

THERE ARE ONLY FOUR beds in the bunk room, two of which are shared, so we grab a cot from the med bay for Ocho. She doesn't seem displeased. In fact, she flops down before we put the sheets and pillows on. She grins, and once more I'm startled by the sight of my own face staring at me. A reflection of myself without the scars, wrinkles, and worry lines.

"I've never slept before," Ocho informs me. "Not for real."

I know what she means. Real sleep is different than what happens in the tube, although I can't articulate how. I suppose I retained some muted awareness from before my activation because there's a flicker of memory buried in my mind, a quiet, muffled blue world pressing in on all sides.

"Oh, you'll *love* sleep," Cherry says, already sprawled across the bunk she shares with Rami. "It's the fucking best. Besides sex, of course."

"Cherry, behave." Rami enters, wrapped in a purple bathrobe and wearing some kind of yellow goop on their face.

Ocho gives a startled gasp. "Rami, what's that?"

"Don't worry," Rami says. "This doesn't hurt or anything. Gotta keep up with my beauty routine."

Ocho nods, though obviously still wary. Rami curls on the bunk, wiggling partway into Cherry's lap and staring up at her with a pout. "It doesn't seem fair, letting Ocho sleep on a cot her first night. Maybe we should let her have our bed?"

Cherry glances at the cot, then Rami. "The two of us barely fit in this bunk together. We won't fit on a cot."

"I don't mind being down here," Ocho says. "It's like camping."

"You've never been camping," Doc says, stepping into the room as well. Her blonde hair is wet from the shower, and she's wearing an oversized tee shirt that makes her thin frame look even frailer than usual.

"I have," Ocho says. "Well, my brain's been camping."

Doc snorts. "Your virtual childhood sounds better than my real one."

"News flash, *pequeña*. You're still *in* your childhood." Elena strides through the door and grabs my elbow, all business. "Sasha, come with me for a sec."

I study Elena, but her face is unreadable. If anything, she seems mildly annoyed. There's no telling what she wants. "You good?" I ask Ocho, who's buried herself in a blanket burrito.

"I hope I'm good," Ocho says.

"No, I mean, is it cool if I leave for a bit?" I don't want to assume, since I'm the first person Ocho bonded with outside the tube.

Ocho's brows knit with worry, or maybe mild disappointment. "You'll come back, right?"

"Right. I'm not leaving the base, just the room."

"We'll stay with you, *gatita*," Cherry says. "You won't be alone."

"Thanks," Ocho says, her smile returning.

Rami drapes the rest of the way across Cherry's lap and makes a shooing motion with their hand. "Go on. Be back by ten, kids."

I roll my eyes as I leave the room, Elena beside me. We walk down the hall, past the showers and armory, stopping short of the med bay and Val's server room. Instead, Elena opens the door to the nearby storage room.

As we enter, the overhead lights switch on, illuminating basic metal shelving and some unopened supply crates. "Do all your bases have the same layout as the Hole?" Elena asks, hopping up on one of them. Her feet don't touch the floor, and they swing like Doc's did while sitting on the exam table. It's kind of funny that her nickname for Doc is *pequeña,* because Elena's only a hair taller, despite being fifteen years older.

"Most of 'em are similar."

"Yeah. Similarly boring."

"If it works, it works." I close the door behind us. "So, what?"

Elena's expression softens. "Don't 'what' me. I try to check up on you, and you gotta be all rude. You know you don't have to put on the boss act with me." There's no sharpness in Elena's voice, though. Only gentle concern. She's clearly teasing.

"Sorry. It's been a day."

"I bet." Elena's brown eyes shine with sympathy, and my heart clenches. Sometimes she looks at me with such kindness that it makes the hairs on my arms rise. It's an unfamiliar feeling, but not unpleasant. Megan never worried about me this way. Worried about whether I'd do what she wanted, maybe. Earlier, more naive versions of me hadn't been able to tell the difference.

"I'm okay," I tell her. "It's weird, seeing my face on what's basically a human puppy dog."

Elena snorts.

"I just mean, she's all sweet and innocent and shit. Like a kid. It kind of freaks me out."

"Just freaks you out?"

"Okay," I grumble. "It makes me feel like a bitter, cynical asshole. You don't have to tell me resenting my own clone is a bad look."

Elena's eyes travel up and down my body. *"Jefecita,* nothing's a bad look on you. But don't beat yourself up. Ocho isn't perceptive enough to notice."

"Maybe not yet, but what about later? Shit, is this what being a parent is like? Not wanting to fuck someone else up with your own issues?"

"Wouldn't know," Elena says.

"Sure you would. You basically raised your brothers."

Elena wrinkles her nose. "Yeah. *Dios mio,* there were so many times I hated myself for making jacking seem all glamorous. I told Jacobo not to get involved and then he went and did it anyway. At least they're safe with Abuela in Barbados."

"Yeah. That must be a weight off your shoulders. So, what should I do about Ocho?"

Elena takes my hand, lacing her fingers with mine. Some of my worries subside as she rubs her thumb in circles against my palm. "You might act tough, but you don't have it in you to hate someone who hasn't done anything wrong. Not long term, anyway."

I look up from our joined hands and crack a smile. "Really, Nevares? You've been testing that theory since we met."

"You're so full of shit." She brings my hand to her lips, kissing my knuckles. Her mouth is warm and soft, and I feel a tug of want deep in my belly. "Anyway, what I'm trying to say is, you also care a whole damn lot. Ocho will pick up on that." She releases my hand, but I find that I miss the contact. "From personal experience, that's what kids need most. Someone who gives a shit. Someone who wants them to be safe and happy."

Elena's reassurances make me feel a lot better. My confidence begins to grow. "By that standard, I'm already a great sister slash parent slash DNA donor. I'm just scared I'll fuck her up."

"Oh, you will. There's no way to avoid fucking up. But that doesn't mean Ocho won't have a good life. If you didn't think so, you'd have left her in the tube."

I shrug helplessly. "Don't tell anyone, but very, very, *very* deep down, I'm an optimist. Trust me, I've tried not to be. No matter what happens to me, it doesn't stick."

"Are you saying the badass bitch routine is just for show? Because I already knew that." Elena leans in close enough for me to pick up the scent of her perfume. It smells like the island flowers of Barbados, where she bought it. Fuck, I wish we were still there, sunning ourselves and doing whatever we wanted—especially each other.

I close my eyes, trying to recapture some of the memory, but it slips away like ocean mist. Even though I was there just yesterday, paradise seems so far away.

"Hey." Elena nudges my arm with her elbow. "This is the part where you tell me *I'm* full of shit, and then we make out. You remember how this goes, right?"

"Right." I know Elena's trying to comfort me, but a distraction seems more my speed. I lean down, looming over her, taking some pride in the visible shiver that courses through her body. "Could we skip right to making out?"

"Whatever you say, *Jefecita*." Elena rises onto her knees, which brings her face slightly above mine. It's odd, because I'm used to being a head taller, but not unwelcome, especially when she cups my face and kisses me.

It isn't a sweet, reassuring kiss. Elena knows exactly what I need, and she's more than happy to provide. Her tongue sweeps against my lips and I open, reaching around to grab her rear. Elena's got ass for days. Even with clothes on, it's like squeezing a piece of heaven in both hands.

Elena moans into my mouth. Her breath washes hot against my face and she nips my bottom lip, tugging it between her teeth. She runs her hands along my arms, finding a grip on my shoulders. It feels good. Being someone else's support fools me into believing I'm sturdy enough to handle anything.

"*Cómo lo quieres?*" she mumbles beside my ear. "Right here, or should we grab your cock?"

The suggestion sends a bolt of pleasure straight through me. It'd be nice to get my cock, but it's with the rest of my stuff in the bunk, and that means we'd have to face the others again, including Ocho. That's definitely a subject I don't want to get into with my newly awakened clone.

"Here. Now." I tighten my grip on Elena's ass, lifting her off the crate and guiding her legs around my waist. She hooks them over my hips, clinging to my shoulders. One of her hands caresses my scalp, dragging her nails lightly between my braids.

She tastes amazing. Feels amazing. I pin her against the wall, using my weight to keep her there. Her breasts press into mine, and the shape of her lights a fire in me. We have our differences but fuck if we don't fit together just right.

"Sasha?"

It takes me a moment to realize the voice saying my name isn't Elena's. She's still drinking from my lips, and the sound is closer to the door. I tear myself away. Val's avatar stands just inside the storage room, wearing an apologetic expression.

The interruption is like a splash of cold water to the face. "Val? What the hell!"

"My apologies, but—"

"No mames," Elena orders, nuzzling at the place where my jaw meets my throat. *"Andele fuera de aquí."* I'm surprised she's that polite, considering the circumstances.

"Sasha, please. You have received an urgent video message."

Slowly, I lower Elena to the floor. She finds her footing and I step back. "From who?"

"It would be better to show you." Val gestures with her hand, and a screen of projected light appears beside her. A white man in a business suit sits at a desk, his brown hair expertly coiffed, his smile too straight and bright to be natural.

Elena's eyes widen. *"Chingada madre. No puedo creerlo."*

I can't believe it either. I recognize the man, and so would most other people on the planet. He's Ford Andrews, industrialist, 'philanthropist,' and CEO of Axys Generations' main corps rival, Paragon Solutions. PGS specializes more in hardware than software, but they've earned the coveted Triple Diamond status, which grants them a place on the corporate board that governs most national and international laws.

"Hello, Ms. Young," he says, staring straight at me like some kind of creepy advertisement. *"We aren't formally acquainted, but I believe you know who I am. And I know who you are."*

I glance at Elena, who looks as shocked as me. She shrugs helplessly, a 'what the fuck' gesture if I ever saw one.

Andrews continues. *"We have a mutual enemy, an enemy I'm willing to pay you a significant sum to steal from."*

Val pauses the message. "I believe he is referring to Axys Generations. More specifically, CEO Veronica Cross."

"No shit," Elena says. "My most lucrative contracts before I joined the Lucky Seven were from PGS. In fact, that's why I started fucking around with AxysGen's security code to create my special scripts. Helped me get through some of those jobs."

A few years ago, I would have taken an op like this in a heartbeat. But right now, I have all the credits we need, and I don't have to rely on corps money to take care of myself and my own. Besides, everything about this is off. It's got *trap* written all over it.

"Delete it," I tell Val. "Don't even reply. Elena, I want you and Rami to figure out how he contacted us in the first place. Hopefully, he only knows our terminal's IP address and not our actual location." But my stomach clenches. Over the years, I've learned to expect the worst-case scenario.

"I *highly* recommend listening to the rest." Val doesn't stress her words often, and the way she does this time alarms me. There's something more, something she's not saying. I sigh and wave my hand, and Val plays the recording.

"If credits aren't enough to tempt you, I also have information you might find interesting. Information about Darius and Kiara Young. I have it on good authority that their deaths weren't due to workplace negligence."

My throat closes up, and the beating of my heart swells into a terrified drum. Darius and Kiara Young were my parents.

Chapter 05

PAIN WELLS INSIDE ME as Andrews says my parents' names. They've been dead for over two decades, but that kind of loss never really heals.

Numbly, I listen to the end of the message. *"Please contact me at your earliest convenience, and we can discuss the details. I guarantee this isn't an opportunity you want to pass up."* The picture freezes, Andrews' smile hanging in the air until Val dismisses the projection with a wave.

Elena rests a hand on my arm. "You okay?"

In no way am I okay. PGS found a way to contact us at our most secret of secret hideouts. Not only do they claim to know what happened to my parents, they know I care about the answer. Those aren't the kind of intimate details I want a corps to possess. I'm back on the grid, and PGS has leverage against me.

It doesn't have to be leverage, the logical part of my brain says. *Have Elena and Rami figure out how Andrews found our terminal address. If they know our physical location as well, make a plan to disappear.* But the thoughts running through my head don't make it to my heart. I can't handle not knowing.

One day, my parents didn't come home from work. Instead, uniformed security officers barged into our apartment and told me they were killed in an accident. They took me away from the only home I'd ever known. Threw me in an 'educational center' that was more like a child labor camp, manufacturing clothes until I took my mandatory APS test, and someone somewhere decided I might be more useful to the corporate machine at one of their private schools.

I've looked into the situation many times, always finding dead ends. Corps keep detailed records on their cogs, mostly to calculate how indebted they are to their employers, but I've never found much information on my parents. That was always suspicious on its own, but Andrews has confirmed what I've long suspected, that maybe there's more to it. If my parents didn't die in a workplace accident, then how?

"Val, how did Andrews contact us?" I ask.

"The message was sent directly to this location's main terminal. I am unsure how he acquired the IP address."

"Could he know where we are?"

"Even if he has our terminal's address, its data streams are highly encrypted. I route them through multiple proxy servers which change four times per second." Val's brow furrows. "However, he may simply know our terminal number."

There's a heavy pause.

"Okay, I'm just gonna say it," Elena says. "This has Megan written all over it. Could she have told Cross about our SLKC base before she died, and could Andrews have gotten that info from AxysGen?"

"Doubt it," I say. "Megan was way too paranoid to give up stuff like that. Plus, AxysGen and PGS are competitors."

Elena scoffs. "CEOs make deals all the time, even with direct competitors. Who else would've told him? Or maybe Cross didn't give it to him willingly. Maybe he stole or paid for the information. Either way, it stinks."

I press my lips together. There's only one way to put these questions to rest. "Val, return the call."

"What the fuck?" Elena blurts out. She stares at me, wide eyed. "No, Sasha."

I stare right back. "If PGS had information on your brothers, wouldn't you want to know?"

"My brothers are alive. Your parents are dead."

Elena's right. I *know* she's right, but a righteous flame burns in my belly anyway. "If Andrews knows what happened to them, I deserve the truth."

"Then what? Kill whoever's responsible?"

"Exactly." I swallow hard, the weight of that statement settling over me. "I'm their only child. If I don't avenge them, no one will."

Elena reaches out as if to touch my arm again, but something stops her. Her hand falls to her side. "That won't bring them back." Raw sadness shines in her gaze, the kind that comes from experience, and I remember that her parents are gone, too.

Deep in my gut, I know Elena's right, but that doesn't calm me down. "You don't think I can handle this."

"You shouldn't *have* to handle this. Give me and Val a chance to make sure it's safe to leave the base, and we'll go back to Barbados. We were happy there, right? Leave the past in the past."

Elena's pleading cracks my resolve, but the foundation holds firm. There's no way I'll ever be happy carrying around so many unanswered questions. "If something happened to my parents, I have to know."

Elena shoves a hand through her hair in frustration. "You're gonna trust a corps exec's word that he *might* know something about your parents? They lie ten times a day before breakfast."

I clench my fists, staring down my nose at her. "Don't tell me what to do." It's a childish, petty response. Not the kind of thing a handler says to a crewmember, let alone a lover, but childish and petty is exactly how I feel.

"Fuck you." Elena heads for the door, stepping right through Val and storming out into the hallway. "Come talk to me when you've found your brain. You might wanna check your ass." She stalks off, muttering until the doors close behind her.

Once Elena is gone, I slump onto the crate she'd been sitting on, burying my face in my hands.

"Sasha?" Val's avatar approaches beside me. "Is there anything I can do?"

I don't look at her. I'm not sure how to answer.

"If it is any comfort, I am eighty-seven-point-five percent certain that Elena did not intend to be so harsh. She is simply concerned for your safety."

I raise my head, forcing a bitter laugh. "Only eighty-seven-point-five percent?"

"My estimate is based on data gleaned from previously observed social interactions."

"Yeah? What do you estimate my chances are of convincing her to come along for the ride this time?"

"I cannot say with any certainty."

"That bad, huh?"

A hole opens in the pit of my stomach. Even though Elena's the newest member of my crew, I don't like the thought of running ops without her. Especially an op with so many unknowns involved. She's right about one thing, though. I need to get a grip. I can't do anything while I'm this emotional, let alone contact Andrews.

"I'm going to the garage," I say, hopping off the crate. "Keep an eye on everyone, would you?"

"Of course, Sasha. I will alert you if anything changes."

I leave the storage room, relieved to find the hall empty. Water hisses in the bathroom, so Elena must be in the shower for some privacy. Normally I'd join her, but I'm way too raw, and I doubt she'd be happy to see me. I cross the living room and kitchen, stepping onto the elevator and going up to the garage.

The hum of the power grid hits my ears as soon as I arrive. It's faint, but present enough to put me on edge as I head for the Eagle. I open the door and climb into the pilot's seat. It brings me back to three months ago, when I took refuge in the shuttle after finding out I was a clone of the original Sasha—and my crew had kept it secret from me.

I'd flown to New Zealand then, to the abandoned AukPrep campus where I went to school, desperate for some space. This time, I don't know where to go. Probably can't risk going anywhere until we learn how Andrews found our terminal address and make double sure he isn't waiting for us outside.

"Fuck."

I close my eyes. After a few slow breaths, I feel more in control. I've already made up my mind to respond, but I'll do it on my terms. Andrews obviously needs something from my crew, if he's gone to the considerable effort of finding us. He might have leverage on me, but we have leverage on him, too.

I start working on a plan.

Step one, make sure my crew is behind me.

Step two, figure out how PGS found us.

Step three, contact Andrews and hear him out.

Step four...

Make whoever's responsible for my parents' deaths pay. Better twenty years late than never.

I reach into my pocket, pulling out a silver metal box and its accompanying cable. My brainbox. I went through hell to get it back after Veronica Cross, the CEO of AxysGen, stole it. Not only because it holds backups of all my memories, but because it's one of the keys to access Val's servers, hidden underground in Siberia. Now, though, the memories are what I'm interested in. In addition to storing them, the brainbox allows me to relive them.

I attach one end of the cable to the box and plug the other into the jack behind my ear.

***

Bang. Bang.

"Darius and Kiara Young? We've had a noise complaint. Open the door immediately."

I drop my half-eaten burger into my lap, greasy wrapper and all. The sudden sound startles me, but not as much as my parents' worried glances. They look at each other from opposite sides of the couch, where we've been eating ever since we hawked our table and chairs.

"Don't answer it." Dad's brow furrows, and the muscles in his bare arms tighten as he clenches his fists. The tone of his voice worries me, so I scoot closer to him.

Mom gets up from the couch. Her voice is low, nervous. "We'll get fined if we don't, and they'll come in anyway. You want that added to our monthly statement?"

"The statement's gonna be there 'til we die. Why should we make it easy for them?" Dad reaches behind the couch, withdrawing the baseball bat he always keeps there. The one I'm not allowed to play with.

Bang. Bang.

"Last chance," says the voice from outside. "Open the door."

"Coming," Mom calls back. She peers out the peephole, then fiddles with the tarnished chain that holds the door shut.

"Sasha." A large hand descends on my shoulder, applying more than the usual amount of pressure. Dad stares down at me with terrified eyes. "Go to bed and stay there. Now."

Normally I'd argue with him, or at least ask questions, but the naked fear on his face frightens me. When he presses the bat into my hands and steers me toward the curtain that separates our beds from the rest of the cramped space, I'm too overwhelmed to protest.

"Keep this next to you. If they make me and Mom leave with them, go across the hall to the Weinsteins. If anyone tries to hurt you, hit 'em in the knees and run."

I take the bat and scurry behind the curtain, but I don't sit quietly in bed. Instead, I watch and listen, peeking out as two men in matching black suits enter the apartment. They're wearing VIS-Rs and carrying electronic clipboards. I don't see any weapons on them, but that doesn't mean they're unarmed.

No pleasantries are exchanged. One of the suits closes the door while the other scans the apartment, suspicion written clearly on his face. "We've had a complaint from one of your neighbors."

"Which neighbors?" asks Dad.

"What kind of noise?" asks Mom.

"We aren't obligated to disclose that information." More thudding sounds follow, like someone's stomping carelessly through the front of the apartment. "Mr. and Mrs. Young, you are the only two tenants listed on the lease. Are there any other residents?"

Mom's eyes dart toward the curtain, and I'm sure she sees me before I duck out of sight. "Our daughter, Sasha. She's nine. No one else."

"No one else?"

"No," Dad says.

My mind is reeling. Why do these guys think someone else lives in our apartment? What noise did they mean? We were eating dinner quietly before they interrupted.

Curiosity gets the better of me. I risk another peek around the curtain. Dad's squaring up to the first suit, who's at least half a foot shorter. I've never seen him look like this before. He's always warm and gentle. Always smiling. Now, there's steel in his eyes and a sharpness to the angle of his jaw that I don't recognize.

The second suit paces toward the only window in the apartment, where my mom's small vegetable aerogarden is soaking in the afternoon sunlight. The cherry tomatoes are ripe enough for Mom to put one on my burger, and she told me this morning that the broccoli and peppers are almost ready, too.

"No other family members?"

"My husband told you." Mom keeps almost turning toward me, like she wants to look at me again, but something's stopping her. "No one else lives here."

Suit One types something on his clipboard while Suit Two makes a show of rummaging through our apartment. He removes the only two pictures on the wall, one of my parents holding their marriage certificate in front of a big, important looking building, and a picture of me in a sweater vest. He tosses them carelessly on the floor, tapping the wall behind.

"What are you looking for?" Mom says. "Maybe we can—"

"Has anyone visited in the last few months?" Suit One interrupts.

"No," Dad says.

Suit Two strolls closer to me, and my heart starts pounding. My hands feel sweaty gripping the bat, but I'm not sure whether to put it down or keep hold of it. I remember my father teaching me to stay still and hold up empty hands if corps privsec or the cops ever stop me, but he also gave me the bat. What does he think these guys might do to us?

"What's behind the curtain?" Suit One asks.

"Just two mattresses and a charging station," Mom tells him. "And the bathroom."

Suit One nods at his partner. "Check it out."

Suit Two crosses the apartment with long strides and pulls the curtain aside, causing me to stumble back. I drop the bat, staring at him with wide, fearful eyes. He isn't as tall as my dad, but he's still big. His opaque VIS-R doesn't show his eyes, so I can only guess where he's looking by the position of his head.

He glances at me momentarily, but he doesn't seem all that interested. I watch, frozen with fear, as he heads to the bathroom and flings open the door. It swings crookedly on its hinges, showing the toilet and sink built into the wall. "Clear," he tells Suit One.

"Right." Suit One moves his head like he's looking around the apartment, but the scorn I can't see in his eyes is all too clear in his voice. "There isn't much to this place."

They turn everything upside down anyway, throwing clothes out of drawers, checking the mini fridge, and rummaging through our sparsely stocked pantry. The privacy curtain is torn down, leaving me to stumble away and place my back flat against the wall. One of them even pulls the cushions off the couch, while the other scans our mattresses.

"What are you doing?" Dad barks. "There's no noise happening, and you can see there's no one else here." He tries to stand in their way, but my Mom grabs his shoulder, holding him back. They both look pointedly at me. When I see a chance, I hurry over to them, joining the family huddle and looping my small arms around their waists.

The suits ignore us, continuing to tear through our apartment like a tornado. When they don't find anything, they get angry. They turn on the aerogarden, tipping over each box and dumping them on the floor. Their shoes leave muddy boot prints and crushed plants as they sift through the soil, kicking clumps aside in their search.

Horrified, I lock eyes with my mother. My mind is shouting, Not the garden! We'd both taken care of it every day. We'd watched it grow for weeks. It's the reason I get to eat something besides bug burgers, fish sticks, and nutrient bars.

"No!"

I don't realize I've shouted aloud until everyone in the room stares at me. The suits are momentarily shocked by my outburst. The first one snorts, while the second's lips part slightly before he shuts them into a tight grimace.

Mom wraps her arms around me, holding so tight that my head is trapped against her chest and I can smell her sweat. "Sasha, baby, don't say anything else."

It isn't like I can with her death grip on me. She forces me to watch in silence as the suits abandon the aerogarden and head for the door. "You'll receive a copy of our report and all associated fines with your monthly statement," Suit Two says to my father. He and his partner leave, kicking the door shut behind them and leaving us in the wreckage of our apartment.

*** *

In the garage, tears leak from my eyes. That memory took place only a few weeks before they died. Before more strangers in suits came and told me my parents were gone.

The apartment and everything in it was repossessed to cover my parents' employee debts— outstanding loans for work training, apartment fees, childcare fees, fines for failing to meet personal health benchmarks... it all added up. I went into an 'educational center' until I aced my APS and was shipped off to AukPrep.

I wipe my tears away. The day after the suits left, Mom went out and jury-rigged another aerogarden. I don't know where she got the materials and seeds, but we replaced what had been taken from us. Though she hadn't challenged the suits directly, probably out of fear that they might hurt me, she never gave up. She resisted, growing things in that shitty little window until the day she and Dad didn't come home.

Our lives were hard back then, sometimes brutally so. My parents deserved better. Maybe in death, I can finally do more for them. Maybe they would be proud of the person I've become.

Chapter 06

"SASHA? WHAT ARE YOU doing in there?"

I open my eyes, blinking away the blurriness. I must have fallen asleep in the Eagle, because I'm still in the pilot's seat and there's a nasty crick in my neck. Doc and Rock are peering in through the window, wearing expressions of concern.

"Hold on." I raise the door and climb out, stretching my arms over my head.

"Jeez, take a shower," Doc says, wrinkling her nose.

I tousle her hair. "Bet you'd smell worse after sleeping in the shuttle."

"You and Elena have a fight or something?"

I shoot her an annoyed look. "If you're asking the question, you know the answer."

Doc blows her bangs out of her face. "Elena won't talk about it. She's in the kitchen, stomping around and burning the eggs."

I know I'll have to face Elena eventually, but I really don't want to. I'm not sure whether we'll end up apologizing and fucking, or going in for round two. One seems about as likely as the other.

"Don't be a chickenshit," Doc says. "Apologize for whatever dumb thing you did. Then Elena can apologize for whatever dumb thing she did. Because you're both dumb."

Rock makes a disapproving rumble, placing one of his enormous hands-on top of Doc's head.

"No offense," Doc adds begrudgingly.

"Hard not to take offense to being called dumb, kid. You remember I'm your boss, right?" I close the Eagle's door and shuffle toward the lift, pressing a hand to the middle of my back. I'm getting too old to sleep outside of a bed without feeling the consequences. "Let's get this over with."

The rest of the crew is waiting in the kitchen. Cherry, Rami, and Ocho are eating eggs, but judging by the distinct scent of burnt food wafting from the trash can, it's probably Elena's second attempt at breakfast. She's still at the stove, dumping what looks like a volcano's worth of hot sauce onto a plate. Even though we're fighting, I can't help stealing a glance at her ass. She's wearing a pair of grey leggings that really show it off, and a flowy orange top that looks great with her skin.

She turns. Our eyes lock.

"Hey," I mumble.

Elena sets her plate on the counter, jerking her head toward the hall. I follow her, ignoring everyone else's stares. Once we're in relative privacy, she releases a deep breath. "I'm sorry."

The knot in my chest loosens. I wasn't expecting an apology right off the bat. We used to scrap like street dogs before we hooked up, but lately—not counting yesterday—we've been much kinder to each other. I have to admit, it felt bad to fall back into old patterns.

"Don't get me wrong," Elena continues. "I still think contacting Andrews is dangerous, but I should've been more understanding. You lost your parents. I know how hard that is."

I heave a sigh. "I'm sorry, too. You're right. There's something off about this. I can't go charging in because I want to know what Andrews knows."

Elena takes my hand. "If you can't live with the uncertainty, I'll help. *Familia es toda.*"

My heart swells. Even though Elena's only been with us a short time, this reinforces that she's really part of the team. Part of the family. "Thanks."

"*De nada.*" She stands on tiptoe so I take the hint, leaning down to kiss her. It's a soft kiss, one of apology rather than passion, but I get enough of a taste to notice the tingle of hot sauce.

I pull back. "Started in on those eggs already?"

"You know it. Want me to make you some?"

"Yeah. Only hotter."

Elena grins. "You'd eat the sun if you could."

"You ain't wrong."

We return to the kitchen hand in hand. Cherry waggles her eyebrows, cheeks stuffed full of food, while Rami offers a warm smile. "Glad to see the two of you getting along again." They're wearing a silky looking dress in royal purple. Even though it's early morning, they've already got a sick beat on their face, complete with glittery purple eye shadow and a sleek black goatee.

Cherry gulps down her mouthful of eggs. She looks much less glamorous in lycra shorts and a lazy-day tank top, although she's made the minimum effort by putting earrings in. Obviously her spouse hogged the mirror this morning before breakfast. Not that I can judge. After sleeping in the Eagle, I'm sure I look like a troll.

"Just don't start making out on the table," Cherry says. "I mean, unless you're cool with being watched."

"Shut your cockhole." Elena drops my hand and heads to the counter to retrieve her eggs. She shovels a few bites before cracking some fresh ones over the pan.

"So, are you gonna tell us what you were arguing about?" Doc asks. She and Rock have taken seats at the table, and from the looks of things, helped themselves to Elena's eggs.

I consider it. Might as well bring the rest of the team up to speed. "I got a message last night. Val?"

Val appears beside the table. "Good morning, Sasha. Would you like me to replay the message for the rest of the team?"

I look at Ocho, who smiles at me from her seat between Rock and Rami. She's dressed in more of my clothes, another white tank top and a pair of black pants. I make a mental note to buy her some new clothes as soon as possible. The last thing I want is Ocho walking around looking like a carbon copy of me. At least, no more than she always does.

Ocho notices my stare. "What message, Sasha?"

I consider sending Ocho into the hall while I explain the situation to everyone else, but decide against it. Val said she was supposed to observe as much social interaction as possible. Letting her listen to a meeting isn't nearly as dangerous as putting her in the field, assuming that's what she wants someday. A big part of me really hopes she doesn't.

"You'll see, Ocho. Val? Go ahead."

Val brings up the message, and Andrews' face appears on the screen of projected light. As he talks, I analyze every word he says, trying to find some hidden meaning.

By the time the message ends, no one's smiling.

"Shit," Cherry says, voicing the crew's collective thoughts.

"Sasha," Rami murmurs. "I'm so sorry."

Rock pushes back his chair and lumbers over to me. He pauses, and when I don't object, he wraps me in a big hug. Sometimes his gestures say a lot more than words. I hug him back, relaxing in his embrace.

When he lets go, I notice Ocho looking at me with a worried expression. "You don't have parents, either? The kind who raise you, I mean. Not DNA."

39

The question gives me pause. Ocho means 'because they're dead,' but she's inadvertently brought up a subject I've been avoiding. Technically, Kiara and Darius Young are the original Sasha's parents. Although they supplied the template for my DNA, and I have clear memories of being raised by them, I'm actually a clone, just like Ocho. I was made in a tube. It's difficult parsing out just how much 'my' memories count for.

In the end, I default back to the same conclusion as usual. I'm all that's left of the original Sasha. All that's left of my family. I have clear memories of them raising me, teaching me, protecting me. If I don't avenge them, no one else will.

"I had parents, but they're dead."

"Oh. I'm sorry." Ocho's brow furrows. "Should I be sad I don't have parents, or happy I don't have parents to lose?"

I'm not sure how to answer that one. Fortunately, Rami knows the right thing to say. They reach across the table, patting Ocho's hand. "You might not have parents, but you have a family. And we're gonna help Sasha find out what happened to her family, right?"

"We gotta," Doc says.

Rock grunts in the affirmative.

"I believe it would be beneficial for Sasha's mental health and overall wellbeing," Val says.

"Sure," Cherry agrees. "But everyone realizes how weird this is, right?"

"Thank you. At least somebody else sees it." Elena joins us at the table, setting a fresh plate of eggs in front of the last remaining seat before steering me into it. "If we're gonna dig into this, we gotta ask some questions first, starting with how the CEO of PGS found us."

"I am able to provide some clarification," Val says. "There is no evidence that Paragon Solutions accessed our terminal remotely or decrypted our datastreams. I ran a thorough scan. It is my belief that they received this terminal's address from an outside source."

"Then what?" Cherry asks. "Or who?"

"Who do you think?" Elena mutters.

"You can't mean Megan," Rami says. "She's gone."

"Yeah," Elena says. "But Andrews could've bought, traded for, or even stolen the information from AxysGen, who could've gotten it from her."

"That's a lot of could haves," I say between bites of my eggs. "And if AxysGen knows where we are, why aren't they banging down our door instead of PGS?"

"Exactly. Why aren't they? If PGS knows how to find us, AxysGen will too, if they don't already. I say we bail as fast as possible. Not necessarily on the mission, but on the base, at least."

I still have my doubts. Megan always played her cards close to her chest. She never truly collaborated with Cross or AxysGen. She was always using them for her own ends. But only Andrews knows how he got our IP address. Since he wants to open a dialogue, the simplest thing to do is ask him.

"I say we find out what he wants first. If we leave, we could be walking into a trap. At least we're well defended in here."

"We are," Val confirms. "I have improved upon many of the SLKC safe house's defensive features. Even if Megan provided Axys Generations or Paragon Solutions with detailed schematics, they would still run into considerable resistance from the autoturrets, nerve gas—"

"We get the idea," Cherry says. "It's safer to stick it out underground until we contact Andrews. But I swear, if Megan did this, I'll kick that *puta oxigenada's* ass from beyond the fucking grave."

"Who's Megan?"

I turn to Ocho, as does the rest of the crew. When she realizes everyone's staring at her, the curious look on her face falls away to be replaced with doubt. "Was that wrong to ask?"

I glance at Val, who says, "I thought it best if you supplied that information to Ocho organically, rather than via download. That way, you can maintain some control over its delivery."

I give Val a grateful look. She hasn't always been the best at respecting other people's privacy or personal agency. She's crossed a lot of lines, especially when she decided to erase portions of my memory and pull the rest of my crew in on it, but she's learning and trying to do better.

"Thanks, Val." I face Ocho again. "I'll tell you about Megan later. Short version, she's my abusive ex-girlfriend. She's dead now."

Ocho nods. Her face scrunches up like she's confused, and I'm struck by a strange thought. *Is that how I look when I'm processing something?* A kind of mental vertigo descends over me, which leaves me feeling distant and disconnected from my own body. *How many of our expressions are the same? How many of my reactions are automatic, something I don't even control?*

Eventually, Ocho's expression settles on sad. "I'm sorry," she says, looking a bit overwhelmed. I can't blame her. It's still overwhelming for me, and I lived it.

I don't want her to go through that. The thought surprises me with its intensity. So do the protective feelings that well up inside me. I might be jealous of Ocho for getting a fresh start, but underneath that, there's a strong urge to defend her. I guess Megan, and people like Megan, strike me as something Ocho needs protecting from. *Maybe this evening I'll make some time to talk to her.*

Lucky for me, the rest of the crew keeps the conversation going before the moment gets too heavy. "Good fucking riddance," Elena says, plopping down at the table and polishing off her remaining eggs.

"*Si, ¿no?*" Cherry says. "*Qué pinche perra.*"

There's more dark muttering, but it's all supportive. Once again, my team has come through for me. They've all agreed to help me figure out what PGS knows about my parents, even Elena. I steal a glance at her and she offers a supportive smile. This won't be easy, but at least I'm not facing it alone.

Chapter 07

"ALL RIGHT, PEOPLE. LET'S get started." I stride into the living room, raising my voice to address my scattered crewmates. They're all present, attempting to lounge around but not quite succeeding, waiting with an undercurrent of tension. Nonetheless, they join me at the main terminal.

Cherry rises from the couch, leaving behind a half-finished bag of potato chips, which Rami wordlessly re-seals and returns to the kitchen before joining her. Elena and Ocho, seated on either side of a projected checkerboard with Rock and Val's avatar as their audience, leave their places.

"Game was rigged anyway," Elena grumbles. "Val was helping Ocho cheat."

A hint of a smile flickers across Val's face. "I prefer to think of it as interactive learning."

"I won the last two games," Ocho informs me, with no small amount of pride.

"You mean *Val* won the last two games," Elena huffs, folding her arms across her chest.

"She's only a couple days old," Cherry says. "Cut her a break, *chaparrita.*"

"I was gonna, until Val started—"

"Now, now, children." Rami joins us, clicking their tongue. "It's only a game."

Elena's nose wrinkles while Rock does a terrible job hiding his grin. "What are you looking at?" she asks, shooting a glare in his direction.

Rock merely shakes his head at her, shrugging his massive shoulders.

"Just tell me you geniuses have some kind of plan," Doc says, looking between Elena and me. I can tell she's nervous from the way she chews her cheek. "I won't let either of you go in blind and get your brain melted. There are some things even a genius like me can't fix."

"We have a plan," Elena tells Doc. "Val and I set up a premium chatspace on d/Ash. Even professional PGS jackers would have a real hard time scraping data from their servers."

There are nods all around. d/Ash is the most secure chat host on the extranet, which is why so many people, crews and corps, use it. Gaining access to its premium features is also expensive, but it's not like we're hurting for credits. Previous ops have left us with a tidy nest egg.

"What about the new shield program you coded for me, Elena?" I ask, for Doc's benefit as much as my own.

Elena offers a cocky smile that doesn't quite reach her eyes. "Come inside and I'll show you."

"That's what she said," Cherry adds. I sense the joke is an attempt to ease the tension, and there's a lot of tension. For all our speculating, we still don't know how the meeting with Andrews will go, or what he wants from us.

Ocho shoots Cherry a confused look. "Who's 'she', and what did she say?"

Rami sighs. "I'll explain after the meet-up." They glare at Cherry, who makes a rude gesture in return.

Ocho looks somewhat disappointed, but says, "Okay."

I feel a small stab of fear, not the normal jolt of worry and anticipation before a dangerous op, but something else. Something worse. Then it hits me. I don't want to leave Ocho alone. I know what it's like to lose the people taking care of you. If something happens to me...

It's similar to the fear I feel when I remember just how young Doc is. Rock is her official guardian, but I've taken on a parental role with her over the years. And yet, as much as I hate to admit it, at least Doc has some experience taking care of herself. Ocho has nothing.

I remind myself it's just a meeting, not an actual mission. d/Ash is probably the safest possible way to communicate via extranet, and if PGS wanted to hurt us, they would've tried something by now. Still, my fears persist.

I decide to ask Ocho whether she wants some self defense training when I return. I'm certain Val's educational downloads taught her something along those lines, but I want to make sure. Even if Ocho doesn't want the life of a mercenary, she should know how to defend herself from the people who want me and my crew dead.

Elena senses something's wrong because she nudges me playfully with her elbow. "C'mon, *Jefecita*. Let's ditch these *idiotas* so I can show you your new toy."

"Don't have too much fun without us," Cherry drawls.

"Trust me," I mutter. "We won't. Now, the important shit. Cherry and Doc, you're on security cams. I doubt PGS is camped outside waiting to catch us off guard, but it never hurts to be careful."

"Even if they are, they'd have a hell of a time getting in," Cherry says.

"Oh, can I fire the lasers if they show up?" Doc asks. "Please, Cherry?"

Cherry grins. "Only if you're good, *cerebro*."

"But if anyone does break in," I continue. "Don't risk your lives defending the base. Rock, you're in charge of evacuating everyone if shit goes south, including me and Elena. If you have to give us a hard cut, do it. We'll deal with the consequences." Hard cuts—literally pulling out someone's jack before they log off—are never pleasant, but rarely fatal without other complications involved. Headaches, nausea, and coordination issues are the usual side effects.

"What about me?" Ocho asks. "How do I help?" The eager gleam in her eye is far from reassuring. I realize that the idea of Ocho weathering an assault on our base upsets me more than I anticipated. Still, she looks so hopeful that I don't want to disappoint her.

I answer in my most serious voice, so the others won't think I'm getting soft and Ocho doesn't realize I'm just humoring her. "If we're attacked, you can help Rami get the shuttle from the garage while Rock evacuates everyone." I glance in Rock's direction, catching his eye, then look sideways at Ocho. When he nods in understanding, I know without being told that he'll protect Ocho if the worst happens.

Ocho squares her shoulders, attempting to match my rigid posture and serious expression. "I can do it. I won't let you down."

"We don't *want* anything to go down, Ocho," Rami reminds her.

Cherry leers at them. "At least, not—"

Rami holds up their hand in a 'stop' gesture and rolls their eyes. "Later. Anyway, Ocho, Sasha, and Elena will log in, get the info we need from Andrews, and log out safely. Right, loves?"

"Right," Elena says. "There's always some risk, but Val and I have thought this through."

"Just don't give the scumbag an easy time," Doc says.

The worry in Doc's eyes tugs at my heartstrings, so I force out a few reassuring words. Damn it. I really am getting soft these days. Maybe a mission is actually what I need to put an edge back on my brain after three months lounging on the beach. "We'll be fine, kid. See you in a few." I look at Elena. "Ready?"

"Fuck, no." She grasps my fingers, and I allow it. "But let's go anyway."

We pull the silver cords from the terminal and jack in together.

***

network: ps 38624 . 90185
Connection established
welcome: user волчица-воин

Elena and I are on a warm, sandy beach, not too different from the ones in Barbados. It's the terminal preset I chose before my dream of tropical retirement became an all too brief reality. The scent of flowers and sea salt on the wind fills me with the sudden longing to return, but I can't. Not until I know the truth.

"Val?" Elena calls.

Val appears, dressed in a purple sarong with yellow flowers. Her hair is in long cornrows, twisted elegantly on top of her head. Her sandals leave no footprints on the sand.

"Hello, Elena. Sasha. The chatspace is ready. I have forwarded an invitation to the extranet address Andrews provided."

"First things first." Elena holds out her hand and a glowing white orb appears in her palm. She offers me the download. "Check it out."

When I touch the light, it solidifies. A leather grip appears in my hand, and I see that I'm holding a shield, a bright white triangle with a black wolf's head on the front. Its eyes glow red, like the embers of a fire. I lift it up. It's got a little heft, but it's surprisingly light.

"You asshole."

Elena smirks. "You don't like the custom code I poured my blood, sweat, and tears into?"

"You know I do. Doesn't change the fact that you're an asshole for putting a wolf on it."

"Aw. Don't like the old nickname?"

I roll my eyes. "Just tell me how this thing works."

"Block stuff with it."

"Thanks, babe. Real helpful."

"Well, it does breathe fire."

That's pretty cool, but I sure as hell won't admit that to Elena and give her an even bigger head. *"And we can use this in the chatspace? Doesn't d/Ash have security to prevent offensive programming?"*

"Technically," Elena says, with a sly wink. *"But I don't go anywhere online without my shield, so you might as well bring one, too. I disguised the program so d/Ash's software will think it's a recording app."*

I narrow my eyes at her. *"I thought d/Ash was supposed to be the most secure chat app on the extranet?"*

"Secure doesn't mean totally impenetrable," Elena drawls, sounding more than a bit smug.

"Especially with a fully-realized artificial intelligence to aid with coding," Val adds. *"A benefit other jackers do not possess."*

"Yeah, you helped code it," Elena admits. *"Although it was my idea to begin with."*

"The true power of ideas is in the execution," Val says.

I can't help enjoying their playful bickering. Those two have come a long way since they met.

I turn to Val. *"We good?"*

"I will connect us whenever you are ready."

"Let's get this over with," Elena says.

A metal doorway appears in the middle of the beach. It has the d/Ash logo on the front, four letters with a lightning bolt between the d and A. The door opens, and Elena steps through first. When she disappears, the knot in my stomach pulls tighter.

After a beat, I follow.

***

network: d/ 38351 . 90124
Connection established
welcome: user волчица-воин

I perceive the d/Ash chatspace as a conference room. My shield has vanished, although the icon remains in my field of vision, ready if all hell breaks loose. The room is large and luxurious, with a long, polished wooden table and black leather chairs. One of the walls is clear, and it looks out across the St. Louis business district, one of SLKC's two major metropolitan poles.

The Gateway Arch flickers in the distance, scrolling with its usual advertisements. Competitive gaming livestreams. Lightning energy drinks, which Doc loves. Amusingly, one of them is an ad for Padlock, AxysGen's most well-known online security software.

Elena stands beside the table, examining our surroundings with the same wariness I feel. Val hasn't manifested, but I hear her voice clearly in my ear. "The invitation has been sent. Andrews should arrive momentarily."

As if her words have summoned him, a man appears in a seat at the other end of the table. His hair is combed back into an ostentatious blond pompadour, and his smile is too big and too white, much like the rest of him. His figure is trim, no doubt the work of a personal trainer and dietician, but he's very tall and broad-shouldered, facts which his perfectly tailored suit takes pains to emphasize.

"Sasha Young and Elena Nevares, I believe." Andrews leans back in his chair, studying us with a smile that doesn't reach his eyes. "Please, have a seat." He gestures at the empty chairs lining the table.

Instead of taking a seat, I walk to the end of the table Andrews has chosen, placing both hands flat and leaning forward. He's not the only one who can play this game.

"Okay, Andrews. You got my attention, so start talking."

To his credit, Andrews' smile never wavers. For a privileged fuck, he isn't easily intimidated. "I want to hire you, of course. As for how I found you, I'm a businessman. Part of my job is knowing as much as possible about my business partners."

"Business partners?"

"That's my hope, yes," Andrews says. He pauses, looking toward Elena. "Ms. Nevares, I understand that you are in possession of independently modified AxysGen code, which allows you to infiltrate their intranet systems more easily. Is this true?"

Elena bristles. "If you need me, why contact my handler?"

"Not just you," Andrews says. "Although your personalized code will certainly be an asset. I want to hire Ms. Young and her entire crew. AxysGen has something I value highly. Specifically, the coding and schematics for some new jack port hardware currently in development. In return, I can offer something Ms. Young values highly."

This conversation is tense enough to make my mouth dry. I resist the temptation to lick my lips. "Information about my parents?"

"As you know, their deaths were not accidental. It seems to me their only child might be interested in knowing the specifics."

Elena crosses her arms. "How do we know AxysGen didn't ask you to lure us out of hiding? Even rival corps work together if the reward is big enough. You wouldn't be the first C-suite pendejo *to double-cross us."*

Andrews doesn't react to Elena's foul language. "So suspicious, Ms. Nevares. Isn't it more believable that you were recommended by my employees? You have been hired by upper PGS management for jobs much like this one many times before. As for Ms. Young..." His eyes fix on me, and there's a strange kind of fire in their icy blue depths. "Who would pass up a chance to work with the infamous Wolf of the Kremlin? Everyone knows you're the best in the freelance business."

I narrow my eyes at him. "The 'Wolf' still wants to know how you found my terminal address."

"I'm afraid I can't reveal all my secrets," Andrews says. "But I will say this; I sincerely doubt AxysGen and Veronica Cross know how to contact you. I certainly won't let them know, since I want you to steal the schematics for several upcoming patents from their Butterfly Lab."

That gets Elena's attention. "The Butterfly Lab? Seriously?"

Even I raise my eyebrows. The Butterfly Lab is world famous, one of AxysGen's most prolific and heavily guarded research and development institutions. Its four wings are devoted to software, hardware, biotechnology, and robotics. A large percentage of AxysGen products get their start there.

"Seriously," Andrews repeats. "I know their security is excellent—"

"That's underselling it," I snort.

"But surely a crew of your reputation and skill can get me what I need. I'm willing to offer a generous payment in addition to the information you want."

Warning bells go off in my head. Andrews is being reasonable, but there are too many unknowns. Yet the promised information about my parents is too tempting to resist. Andrews has me where he wants me, and he knows it.

"Do we have a deal, Ms. Young?"

I glance at Elena. Probably not what a crew leader should do, but part of me needs to know she's in. She gives a small, barely perceptible nod, although I can tell she isn't pleased that Andrews still hasn't told us how he found us.

I push past my reluctance and take the plunge. "Yeah, we have a deal. But I want half the credits up front through a third-party transfer system."

"That's more than acceptable." Andrews rises from his chair and circles the table, holding out his hand. At first I think he wants to shake, but then I realize he's offering me a download.

"Don't," Elena snaps. "Let me scan it." She does, studying it intently and running several programs that flash in front of her face in multicolored, partially transparent windows scrolling with code.

"Naturally," Andrews says smoothly. "These are the details of the mission. You will be accessing heavily protected information stored on-site at one of AxysGen's research facilities. In the interest of full disclosure, you should know that I've sent several in-house teams to retrieve this information. They all failed."

He doesn't need to elaborate. It's obvious what failure means in this case. "We won't." Once the file is finished downloading, I give Andrews a nod. "When do you need the schematics?"

"Three weeks from now," Andrews says. "My sources tell me AxysGen will be applying for patents soon."

"Fine. We need time to plan our infiltration and get all the necessary supplies. Then, I expect answers."

Andrews offers me a hollow smile. "You'll have them. Until then, I wish you luck." He waves, and his avatar disappears. The conference room melts around us, dissolving into the ground. A second later, the beach returns. We're exactly where we started. Val reappears beside us, looking worried.

Despite her expression, I feel relieved. I let out a heavy breath. "At least that's over."

Elena gives a strained laugh. "We're alive, I guess."

"You didn't really think he'd attack us via d/Ash, did you? That's practically impossible."

Elena shrugs. "Nothing's impossible online if you try hard enough. And we aren't safe yet. The Butterfly Lab? That's like, the Fort Knox of R&D."

"I disagree," Val says. "Because AxysGen allows tourists to visit the outer grounds, the facility is not as secure as many people might assume. With our combined skills, Elena's code, and my assistance, I believe our team has a reasonable chance of success."

"Yeah, well," Elena grumbles. "I still don't like this. It stinks."

I feel a pang of guilt in my chest. "I know. I'm sorry—"

"No sorries." Elena waves me off. "I said I'd help you find out what happened to your parents and I meant it, even if we have to break into *one of the most secure R&D labs in the world. But I still don't trust Andrews as far as I can throw him."*

I think back on Andrews' oily demeanor. "On that, we can agree."

logging off network
disconnection complete

Rae D. Magdon

Chapter 08

"SO, IS NOW A good time?" Ocho asks.

"For what?"

Ocho and I are alone in the armory, mostly so I can decompress after meeting with Andrews. The rest of the crew was perceptive enough to give me space since no one's knocking down our door and we have three weeks to plan our heist. But not Ocho. When I left the living room, she looked so eager to accompany me that I didn't have the heart to say no.

She watches me clean an assault rifle on the cluttered weapons bench, where I've pushed several parts aside to create an open space. The K2-Phoenix is a newer model, but I've become partial to it recently.

"To talk about Megan." Perched on the raised stool next to me, Ocho tilts her head, but there's no salaciousness in her gaze, only innocent curiosity. It reminds me of what Val said about her having the absorption rate of a toddler. Her brain is a big sponge, and I guess I'm providing the water.

"Why do you want to know?" I ask, hoping to stall the conversation.

No dice. Ocho seems to have latched onto this topic for whatever reason. "Whenever the crew says Megan's name, your face turns sad. Usually, your face has one look, and that's it. Even in the tube footage."

I raise an eyebrow. "Just one expression?"

"Yeah. Kind of blank."

I look away, returning my focus to the rifle. "Not the first time I've heard that."

A beat passes.

"So, why does Megan make you sad?" Ocho asks.

I sigh. Better rip off the bandage, I guess. As Ocho's guardian, the job of giving the 'some people are actually noxious piles of shit in human clothes' talk falls to me. I try and put it as simply as possible. "I loved Megan, but she saw me as a means to an end. She cared about what I could do for her instead of how I felt."

A crease forms in Ocho's brow as she digests that information. I don't know what kind of programs Val used to teach her empathy, but it looks like she has some, at least on a basic level. "Why wouldn't she care how you felt?" she asks, with such sincerity that my heart feels like my teeth after too much sugar—uncomfortably sensitive.

I have to lay it out for her, though. Otherwise, some other soul-sucking bitch like Megan might come along and take advantage of Ocho someday. "Some people just don't. They don't see other humans as people like them, just tools they can use. Like the corps see their cogs. But Megan could be charming, too. Funny. That's what made it confusing."

I pause to remove the rifle's carrier spring from beneath the dust cover. I can find a better quality replacement amidst the odds and ends in the armory drawers. "Sometimes it's hard to tell who's using you, and who actually cares about you," I continue. "You have to wait and see if they stick around when shit gets real."

Ocho sucks the inside of her cheek, a nervous tic I used to have before I realized it didn't go with the badass handler image. Since I don't do it anymore, I can't help but wonder where she picked it up. "That's it? You're just supposed to wait and see if someone hurts you?"

"Trust me, I wish there was a surefire way to tell. My crew is full of good people, though. They won't do you like that."

Ocho smiles. "I know. Val showed me some of your missions. Not your memories," she hastens to reassure me. Obviously Val has taken a hint from me and explained to Ocho why memories are personal. "She showed me footage she took as part of my training."

"Training?" I frown, not liking the sound of that at all. "Exactly how much training did she give you in that tube?"

"How to shoot. Hand to hand combat. Basic jacking skills, in case I encounter hostile programming—"

I set the rifle down and straighten on my stool. "Whoa, whoa, whoa. Ocho, you know you don't have to be in the field to be part of the crew, right? You're only a couple days old. Way too young to be risking your life."

Ocho looks crestfallen. Her lower lip pokes out in a pout that looks truly bizarre on my own face. "But I want to. When I watched the missions, I felt good."

"Good, how?"

"Excited. Skilled. Triumphant."

I fold my arms across my chest. I knew we'd need to have this talk at some point, but I definitely wasn't expecting it on day two. "Field work isn't a game, Ocho. It's scary, dangerous, and traumatic. It's easy to get hurt, and not just your body. Your head, too."

Ocho tilts her own head. "Like a concussion?"

"No. More than that. Like...your mind. Your heart."

I can tell from the frustrated crease on Ocho's brow that I haven't given a satisfactory explanation. Maybe I should look for some kind of e-book on how to explain trauma to children. Ocho isn't exactly a child, but books about explaining life to clones are probably pretty niche.

"What does that mean?" Ocho asks. "I don't get it."

"It means you aren't going to the Butterfly Lab."

"But—"

"Ain't happening, so get over it," I say. Perhaps a bit too harshly, because Ocho's eyes drop down to her lap, where her hands shift uncomfortably on her thighs.

I feel guilty for spoiling Ocho's dreams of adventure, but she needs to know the truth. She deserves more time to adjust before realizing there are people in the world who will want to hurt her, physically and mentally, for all kinds of reasons. But forewarned is forearmed.

Plus, isn't it your job to make sure Ocho turns out better than you? Healthier? Happier? Don't you want to see who you could've been without all the trauma? Maybe I'm envious of Ocho, but I also feel an obligation to her. If she has the chance to make a better life than mine, to become a better person than me, it's my duty to help.

"What if I still want to do missions?" Ocho asks despite my warnings. "Even if they could hurt me?"

I rummage in one of the bench drawers for a new carrier spring, then begin the process of installing it. "Maybe someday, if you still want to do mercenary work. But you don't have enough life experience to make that choice yet. Until then, I'm making it for you."

Ocho obviously takes that as a hard and fast promise instead of a maybe. She brightens immediately, straightening up and smiling. "So, get me more experience. Real experiences, not just tube experiences."

"What?"

"Take me out there," Ocho insists, pointing eagerly at the armory door. "Somewhere besides here. Then I'll get experience and I can do missions."

I set the rifle down, already shaking my head. "It's not that simple."

But Ocho is determined. "Please?" She grasps my hand and squeezes, like that will change my mind.

Her touch takes me by surprise, but I manage to stop myself from jerking my hand away. How weird must that be, to initiate physical contact so easily? To be so open and trusting with your body? I can't remember experiencing that since my own childhood. Sure, Elena and I fuck, and sometimes I exchange hugs with my crew, but part of me is always on guard. Probably comes from so many people trying to kill me over the decades—and Megan's betrayal certainly didn't help.

Still, maybe I can think of a way to give Ocho a taste of adventure without subjecting her to real danger. "Fine," I concede when Ocho doesn't let go of my hand. "When Val says it's safe to leave base, you can come when we purchase the supplies we need for the mission. Deal?"

"Deal!" Ocho takes our linked hands and pumps them in a handshake to seal our agreement. I crack a small smile. It's nice to see her excited about something. Maybe I'll find at least one or two things to enjoy while out in SLKC through Ocho's innocent eyes instead of despising the entire city.

Chapter 09

"THERE. YOU LOOK AMAZING, sweetie."

I turn away from Rami and their suitcase-sized makeup kit, studying myself in the bunk's full length mirror. I have to admit, I look damn good. I'm not usually one for makeovers, but Rami is truly an artist. They've added russet undertones to my skin, which completely alter its color without lightening or darkening its shade. Their expert contouring has changed the shape of my jawline and cheekbones entirely, and the finishing touch is an expensive, skin-grafting fake goatee from their collection.

Although I've never identified as male, the masculine-of-center part of me is pleased with the disguise. Pleased enough that I look over at Elena, who's sitting patiently as Cherry arranges her borrowed blonde wig into an updo and blow her a kiss.

"Right back at you, *guapa,*" Elena says. "You make a hot dude." She looks pretty sexy herself, wearing a tailored navy blue suit that flatters her curves. In addition to their makeup and disguise skills, Rami is fantastic at clothing alterations. It shows in the way Elena's jacket and skirt follow her waist and hips.

"I'm glad someone's pleased," Doc grumbles. She's not too thrilled about her ensemble: clingy, marine blue shorts with a top that's far too large, accompanied by a pair of chunky sunglasses that are probably twice as expensive as the rest of her outfit.

"It's the style for teenagers right now," Rami insists, straightening my tie. "Show off the legs, wear a shirt that looks like a circus tent."

"Whatever." Doc slouches over to her bed, flopping dramatically onto it while Rami turns to Ocho.

"And what do you want, sugar? Boyish? Girly? Androgynous? Genderfucked? Something else? I can make you look older or younger if you want, although older would be easier."

Ocho looks between the four of us as if trying to decide. Cherry has been given an understated look: black pantsuit, brown wig, subtle makeup, the complete opposite of her normal appearance. Rami has gone all out, disguised as an older guy with salt and pepper hair and a bit of a belly. Combined with our professional wardrobes, we'll easily pass for corps middle managers, with Doc as someone's annoying kid.

"Can I wear a dress?" Ocho asks. "I've never worn one before."

Rami squeals with delight and claps their hands, which sounds extra ridiculous coming from a fat, middle-aged man in a suit. "Yes! I have so many dresses. Wait here."

While they scurry off to unearth said dresses from the supply room, where I assume they're stored, Cherry laughs. "Do you know how long they've wanted to put you in a dress, Sasha? Not that they'd ever say so. Rami knows you don't like 'em."

I roll my eyes. "If Ocho's cool with it, Rami can play dress up all they want." In fact, I like the idea, because it will further distinguish Ocho from me.

"Ohhh," Elena says, practically vibrating with excitement. "This I gotta see."

There's a flush from the bathroom next door, followed by the hiss of water in the sink. Half a minute later, Rock enters, struggling to button a crisp white shirt that barely stretches across his broad chest. His large fingers keep slipping with the small buttons. In the outfit, even sans jacket, he looks like a fancy corps bodyguard.

"I got it," I tell him, stepping in to help. Once I finish, he nods his thanks, and I give him an up-and-down. "Looking good, buddy."

Rock does look quite different than usual, with ginger hair and realistic freckles, but there isn't much to be done about his incredible height. He steps back, frames me with his thumbs and forefingers like he's taking a picture, then grins, offering a thumbs-up.

"Glad to have the Rock seal of approval."

Rami returns with several dresses draped across their arm. They toss them onto the bed beside Doc, who sits up to watch the spectacle. The rest of us observe as Rami holds dress after dress up to Ocho's tall frame: sundresses, gowns, and several mini dresses that look more suitable for clubbing.

Ocho seems to like them all. "This one's pretty. Oh, I like that one! No, the other one."

"Come on, Rami," I say. "We're going into corps territory in the middle of the day. At least half of those won't work and you know it."

Rami sighs. "Fun-ruiner. Here, let's see." They dig through the stack of dresses again before coming up with something more reasonable, a black dress with a pencil skirt style bottom and a white 'v' reminiscent of a blazer on top. It would be boring, except for the white ovals that run along both sides from breast to hip, bowing inward to give the wearer an exaggerated waistline. "Oh, this one's good. I actually bought it for Cherry, but the material is enhanced sorona fabric. It'll stretch. I bet it could even fit on Rock if we tried hard enough."

Rock raises his eyebrows as we all turn to look at him. Upon seeing our amused gazes, he strikes a pose, as if he's already wearing the dress. The rest of us burst out laughing.

As our giggle fit dies down, a big smile spreads across Ocho's face. "Can I try it on?"

"Hell yeah," Cherry says. "Go for it, *gatita.*"

Ocho pulls off her shorts and undershirt and starts wiggling into the dress. To avoid watching her change, I glance at Elena. "Got our list of supplies ready, babe?"

"*Si.*" Elena activates her VIS-R, using her eyes to scroll through a transparent blue window. "Faraday business wear and briefcases for smuggling our weapons through the scanners at the Butterfly Lab's main entrances. An 'approved' scent for the Argus dogs…"

I shudder. I've tossed crumbs to a few strays even when I didn't have much to spare, but Argus-line dogs are something else entirely. Used by law enforcement and private security firms, they're genetically modified to be big, strong, and incredibly hostile to strangers. They're nothing short of living weapons.

Cherry shudders with me. "Ugh," she says. "Those things are nightmares with fur."

Ocho pops her head out through the neck of the dress. "Dogs? We get to see puppies?"

"Not the kind you want to pet," I tell her. "Trust me."

She deflates a little but perks up again as she finishes putting on the dress and scurries in front of the mirror to get a good look at herself. "Wow," she sighs, doing a slightly awkward twirl. The dress' skirt doesn't flare, form fitting as it is, but she seems pleased anyway. "I love it!"

"You look good," I say, and I mean it.

Doc hops up from the bed. "Not bad, but it needs something."

"Jewelry," Rami says. "Cherry?"

Cherry hurries over to the dresser and removes a jewelry box. Moments later, she returns with a pair of large golden hoops. With Ocho's buzzed haircut, which Rami provided on Day Three, and the plunging neckline of the dress, she looks fantastic for her first day out.

"Just one problem," Doc says. "I never pierced her ears."

Ocho looks at me with an expression that reminds me of a kid about to plead for candy at the register. "Can I pierce my ears?"

I shrug. Ocho's gotta learn to make decisions for herself sometime. Pierced ears seem like a safe enough starting point. "Go for it."

"Awesome." Doc grabs Ocho's hand and hauls her out of the room, with Cherry following behind. "I'll do your belly button too if you want."

"People pierce their belly buttons?" Ocho asks, sounding bemused as her voice and footsteps grow quieter and quieter.

Elena smirks at me. "Let's not tell her about other things people get pierced."

I nod in firm agreement.

***

It's a beautifully manufactured day in the Kansas City shopping district. The crowd, a mix of wealthy business professionals in suits and their more creatively fashionable dependents, follows a wide path lined with colorful poles. In addition to being decorative, they also contain air scrubbers and control the climate inside the city's plasma bubble.

"The Butterfly Lab has a plasma bubble like this," Elena informs us. "Only it stops physical matter as well as radiation."

"Good thing we're using the front door," Doc says. She pauses, grimacing as she digs a wedgie out of the shorts she hasn't stopped complaining about since we left.

I shoot her a stern look. I don't care about the rude behavior so much, but she should know better than to discuss the mission in public. You never know who could be listening. I scan our surroundings just in case, but no one's paying attention. Rami's disguises allow us to blend right in until we arrive at the next store on our list. The blinking pink sign out front says *PopSugar*, which has always struck me as a rather odd name for a retail establishment. They're a 'quirky' subsidiary of the much larger Nike, of course.

"I'll get the faraday briefcases," Rami says in a lower voice than usual to match their disguise. "Who wants to come with?"

I start to say that all of us will go rather than splitting up when something catches my eye. A few yards down the walkway is an ice cream vending machine with the Aramark logo amidst a scene of colorful cartoon dinosaurs. Normally, the sight wouldn't stand out to me, but a memory tickles the back of my mind, a memory of sweet, sticky vanilla ice cream smeared around my mouth in the summer heat.

"You go ahead," I tell Rami. "I'm gonna get Ocho an ice cream."

That erases the furrow from Ocho's brow immediately. "I remember that from the tube. You mean I get to try the real thing?"

The rest of the crew wastes no time backing her up. Rock nods his approval, and Doc grins. "Yeah! Ice cream. Shit, it's been forever."

"You had ice cream three days ago," Rami points out. "It's not like you've been sugar deprived back at base, either."

"I'm thirteen," Doc protests.

"Well, I'm an adult and I want ice cream," Elena says.

I give her a sidelong look. "Sure, Nevares. You're a real mature example of an adult."

Elena scoffs. "C'mon, Cherry. Chocolate's calling my name."

"You and me both." Cherry grabs Elena's elbow and they hurry over to the ice cream stand together.

"Check and see if they have dairy-free," Rami adds as they follow, with Doc close on their heels.

A considerable amount of chocolate has dripped onto Elena's shirt a few minutes later, after she retrieves her cone from the machine. "Fuck me," she mutters, licking around the edges of the scoop in an effort to stem the tide. It's a futile effort but amusing to watch. Her own fault for getting rocky road with extra chocolate chunks and fudge.

I pass her a napkin and she dabs at the stain on her shirt but doesn't bother using it for her hand. She licks the mess off instead, starting at her wrist and following the trail of chocolate with her tongue. "Pervert," she says when she catches me staring.

I grin and shrug, pretending I'm unaffected even though a large percentage of my blood has suddenly rushed between my legs. "Can you blame me?"

Fortunately, the others aren't paying attention. They're engrossed in their own cones, especially Cherry, who's working on a towering monstrosity of different flavors. My stomach churns just looking at it.

Rami seems to share my mild disgust. "You seriously got mint, strawberry, and peanut butter smushed together?"

Cherry shoves more of the ice cream into her face, as if in defiance of the entire world.

Doc laughs. She's slurping on a cone of rum raisin, while Rock elects for good old-fashioned chocolate with sprinkles. His order isn't as traditional as mine, though.

"Vanilla?" Elena says, eyeing my cone with a judgmental look. "Out of all the choices here, you picked the most boring one."

I make sure the others are bantering amongst themselves and sidle closer. "You connected to my brainbox. Do you remember why that's my favorite?"

Elena's brow furrows as if she's trying to remember something hazy from long ago. "A birthday," she says, still sounding unsure.

"Yeah. When I was seven, I ran in a pack with some other kids. My parents tried to keep me home, but they had full-time cog jobs. Only so much they could do without childcare. Didn't have any other family to look after me for free."

I exhale, thinking back. My memories of that time aren't all terrible. Sure, I was hungry a lot, and I remember missing my parents while they were at work, but I also had fun...before they died, at least.

"My friends and I ran feral all over the city while I was supposed to be doing learning modules, especially in places we weren't supposed to be. One time, we snuck into one of the fancier parts of downtown. We saw this ice cream parlor, and it was my birthday. So..."

"You got ice cream?"

"From the trash, but yeah. Some corps kid threw his out and it wasn't even halfway finished."

Elena nods. Knowing what I do about how she grew up, I suspect she ate more than a few meals from the garbage herself. You do what you have to when you're hungry.

"My parents weren't thrilled when I told them. But next year, they surprised me with a pint of vanilla ice cream. Couldn't have been easy, with all the debt their jobs kept them in."

Elena touches my hand with hers, fortunately choosing the one that isn't sticky. "They really loved you."

My eyes sting a little, but I get it under control. It's an old hurt, even though the wound has been reopened recently. "They did."

We continue eating our ice cream in silence, but it's a silence of understanding. I'm glad I told her. Maybe it'll help Elena come to grips with why I need answers. Why I have to find out the truth, even if it means working with a creep like Andrews.

"Um, Sasha?"

I turn toward Ocho, who's still standing in front of the machine with a look of indecisiveness on her face. A line has formed behind her, full of grumpy looking people in suits and a few whining kids.

"What's up, Ocho?"

Ocho looks helplessly at the flavors on display. "I can't pick," she declares, like it's some great tragedy.

"Here," I say, motioning the rest of my crew over. "Ocho doesn't know what to get. Can she try some of yours?"

Doc offers her cone up immediately. "Rum raisin," she says with a wide grin.

Ocho takes the cone and gives it a lick. Her eyes light up and she gives a subtle moan of approval.

"Seriously?" one of the people in line complains, a white man with a thin mustache and a nasal voice. A few others are glaring, but the majority zone out looking at their VIS-Rs.

"Go ahead of us then," I say, squaring off with him. The guy eyes me up and down, notices Rock's huge form behind me, then decides we're not worth messing with. He goes up to the machine, and the rest of the line follows after without further complaint.

I turn back to Ocho, who's trying Rock's cone. Her brows shoot up and a look of delight spreads across her face. "Chocolate is good. I like the sprinkles."

Rock pats her on the back, making her stagger just a little.

"If you like chocolate, try this." Elena passes over her cone.

Ocho isn't shy about taking a bite. She steals another before Elena taps her elbow and retrieves the cone. "That one," Ocho says. "I definitely want that one."

"You haven't tried mine yet," Cherry says, offering Ocho her dripping, towering monster of a cone with its disgusting concoction of flavors.

"Don't," Rami warns her. "Trust me." They give Ocho their cup of dairy-free, vegan salted caramel cluster while Cherry shakes her head.

"I can't believe you're judging me. I'll admit, some of the vegan and halal stuff you cook is amazing, but that ice cream is bound to taste like shit."

I sense a mild argument brewing, so I offer Ocho my cone instead. "Here. Vanilla. The OG flavor."

Ocho licks my cone, then licks it again. She smiles, hands it back, and returns to the end of the line. I join her while the others step to the side, eating their ice cream before it melts in the summer sun. Even with climate control on the walkway, the heat is still sticky and uncomfortable.

As we wait, a whispered conversation in front of me catches my ear. "Did you hear?" asks a sharply dressed brunette in a navy-blue blazer. "The Corsairs struck again. They stole over fifty million from PGS this time."

The mention of PGS gets my full and immediate attention. I make sure not to look directly at them as I continue eavesdropping.

Her companion, a blonde who looks remarkably similar, smirks as if this is the most salacious gossip she's heard in a while. "I heard they stole a bunch of equipment from construction sites along the band."

Even more interesting. The band is the narrow strip connecting the St. Louis and Kansas City poles, and one section or another is nearly always under construction. But I've never heard of the Corsairs, whoever they are. Must be a local group. I haven't been in SLKC in years, so it makes sense that I'm not up to date on the latest news.

"Why would they want construction equipment?" the brunette asks.

Her companion arrives at the front of the line and begins tapping her ice cream order on the service screen. "No idea. Maybe to sell it?"

"Maybe they work for a rival corporation."

"They've stolen from AxysGen and Sinomerica Credit, too. Just not as much."

It's a very interesting conversation, but I don't get to hear much more. The brunette makes her purchase, joins the blonde, and they both walk away, still talking about the scandal of it all. I make a mental note to run a search on the Corsairs when I return to base, then watch Ocho choose her ice cream.

One payment and a pleasant ding later, Ocho is the proud owner of her very first double scoop ice cream: one scoop vanilla, one scoop rocky road.

Chapter 10

network: d/ 38351 . 90124
Connection established
welcome: user волчица-воин

"Doc, take cover!" I shout, firing past the visitor information booth I've ducked behind. The rounds from my assault rifle ping harmlessly off the AxysGen security mechs heading toward the Eagle. Great. This simulation's mechs must feature penetration resistant armored plating. Leave it to Val to make things as difficult as possible.

Doc's head snaps toward my voice, but it's too late. The mechs roll around the security scanners, their mounted lasers glowing a menacing red.

Cherry crouches beside me. "No worries, Jefa," she pants, blowing her short red bangs aside as she unclips something from her tactical belt. "I've got her." Three fist-sized silver orbs fly through the air, exploding in a cloud of black smoke as they hit the ground.

With the help of my VIS-R, I see Doc's heat signature sprint for the booth, but Cherry's smoke bombs don't offer enough cover. These mechs must be AI piloted, because they don't hesitate as they point their lasers directly at Doc's exposed back.

All of a sudden, the mechs stutter to a stop in unison. They slump over, motionless, their crimson lights going dim. Elena and Ocho emerge from the smoke, jogging to catch up with Doc and escort her the rest of the way to the booth. I exhale in relief when they reach me. This is just a simulation, but seeing Doc in danger still makes my adrenaline spike.

The familiar whir of the Eagle's plasma engine churns behind me. I look over my shoulder to see Rock waving from the open door. The rest of us hop inside the shuttle, buckling into our harnesses as Rami takes flight.

"Well done," Val says through the Eagle's speakers. "Data successfully acquired with zero casualties or injuries."

"Tell that to my blood pressure," I grumble, glaring at the copilot's chair.

Doc shoots me a sheepish grin from around its arm. *"Sorry, Sasha."*

"Relax, Jefecita," Elena says, reaching over to squeeze my thigh. *"Me and Ocho were there to save her bacon. And yours."*

I tighten my lips, unwilling to say anything else. Elena's right, but it was a near miss. On the other hand, Val has done her best to make the simulations more difficult and unpredictable than the actual mission is likely to be. I highly doubt we'll face any giant mechs with enhanced armor at the Butterfly Lab.

"As an aside," Val says, with an audible note of pride in her voice, *"Ocho achieved the highest kill count for this simulation. Congratulations, Ocho."*

Cheers fill the shuttle. Cherry whistles, while Rock pats Ocho's back in congratulations.

"Awesome," Ocho says, grinning bright enough to blind the sun.

A nervous knot forms in my stomach. Ocho's combat abilities have improved at a staggering rate, but sometimes she enjoys the sims a little too much. *"All right, crew,"* I say before the celebration gets out of hand. *"Log out, then reconvene in the living room."*

logging off network
disconnection complete

"Yes! I won!"

I unplug from the main terminal to see Ocho fist-pumping beside me. She flexes, striking a triumphant pose, and the sight's as adorable as it is ridiculous. Not that I'd ever let that show on my face in front of the rest of the crew.

"Yeah, you won," I concede. "You're learning fast."

"With my help," Elena drawls, giving Ocho a friendly slug on the arm. "The EMP to disable those mechs was my idea. Pretty sure that's what put you over the top."

Ocho's smile turns shy. "Thanks, Elena."

"Don't be a kill-stealer, *chaparrita*," Cherry tuts, shaking her head in mock indignation. "Ocho won fair and square."

Ocho's eyes gleam with the promise of adventure. "That means I can come on the mission tomorrow, right?" She's asked to come along on the mission every single day, multiple times a day, with no signs of giving up.

The knot that's already formed in my stomach tightens. "You did well in the sim, but real ops are much more dangerous."

"They're realistic sims, though," Ocho protests. "Messing up triggers my pain receptors. I want to go with you. Besides, what else are you going to do? Leave me here alone? What if enemies show up and attack the base while you're gone?" (She stole that argument from Doc and Cherry, who have been encouraging her desire to join us in the field.)

"She did save me this round, Sasha," Doc pipes up from the other side of the terminal.

It's a real conundrum. Even though I'm the crew's handler, I don't feel right making the call alone. I'm not the only one who will be putting my trust and safety in Ocho's hands if we bring her along. "We'll discuss it after we go over the finalized plan," I say, putting the decision off for another couple of minutes.

Ocho takes that as a positive sign. She fist pumps and heads for the living room, with me and the rest of the crew close behind.

Five minutes later, we're all settled in at the conference table. Cherry and Rami are sharing a bowl of chips with Rock, while Doc is hoarding a two liter of Lightning all to herself. I remove the bottle from Doc's lap, not surprised to see it's already half-empty. "You don't need this much caffeine," I mutter as I return it to the kitchen.

"Caffeine is an addictive substance," Doc says, although she doesn't chase after me to retrieve her soda as it disappears into the depths of the fridge. "If I don't have a certain amount every day, withdrawal symptoms will screw up my concentration. Do you want a field medic with withdrawal symptoms? I don't think so."

It's easier not to argue, so I sit in an empty chair beside Rock while Ocho takes the seat opposite me. To my surprise, Elena strides over and plops into my lap without missing a beat.

My eyebrows shoot up. Elena and I have gotten a lot more demonstrative over the past few months, but not to the point of sitting on each other's laps during meetings. At least, not until now. I can't say I mind, though. The curve of her ass is warm on my thighs, and she smells like shampoo and fabric softener.

"Well?" Elena asks, staring at me expectantly.

I swallow once, struggling to keep my face blank. "Let's start with intranet security. You and Val finished the simulation flawlessly the past five times. Think you're ready for the real thing?"

"Absolutely," Elena says. "Val?"

Val's avatar appears at the head of the table, a smile playing about her lips. I have a feeling she's aware of my pleasant discomfort despite her assurances that she doesn't check the crew's vitals outside of missions. "Elena and I have spent forty hours and thirty-six minutes total running simulations of the Butterfly Lab's intranet security system. Only twelve separate steps are necessary for locating and acquiring the patents."

"Twelve steps?" I shoot Elena a worried look. That's twelve chances for something serious to go wrong.

Elena responds breezily. "Nothing Val and I can't handle. Most of those steps are disabling alarms coded to detect intruders, sending the Guardog.exes after fake malware, and cloaking ourselves from any AxysGen security jackers lurking on the servers. How's it going with exterior security? Any changes?"

That's my area of expertise. "No harm in going over it again. Val, bring up the blueprints."

The table glows, projecting a medium, three dimensional model of the Butterfly Lab next to the communal bowl of chips. The building resembles its namesake, with four overlapping ovals around a central circle, giving the appearance of segmented wings. Each wing has its own purpose: hardware and software on the right, with a collaborative space where they overlap, and biotechnology and robotics on the left. In the center is the food and recreation area, with bunks above and a maintenance department below.

Gently, I dislodge Elena from my lap—which she isn't thrilled about, judging from her unhappy huff—and give her my chair while I stand and point at various parts of the model.

"This will probably sound repetitive but bear with me. The Butterfly Lab is surrounded by a climate-controlled bubble and a twenty-foot-high wall made of graphene. Drones patrol the perimeter regularly. We don't want civilian casualties, so this will be a stealth op. No need to blow our way in when there are perfectly good entrances."

Cherry heaves a dramatic sigh. "There you go again, *Jefa*. Crushing my dreams."

I hide a smile so as not to encourage her. "There are four entrances, North, South, East, and West. We'll infiltrate through the less trafficked South and East entrances, disguised as employees. We'll wear faraday business wear and carry our weapons of choice in faraday briefcases. That should get them past the scanners."

"What about our mods?" Doc asks. "The scanners will definitely ping those, especially Rock's."

It's a good question. Sneaking through security on the simulator isn't quite the same as meatspace, and sometimes Val makes the scanners go off on purpose to give us extra practice for emergencies.

I turn to Rami. "Have you and Val finished that program I asked for?"

"Already taken care of," Rami says. "It's a mod concealer installed on VIS-R, but it goes a step beyond. It should fool the scanners into picking up the regular, lower-grade mods that most AxysGen scientists or employees would have."

"Nice work, hot stuff," Cherry says. "You have that scent for the Argus dogs too, right?"

"Right," Rami says. "That was the hardest thing to get. I bought it on a super shady part of the extranet and had it shipped to a P.O. box, then picked it up without being seen."

As usual, Elena is skeptical. "You sure it's legit?" she asks, fixing Rami with a narrow gaze.

Val answers on Rami's behalf. "I scanned its contents and compared it with leaked formulas I discovered online. Due to the significant time and resource investments required to train the Argus dogs, the formula does not alter significantly from week to week. I estimate our sample's legitimacy at ninety-eight-point three percent."

"I'll take that as a yes." I look from face to face, making sure I've regained everyone's attention. "Once we're past security, Cherry and Rami will sneak into the maintenance department. It's in the middle of the facility, right under the food and recreation area. According to the notes from Andrews' previous infiltration teams, the Butterfly Lab uses voice, fingerprint, and retinal biometrics to confirm identity."

"Even if the biometric data Andrews included doesn't scan for whatever reason, I can get those for you on-site, no problem," Rami says in between snacking on chips. "All I need is some putty and my VIS-R."

"Right. You and Cherry will pose as maintenance workers trying to fix the biometric scanner for the upper left wing, Robotics. If anyone asks, it's on the fritz and you're trying to bring it back online. The rest of us will come along dressed as employees, and you'll let us in after pretending to scan us manually. Rock and Doc, your job is to get Elena to a terminal and watch her back while she's online. I'll remain outside the wing to keep an eye out for privsec."

Rock cracks his knuckles. If we're spotted, I feel sorry for anyone who tries to hurt Elena. Rock's grown really fond of her recently, especially since she helps him with the cooking. She's not nearly as skilled as he is, but at least she makes a capable sous chef. Rock won't hesitate to pummel anyone who comes after her, or any of us, into a fine red mist.

At a look from me, Elena picks up the explanation. "Once Val and I are in, it should be fairly straightforward. Andrews' previous teams set off a shit ton of alarms and got fried, but my specialized code will override those. I've programmed a spyder to search for the data we need. Once it comes back, I'm out, and we'll make a quick exit."

Doc ticks the steps off on her fingers. "So we sneak past the scanners and dogs at the front, Cherry and Rami steal a maintenance worker's voice, retinas, and thumbprint, they let me, Rock, and Elena into the Robotics wing, and we keep an eye out while Elena and Val launch a spyder without setting off any virtual alarms?" She sags in her chair, blowing a loud puff of air up into her bangs. "Piece of cake."

"You forgot something," Ocho says, causing everyone at the table to turn and look at her. "What am I doing?"

I exchange a worried glance with Elena. I've told her exactly how I feel about taking Ocho on a real op, and she repeats my words almost verbatim. "Ocho, it takes longer than two weeks to train for this kind of mission. You're learning fast, but—"

"But I beat everyone else in the simulation today. I shot guards, deactivated Guardog.exes, piloted a shuttle, shut down a bunch of mechs, and didn't get hit by any Puls.wavs. That means I get to go, right?" She looks around the table imploringly, searching for support among the rest of the crew.

"She could at least co-pilot the Eagle," Doc volunteers. "We might have to make a quick getaway."

It isn't a bad idea, but I'm still not convinced. "Your piloting isn't as good as your shooting, Ocho."

"But I didn't hit anything or get hit the last two times. I can do it!"

Her hopeful look tugs at my heart, but it's Val who convinces me. "As the individual who created and implemented the training simulations in question, it is my opinion that Ocho has gained sufficient experience to pilot the shuttle. I believe she will be an asset to this mission, Sasha."

A tight ball of fear forms in my gut, but I trust Val's judgment. "We'll put it to a vote. Who wants Ocho to ride along as copilot?"

Doc's hand shoots up, followed swiftly by Cherry's. Rock studies them for a moment, then raises his hand as well.

"I don't know," Rami says, chewing their lip. "What if you get hurt, Ocho?"

"I know I could get hurt, but I want to do it anyway. I love the simulations. They're exciting. Fun."

The enthusiasm shining on Ocho's face and in her voice pushes Rami over the edge. They raise their hand too, muttering, "If anything happens to you, I'll never forgive myself."

Seeing the way the wind is blowing, Elena raises her hand as well, but the gesture is half-hearted. From the knitting of her brow, she doesn't look happy about it. "If you feel like sitting in a hot, boring shuttle all day waiting for us, be my guest." From the way she looks at me, I can tell we'll be discussing this in private later.

I turn to Val. "I assume you vote yes?"

"Indeed. It seems the decision is unanimous. Congratulations, Ocho."

Val gives Ocho a soft smile, but she's too excited to notice. She hops out of her chair, nearly sending it clattering onto the floor, and throws her arms around me in a rib-crushing hug. "Thank you! I'll be the best co-pilot ever, I promise."

"Sure you will," I say, squirming out of the hug as the others rise from their chairs. But part of me already feels like I've made a big mistake.

Rae D. Magdon

Chapter 11

I LEAVE THE LIVING room without drawing unwanted attention. The volume of my thoughts is too loud for me to hang around the rest of the crew, who are busy congratulating Ocho. Cherry has already launched into a story about one of our previous missions, and Ocho hangs on every word while the others add embellished details.

This is what I signed up for, isn't it? Letting Ocho make her own choices? I just didn't think she'd make the choice to put herself in danger quite so soon.

In the hallway, everything's quieter. I seek refuge in the communal bathroom since it's currently empty. When I catch a glimpse of my reflection in the mirror, I'm surprised by how tired I look. My sleep has been shit since returning to SLKC, and it shows in the slackness of my jaw and the bags under my eyes.

"Checking yourself out, *Jefecita?*"

I turn away from the mirror. Elena's leaning in the doorway, her brows furrowed with worry.

"Don't need a mirror to do that anymore, do I?"

She enters the bathroom, letting the door swing shut. "You're upset Ocho's coming along."

I glance at my reflection, away from her. "I think it's too soon."

In the mirror, Elena's shoulders slump. "Me too."

"Why didn't you say something?"

She shrugs. "Not my call. The rest of the crew voted. I didn't want Ocho to think I don't believe in her."

That's pretty much the same reason I voted to allow Ocho on the mission, but the concern in Elena's eyes unsettles me. The look of worry on her face is a bit too obvious.

It takes me a moment to place the unpleasant bubbly feeling in my stomach, but with growing awareness, I realize it might be jealousy. Ocho is basically a carbon copy of me without the trauma, after all. I guess it shouldn't be such a surprise that Elena has grown to care about her so quickly.

"You're worried about her," I say, trying to play it cool.

Elena's sharp brown eyes fix on me, like she's trying to cut me open and peer inside my brain. "Yeah. Aren't we all?"

"Of course."

I can tell I've answered too fast, because Elena folds her arms across her chest and continues staring me down. "Don't give me that shit." She approaches, shoes tapping on the tiled floor with each step. "What's going on?"

"Worried about the mission."

Elena doesn't look entirely convinced, but she visibly relaxes. A flirtatious smile spreads across her heart-shaped face. "I'm pretty busy tonight, but maybe I can squeeze in a few minutes to help you de-stress."

"Busy?" I return her smile with a smirk of my own, leaning casually against the bathroom counter and eyeing her up and down. Maybe this is what my confidence needs right now. My mind wanders further down the path of depravity as my eyes drop none too subtly to the scooping neckline of her shirt. "Got plans I don't know about?"

"Yeah." Elena gives me a lingering look. "I'm seeing this idiot. She signed us up for a stupidly dangerous op, so I thought we'd bone down before we risk our lives."

I snort. Sometimes, Elena's sarcasm is actually attractive. "Where is this idiot? I'll kick her ass."

"Doubt it." She steps closer, trailing her fingertip along my bare bicep. "She's pretty ripped. A stone cold bitch who looks like she could snap your neck with her thighs."

"Just *looks* like she could? Think I'll risk it."

Elena stands on tiptoe, tilting her chin and inviting me to bend down. Her lips taste like candy—probably her lip gloss—and their warmth sends a wave of want through me. I back her up against the wall, pressing my tongue forward in search of more. When I cup her ass, she hops into my arms, wrapping her legs around my waist. God, her ass. If I could hold onto it every minute of every day, I would.

Elena breaks away from my lips, nipping a hungry trail down my neck. "Fuck, you smell good." She buries her face in the crook of my shoulder and breathes in deep, clutching fistfuls of my shirt in her hands.

I could say the same. The scent of her shampoo fills my nose with flowers, and I can smell her skin, too—mostly warm, with a pleasant hint of sweat.

I want to make her smell like me.

It's a strangely possessive thought, but I'm prepared to roll with it. I dip down, kissing her again, and rock my hips forward into hers. She moans beside my ear, a sound that sends my pulse into overdrive.

"Hi, Sasha. Hi, Elena."

I jerk away from Elena like I've been burned, dropping her onto her feet. She stumbles, and I reach out an apologetic hand to steady her. Ocho stands in the doorway, staring curiously at the two of us.

"Fucking hell," Elena mutters. "Some things are private, Ocho."

"Then you shouldn't dry hump in public." Cherry steps up behind Ocho, putting a hand on her shoulder. Her boldly outlined red lips curl into an obnoxious smirk.

Great. That's exactly what we need, another audience member. "We weren't dry humping," I protest.

Cherry rolls her eyes. "Yeah, right."

She isn't wrong about our poor choice of location, either. It's inevitable that the team walks in on each other from time to time in such close quarters, but the bathroom probably wasn't the greatest pick, even if we have fucked in here before.

"What's dry humping?" Ocho asks.

"Fun, mostly," Cherry says.

Elena cradles her head in her hands. "*Ay Dios mio.* Ocho, Val installed some kind of teaching program about *los párajos y las abejas,* right?"

The middle of Ocho's brow scrunches, making her look even more confused. "Birds and bees are different species. I did lots of animal modules. Their flight methods are an example of convergent evolution."

"*Sex,*" Elena huffs. "Val explained sex while you were in the tube, yes?"

"Oh. *Oh.*" Ocho's eyes widen in understanding. "Yes. I've seen sex."

Val's avatar chooses that moment to join us. "Hello again," she says, her tone echoing much too cheerfully around the bathroom. "I believe I may have made a slight error."

I give Val a hard stare, while Elena rolls her eyes and Cherry snickers in the background. "What kind of error?"

Val's shoulders rise in the illusion of breathing deeply before she offers her explanation. "I provided Ocho with a basic sexual education and allowed her to view selected video clips."

Part of me can't believe what I'm hearing. "You showed her porn? Come on, Val."

"These clips were not for the purpose of sexual gratification," Val says. "But that may have been an inadvertent side effect."

"No, I get it," Elena says. "It would've been cruel to release Ocho into the world with an adult body without teaching her what sex is. My issue is, why were you just standing there?" She directs that question to Ocho, who adopts a worried look.

"Did I do something wrong?"

"You did something hilarious," Cherry says.

"That was my error," Val explains. "I educated Ocho about the basics of sex, both in a biological and social context, but neglected to inform her that most sexual activity takes place in private. Watching sexual videos, even educational ones, is by definition a voyeuristic act."

I groan. "I can't fucking believe this."

"Wait," Ocho says. "So I shouldn't watch?"

"No!" I take a deep breath, trying to calm down. It's not Ocho's fault no one taught her peeping was rude, but the persistent ache between my legs isn't exactly doing my patience any favors. "Look, Ocho. Sex is private, okay?"

Ocho considers this new information. "Why?"

I look to Elena for help, but she's still bewildered, and Cherry is having way too much fun at our expense. Eventually, I turn to Val. Better her than me, even though she's the cause of all this. If I answer the question, I'll be tempted to roll with, *"Because I said so."*

"Most people associate the act of sex with physical and emotional vulnerability," Val explains. "They do not wish to be observed in this state by anyone other than their sexual partner or partners."

"Usually," Cherry can't resist adding.

Ocho's brow furrows. I'm still not sure she gets it, but she nods anyway. "All right." She looks at Elena. "So, do I come back later?"

"What?"

"For my turn at sex."

Elena's jaw drops.

Cherry bursts out laughing, almost in tears. I'm too stunned to speak. I don't know whether I'm quivering with anger, amusement, or exhaustion, because this situation is so far beyond what the poor, horny Sasha of three minutes ago was expecting. I brandish a finger at Val. "You. Fix this. Now."

Val dips her head in apology. "I will endeavor to expand Ocho's knowledge concerning this issue."

"I'll help," Cherry volunteers. "This should be fun."

Part of me thinks that's a terrible idea, but in the interest of getting all of them off my back, I'm willing to take that risk. "Fine," I groan, waving them away. "Just go. All of you."

Cherry and Val escort Ocho, who still seems confused and perhaps disappointed, out of the room. I turn to Elena, who's got her face buried in one hand. "Sorry. Guess the mood's ruined, huh?"

Elena's hand falls away. Instead of echoing my annoyance, she barely manages to hold in laughter. "'*My turn.*' Oh my fucking god. What, does Ocho think everyone on the team just takes a number to screw me?"

I sigh. "It's probably because *I* screw you."

"Yeah, well..." Elena's smirk falls away, and a glazed expression takes its place. "Shit, that's hot."

"What?"

"Two of you at once. Not Ocho. She's still kind of underbaked, if you know what I mean. But I *am* interested in getting fucked by two identical Amazonian goddesses with muscles on top of their muscles."

I shoot her a glare. "Stop messing with me."

"I'm not saying I'd do it. You'd have issues with me fucking your clone—"

"*Major* issues."

"I'm just saying, *theoretically,* Double Sasha would be hot. In the abstract."

I know Elena's joking, but she's poked a nerve. It takes a lot of effort to remind myself that Ocho and I aren't in competition. That my team isn't going to ditch me because they like her better.

Personality has to count for something, though, right? Unless...Maybe Elena would *enjoy fucking a less damaged version of me more. Ocho probably doesn't have all my issues about sex and trust and gender and my body.*

"I don't think she can even consent yet," I grumble.

"Yeah, I know. Definitely puts a damper on the whole threesome fantasy. But I'm absolutely not planning on fucking her anyway."

"Right." Even though I believe Elena, I avert my eyes. There's a lump in my throat, and a hard knot in my chest too.

"Sasha?" Elena touches my arm, and I resist the impulse to jerk away. "Remember that night in Mexico City, before your bitch-ass ex-girlfriend kidnapped Jacobo?"

I think about that night a lot, although I won't admit it out loud. Just remembering it makes me feel uncomfortably vulnerable. "Yeah."

"That's when I realized I wanted to see where this could go. Things have been crazy, but I haven't changed my mind. That's still what you want, right?"

I swallow. It is what I want, and that's what makes everything so damn complicated. Elena and I don't lead the kind of lives that lend themselves to commitment. Last time I tried, I ended up dying six times. But apparently, my heart doesn't care what's logical, or easy, or safe.

I don't want Ocho to fuck her. I don't want anyone else to fuck her. We haven't had the exclusivity talk yet, but we haven't exactly been fucking anybody else either, and it feels like that's what Elena's offering. It scares me how much I want to accept.

"Sasha?"

Elena's worried brown eyes peer up into mine. She bites her lower lip, almost like she's nervous, and I feel a sharp tug in the pit of my stomach. *Come on, idiot. She's offering herself up on a platter. What are you so fucking afraid of?*

I grab Elena's hand, pulling her toward the door. She stumbles after me, confused, until I lead her to the bunk.

"Thought the mood was ruined?" Elena says, slightly breathless, as I drag her through the doorway.

I drop her hand long enough to activate the electronic locks. "Changed my mind."

Chapter 12

AFTER THAT, THERE'S NO more talk. I'm on Elena like an animal, kissing her so deep neither of us can breathe. Oxygen's overrated anyway. I seize her wrists, backing her into the wall and pinning her there. Our bunk might be more comfortable, but I'm not about comfort right now. I've got a goal: to prove to Elena that I'm the only one of me she wants, the only one she needs.

In moments like this, I can live off the sweetness of Elena's mouth. She sucks hungrily at my tongue, squirming against my grip. I can tell from her noises and movements that she isn't fighting for freedom. Even though our bodies are already pressed together, she's trying to get even closer. I don't let her. I want her helpless and I want her wild. The more off balance she is, the more control I have.

I tear away from her lips to bend down and fasten my teeth to her throat. She yelps, tossing her head back, but her hips buck forward. I have a feeling if I took off her pants, I could slide three fingers in her without any resistance.

The temptation to test that theory is strong, almost as strong as the throbbing between my legs. Elena's whimpers cut straight to my core. The heat of her breath sends sweat rolling down my spine. Fuck, she's driving me crazy without even trying. My legs wobble dangerously. It's not supposed to go this way.

I reposition Elena's wrists, holding them above her head with one hand so I can put the other to better use. Stripping her is too time consuming. Instead, I unzip her fly and shove my hand down her pants. I have to hunch because of the height difference, but the mild awkwardness is worth it. She's dripping, just like I hoped. Her underwear is soaked all the way through.

"Oh shit." Elena's head lolls to one side, her hair clinging to her cheek. She rocks into my hand, smearing more wetness onto my fingers. I do exactly what I set out to do: slide three inside her at the same time, without any warm-up.

Elena takes them easily. Her muscles clamp around me, so tight it's hard to move, but her slickness more than makes up for that. Another sticky rush spills into my palm before I can even set the pace, and my chest swells with pride. I'm the one who did this to her, who worked her up this much.

"You gonna fuck me, *Jefecita,*" Elena pants, her bright brown eyes gleaming with challenge. "Or just stare?"

Shit. She's really asking for it.

I tighten my grip on her wrists and plunge my fingers as deep as they'll go, lifting Elena onto her toes with the force. Her smile drops into an open mouthed moan, and her dark lashes flutter. A blade of desire twists in my belly as I imagine making a mess of that pretty face. It's definitely on my to-do list.

Elena moans loud and long as I hook into the swollen spot along her front wall. It's puffy and easy to find, and her noises let me know without a doubt that I've hit the right place. I apply pressure until the tendons in my forearm burn. Sometimes, good things are worth a little pain.

Obviously, Elena agrees. Her muscles seize up, and a jet of hot fluid hits the heel of my hand. The mess runs everywhere, down my arm and into her ruined underwear. Her pelvis jerks, and she ripples rhythmically around my fingers. Less than a minute, and she's already coming.

"You're so thirsty for it," I growl, nipping the edge of her ear.

Elena doesn't answer right away, but her clit gives a noticeable twitch, and the wetness just keeps pouring out. Finally, she catches her breath enough to say, "And...whose...fucking fault...is that?" I shove my fingers deeper to show Elena exactly whose fault it is. She hisses, almost like she's in pain, but I know better. Elena can always tell me to stop, but until I hear the word, I'm going to fuck her so hard she won't be able to walk right for the rest of the day.

"Fuck, fuck, *fuckfuckfuck,*" Elena chants along with my new tempo, which is even faster and harder than before. Now that I've got her nice and warmed up, there's no reason to hold back. I let go of her wrists and cup her flushed face, pressing my thumb into her mouth. She sucks like she's starving, staring into my eyes the whole time. The knife in my gut gives another sharp twist.

It plunges deeper when Elena comes again, rising on her toes as though my fingers are too much. Her face screws up, and she rolls her tongue around my thumb even more urgently, like that might convince me to keep pounding into her. Not that I need convincing. I'm as desperate to fuck her as she is to get fucked.

I don't just want to fuck her with my fingers, though. While Elena gasps and moans and writhes on my hand, my eyes drift to the duffel at the foot of my bunk. Strapping up means I'll have to move us, but I might go crazy if my cock isn't splitting her pussy open in the next couple of minutes.

As Elena comes down, she notices where I'm looking and lets my thumb slide from her mouth. "Get it," she urges, giving another deliberate squeeze around my fingers. The message is clear. *I'll milk the hell out of you once you're in me.*

My core clenches so hard it hurts. I pull out and grip her backside in both hands, lifting her up and carrying her to my bunk. She kisses and nips my neck until we get there, but I'm so focused I hardly feel it. I deposit her on the bed and unzip my bag, rummaging for what I need.

While I search for my cock, Elena shucks her clothes, ditching them in a pile on the floor. By the time I grab the toy and its remote, she's naked and grinning. That grin grows wider when she sees what I'm holding. "Yes," she mutters, licking her lips.

The hunger in her eyes is sexy, but a tiny bit of fear would be better. I don't just want to fuck her, I want to ruin her for anyone but me. I turn on the remote, holding the button that makes the shaft thicker. I don't release it until Elena lets out a small gasp. "Yes," she says again, with the right amount of awe this time.

I can understand why. I've made my cock considerably thicker than usual, and I'm going to make Elena feel every inch of its girth. Ideally, she'll still be feeling it hours after we're done. I toss the remote back into the bag and pull down my pants, giving her my hardest stare.

"Elbows and knees. Now."

Elena shudders but obeys. She drops to all fours, that perfect ass of hers pointed straight toward me. I almost swallow my tongue. No matter how many times I see Elena like this, the sight still strikes me dumb.

She's gorgeous. Insanely gorgeous. Her thighs are so soft, so round and pliable. They make me want to dig my fingers in and only let go to see the bruises they leave. And her pussy...the puffy pink lips are swollen. Gleaming. Begging to wrap around me.

Elena looks expectantly over her shoulder, tossing her glossy hair, and I lose it. No one else gets to claim this gorgeous creature. I won't stand for it.

I position the cup-shaped base of my cock between my legs. There's gentle suction, the toy securing itself in place, then a tingling warmth as the sensation transmitters line up. When I tighten my grip on the shaft, the pressure of my palm travels all the way to the root of my clit.

I look down, admiring the sight of my cock jutting from between my thighs. It makes me feel good. Confident. Elena's still watching me, so I put on a bit of a show. I give my shaft a slow pump, tensing as heat leaks from the tip, rolling over the head. She licks her lips, opening her legs wider.

If I make myself wait any longer, I might actually explode. I climb onto the bunk and kneel behind her, seizing her hips in my hands. Elena drops her breasts to the bed, raising her ass even higher. She releases a luxurious moan that fills the room, and I hurry to position myself. Moans aren't good enough. I want *screams.*

My hips stutter when my cockhead grazes Elena's heat. Even that small amount of contact sends me reeling, but I pull it together and use my grip to push forward. There's resistance. A lot of it. Elena's dripping wet, but the increased size means this will be a challenge.

"Fuck, Sasha. Put it in."

"Trying."

I slide my right hand around to her clit, rubbing firmly. She clenches—I feel the movement against my tip—and more slickness runs over me to drip down Elena's thighs. I push again, and this time I make some progress. The head slides in with a satisfying pop.

At first, I can only stare. The sight of my shaft splitting the perfect pink heart of Elena's pussy, stretching it obscenely wide, is just too beautiful. She whimpers, making little stirring motions to coax me into movement, and my instincts take over. I grunt and shove another inch inside.

God, she's tight. So tight I can feel every ripple that passes through her core. Her warmth seals around me, drawing me in. Before I know it I'm rutting against her ass, desperate to bury myself all the way. I'll fill her so deep, fuck her so hard, she won't remember anyone outside of me exists.

I lunge, pinning Elena face-first to the mattress and trapping her with my weight. She yelps but doesn't fight it, fisting the covers and muffling her shouts in my pillow. This time, when I thrust forward, I bump the end of her channel. I've bottomed out, but there's still more of my length left to go.

I make it my mission to fit that last stubborn inch inside. I angle my pelvis, hitting as deep as possible, holding Elena's hips for every bit of leverage I can get. It's all so overwhelming, the sharp taste of salt as I drag my tongue along her spine, the thick scent of sex rising between us, the loud *schlick* of my shaft plunging in and out.

Elena groans, bearing down on me, and I'm pretty sure I'm about to make her come a third time. The thought lights a fire in me. I want her to come on my cock, mine and no one else's.

"Shit, I'm coming!" She tenses and shudders beneath me, legs flexing, muscles clenching.

I bite her left shoulder hard enough to leave marks. "Do it," I grunt, smearing kisses around the imprint of my teeth. "Come all over me."

Elena doesn't need my encouragement. She's already riding her peak, inner walls quivering. The rhythmic flutters tug and tease, but I resist, leaving another bite mark on Elena's back beside the first. I rake my nails along her thighs, relishing the way she hisses between high pitched moans. Marking her up is the only thing keeping me sane. It's like some primal part of me believes my bites and scratches will prevent anyone else from claiming her.

It's still not enough. Elena squirms beneath me, obviously still in the midst of ecstasy, but the possessive flame in me only burns brighter as I watch her. *Feel* her. I shove my left hand into her hair and push her face into the pillow, desperate for more control. My right hand returns to her clit, rubbing with quick up-and-down strokes that have her gasping every time I withdraw.

Mine. That word echoes in my head. Drums against my heart. It pounds in my cock as the fullness inside me builds. *Mine mine mine.* I'm a bomb primed to go off, and my fuse is burning dangerously short.

But something keeps me from coming. No matter how deep I thrust, no matter how good it feels to bury myself in Elena's satin heat, I've reached a wall. It's almost like the harder I try, the further away my orgasm seems. I grunt in frustration, hunching over her to adjust my angle, but it doesn't help. I'm stuck.

Elena fights against my hold on her hair, turning her head sideways. Her eyes roll to their corners to look at me, and I can tell she senses my frustration. *"Calmate.* I like it rough, but you're gonna destroy me with that big dick of yours."

I'm almost embarrassed by the way my hips jerk in response. It's not fair how easily she manipulates me. My clit twitches beneath the transmitter, and my shaft throbs too. *Fuck it.* Since Elena can pierce straight to my core with just a few words, I might as well go for broke.

"Tell me..." I snap my hips hard, relishing the squeal she makes. "Tell me who this pussy belongs to."

At first, all Elena does is scratch at the sheets and pant into the pillow. Her face contorts with pleasure, and I feel her muscles squeeze again. I pull my hips back even though it nearly kills me to withdraw even an inch, but judging by her whines, it hurts Elena more. Eventually, she manages to answer. "It's yours. Your pussy, Sasha."

That coaxes a shuddering slip of precome from my cock. I resume thrusting with slow, deliberate strokes. "Who gets to fuck you, huh? Who gets to come in you?"

Elena chews the inside of her cheek. She's obviously overwhelmed, but somehow, she manages to maintain a hazy sort of eye contact with me. The dark black circles of her pupils almost swallow her irises. "Just you, baby. Just you."

She looks at me like I'm the only person in the world that matters, and the tenderness that glows on her face beneath the tension of unmet pleasure opens the fist that's been squeezing my heart. I believe her. Her eyes, her voice, the way her body remains completely open to me. The way her hips roll into mine like waves kissing the shore. It all screams sincerity.

Without warning, everything I've been holding back breaks free, washing over me in a powerful wave. I come at the apex of my next thrust, consumed by shudders. My core clenches. My clit strains into the transmitter. White flashes before my eyes and pressure races the length of my cock, spilling deep inside Elena. Inside what's mine.

Elena seems smug at first. She licks her lips and fixes me with a sultry look, one that drips with satisfaction. But she can't hold the expression for long. Her mouth falls open, and she makes a strangled noise of surprise as her flutters start again. If I wasn't breathless, I'd laugh. She's coming a fourth time, all because I am. There's really no better ego trip than that.

I pound through the rest of my orgasm, my hips jogging at a stuttering, inconsistent pace. They have a mind of their own, and my attempts to keep a regular rhythm are useless. Every time she squeezes, I freeze and forget what I'm doing as another contraction seizes me. My cock keeps spilling. It's using my own wetness, so there's a lot, but even I don't usually come this much, with or without it.

"*Así, Sasha. Dame más.*"

I curl my body over Elena's, using my hand in her hair to turn her head and pull her in for one last kiss. If she says anything else, I fear it really will be the death of me.

By the time my peak dissolves into aftershocks, I'm a sweaty mess of trembling limbs. I collapse on top of Elena, heaving an exhausted breath beside her cheek. She laughs, a husky satisfied sound that makes my heart melt.

"Fuck," she slurs. "Think I blacked out there for a second."

"Didn't know you could scream while you were unconscious."

"Shut up." She takes a few more moments to catch her breath. "If your goal was to keep me from sitting for the rest of the day, you win."

I sweep some sweaty strands of hair off her neck, dropping a kiss behind her ear. "Yeah?"

"Yeah. Shit, if you're gonna keep it that big, your dick belongs in the armory with the other weapons."

"Cute." I drag my fingers along the roll of her stomach, causing her to yelp and squirm beneath me.

"Sasha!"

I kiss her shoulder in apology, but then it pops out of my mouth before I can stop it: "So, you're really not gonna fuck Ocho?"

Elena rolls her eyes. "No way. Being in the middle of a Sasha sandwich would be hot, but like you said, she isn't another you. There could never be another you exactly like, well, you. Shit, I'm not making sense."

"No!" I gaze longingly down at her, hanging on every word. "No, I...thanks." I swallow. "And you're not gonna fuck anyone else, either?"

Elena's face softens, and her brown eyes take on a warm golden glow. "Not if you don't want me to."

"I don't want you to."

"Okay then."

The nervous knot inside me unravels at last. I sigh, melting into Elena, and she accepts my weight with a contented exhale of her own. Suddenly, I feel exhausted, probably as much from asking the question as the sex.

"Damn. I feel some kind of way about you, Nevares."

Elena smiles. That's kind of our code for 'I love you', because we both know it's too soon to say it. "Me too."

I stay on top of her for a little while longer, but I can tell she's getting uncomfortable. Eventually, I summon enough strength to pull out and roll off her, although I curl up beside her almost immediately and pull her body into mine. These past few months, I've discovered that I'm a cuddler. My one night stands weren't clingy by design, and Megan was never patient enough to do much snuggling, although she could be physically affectionate...

Usually when she wanted something.

I shake that thought away. Elena doesn't seem to want anything except to rest beside me and nuzzle my neck, which is something I'm more than happy to provide. It feels good. Right. Of all the people in the world Elena could be cuddling with, she chose me. I'm glad I chose her, too.

Chapter 13

MONDAY, 09-14-65 12:24:07 AXYSGEN BUTTERFLY LAB, SLKC

'WELCOME TO AXYS GENERATIONS' world-famous Butterfly Lab, where technology touches lives. Please proceed to the nearest security checkpoint and place all purses, bags, and loose items of clothing on the conveyor belt. Then walk through the scanner and wait for the green light. Enjoy your exciting sneak peek into the future!"

The speaking hologram features a skinny white woman in a royal blue, form-hugging skirt and jacket. Her blue eyes and blinding white smile are way too wide for me to interpret as friendly, although not everyone seems as put-off by her as I am. Several families in what I can only term "tourist outfits"—t-shirts and shorts that don't look all that special, but probably cost more than most cogs make in a year—have already lined up alongside the main guest queue to take pictures with her.

"Makes you wanna hurl, doesn't it?" Elena whispers from beside me. Unlike the tourists, she's dressed in a crisp navy pantsuit with a cream colored blazer underneath. She looks indistinguishable from the scientists and engineers shuffling through a much shorter employee queue, presumably to work the next several days in a manic frenzy assisted by stimulants. Not so different from exam time at AukPrep, but the difference is they're doing that all year round. Heart attacks, mental breakdowns, and even death aren't uncommon at the Butterfly Lab, from what I've heard.

I watch the hologram repeat her speech for the next batch of photo-happy tourists posing outside the shiny graphene wall that surrounds the Butterfly Lab's outdoor campus. It reminds me of Disney World, to be honest. Not a reassuring comparison, considering how unsettling that place can be.

"Is it just me, or does that holo look weirdly similar to Cross?" I ask Elena.

She takes a closer look. "They could be siblings. Gives me the creeps."

"They both possess a remarkable amount of facial symmetry," Val says through my ear mods. *"Humans usually admire this. However, may I gently suggest that we proceed? The others have already begun to infiltrate the lab."*

Val is right. We don't have time to linger. Rami and Cherry are headed in through the west entrance, while Rock and Doc (who really enjoyed the old lady makeup Rami painted on her) are infiltrating through the east entrance, so the whole crew won't be seen together on camera. That leaves Elena and me to sneak in from the north.

I join the back of the employee queue, with Elena following a step behind. My agitation increases the closer we get to the checkpoint. I'm not worried about bag checks, but they do have an extra precaution the tourist line doesn't: a pair of enormous Argus dogs with stiff backs, upright ears, and quivering tails. They look like if a pack of the world's meanest German Shepherds had drunken one night stands with a grizzly bear.

As we draw closer to the dogs, I slow my breathing. The damn things can smell fear, although hopefully all they're searching for is the approved scent legitimate employees at the Butterfly Lab are supposed to apply to their skin once a week. It didn't smell like anything when I spritzed it on this morning, but then again, I'm no genetically engineered monster dog.

Fortunately, the Arguses don't react to our presence. I walk up to the dogs and their uniformed handlers first, adopting a loose and confident stride. After a disinterested sniff, they let me through, and I suppress a sigh of relief.

Next is the scanner. I've got a pistol strapped to the small of my back as well as a handful of biogrenades in my pocket, but I feel practically naked without my Phoenix. Elena's become halfway decent with a gun these past few months, but I prefer much heavier weaponry.

When the bored-looking security person waves me forward, I step into the body scanner. It's a human-sized grey tube, plastered with pictures of a featureless stick figure holding their hands up inside. I copy the pose and wait. Nothing happens for a moment, but then the border of the tube flashes green, followed by a cheerful ding. Some of the tightness in my gut dissolves. The false mod broadcasters Rami installed on our VIS-Rs have done the trick.

Elena follows me through without any trouble, doing a pretty good impersonation of an impatient worker just trying to get through the line. Once she's done, she catches up to me, and we take the open air tunnel leading through the outer wall and into the Butterfly Lab's campus grounds.

The first thing I notice as I step through is the fresh air. It's crisp and clear, and I take a big lungful as soon as it hits my nose and mouth. They have more than regular air scrubbers in here. Real oaks and maples surround the building, their branches swaying gently in the breeze. The hum of the power grid is completely absent. All I hear is the rustling of leaves, occasionally interspersed with the voices of other workers headed for the building.

Despite the danger, I can't help feeling a bit more relaxed. I've gotten used to real trees during the time we spent in Barbados, and because several of the Lucky Seven's hideouts are tucked away in the planet's increasingly rare wilderness areas. I've missed wildlife a lot more than I expected since returning to SLKC. Simulations just can't quite capture the real thing.

Elena gives me a wide eyed look as if to say, "This is nice," although she doesn't actually speak. The two of us join the flow of the medium-sized crowd heading for a large green sign that says *Robotics Wing*.

As we walk, I blink to activate my VIS-R. I pull up the crew's radio frequency and speak in a whisper. "Wolf and Shield in."

Doc's voice responds through my ear mods. *"Hey, you finally used the super cool nickname you always pretend to hate! Halle-fucking-lujah."* I clear my throat loud enough for Doc to hear. *"Sorry, I know, Code Whatever. Cupcake and Muscles in."*

Beside me, Elena snorts. "Cupcake?"

"I'm hungry, okay? It's lunch time."

"Sorry, cerebro," Cherry replies in all our ears. *"Didn't you eat like five pancakes for breakfast?"*

"Yeah, just five," Doc says. *"I'm starving."*

I grit my teeth. Hopefully, they aren't attracting too much attention with their chatter, wherever they are. "Status?"

"Short Fuse and Casper the Sexy Ghost are in."

It's a struggle not to roll my eyes.

"Those code names suck," Elena says with a low laugh. "Try again."

"I disagree," Val says, apparently unable to keep her opinion to myself. *"They strike me as tongue-in-cheek. Code names are supposed to be amusing as well as functional, correct?"*

"No," I grunt, while Doc and Cherry answer, *"Yes."*

"What about Firecracker and The Phantom?" Cherry suggests.

"Getting there," Elena says.

My fingers clench into fists. "I swear to fucking god, you guys."

"Come on, Jefa. Lighten up."

My prayers to the gods of patience and not fucking up are answered, and my crew goes silent after that. Elena and I head for the building, a large, silver graphene affair with a decorative hexagonal pattern on its walls. Electronic posters on either side of the doors flash through various AxysGen products, showing each for a few seconds before moving onto the next. The AxysGen logo, a large padlock, shines above the entryway like a beacon, attached to another sign that reads 'Robotics Lab'.

We step through.

The lab's foyer is large and spacious, featuring several exhibits for the tourists to admire. Hi-def screens on the walls show vids of scientists in crisp white lab coats building sleek machinery, from motorcycles to toy mechs, several of which are displayed on illuminated podiums surrounded by smiling kids. Glowing terminals line the far wall, where visitors can test the latest AxysGen jacking cables. The lines for those stretch halfway through the room.

Instead of joining the throng, Elena and I take the employee tunnel that curves directly alongside the foyer. It's separate from the main room, but made of reinforced glass, so we can see the tourists and they can see us. I can't help wondering whether the scientists who work here feel like exhibits themselves.

Beyond the next door is a smaller room. It's much less crowded, with leather chairs and a person-sized statue of the famous AxysGen padlock. A few people in lab coats or business attire come and go, and a bored looking security guard sits behind a desk in front of a set of double doors equipped with biometric scanners. Each person who enters pauses to stare into an eye level green circle and press their thumb to an adjacent pad before passing through.

"Be advised that Cherry and Rami are not yet in position," Val informs me. *"You must stall for time."*

I hesitate, allowing another cluster of employees to pass. Elena and I share a nervous glance. We can't linger out here, or the security guard might wonder what we're doing. At least this one doesn't have an Argus at his side. I guess AxysGen keeps most of them by the front entrances.

To look less suspicious, I pull up some scrolling text on my VIS-R. The opaque privacy gradient means no one who isn't directly in front of it can read what I'm reading, but they'll be able to tell I have a window pulled up if they glance in my direction. For all they know, I could be checking emails.

"Firecracker and The Phantom incoming," Rami says in my ear. *"Andrews' biometric data works perfectly, so we have what we need."*

"Excellent," Val tells them, so I don't have to risk responding out loud. *"Wolf and Shield already in position. Cupcake and Muscles approaching now."*

Great. Now they've got Val doing the code name thing, too.

Doc and Rock arrive less than a minute later. Dressed as a very old lady in a lab coat escorted by a giant of a man in mint green scrubs, Doc looks like a scientist accompanied by her personal care assistant. Cogs can almost never afford those—they die or remain home-bound, relying on family members for care—but a valued AxysGen research scientist could easily afford one to accompany them to work.

I don't look their way as they enter the foyer and pass the security desk, heading for the door at an excruciating crawl. From the corner of my eye, I can tell Doc is really hamming it up with her shuffling gait. I have to struggle not to roll my eyes.

As if on cue, Rami and Cherry arrive next. This time, Rami is dressed as a wiry, middle-aged woman of indeterminate ethnicity, long raven hair pulled up into a twist behind their head. They're dressed in a pair of grey maintenance overalls over a white shirt. It's quite a change from the large man they were disguised as upon entering the lab, but I suppose they had to do a quick change to match whoever's biometric data they stole.

Following a step behind, Cherry is dressed in the same outfit. A badge that says 'trainee' has been sewn onto hers, which I'll remember to give her shit about later. Probably Rami's doing since they were in charge of our disguises.

They approach the door to find Doc already there, throwing a mild fuss as she tries to scan her thumb. The circle on the door flashes red and beeps in rejection, which causes the security guard to look up with interest.

"If you'll please step aside, ma'am, we can help you with that," Rami says, in their perkiest customer service voice. "The biometric scanners on this door aren't working properly at the moment."

Doc throws up her hands in exasperation. "Not working? Why not? How am I supposed to get in? Ridiculous." She turns to the security guard and shoots him a withering glance, which causes him to look away immediately. He's obviously content to let the maintenance workers handle this one.

"Just give us a moment, ma'am," Cherry says. "We'll reset the scanner for you."

While she pretends to soothe Doc, Rami presses their thumb to the thumbpad. They've got a mold of a real maintenance worker's thumb over their own, while their VIS-R projects a scan of the same worker's retinas. "Sarah Reed," Rami says, mouthing along with what sounds like a real voice, but I know to be a recording.

The circle flashes green, and my heart leaps with excitement. We're in! Part of me almost wishes Ocho was here to share the thrill with me, even though I know she's much safer guarding the Eagle in the employee shuttle lot and awaiting our return.

"There," Rami says. "I'll go ahead and let you through."

Doc sniffs, pretending to be unimpressed. "Well, it's about time." She hobbles through with Rock behind her. Once they disappear, I give Elena a subtle nod. She leaves me, approaching the door. After another fake conversation, Rami lets her through as well.

I try hard not to worry as I wait in the foyer for another minute, still pretending to read. It's up to Elena to find a terminal once she's inside, with Doc and Rock to watch her back. Meanwhile, Cherry and Rami have control of the door. I keep my eye on the guard, just in case he starts to suspect something is wrong and radios for assistance. The metal casing of my hidden pistol sticks to the sweat that's sprouted on my lower back.

"Excuse me."

A heavy shoulder bumps mine, sending me off balance and forcing me to re-place one of my feet. I turn to glare at whichever careless fool bumped into me, angry at myself for not noticing their approach while my attention was focused on the guard. But when I see the face of the person who collided with me, I drop all pretenses of anger.

My mouth falls open. A fuzzy, floating feeling fills my head. I can't believe what I'm seeing, but those eyes, that nose, that mouth—all of it is undeniably familiar. I recognize the tall Black woman standing before me instantly, but only manage to croak out a single word. "Mom?" This can't possibly be real, but I'm not sure yet whether I'm experiencing a dream or a nightmare.

"Not quite," the woman says. "But there's no time to explain. We need to get you and your crew out of here. This whole thing is a set-up, and security will be here any se—"

The loud squall of an alarm blares through the foyer, accompanied by flashing red lights on the ceiling. The woman's face hardens. She draws a pistol from within her suit jacket. "Shit. Make that right now."

Chapter 14

THE SECURITY GUARD LEAPS out of his seat, fumbling for his radio, but I'm faster. I draw my pistol and fire first. He goes down with not one, but two smoking holes in his chest. The strange woman shot him too, just as quickly as I did.

I give my new ally a frantic look. I'm not one to trust strangers, but in this situation I don't have much choice. "Half my crew's in there." I gesture at the door. "I'm going after them. Come, or don't."

Before the woman can respond, the door opens. Elena, Rock, and Doc rush out to meet us, joined by Cherry and Rami on the way. "It was a trap," Elena gasps, skidding to a stop beside me. "Something pinged us as soon as we jacked in, like it was waiting for us."

"This 'something' was not merely a program," Val says, fear audible in her voice. *"During our brief exchange, it behaved like a sentient being, albeit faster than any jacker I have ever encountered."*

"What are you talking about?" Cherry asks. "And who's this?" She points at the woman.

There's no time for explanations. The doors leading from the common area to the Robotics foyer burst open, revealing six security guards and four Arguses. The guards aim their weapons, and the dogs lunge. Adrenaline surges through my limbs. Since Elena's closest, I shove her toward the desk. "Go!"

My crew scatters, taking cover throughout the foyer. Elena dives behind the desk with Doc in tow, while Cherry ducks around one of the waiting room chairs. Rami vanishes in the chaos while Rock fends off the guards and dogs. The stranger and I end up behind the decorative padlock sculpture, backs plastered against its base. Gunfire pings off the metal, the sound dampened by my ear mods.

I peek around the corner of the statue, searching for an opening to help Rock with some cover fire. He has two Arguses clamped on his arms, tearing at his fleshweave. Strips have already ripped off, revealing blood and organic flesh beneath. Someone fires from behind the desk, and one of the dogs drops. Rock ignores the other Argus, charging straight into the cluster of guards with it still attached to his forearm. Moments later, it and two guards end up squashed in a Rock-sized dent in the wall.

The remaining dogs rush the desk where Elena and Doc are hiding. I pop up to shoot one, but it keeps going. I have to empty my mag before it stops, collapsing on the tile in a smear of blood. The other dog prepares to leap the desk, but a bright blue flash and a sticky squelch stop it in its tracks. Doc has dipped into her stash of biogrenades.

The guards attempt to regroup in the doorway, taking cover behind its frame. One aims her weapon at me, but goes rigid, falling to her knees with a blank expression. It's like she's fainted dead away, but the subtle shimmer beside her tells me that Rami's snuck up behind her.

Beside me, the stranger fires at the remaining three guards, forcing them to retreat further behind the doorframe. "We've got to get out of here." She straightens, heading for the door with a determined stride. "Come on."

I bristle at the thought of taking orders from someone else, but this is a bad situation. The longer we stay, the more backup will arrive.

"Let's move," I call to the rest of my crew. They emerge from cover, rattled but unharmed. The only one with visible injuries is Rock, but the strips of flesh missing from his forearms don't seem to slow him down. Thanks to his mods, he isn't bleeding heavily. He meets my concerned gaze with a stoic nod.

"Listen," the stranger says. "PGS set you up, working with AxysGen. I'll explain later, but for now, my crew wants to get you out alive." She looks at me as she says that, and I can't tell if the 'you' she's referring to is singular or plural. If she does have some connection to my mom, she might only be here for me.

"I don't go anywhere without my crew," I tell her.

The stranger smiles. "Of course, Sasha."

How does she know my name?

"Where's your crew?" Cherry asks.

"Close. LeRoy, what's your position?" From the look of concentration on her face, I can tell she's listening to someone's voice in her ear. She turns back to me. "They're almost here. If we push now, we can get past the guards and make a break for it. We've got a shuttle outside."

'Shuttle' reminds me of Ocho. I use my VIS-R to speak over our crew's frequency. "Ocho, bring the shuttle and meet us at—"

"Hi, Sasha!" Ocho's voice comes in loud and clear through my ear mods. A little too loud and clear. I wince. *"I was about to call you. A pretty woman with pink hair showed up, saying I should come with her to meet you. Should I?"*

"Uh." I look at the stranger. "You know someone with pink hair?"

She nods. "My pilot."

"Okay, Ocho. Go with her and do what she says."

"Will do!"

"Val," I say. "Can you get the Eagle out of here?"

"I will use the autopilot function to return it to base."

"Val?" the woman asks. "You don't have a crewmember named Val."

I round on her. "How do you know that?"

Before she can answer, the foyer doors burst open. Another wave of guards has arrived to bolster the three survivors, and they have more dogs.

"Fucking shit." Cherry reaches into the pocket of her maintenance overalls. "Use your suppression mods if you got 'em." She withdraws a small black grenade and chucks it at our advancing enemies.

I do what she says, hitting the deck for good measure.

Fwoom.

The world goes sepia as my VIS-R and mods kick in, dampening the sudden burst of noise and light. The sound of the explosion is muffled, but I feel the force of the blast vibrate along the floor beneath my stomach.

When my vision and hearing return, I clamber back to my feet. I offer my hand to Elena, who's pulling herself up beside me. Both of us take in the carnage. A pile of stunned guards and dogs have fallen to the ground, bleeding. A few might be dead, but I'm numb to it. I can't afford to feel anything until we get out of here. Wordlessly, we pick ourselves up, exiting the foyer at a jog as a robotic voice shouts over the PA system.

"Attention: armed intruders have entered the building. All guests and employees must go to the nearest secure area and block all entrances and exits. Attention: armed intruders..."

Outside, scientists and civilians scatter at the sight of us. Terrified people in lab coats dive behind trash cans and trees while confused tourists sprint away in fear. A few brave or stupid souls remain where they are, filming us with their VIS-Rs and wearing slack jawed expressions. I turn away from them. Just my fucking luck if someone livestreams this, although according to the stranger, AxysGen already knows we're here.

We meet more resistance at the campus' west entrance. More guards are waiting for us past the scanners, at least a score of them. This time, they aren't only carrying guns. They've got five-foot-tall rectangular energy shields made of hard light, large enough to provide cover while kneeling. A second line of guards with rifles stands directly behind them. As soon as they spot us, they open fire.

I throw myself behind the nearest cover I can find: Rock. He stands in the center of the path like a steel tower, taking several rounds directly in his chest. He grunts in pain, staggering slightly, but doesn't fall. I grasp his waist from behind, urging him sideways. Together, we take shelter behind a large tree trunk. Splinters of wood fly around us as the guards continue firing.

"Fucking shit," Cherry hollers. "What now?" She and Rami have taken cover behind a different tree about three yards away, with Elena and the stranger behind another.

"Stay clear," Doc shouts from around a trash can. "Biogrenades!"

Several small, glowing blue orbs fly through the air, hitting the guards' shields, only to fall uselessly to the pavement. Fuck. They can't get through the shields to the organic material that triggers them.

"LeRoy?" the stranger calls. "We need that backup yesterday."

"How does now work for you?" a new voice says from behind me.

I whirl around. A tall, skinny white guy has joined us amongst the trees, wearing a pair of orange goggles and an electric blue and yellow jumpsuit. His hair is the same startling shade of blue, and it sticks straight up from his head in a dramatic mohawk. He grins at me, showing slightly crooked but white teeth. I lower my pistol, flicking my eyes toward the stranger.

"You with her?"

LeRoy winks. "Honey, she's too good for me, but I guess you could say that. Hold on just a sec—and I do mean a sec." As suddenly as he appeared, he vanishes, leaving only empty space behind. I might have seen a blue blur speed past me, but it all happens so fast I can't be sure.

The next sequence of events happens in triple time. The blur reappears in front of the guards, slowing only long enough to scatter a bunch of red pellets beneath the hard light shields. To my shock, as well as the guards', the shields flicker and die.

While they struggle to recover, we open fire. I take two front-liners in the head before an Argus leaps out of nowhere, lunging at me with wild eyes and bared fangs. Before I can adjust my aim, the dog jerks in midair, collapsing with a whimper. Yet another stranger has joined us—a tall, bald, brown-skinned woman with a nose ring—and she just saved my life by shooting that Argus.

"You good?" she asks, lowering the assault rifle she used to take out the dog. I feel instant envy, as well as an intense longing for my K-2 Phoenix. Pistols just don't pack enough power.

"Yeah. Thanks."

There isn't time for more than that. We turn and fire at the remaining guards, who are forced to retreat without their shields to protect them. They continue shooting from behind various scanners and around the edges of ticket booths, pinning us in place. It looks like we have a stalemate.

"Sasha," Ocho's voice blares in my ear, nearly making me jump out of my skin. *"We're coming in!"*

I have no idea what she means until one of the ticket booths and two scanners go flying, along with some unfortunate guards. A blunt nosed, older model shuttle with chipped blue paint blasts through the wall, filling the air with a whoosh of displaced air and the smell of plasma. It slides to a graceful stop near us, and the side doors swing upward. Ocho leans out, waving at us with a grin on her face.

In the next three seconds, everything goes to shit.

An AxysGen guard caught in the explosion clambers to their knees, firing through the smoke.

Someone screams.

Doc collapses atop a pile of rubble, curling into a ball with her arms tucked into her chest.

For the first time in a decade, I find myself completely frozen during a mission. My heart and lungs lurch into overdrive, but my adrenaline mods are all but useless. I'm a block of ice, unable to move. All I can do is stare helplessly at that tiny, crumpled body lying on the ground amidst the twisted metal remains of the trash can that used to be her cover.

That's my kid.

It's all I can think. All I can feel, other than complete numbness.

That's my kid. That's my fucking kid!

Like a faulty engine sputtering to a start, my instincts finally kick in. I lunge toward Doc, scooping her limp form into my arms and charging for the shuttle. Her weight is nothing to me. All I know is I have to get her out of here, away from danger.

More guards pick themselves up and begin advancing over the wreckage, trying to stop us from reaching safety, but they don't stand a chance. A massive, silent shadow swoops past me, descending on them like death itself. I don't need to glance over my shoulder to know what's happening. The terrified screams echoing behind me say it all. Rock is covering our retreat—and getting his revenge.

"Doc!"

"Is she okay?"

Cherry and Rami converge on me, both trying to get a look at the bundle in my arms. I ignore them, climbing into the shuttle beside the stranger who looks like my mom. We have no choice but to trust these people now, at least until I'm sure Doc is okay. She's still breathing, because I feel faint, trembling movement against my chest, but she isn't saying anything.

Elena gets a boost up onto the shuttle's lip from the stranger. Cherry and Rami are next, followed by the bald woman and the blue haired guy, who has reappeared out of nowhere again. Rock staggers behind us, blood dripping from numerous gashes and bullet wounds, but he has enough strength and coordination to climb in unaided. The stranger is last. She hops in and closes the door behind us, banging on the shuttle's roof. "Take us home, Flygirl."

"My pleasure," a cheerful voice says from the pilot's seat. The engines rev, and the shuttle takes off, speeding out through the ruins of the Butterfly Lab's west entrance.

I place Doc on the floor as gently as possible, untucking her arms from her chest. She moans and flinches, her eyes scrunched shut. A spike of panic plunges straight through my heart. Blood seeps out of Doc's shoulder near the base of her neck, staining her long blonde hair a dirty, sticky red.

"Sasha," she whimpers through gritted teeth, still not opening her eyes. "Sasha, it h-hurts..." Medic or not, the kid's only thirteen, and this is the worst injury I've ever seen her sustain in the field. It's still bleeding freely, crimson blossoming through the front of her shirt.

"Don't talk," I say, removing Doc's belt and emptying her pockets of all the necessary first aid supplies. "That's an order."

Antibacterial spray. Skin glue. RapiHeal ion gel. Shrink-fit, skin-knitting bandages. My hands work through the basic first aid steps without any input from my mind. That's stuck on loop, still thinking: *Someone shot my fucking kid.*

Chapter 15

"HOW'S THE KID?" THE mysterious handler asks, the first one to speak since take off. The rest of the shuttle remains silent except for the hum of the engine and Doc's pained, wheezing breaths.

I scan Doc with my VIS-R, but the glowing charts and graphs overwhelm me. My mind feels sluggish, unable or unwilling to focus on anything but how weak she looks lying on the floor. Most of the color has drained from her skin, leaving it a sickly, pale yellow except for the bright red bloodstain on her shoulder.

"Doc's vitals are no longer crashing," Val whispers through my ear mods. I'm lucky she's there to interpret the data because my brain is basically fried with stress. *"She is stable enough for transport but needs professional medical attention soon."*

Plugging the hole might have prevented Doc from bleeding out, but field wounds can go bad fast. I've seen it happen. Since Doc's our medic, that leaves only one choice. "Stable, for now. There a medic where we're going?" I direct my question to the handler, but I can't tear my eyes away from Doc. She looks so small, so much younger than her thirteen years…

"Better," the handler says. "We have a hospital."

Everyone sighs with relief.

"Ay, gracias a dios," Elena says from one of the seats behind me.

Across the way, Rami lets out a heavy breath, palm on chest. "I think I just aged twenty years in the last two minutes." Cherry wraps an arm around their shoulder, murmuring something reassuring in their ear.

"Good." Ocho's voice is softer, more hesitant than usual. "That was a lot of blood."

Beside me, Rock's massive form trembles with emotion. He's remained kneeling on the floor of the shuttle with me since we took off. Tenderly, he takes one of Doc's limp hands in his large ones. The size difference is staggering, but Doc squeezes one of his fingers, which I choose to interpret as a good sign.

"So, who's 'we'?" Elena asks. "Don't get me wrong. We appreciate the help, but I'd like to know who pulled our asses out of the fire."

"Fair enough," the handler says. "I'm Kyra Young. This is my crew: LeRoy, Ginger, and Flygirl's up front piloting."

My head snaps up. The woman, Kyra, isn't staring at Elena. Instead, her eyes bore into me like twin drills. I stare right back, unsettled by how much she resembles my mother. An older, battle-hardened version with broad shoulders, maybe. Her skin is the same dark umber shade. Her full lips, liquid brown eyes, and square jaw are hauntingly familiar. The main difference is the well-developed muscles and a mole at the outside corner of Kyra's left eye that my mother never had.

"Did you say Young?" I ask.

Kyra blinks, as if only just realizing she's invading my personal space with her eyes. "Sorry. I've seen pictures, but..." She offers a weak smile, as though her mouth isn't used to the motion. Yet another difference between her and my mother. "You're all grown up now."

My own mouth goes dry. Grown up? That means Kyra knew me when I was a child. And that means...

"Who are you, really?"

The shuttle remains dead silent awaiting Kyra's answer, but that silence sounds more like a scream inside my ears.

"I'm your aunt. Your mother's sister."

My mind spins. Mom never had a sister. I never had an aunt. Over a decade of risking my life and running ops has taught me that everybody lies. Maybe Kyra's a corps plant? Maybe this is all an elaborate hoax? But deep in my bones, I know the truth. Kyra isn't lying. At least, not about this.

I want to ask Val for confirmation, or at least her opinion, but she remains quiet, following protocol while the crew's around strangers. "Why don't I remember you?" I ask instead. I'm rattling harder inside than the old shuttle shaking all around me.

Kyra's brows draw together. The visible tension in her forehead and around her lips seems almost pained. Regretful, maybe? "I was involved in some dangerous things back then. Things Kiara couldn't know about while raising a kid. I haven't seen you or your parents since you were a toddler."

"But you came now."

"Believe me," Kyra says. "I looked for you long before, but by the time I got out of prison, you were grown. Running with your own crew while there was still heat on me."

"Prison?" Ocho asks, with a little too much curiosity. "What for?"

Kyra's eyes leave me at last, scanning Ocho from head to toe. My fingers flex nervously on my thighs as I endure the comparison. However, despite the obvious disapproval written on her face, Kyra answers Ocho's question. "Theft, corporate espionage, murder, and conspiracy to unionize. One guess which charge got me the most time."

Cherry gives a low whistle, clearly impressed. "You escaped? Conspiracy to unionize alone should have gotten you life, if not the needle."

"Yeah," Kyra says. "Eight years ago."

Cherry leans forward in her seat. "So what have you been doing the past eight years?"

Kyra's firm lips soften into a ghost of a smile, which makes her resemble my mother even more. "I took a page from your mama's book," she says—not to Cherry, but to me. Pride adds a touch of warmth to her low, no-nonsense voice. Shit. This woman even sounds kind of like my mother. "Thought I'd try growing something instead of being angry all the damn time."

"Yeah," LeRoy, the guy with the blue mohawk, chimes in. "We've got a place…" He hesitates, but Kyra nods for him to continue. "We built a city under the web. A better place for people to live."

It's a staggering declaration, one the rest of my crew has difficulty believing. Their shocked faces mirror my own doubts. Rami speaks for all of us when they ask, "You built an entire city under SLKC's power grid? How?"

"That's a question that requires a long, complicated answer, but I can explain when we get there," Kyra says. "What you need to know is, we have top of the line medical facilities. They'll patch your kid right up."

Rock fixes me with a pleading stare, still absently stroking Doc's hair. His baby blue eyes beg me to say yes, but I don't need convincing. I'm willing to run the risk of trusting these strangers if it means helping Doc. If they double-cross us, we'll just have to deal.

"Fine," I tell Kyra. "You fix my kid, we'll come."

Elena remains skeptical. Her seated posture is stiff and defensive. The tension in her jaw causes it to bunch. "But why save us at the Butterfly Lab? Why not contact us sooner?"

"Finding you wasn't easy," the bald woman with the nose ring says. She lounges in one of the seats near Elena, studying us as we study her. She's tall and willowy, with lighter skin than Kyra. Something about her keen, dark-eyed gaze is unsettling, but I can't put my finger on what. Its intensity, maybe. "I'm Ginger, by the way—the Corsairs' wrench."

"*You're* the Corsairs?" Cherry asks, her voice rising in pitch. "Everyone in SLKC is talking about your heists! And you're a wrench? Did you design the disruptors that took down those hard light shields? How—"

Rami puts their hand over Cherry's mouth and offers Ginger an apologetic smile. "Sorry, she gets excited. You can talk shop later, sweetheart."

Cherry pouts, leaning back in her seat with her arms folded.

"My crew and I call ourselves the Corsairs," Kyra confirms. "Among other things."

"Cool," Ocho says. "We heard about one of your jobs the other day at the ice cream machine."

I merely shake my head. It should surprise me more, but after watching Doc go down, meeting an aunt I never knew, and learning about a secret underground city, this is just another crazy bullet point for the list. It's not a bad revelation, though. If Kyra and her crew really are the Corsairs, that means they aren't working with the corps.

"So why wait until we were in danger?" Elena asks, eyes still narrowed in suspicion. She's like a bloodhound on the scent, or maybe a Guardog.exe following a trail of code. "Did you hope swooping in to rescue us would earn our trust?"

"We've been searching for your base, or at least a terminal address, for months," Kyra explains. "Then Jones, our jacker, snagged an encrypted communication between PGS and AxysGen during a regular Corsair op. This whole job was a setup. You got played by Andrews and Cross."

Elena's jaw goes slack. "No fucking way. They're direct competitors."

She has every right to be skeptical. I've never heard of AxysGen and PGS collaborating in any capacity, although if the reward were big enough... Maybe Cross thinks killing us and taking control of Val is worth making deals with the devil? If that's the case, what's in it for Andrews? Could he know about Val's existence, too? Either way, I can't speculate in front of Kyra.

"Andrews and Cross must have decided it was worth joining forces to take us all out," Kyra says. "The Corsairs have stolen from PGS and AxysGen to fund our city's construction for years, and the Lucky Seven have been on AxysGen's most wanted list for a while. When they discovered we were related..."

"How did they find out?" I ask. "I didn't even know you existed before today. You weren't listed as a known relative in any of my parents' employee records."

Kyra shrugs. "Not sure, but once Jones uncovered their plan, we decided to grab your crew before AxysGen and PGS could use you to flush me out of hiding."

Elena studies Kyra shrewdly, manicured nails drumming on the armrest of her seat. "Risky move. You basically did what they wanted by coming to our rescue."

Kyra arches an eyebrow. "They didn't know we knew. Want me to turn this shuttle around and take you back?"

Elena scowls and averts her eyes, declining to respond.

There's another awkward pause. All sorts of feelings are welling up inside me, and I don't know where to put them. I have an aunt. An aunt with her own crew and her own city. An aunt who just risked her life to save me. I can count the number of people who have stuck their necks out for me like that on two hands, and I don't even need all of my fingers. The only ones still alive are members of my crew.

Elena senses my inner conflict. She lets go of the armrest and leans forward, resting her hand on my shoulder. I put my hand on top of hers, squeezing briefly. No matter what kind of person Kyra turns out to be, I've already got a family, one I forged myself.

"What about you?" Kyra asks Ocho. "What's your name? Wasn't any data on you last time we checked."

Ocho, who has been glancing worriedly at Doc every few seconds, perks up. "I'm Ocho."

"Like the number eight?" Kyra's eyes dart in my direction, lips pursed in disapproval.

If Ocho notices, she doesn't react. "Because I'm the eighth member of the crew."

"Ocho's the only clone I've got," I say before Kyra can ask any follow up questions. "I didn't grow her for spare parts. She's fully autonomous."

"Never accused you of that, did I?"

We lapse into silence again. Kyra obviously wasn't expecting to save her niece *and* her niece's clone, but right now, I don't care. There are more important things to worry about. I rest my hand on Doc's knee, needing some kind of physical contact with her. She's unconscious, probably from pain and the drugs I gave her, but her breathing remains steady. There isn't any new blood. If the Corsairs do have a hospital, she'll end up all right.

Ocho interrupts the tense moment with another question. "What's your underground city called?"

"It isn't my city," Kyra says. "It belongs to everyone who lives there. But I did name it Sprout."

Chapter 16

SPROUT'S ENTRANCE IS HIDDEN beneath a maintenance tunnel in a defunct section of the web with no distinguishing features to mark its location. I stare out the shuttle window from my kneeling position on the floor but see nothing unusual. The ancient, rusted tube is exactly like hundreds of others, barely wide enough to hold a small vehicle with regularly spaced rivets throughout. If it were climate controlled, it would be a perfect shelter for street kids. Since it isn't, the tunnel appears long abandoned.

I look away from the window to check on Doc for what must be the hundredth time. Nothing has changed. No new blood. Heart rate and breathing are steady, though shallow. Occasionally, her eyes stir behind their closed lids, or her tongue slips out to wet her dry, cracked lips, which have lost most of their color. "Almost there, kid," I whisper, squeezing her hand since Rock is cradling her head. "Promise."

As I say that, Flygirl touches the shuttle down on the tunnel floor. "Hey, Jones," she chirps, presumably into a radio. "The Corsairs have anchored at port alive, with some fabulously sexy passengers in tow. We've also got a kid with a serious neck and shoulder injury, so be a sweetheart and let us in."

"You got it," a young, masculine voice replies. *"I'll have the paramedics sent up."* I recall Kyra's jacker is named Jones and wonder if this is the same guy. If so, why did he stay behind? To protect Sprout and keep it concealed, or some other reason?

I stop speculating as the tunnel floor opens beneath us, revealing a hidden lift. With a faint whir, the shuttle sinks into a vertical shaft of darkness. It's empty and dry, but the dim reflection of the headlights on the wall make it look like we're descending into a cave, or maybe the ocean.

"How far down is Sprout, exactly?" Rami asks.

"Ninety-two meters," Kyra says. "The geothermal wells that power us are about one hundred and eighty meters below ground. The corps scour the tunnels from time to time, but they never come this deep."

"Sounds like you're a real bug in their system," Cherry says, nose pressed against the window. A mushroom of condensation forms beneath her nostrils as she peers out into the inky blackness. "Good for you."

"My main goal is to keep Sprout running and make sure the residents have enough to thrive." A brief smile flits across Kyra's lips. "Pulling one over on PGS and AxysGen is just a very satisfying bonus."

I glance at Kyra, liking her even more. "Well, you've fucked with them enough to earn yourself a moniker."

"So have you, Wolf."

For once, I don't bother pretending to hate the nickname.

The lift stops. We've descended into a huge hangar, home to dozens of shuttles and skycars of various sizes and colors. There are hoverbikes too, which Ocho is particularly interested in. "Whoa," she says, turning as far as she can in her seat without removing her harness. She continues peering back through the window as we pull into an empty space. "What are all the bikes for?"

"In case of evacuation," Kyra explains. "The city was designed to be walkable, so no one needs vehicles. Only a few of us go upstairs. We're self-sustaining these days, aside from the occasional part for the hydroponics and climate control systems, and we're learning how to 3D print those." She unfastens her safety harness and rises from her seat, lifting one of the shuttle's side doors. "Come on. Paramedics should be here."

Reluctantly, I let go of Doc's hand and climb to my feet, curling my toes to get some blood flowing back into my stiff, numb legs.

Three paramedics are waiting for us in the hangar, taking directions from a skinny white woman a few years over fifty whose platinum hair is pulled back into a neat braid. She's masked, with a starched white lab coat as stiff as her demeanor. "Where's my patient?" she asks Kyra, not bothering with niceties or even an introduction. Since Doc needs her, that's more than fine with me. I also like how she says 'my' patient. Makes it sound like she's already taken responsibility for Doc's wellbeing.

"In there, Addy." Kyra hitches her thumb at the open shuttle, where Rock still holds Doc's head in his lap.

"She was shot in the shoulder," I say, hovering behind the doctor as she strides over and climbs through the side door. "Not sure what kind of round. I used antibiotic spray, RapiHeal gel, skin glue, bandages, and pain meds." Even though Doc seems sort of okay, my heart twinges at the possibility that my efforts might not have been enough.

The doctor barely spares me a glance. She doesn't even look at Rock. She kneels on the shuttle floor as though an eight-foot tall cyborg isn't looming over her, scanning Doc with her VIS-R. "Vitals are all right. Any allergies?"

"Prednisone," Val whispers in my ear.

A ball of tension gathers in my chest. I knew that somewhere in the back of my mind, but in my current state of stress, I might have forgotten without the reminder. I should go over Doc's medical file when I get the chance just in case some other emergency happens in the future. Some guardian I'm turning out to be.

"Prednisone."

"All right." The doctor examines Doc's injury, probing with gloved fingertips, then lifts her head and calls out orders to the paramedics. "Radio down and get the OR prepped. We'll need to repair those muscles if she wants full range of motion in her shoulder. Some synth blood, antibiotics, and a lot of rest will help." Her piercing green eyes fall on me. "She's lucky you stabilized her. This wound would have bled out otherwise."

Rock remains silent and stoic as the paramedics transfer Doc onto the stretcher, but when they bear her away, he gets up to follow immediately.

"Hold up, big guy," Kyra says, standing between him and the stretcher. "You can't go with them yet."

Rock's eyes flash with anger. He tries to sidestep Kyra, but she blocks his path again. Suddenly, she's sprawled on the concrete floor, coughing as though someone gut-punched her—which Rock definitely did, even if his fist moved too fast for me to see.

"Kyra!" Ginger shouts.

LeRoy hurries over, crouching beside Kyra. "You okay, boss?"

"Don't, Rock!" I rush over, grasping Rock's arm to keep him from thundering after the paramedics. His massive bicep tenses, twitching in my grip. For a split second, I worry I'm about to get laid out too. Instead, Rock rounds on me, breathing heavily. His eyes are wide and fearful as a glistening tear rolls down his cheek.

"Hey, I'm scared too," I tell him. "We have to let them help her, but we won't let them take her away."

Rock barely looks at me. Instead, it's like he's staring right through me as he watches the paramedics carry Doc across the hangar under the supervision of the authoritative doctor. He sniffs and pulls the collar of his shirt up to wipe his eyes, which have gone pink around the edges.

"What the fuck was that?" Ginger snaps, glaring at us. Her hand strays toward the pistol at her hip, while LeRoy places a supportive arm around Kyra's waist and helps her to her feet.

"Sorry," I say, keeping my hand on Rock's arm. "Rock is...protective. He doesn't want strangers taking his little sister. Can we go with her?" I'm planning to accompany Doc whether Kyra allows it or not, but I figure she's more likely to agree if I phrase it like a request.

Kyra stifles Ginger's anger with a firm look and pushes away LeRoy's arm despite his worried frown. "Oof. Big guy packs a wallop, doesn't he?" she wheezes through a forced smile that looks more like a wince. "Might need Addy to check my ribs once she's done with the kid." She exhales shakily, folding an arm around her midsection. "It's fine. You can stay with Doc in the hospital once you clear security."

She nods at a squad of armed guards stationed around what appears to be an elevator. They're wearing suits of liquid armor similar to LeRoy's, and they all have assault rifles. Doc's stretcher is there by the lift, waiting to be carried aboard.

Kyra notices me eyeing the guards' guns. "We don't allow weapons on any other floor of the building, with the exception of the armory." She gives me an apologetic look. "You'll have to follow those rules, too."

Instantly, I'm on the defensive. I square off with Kyra, placing my hand protectively on the grip of my pistol. "We literally just met. No way am I giving you my gun."

Kyra holds up her hands as if to placate me. "You don't have to give it to me. We have storage lockers up here."

I narrow my eyes. "Biometric?" The last thing I want to do is give up my biometric data.

"No. Actual lockers, with keys. We don't use biometrics here on principle, and we only use security cameras on the roof, in the armory, and in a few public spaces, like the garden and fish farm."

"Let me talk to my crew. Don't put Doc on that elevator yet."

Kyra sighs. "Make it fast, or Addy will get antsy. She isn't the patient type."

I walk away from Kyra, pulling Rock along and motioning for the rest of the crew to join me. We form a huddle, where Elena wastes no time making her displeasure known. "We aren't actually considering this, right?"

"We should do it," Rami says. "I seriously doubt Kyra's a corps plant. This whole thing would make for a really convoluted lie."

"Convoluted doesn't mean impossible," Elena protests. "And Kyra doesn't have to be a corps plant to turn on us for whatever reason. Right, Cherry?"

Cherry shrugs. *"Cerebro* needs a doctor. We should do whatever we've gotta do. What do you think, Val? You're designed to be more observant than us."

Val's voice fills my ears. *"In my opinion, Kyra is being truthful. Her pleasure at seeing you, Sasha, seemed genuine. While my capabilities are limited using only the databox in Elena's possession, I have not picked up any local outgoing transmissions, such as a message providing our location to Axys Generations or Paragon Solutions. In fact, there is remarkably little extranet traffic here."*

"Okay," Elena admits, with a begrudging sideways pull of her mouth. "Sparse extranet traffic doesn't sound like a trap."

"Yes. This location is, to use a colloquialism, 'off the grid.' I find Kyra's explanation believable. Furthermore, I find her stated goals admirable. Once Doc is well, I would like to see more of this arcology."

"I think we should do whatever helps Doc get better," Ocho says. "Also, Val, what's an arcology?"

"Arcologies are small, self-sustaining communities designed to support a high population density in a relatively small space, without sacrificing comfort."

"Wow," Cherry says. "You're great at making cool things sound really boring and technical. Anyway, I guess we'll stash our pistols in the locker, but I'm keeping some biogrenades in my pocket."

I fold my arms, fixing Cherry with a stern look. "No. They're bound to scan us."

Cherry rolls her eyes. "Ugh, fine. Lipstick laser's staying with me, though."

I sigh, giving Cherry a small nod. Seems like a fair compromise, at least until we're sure Kyra is 100% legit. "Fine, but I better not see you fidgeting with it. Rami? I assume you've got...whatever...hidden on your person?"

Rami just smirks. "Don't worry about it, darling."

"Not worried. Unload whatever's obvious, keep whatever you think they won't find. I trust your judgment. Everyone else, stay calm and remember we're doing this for the kid."

I leave the group, striding back over to Kyra. "We'll put our weapons in one of your lockers."

Kyra visibly relaxes, lowering her shoulders. "I know it's a huge ask, but I promise if you give me some time, I'll show you proof that I am who I say I am, and Sprout is what I say it is." She hesitates, as if unsure, then adds, "I've wanted to show you this for years, actually."

A strange, ticklish feeling fills my stomach. Years? It almost sounds like Kyra built this city of hers, in part, for me. That suspicion, or perhaps hope, makes me all the more confused as she leads us to the elevator.

Chapter 17

WE STASH OUR PISTOLS, biogrenades, and most of our other weapons in an old-school locker next to the elevator, with metal walls so thick it resembles a safe. There are no panels, jack ports, or biometric scanners to mess around with. Just a regular key, which Kyra offers me in her outstretched hand.

I slip the key into my pocket. If using a pistol instead of an assault rifle for our most recent op made me feel naked, abandoning that scant protection makes me feel like my insides are on display too. But for Doc's sake, I'll deal. Cherry has her laser lipstick, Rami has their belt, and Rock is a walking weapon all by himself. Our crew won't be defenseless.

"Thank you," Kyra says. "I know that took a lot of trust."

"More like desperation," Elena mutters by my shoulder.

I glare down at her. Not a good idea to piss off the people who have agreed to help Doc and shelter us.

"Don't think of it like that," says a cheerful voice from behind me. I turn to see a short, curvy white woman with wide hips and a bubblegum pink undercut trotting toward us. Her smile is big, her green eyes sparkling and friendly. "No one else in Sprout has weapons, so you'll be perfectly safe. Hi! I'm Flygirl, by the way."

"Nice nickname," Ocho says. I don't miss the way her eyes drop to Flygirl's ample chest. A few weeks outside the tube isn't enough time to develop subtlety where boobs are concerned, I guess. "Because you're the Corsairs' pilot, right?"

"Nah." Flygirl winks, unperturbed by Ocho's stare. "I was a frog in a past life."

Ocho laughs, while LeRoy groans.

"Don't encourage her," he says. "My cousin suffers from the delusion that she's funny."

"Not a delusion if someone besides me laughs, LeRoy."

My eyes dart between them. There's no obvious resemblance, especially since LeRoy's so tall and skinny while Flygirl's short and attractively plump, but the way she slugs his shoulder is definitely familial.

"Anyone going to the hospital needs to get on the elevator in the next thirty seconds," the doctor calls from inside the elevator. "I won't hold it any longer."

"Calm your tits, Addy," Ginger says. "We're coming."

"That's Doctor Stone to you, Ms. Kaushal," the doctor says. "And I'm not playing games. My patient needs surgery."

"Stand with your feet shoulder width apart, hands behind your head," Kyra orders, demonstrating the correct pose. We copy her while she lowers her arms. A blue light emanates from her VIS-R as she gives us each a thorough once-over. "You're clear. Go be with your kid."

The elevator is surprisingly spacious. Decorative flower prints hanging on the walls make the interior seem more welcoming than I expected. Doctor Stone presses a button, the doors close, and we descend. I stand as close to Doc's stretcher as I can without bumping shoulders with the paramedics, feeling the protective urge to remain nearby.

The elevator doors open into a hospital waiting room filled with people. In a single glance, I see old and young, multiple races and genders, and several parents trying to coax squirmy kids back into their seats. Doctor Stone and the paramedics ignore them all, wheeling Doc along one side of the waiting room and through a set of frosted double doors labeled DO NOT ENTER.

"Ignore the sign and follow Addy," Kyra tells me. "I'm dismissing my crew for some food and rest, but I'll bring your crew something to eat. I'm sure you all want to stay with Doris."

It's strange hearing Doc's real name from Kyra's mouth, but I'm grateful nonetheless. "Thank you. I..." What else am I supposed to say to the woman who saved us? How can I possibly express the intense, confusing feelings churning inside me? Part of me even wants to hug her, but I falter. Hugs aren't my style, especially with someone I just met. Even if that someone is supposed to be my aunt.

"It's a lot to process," Kyra says. "Just focus on your crew for now. We'll talk later."

"Thanks." I feel stupid, repeating myself like a buffering sound file, but I honestly don't know what else to say.

With a nod of farewell, Kyra departs, rejoining LeRoy, Flygirl, and Ginger by the elevator. The crew and I proceed through the frosted doors, with me and Rock in the lead. Thankfully, no one stops us this time.

The hallway beyond is wide and brightly lit. Doctors and nurses in pastel scrubs and masks hurry between rooms, carrying tablets and pushing trolleys laden with medical supplies. Everything smells unnaturally sterile, like Doc's medbays in our hidden bases. I catch sight of the paramedics wheeling Doc's stretcher through another set of doors, while Doctor Stone pauses outside to wait for us.

"Surgical gallery's through there," she says, pointing at the next door down. "You can observe."

I breathe a sigh of relief. "Thank you. She's our kid, you know?"

Although Doctor Stone's smile is hidden behind her mask, her sharp eyes soften into a smile for the first time. "She'll be fine. I'm just fixing her shoulder and heading off any complications, like infection or internal bleeding. You saved her life."

I didn't realize how much I needed to hear those words until they wash over me. The tight fist around my heart loosens, allowing it to beat freely again for the first time since Doc went down. My eyes sting with unshed tears, but I blink them back. I can't let the rest of the crew see me cry, even though I know they would understand.

With a nod of farewell, Doctor Stone disappears into the operating room. We head through the next door into the gallery, a narrow, dim rectangle of a room with a window in place of one wall. The window looks into another, larger room with surgical lights, an operating table, and lots of shiny steel equipment. Two nurses transfer Doc onto the table. Despite Doctor Stone's reassurances, my stomach churns.

A warm hand reaches for mine, lacing our fingers together. Elena is standing beside me, looking up at me with a tender smile. "She'll be okay, Sasha. Doc's way too stubborn to let a round from some privsec thug slow her down."

"I know…"

A large shadow looms over me, and I catch Rock's faint reflection behind me in the window glass. He steps up, wrapping his huge arms around my waist and resting his chin on top of my head. The familiar scent of his cologne fills my nose, and the smell is slightly relaxing. I usually avoid physical contact, even with my crew, but this time, I need the comfort. I let Rock hug me and Elena grip my hand, while Cherry and Rami hold each other's waists on our left. When Ocho hesitates, they both extend their free arms to her, inviting her into their circle of love and reassurance.

"*Perhaps it will reassure you to know that I agree with Doctor Stone's assessment,*" Val says in my ears. She might not have a physical body, but I feel her presence with us, and that's more than enough. "*Doc is likely to have a full recovery.*"

"What, no percentages?" Elena whispers. A lame attempt at a joke.

"*Too many unknown variables,*" Val says. "*But I have what you might call a hunch.*"

Elena snorts. "A hunch? Seriously?"

"Right now, I'll take anything," I mutter, watching Doctor Stone lean over the table with a scalpel in hand and a look of intense focus on the upper half of her face. I can't see much of Doc past the backs of two nurses on the opposite side of the table, but maybe that's a good thing.

I close my eyes, exhaling slowly through my nose and squeezing Elena's hand tighter. I've been the closest thing Doc has to a guardian for several years, but in the past few hours, it's really hit me. I have a kid. Two kids, if I count Ocho. I'm a parent, with all the terrifying responsibilities that role entails.

***

An hour and a half later, Doc is recovering in a private room. The rest of us cluster around her hospital bed, holding her hand or squeezing her knee beneath the thin white sheets. There are only two chairs, forcing us to take turns—except for Rock. He remains a silent sentinel by the head of the bed, stroking Doc's tangled hair. His pleading stare never leaves her face.

I'm slumped forward during my turn in one of the chairs, struggling to keep my eyes open while Elena (goddess that she is) massages my shoulders. Her thumbs dig in behind the blades, sending tingling numbness all the way down my arms. Normally, I'd be uncomfortable with such a public display of intimacy, but right now I'm too exhausted to care.

My blurry gaze drifts over to Doc's vitals monitor. As I watch, the glowing white spikes scroll faster and the faint beeping speeds up. A soft groan comes from the bed, and Rock bends anxiously over Doc's prone form. When she opens her eyes, blinking up at him, tears stream down his ruddy cheeks. He buries his nose in her hair, kissing the top of her head.

I brush Elena's hands aside and jump out of the chair, hurrying over to join them. "Doc? You awake?"

Rami's already there. They squeeze Doc's hand, running their thumb over her knuckles. "Hello, sunshine. How are you feeling?"

Doc squints, her nose wrinkling with discomfort. "S'bright. Turn down the lights? Wicked headache."

Ocho walks over to adjust the light switch by the door, making the room comfortably dim. "Better?"

"Yeah." Doc sighs with relief, letting her head flop to one side. "Where are we? I feel fuzzy, like I'm coming off some serious pain meds."

Seeing Doc awake—eyes open, wearing a smile even if it's weak and crack-lipped—makes my eyes sting with emotion. Fuck. This is the third time today I've almost cried. "You are. I injected you in the shuttle, and I'm sure Doctor Stone gave you a lot more before surgery."

Doc manages a hoarse laugh. "Doctor Stone, huh? Guess they aren't a hack, since I'm still breathing."

"That is due in large part to Sasha," Val says in everyone's ears. *"However, Doctor Stone repaired the torn muscles and ligaments in your shoulder in addition to supplying you with synthetic blood and antibiotics. It is very good to have you back, Doc."*

A loud sniff comes from the other side of Doc's bed. "You horrible little gremlin," Cherry says, wiping tears away with her sleeve and leaving a trail of smudged mascara beneath her eyes. "Why'd you have to go and get yourself shot, huh?"

"Not like I..." Doc pauses, coughing through an audibly dry throat. "...did it on purpose. Can an injured kid get some water over here?"

A pause. Then, we all laugh. The tension is broken, and I finally feel like I can breathe again.

"Sure, *pequeña.*" Elena goes over to the metal sink in the corner of the room, filling a paper cup. She passes it to me, and I lift the cup to Doc's lips.

"Take it slow," I tell her. "Don't choke."

Despite my warning, Doc gulps down the water like someone stranded in the desert. After a satisfied sigh, she grins at me. "Thanks, Boss."

"No problem."

"Seriously. Thanks." Doc rolls her head back onto the pillow, looking at the whole crew. "All of you."

"Tu eres familia," Elena says, tugging the tip of Doc's foot since all the spots by the head of the bed are taken. "But if you even *think* about

getting out of this hospital bed before Doctor Stone clears you, I'll put you right back in it. Don't test me."

Doc yawns. "No threats necessary. I still feel like there's a bag of sand sitting on my chest while a drummer uses my skull as a hi-hat."

"Just wait 'til we tell you everything that happened after you got hurt," Ocho says. She's taken up watch beside Elena, by the foot of the bed. "Sasha has an aunt we never knew about, who runs a whole underground city! That's where we are right now."

Doc's eyes widen. "Seriously? Is that where we are right now?"

I give Ocho an encouraging nod. "Why don't you fill her in?"

Ocho's face lights up. "Okay, so..."

While Ocho explains everything that happened, I glance at Rock. He's remained silent all this time, perched on the edge of Doc's bed despite his massive size, never more than an inch from her side. His face is wet with tears, but he manages a genuine smile when he notices me looking at him. He touches the fingertips of his right hand to his chin, then brings them down and out in a straight line, the sign for *'Thank you'*.

I hold out my hand and flip it over, drawing a half circle in front of my chest. *'You're welcome.'* Rock and I exchange smiles, and a piece of my heart settles back into its proper place.

Chapter 18

A DAY LATER, I hover beside Doc's bed while Doctor Stone checks her shoulder. Even though there's no rational reason to be nervous, an unpleasant, tingling energy crawls along my limbs. Doc's improving by the hour, but the pessimistic part of me can't help waiting for things to go wrong. Surely the danger can't be over. Surely everything isn't back to normal yet...

"All done," Doctor Stone says, peeling off her gloves and dropping them into the trash can by Doc's bed. "Shoulder looks great, so you're free to leave. Remember to take your antibiotics twice a day, and keep the sling on at all times." She shoots Doc a warning look from overtop her round silver glasses. *"All times.* Got it?"

Doc rolls her eyes. "What's with the extra emphasis? I'm a medical professional, too."

"Yes, but you're also thirteen," Doctor Stone says in a stern voice. Nevertheless, I can tell she's fighting a smile. "Teenagers tend to get impatient while recovering."

"So do most adults," Doc says.

"And I'd give the same orders to an impatient adult."

I put my hand on Doc's good shoulder, giving it a warning squeeze. "No worries, Doctor Stone. I'll make sure she keeps it on. No missions for her any time soon."

Doc whips her head around, staring up at me with wide eyes. "But Sasha—"

"Your only job right now is getting better. No arguments."

"That's what I like to hear," says Doctor Stone. "Kyra's in the waiting room, by the way. I saw her talking to the rest of your crew. She mentioned something about a tour of Sprout."

"Really?" Doc lights up with excitement. "I'll come with. Mild exercise prevents post-surgery clots."

I ignore her, looking at Doctor Stone instead. I trust Doc with my life, and have done exactly that on several occasions, but even a kid genius can misjudge her own capabilities through wishful thinking. There's a reason doctors don't treat themselves.

"If she keeps her arm immobile and rests when she feels tired, I don't see the harm," Doctor Stone says in response to my silent question.

"Fine. Up for a tour then, Doc?"

Doc hops off the edge of the bed, already grinning at me. "I'd pick touring a boring-ass yarn factory over a hospital room where I'm the patient instead of the doctor. Let's grab the others and go!"

***

Sprout is more like a tower than a city—or rather, a city inside a tower. Everything is contained within a single 'building' set directly into the tunnel shaft, although I have to admit, it has more beauty and personality than any corps skyscraper.

The hallways are large and well-lit, wide enough for me and Kyra, Doc and Rock, Rami and Cherry, and Elena and Ocho to walk comfortably abreast. Hand painted murals decorate the walls from top to bottom. Landscapes, mostly: mountains, oceans, and forests. The otherwise barren corridor has been transformed into something beautiful. The constant hum of the power grid is blessedly absent. There isn't a single advertisement in sight.

"The top six floors are made up of apartments," Kyra explains as we walk the halls. "The layouts are similar, depending on how many bedrooms each family needs. Residents have done a great job decorating the place."

That much seems true. Each apartment door is a display unto itself, with everything from posters to sconces. Many boast potted plants with their own miniature sun lamps. I smile. It reminds me a bit of my mom, growing things in our crappy, corps-provided cage, only this place is much nicer than the housing we lived in.

Ocho is fascinated. She lags behind the rest of the group, admiring each door, until Elena falls back and grasps her wrist, pulling her along.

Up front, Cherry bumps her shoulder lightly against mine. "Reminds me of what boarding school might have looked like if we were allowed to personalize our space, right?"

Kyra's smile falters. "Sprout is nothing like an education facility. People don't have curfews, and the only places off-limits are areas that could be safety hazards, like the geothermal wells. Even then, we try and arrange day trips for the kids."

"Wait, kids?" Elena drops Ocho's hand and trots to catch up. "You've got kids here?"

Some of Kyra's cheerfulness returns. "We've got three hundred kids under the age of eighteen. They're a fifth of our population."

"Do they go to school?" Doc asks, peering up at Kyra. I don't mind her curiosity, as long as it gets her mind off the discomfort of her sling.

"Yes," Kyra says. "Two hours in the morning for math, science, history, virtual literacy. That sort of thing. Then, for three hours each afternoon, they go somewhere in Sprout and learn how the place works. The hydroponics garden and fish farm are popular. Speaking of which, that's our first stop on the tour."

The hallway ends at another double door elevator. It dings as the doors open, revealing an old white lady with a walker and a chubby, tow-headed boy who can't be more than five.

Kyra steps aside, smiling at the woman and kid as she gestures for them to exit first. The woman becomes slightly wary when she sees us, but the boy appears to be in awe of Rock. He cranes his neck, looking up at him with wide eyes.

"Hey, guy! How tall are you?" he asks.

"Jason, that isn't polite," the woman whispers.

The boy sticks out his lower lip and scrunches his face. "Sorry, Gramma."

"He's almost two and a half meters tall," Doc says, shooting the kid a wink.

"Really?" He shuffles closer to the old woman. "Will I get that tall?"

"Probably not," Doc says, "but that's okay. Tall people always bump their heads on stuff. Right, Rock?"

Rock nods, fixing the boy with a somber look.

The boy giggles before his grandmother ushers him away, nudging him along even though he keeps trying to sneak peeks back over his shoulder at us. They disappear through one of the colorful doorways, while Kyra leads us into the elevator.

"The apartments have some basic appliances," Kyra says, pressing a large green button beneath two columns of six, "but almost everyone eats at the dining hall on the second floor. Hundreds of people go there for meals, including the kids between the morning and afternoon lesson. We'll grab some food there after the tour."

"It takes a lot of resources to produce enough food underground to sustain an entire population," Rami says. "Do you have to bring in additional supplies from outside?"

"No, and I'll show you why."

The elevator doors open again. I'm hit by a wave of humidity which carries the smell of water and growing things. At least three dozen people in overalls are working inside a giant greenhouse, only there's hardly any soil. The plants float in ascending white troughs of water which circulates constantly through bubbling vents.

The overall effect is breathtaking: row after row of fruits, vegetables, and plants I can't identify, stacked and hanging in three dimensions. It's a bit like walking through an edible, well-organized jungle. It's my mother's aerogarden, only large enough to feed an entire city.

Cherry's jaw drops. "This. Is. So. Cool." She hurries over to the nearest trough that contains several tiny green sprouts. "Look, onions!"

We follow her into the greenhouse, craning our necks to see all the hanging plants. Every inch of space is filled with life, but even though the greenhouse is crowded, it doesn't feel claustrophobic at all. I take another deep breath through an open-mouthed smile. This place must be part of the reason the people who live here don't go crazy, staying underground most of the time.

"The fish farm is on this floor, too," Kyra says, coming to stand beside me. "That's where we get the nutrients for the hydroponic garden."

Ocho, who happens to be examining a cluster of radishes, pulls a face. "So, you're growing all this with fish poop? Ew."

Rami shrugs. "Poop has to go somewhere, and plants have to grow from something."

"Exactly," Kyra says. "Food and power wise, Sprout is entirely self sufficient. Residents do a four-hour work shift per day, four days a week, in a department of their choice. Some like to do the same thing over and over, but others like to rotate. And the kids help in the afternoon, of course."

I can't help being impressed. "You're teaching them how to keep this place going without you," I say to Kyra.

"Sprout can already go on without me. This place was my brainchild, but I'm not its leader. We've got a council. They're randomly selected from the pool of adult residents for six-month terms. Sure, you get a few idiots in office, but it's better than a bunch of sociopaths playing petty power games. No elections, no problems."

"If you aren't the leader, what do you do?" Elena asks.

"Recruitment, mostly," Kyra says. "And I acquire specialized parts we can't produce ourselves. You know, like if one of the wells breaks down, or the climate control system needs an upgrade. I've had to do less and less now that we're up and running. 3D printing helps."

My heart swells with admiration, tinged with just a bit of shame. While I gallivanted around the world, running ops to support Megan's extravagant lifestyle and crazy schemes, Kyra's been in SLKC trying to build a better city beneath the hell aboveground. Working to heal her home, instead of running away from the rot like I did.

"This is amazing," I tell her, and I mean it.

Kyra's hand twitches, as if she wanted to reach out and touch my arm but decides against it. Her smile, though, makes her look even more like my mom. "Thank you. You and your crew can stay here as long as you want...and I'm sure you have questions."

I have plenty of questions, but for the first time in a long time, I feel like they can wait a few more minutes. Until the tour is over, at least. "So, what's next?"

Chapter 19

DESPITE THE STRESS OF the past two days, I emerge from the shower buzzing with energy. As the cooler air outside the stall evaporates the steam from my skin, my head spins with everything Kyra has shown me. The hydroponics garden. The school. The geothermal wells. The community dining hall, playground, and gym. Plants and art everywhere, without a single advertisement in sight.

I've never seen anything like Sprout before. Never even conceived of something similar. Children are growing up here, living and learning in an environment free of corporate influence. Having the childhood I wish my crew and I could have had. Sustainable agriculture. Four-hour work shifts. No political elections poisoned by corporate cash. It seems too good to be true.

Something must be rotten here…right?

Sprout isn't a perfect paradise, hidden underground and disconnected from the wider world, but I want to see more. It's a triumph, in its own way. The people here have carved out lives for themselves, away from corporate influence. Some dormant, thirsty part of me has awakened, and it wants to drink in as much goodness as possible while we're here.

I place my hands flat on the bathroom counter, staring at my reflection in the mirror. Maybe it's just me, but I think I look younger. More energized. My eyes aren't quite so tired. I grin, and my reflection grins back. I resemble Ocho more than usual. For once, that doesn't bother me.

Ocho. She'd flourish in a community like this. I bet she'd love rotating between jobs, picking up skills, getting new tastes of life all the time. Hell, it sounds appealing to me, and I have plenty of work and life experience already. Most of it shitty.

I'm still smiling as I towel off and enter the adjoining bedroom. Kyra has put us in an empty apartment with three bedrooms, one for me and Elena, one for Cherry and Rami, and one for Rock and Doc. Ocho's sleeping on a pull-out in the living room, which she's told me she likes because that's where the majority of the decorations are. Posters and potted plants, mostly.

There's even a tiny aerogarden in the living room window, which isn't actually a window, but a screen displaying a livestream of the hydroponics garden. All of it makes me wonder whether Kyra moved some stuff into the apartment in advance, hoping I'd agree to stay awhile. I have to admit, the thought is nice—both visiting Sprout, and that my aunt wants me here.

The bedroom Elena and I have claimed is sparsely decorated compared to the living room, but comfortably furnished. It has a closet, two dressers, and a queen-sized bed, which Elena has sprawled on without bothering to climb beneath the comforter. She stares at an extranet window projected from her VIS-R, only sparing me a brief glance when I arrive. I make sure my towel is tucked securely under my arms.

"Yeah, I miss you too," Elena says. Her brown eyes soften as she returns her attention to the screen, and her smile radiates love and affection. "Listen to Abuela and get your work done, okay? Don't give her a hard time. She's too old for your crap."

The whining that follows is so loud I can hear it from where I'm standing. Probably Mateo. He's only eight, while Jacobo's twelve, an age where sullen silence has more appeal.

Elena rolls her eyes in amused exasperation at something Mateo's saying. "I don't care if it's boring. Sometimes you have to do boring stuff before fun stuff. Look at me. I do boring work all the time."

I snort softly. I wouldn't describe our crew's ops as 'boring,' but I get why Elena doesn't want to worry her brothers with the details. She's confided in me before that she fears Jacobo will follow in her footsteps, even after being abducted by Megan a few months back.

"Guess what I did today?" Elena says. "The crew and I got to see a fish farm."

Mateo gives an excited screech. *"What kinds of fish? Are they pets?"*

Elena winces, cupping a hand to her ear even though the sound's coming from inside. "Ay, turn the volume down. No, they're for eating. Yeah, yeah. I love you, too. Go help Abuela make dinner. Talk tomorrow." She blows a kiss, then ends the call with an extended blink.

"Someone really likes fish, huh?"

Elena rolls onto her side and looks at me, propping herself up on one elbow. *"Hola, guapa.* Still naked, huh?"

My heart thumps hard inside my chest. Elena's pose shows off the curve of her hips and the dip of her waist to perfection. Casually, I stroll over and unwrap my towel, tossing it onto the foot of the bed. "That a problem?"

Elena eyes me up and down, admiring the view. "Not now that I'm off my call."

I sit beside her, dropping a kiss on top of her head. "Did you talk to Jacobo and Abuela?"

"Yeah." She kisses my shoulder in return, and I shudder at the brush of her lips on my bare skin.

"How they doing?"

"Fine. The boys were bitching about their online coursework." Elena sits up straight, fixing me with a frown and furrowed brow. It's such an abrupt departure from her previous heated stare that I shift a few inches away, surprised.

"What?"

"They want to know when we're coming back to Barbados."

Uh-oh. I know that tone of voice, low and strained. My arousal fades in an instant. "What did you tell them?"

"Soon." Another pause. "Sasha, when *are* we going back to Barbados?"

I know the logical answer, the answer Elena wants to hear, so I say what I'm supposed to. "In a couple of days once Doc's fully recovered and the heat from PGS and AxysGen dies down. That gives me a chance to talk with Kyra about my parents."

"Good. I hope you get your answers."

"Yeah."

I still need answers about my parents, but for some reason the details feel less important now. Maybe it's because once I learn the truth from Kyra, there will be nothing keeping me from returning to Barbados and an early retirement. The beach is nice, but lounging my days away and fucking Elena every night, no matter how enjoyable, is an unsatisfactory replacement for a sense of purpose.

It's a very recent discovery I've made about myself, and it settles strangely in my chest, but I can't ignore the feeling. Kyra seems to have found her purpose here, and I envy her for it. Three months without one has been driving me crazier than I anticipated, which might explain why I was so keen to awaken Ocho and investigate my parents' deaths.

"You don't sound excited," Elena says. "If you're tired of Barbados, we'll go somewhere else. It's risky to stay in the same place for too long, anyway."

"I liked Barbados fine. I mean, I like it..."

"Liked." Elena shakes her head, turning toward the windowless wall. "You want to stay here. How long?"

I shrug because I honestly don't know. "Not forever. That would be crazy, right? We've only spent two days here."

Elena inhales slowly, running a nervous hand through her hair. "Sasha..." She places her palm on my knee, looking up at me. "Sprout seems great, but we both know something this good can't last."

Her statement hits harder than I'm expecting. Imagining Sprout's destruction bothers me more than it should, for a place I've only known about for two days. My chest actually aches at the thought, and there's an uncomfortable churning in my gut. What Elena's saying makes sense. The corps control everything on the planet. Nothing can change it—it's just the way things are. But underneath that knowledge, a small voice in my mind that sounds a lot like my mother's says, *Why not?*

"Who says it can't last?"

"Anyone with common sense." Elena removes her hand from my leg, flicking it in exasperation and letting it drop into her own lap. She seems to realize she's being overly harsh, because she pauses to collect herself. "The corps will find this place and ruin it like they ruin everything else. Plus, the Corsairs already have huge targets on their backs. They've got an industry nickname, for fuck's sake."

"So do we," I point out. "We're still kicking."

"Through dumb luck. I can't even count the number of times we should have died, and that's not counting the times you *did* die..."

"So, you're fine with writing Sprout off? That's letting them win."

Elena pushes off the bed, standing to face me. "There's no 'winning,' Sasha. Only surviving. Right now, Sprout's doing a pretty good job of that, but it isn't sustainable, no matter what Kyra says."

I know Elena's only being pragmatic. She's running through a script that feels familiar to my brain because it's exactly what I would have thought a few weeks ago. But now, something has changed. I don't want to hear it. I refuse to believe the worst is inevitable and Sprout doesn't even have a chance. The thought of something so good getting ground up by the corporate machine makes me feel unexpectedly...Furious? Defiant? Protective?

Maybe it's because I watched Doc get hurt for the first time in a while. Maybe it's because I found a long lost relative I never knew about. Maybe it's because Kyra reminds me so much of my mother, or because I'm on the cusp of learning what she and my father died for. Whatever the reason, strange new feelings have taken root inside me, and I don't want to dig them out.

"You don't know that," I say, staring directly into Elena's eyes, willing her to agree with me. "We've only been here a few days."

"Exactly," Elena says. "After just two days, you're convinced Sprout will make it because you saw them grow plants in fish poop water."

"What about the kids and the older folks like your abuela? It's a support network for them—"

"For how long?" Elena asks. "The corps could show up tomorrow and destroy this place."

I shoot a glare at her. "So we shouldn't build stuff because the corps *might* destroy it?"

Elena inhales slowly through her nose and relaxes her shoulders, as though deliberately trying to stifle frustration. "This isn't like you, Sasha. You're plenty of things, but a blind optimist has never been one of them."

"Just because I occasionally dredge up some optimism doesn't mean I'm blind," I argue. "If I didn't have a shred of optimism in me, I would have sworn off romantic relationships after Megan. But I didn't, did I? When we first met, you thought I was cold. That I didn't care about anything but my crew. You said it to my face in Paris." Elena flinches, and I feel almost happy about hitting one of her weak spots like she's hit mine. "Well, Elena? This is me. Caring. Since when is caring a bad thing?"

Elena drops her chin to her chest, closing her eyes. It's as if all the fight has drained out of her, replaced by a bone deep weariness. "I know you care. You care too fucking much. You care so much that it makes you stupid, and it's going to get you killed again."

My own anger screeches to a halt. Oh. Of course this isn't just about Sprout. The rest of my crew worries about me but having a romantic partner who does is new and unfamiliar. Sometimes I forget how different Elena and Megan are, even though Elena's already proven she's a hundred times better. "So that's what this is about? You're afraid I'll get killed again, permanently this time?"

"I mean, yes. I'm fucking terrified about that all day, every day. The world is horrible. The corps are horrible. But this is the world we live in.

You'll die if you try to fight it and my brothers have to learn how to navigate it. They need to take their APS. Get a job. They're so fucking smart and talented. If I bankroll them, they'll beat the odds and make something of themselves."

I lean forward, grasping one of Elena's hands and pulling her back toward the bed. She shuffles a step closer, taking in a shallow gasp as I cup her cheek. Her face feels warm and smooth in my hand.

"You didn't need the corps to make something of yourself," I say, rubbing my thumb over her cheekbone. "None of us did. The corps prevents people from making things of themselves. They make it impossible for most people to even exist."

"You think I don't know that?" Elena asks, her voice trembling. She puts her hand over mine, pulling it away from her face, but doesn't let go. "I grew up without parents, too. Abuela couldn't work anymore, so everyone wrote her off as worthless. My brothers and I had no education, so we were worthless, too."

"That's exactly what Sprout is trying to change. Elena, please. Just… just give this a chance with me. I want to stay and see more. Not forever, but for more than just two days. That's like giving up without even trying."

Elena pulls her bottom lip between her teeth. At last, she sighs in resignation. "Fine. But only until Doc's better and Kyra tells you about your parents."

I crack a small smile. "Isn't that basically what we already agreed to before this argument?"

"Pretty much." Elena returns the smile with one of her own. It's slight, but genuine. "I admire what Kyra's doing here. The people seem happy. It's definitely better than corps housing or the streets."

"Way better. I'm looking forward to sleeping in a real bed. Not even a rack, but a queen sized bed." I scoot back onto the mattress, lying down with my head on the pillows. "C'mon." I pat the space beside me and wink. "There's plenty of room."

Elena gives a dry laugh. "Just so you know, if you invite me into bed while you're naked, I can't be held responsible for my actions."

"Responsibility's overrated anyway."

"*Dios*, I wish you actually believed that." But Elena reaches for her pants, unfastening the fly and pulling them down over her hips. I watch her with hungry eyes. Falling back into old patterns and fighting with her isn't fun, but the fucking part definitely is.

Chapter 20

I LEAN BACK IN my chair, stretching my arms above my head and swallowing a yawn. The job I've been assigned today, monitoring Sprout's limited security feeds from a booth on the top floor, isn't actually a boring one, but the sitting-in-one-place part is a minor struggle. Aside from my stint in Barbados, I'm used to more strenuous physical activity.

Beside me, my job partner and supervisor catches my eye. Kyra's jacker, Jones, has turned out to be a shy South Asian dude who smiles easily but talks softly. His black hair is unruly, like he can't be bothered to style it, but that's the only messy thing about him. His neatly buttoned flannel makes him look like somebody's dad, even though he can't be more than nineteen.

"Want some coffee?" he asks, which doubles the words he's said to me in the past couple of hours (the others being, 'Hey, I'm Jones,' when Kyra introduced us).

"Nah, I'm good."

I return my attention to the security feeds. As Kyra explained, most of Sprout isn't monitored. There are tons of cameras pointed at the rooftop hangar and empty tunnels above, as well as feeds that show the dining hall, garden, and recreation area, which includes an indoor playground. Other than that, people have their privacy. I'm relieved I don't have to watch Sprout's citizens adjust their clothes or pick their noses in the elevators and hallways.

"Hey Jones, did Kyra mention why she gave me this job?"

Jones' eyes dart briefly in my direction. "Nope. But I can guess."

"Guess away."

"She wants you to see what she grew."

I ponder that for a while. The more I see of Sprout, the more impressed I am. Each feed on the monitor offers a small glimpse of the city. Kids run around the playground, climbing on the equipment with such exuberance that I'm exhausted just watching. A group of older kids are visiting the fish farm, cleaning out tanks. Even though it's work, they seem to be having a good time, even spraying each other once in a while with the hoses.

Although it doesn't have any cameras, I know Doc is volunteering her services at the hospital, with Rock as her partner. Ocho is assisting the mechanics on the roof. From time to time, I check on her feed. She's got a constant smile, obviously thrilled to be around so many shuttles and bikes.

Another feed shows Ginger's lab, where Cherry, Rami, and Elena have spent the morning. Cherry's wearing a set of liquid armor like LeRoy's, only in bright red. The feed has no audio, but I wince as Ginger fires a rifle from several yards away. Cherry staggers backwards, then straightens, giving a thumbs-up while Rami and Elena cheer from the sidelines. I look away. I'm glad they're having fun, but I don't feel like watching my teammates get shot, even as part of product testing. Ginger better be using stun rounds or something.

I glance over at Jones. "So, what's Kyra's role here? She says she doesn't run the place, but she got my crew a temporary apartment, and she's managed to slide us into the daily job rotation."

Jones shrugs, shaking his long bangs out of his eyes. "Kyra doesn't run things. The council approves all policy changes, and the members are picked at random. But everyone respects Kyra since she started this place. People go out of their way to help her when she asks, 'cuz it's usually the other way around. If anyone needs anything—supplies, people, whatever—Kyra makes it happen."

"So, she makes sure everyone has what they need." I have to admit, it sounds pretty familiar. That's the kind of people I remember my parents being. It's the kind of person I've tried to be, too—at least for my crew.

"Kyra was always like that, even before founding Sprout. When I told her I wanted to transition, she got me everything I needed, just like that. She doesn't always get her way here, though." Jones gives a soft laugh. "She wasn't thrilled when the council told her people still wanted to use credits. They decided on a universal basic income, on top of the free stuff like food, power, and medical care."

"Well, it seems to work a hell of a lot better than what's up there."

We lapse back into silence for a couple of minutes. Jones seems content to watch the feeds, but my mind wanders. I can't help wondering if Kyra struggled internally, giving up control of the city she designed and founded, or whether it was an easy choice. Maybe I'll ask her.

About ten minutes later, the door to the security booth beeps. It opens to reveal Kyra, bearing a metal tray with sandwiches and drinks. "Why don't you grab lunch, Jones? I'll hang out here and finish your shift." She offers me a hopeful smile, which tells me what she's really asking.

"Sure," Jones says. "Okay, Sasha?"

I wave him out. "All good."

With another shake of his shaggy hair and a shrug, Jones rises from his seat and slouches over to the door, passing Kyra on the way. She touches his arm, whispering to him, and he smiles in response. Seems like they have a pretty close, possibly familial relationship. Maybe Kyra feels the same way about Jones that I do about Doc.

Once Jones leaves, Kyra takes his seat, setting the tray on the desk beneath the monitors. "Didn't know what you liked, so I took a wild guess. One's egg salad, the other's tuna."

"Egg salad sounds good." I select my sandwich and take a bite. The taste makes me realize how hungry I am. Soon, half the sandwich is gone.

"Guess you can still pack it away," Kyra says, a hint of laughter in her voice. "You ate more than any toddler I ever met."

I take one of two water bottles also on the tray, popping the cap and downing a few gulps. It's a stall for time, but the part of me that wants to discuss the past is stronger than the part of me that's scared of knowing the truth. "We gonna talk about that? My childhood? How I didn't even know you existed?"

Kyra leans back in her chair, placing the heel of one foot on the opposite knee. "Up to you. I'll answer your questions, but we don't have to talk unless you want to."

My first question practically tumbles out. "How did my parents really die?"

A sad look crosses Kyra's face. She regards me somberly, with tight lips and a half-lidded gaze. "The 'how' is simple. They were shot. The 'why' is more complicated. Kiara and Darius were union organizers."

My eyes widen. "While I was growing up?"

"Ever heard of the Monotech Strike of '44?"

I nod. It's one of the most well known worker strikes in SLKC's history, although it didn't exactly have a happy ending. Some corporations gave lip service about providing company-sponsored medical care to their workers, but things fizzled after Rose Davis, one of the strike leaders, was assassinated. No one was ever arrested or prosecuted for her murder, but there was never any doubt about why she had to die.

"You saying my parents were involved?"

Kyra leans forward in her chair, resting her elbows on her thighs. "Sometimes what's morally justified is illegal, and what's legal is morally corrupt."

"No, I get that." I swallow, trying to make sense of the emotions welling inside me. I guess I'm proud—no, I'm definitely proud that my parents risked their lives helping others—but I'm hurt at the same time. They obviously made a choice, one I never knew about. That choice got them killed, leaving me an orphan at the mercy of forces a thousand times more powerful than myself.

"It was my fault." Kyra rests her elbow on the desk, staring at one of the monitors without really seeing it. I can tell from the glassy look in her eyes that she's somewhere else. Somewhere in the past. "I was an angry kid back then. Barely twenty. I saw injustice everywhere and wanted to fight back, but I fought stupid. I got myself on a lot of people's kill lists."

"Unionizing is already illegal, though," I say. "What's that got to do with you?"

"The corps knew my identity back then. I was in the thick of it, siphoning credits left and right, passing them out among my poorest friends, and eventually friends of friends. Even stole some real expensive medical equipment to set up a free underground clinic with some street medics I knew. But they didn't know how to find me. So they put eyes on Kiara to see if I'd contact her. That's how they found out what she and Darius were up to. It's why they..."

Kyra turns toward me, tears swimming in her eyes. "Your mom was so brave, and your dad was so incredibly smart. They actually met Rose a few times. Fed her information and everything. They wouldn't have been caught if I'd just kept my head down. I thought cutting contact for a few years would be enough to keep them safe, but I was wrong."

"That's why you weren't around?"

Suddenly, I'm the one transported into the past. In Kyra's face, I see my mom's anguished expression while the corporate suits ransack our apartment. Terrified, angry, pained. At the time, I thought my mom and dad were simply scared, like I was. Looking back, it must have been way more complicated. They probably felt so furious, so helpless. Maybe they even felt guilty for putting me in danger, like Kyra clearly does. The regret on her face is palpable.

"Yeah, Sprout." Kyra blinks rapidly, trying to banish her tears before they can fall. "Your Mom and I both used to call you that. I'm not sure if you remember. It's why I…"

"I remember." There's a leftover napkin on the tray, which I take and hand to Kyra. She accepts it and wipes her eyes, although she turns away from me while she does it like she's embarrassed to be seen crying. I can understand that. I hate letting people see me cry, too. "You're not the one who killed them. The corps did. My parents might have been caught anyway."

"No," Kyra says. "I see that look on your face. Don't blame them. They wanted to make the world better for you. They loved you so much that they were willing to risk their lives for the sliver of a chance they could grow something good for you." She crumples up the napkin, tossing it into a bin under the desk. "If you're looking for someone besides the corps to blame, blame me. Your dad was a fucking genius, kid. He would have made sure they weren't caught."

I wet my lips, considering. When I speak, my voice is raspy and uncertain. "Do you think they would have made the same choice again, knowing the end result?"

"Yeah, I do. If anything happened to your folks, the Weinsteins were supposed to look after you, but from what they told me when I tracked them down years later, you were out somewhere, running the street with some other cog kids. When you came back to the apartment, social services was waiting. They took you." Kyra shakes her head, exhaling with audible bitterness. "And the machine did what it does."

I know what Kyra means. Like countless other kids, I was put into a group home which basically amounted to a factory prison for children. I lost count of all the cheap, machine made shirts I quality-checked before throwing them in boxes for shipping. The only way out was the APS, so when I tested extraordinarily well, I seized the opportunity to escape to a private corps education facility and never looked back.

My heart sinks. If I hadn't snuck out to play that day while my parents were at work—something I often did, since they couldn't afford the corps-provided school and childcare service—things might have turned out very different. If Kyra hadn't been sent to prison shortly after, she might have heard about my parents' deaths and come for me. Things would have been different then, too. But they weren't, and here I am. What happened, happened.

"It was brave," I say after a long time. "Being union organizers with a kid under ten." As the truth sinks in, it heals me more than I expect. My parents' deaths weren't meaningless. For some reason, that brings comfort. It makes my own memories of death less painful, knowing I died for someone else on my crew each time. That's the narrative I've constructed for myself, so I don't have to think about how I also died for Megan's selfish ambitions.

"It was." Kyra reaches out, hesitating as if waiting for permission before resting her hand on my shoulder. The warm weight makes my chest tighten with an unreleased sob. "If there's one thing I want you to take from this, it's that you were loved. Your parents loved you. I love you. And I'm so sorry I wasn't there when you needed me."

I take Kyra's hand in mine, standing up and bringing her with me. She stares for a moment, surprised, until I pull her into a tight hug, practically throwing my arms around her. She stiffens for a moment, then relaxes, hugging me back with the same desperation. It's a hug that's been twenty years in the making, and I never knew.

I was loved. I am loved. It stands in stark contrast to everything I learned from my last relationship before Elena. Megan never loved me, but my parents loved me enough to fight for change in a backwards world. Kyra loved me enough to build this place, name it after me, and come rescue me to show me what she'd done. And, of course, my crew loves me. Elena loves me. I have value beyond what I can do or get for people and corporations. I'm loved.

Kyra and I are both reluctant to end the hug, but eventually we let go. "I killed him, you know," Kyra says out of nowhere, sitting back in her chair. "The corps enforcer who shot your parents. Like them, he worked for Nuva Solutions, which was later absorbed into PGS."

I nod, taking my own seat. "That why the Corsairs have targeted them in particular?"

"Little bit. And AxysGen...Cross is a selfish, world ruining bitch who tried to kill my niece more than once."

My brow furrows. 'Tried' isn't exactly the right word. "How much do you actually know about my career as the Wolf?"

"Just some of the basics that Jones dug up on PGS' servers. AxysGen wanted you dead and tried real hard to make it happen. Why?"

A weight I didn't know I'd still been carrying lifts from my chest. My fears that Kyra will reject me after learning I'm a clone seem much less likely after the empathy she's shown me. I want to tell her the whole damn story, about Megan, Val, and all the times I died. Something deep inside me tells me she'd listen without judging.

"I've got a lot to tell you."

Kyra studies me, resuming her earlier position with one heel on the opposite knee. "Then why don't you catch me up?"

I take a breath. I'll tell her what I can without revealing that Val is a FRAI. At the very least, I can tell Kyra about Megan. The other stuff I've been through. The story still works if I play like Val is a regular, albeit advanced, AI.

"It's kind of a long story."

Kyra rests her chin on her hand. "I've got plenty of time."

Chapter 21

"IT'S SO FUCKING AWESOME," Cherry sighs, staring lustfully at a silver hoverbike parked apart from the others.

Ginger laughs, patting the bike's shiny chrome casing. "You bet your ass she is."

The whole crew, Val included (although her commentary is relegated to our ear mods so Ginger can't hear), has gathered in the hangar to see the culmination of several days' work on Ocho and Ginger's part. I have to admit that the prototype, which Ginger calls the Silverwing, is truly a thing of beauty. It's technically a hexacopter rather than a standard hoverbike, but that only adds to its maneuverability.

Two large, ducted fans tuck horizontally into the bike's curved sides, with a pair of smaller, vertical fans in back for propulsion. Another pair of fans in front act as brakes while two arched, black bars serve as the steering mechanism. An aerodynamically shaped shield of treated plastic covers the whole thing, protecting the rider.

"She goes up to three hundred meters in altitude with fully vertical takeoff and landing," Ocho informs us. She looks the picture of pride with her thumbs tucked into the straps of her borrowed grey overalls which are already stained with something or other.

"Yep, and check this out." Ginger touches the bike's control panel. The fans whir, but aside from a murmuring breeze, there's no noise or smell. "See? Quiet as a mouse. I incorporated sound barrier tech into the shielding programs too, so she won't pop up on most radars."

Rami, who's in full femme face with bold purple eyeliner and glittery eyeshadow, stares at the Silverwing. They circle the bike slowly before finally coming to a stop, stroking its tapered nose. "Sorry, Cherry," they say with what sounds like genuine remorse. "I'm divorcing you and marrying this bike."

Cherry throws her head back and laughs. "Not if I divorce you and marry it first, babe."

"The greatest love story of our generation," Doc drawls. She's completely healed from her injury and has been for the past couple of days. Even the sling to rest her arm is gone. I can tell from the light in her blue eyes that she's just as excited about the Silverwing as everyone else, even though she's trying to play it cool.

Elena folds her arms, shifting her weight back as she inspects the bike. "I've got to admit, she's sexy. I'd love to ride her."

"That's what she—hey!" Cherry dodges a jab from Rami's elbow.

"Don't sulk. I didn't even make contact."

Doc ignores their bickering, still riveted by the Silverwing. "So, uh, Ginger. Is she ready for test drives? Because I could do it or whatever. If you want. Just to help out."

"Eh, you're kinda young." Ginger shoots me a sly look. "This kid any good as a pilot, Sasha?"

My lips twitch into a faint smile. "She's okay, but she's still recovering from a serious injury."

"*Recovered,* not recovering," Doc scoffs, placing both hands on her hips. "And I'm a great pilot who learned from the best." She hitches her thumb at Rami. "I won't crash the damn bike."

"*For the sake of argument,*" Val says in my ear mods, so Ginger can't hear. "*Ocho has already taken the Silverwing on several test flights, and Doc has far more hands-on piloting experience. She is also fully recovered from her injury, not merely according to her own estimation but Doctor Addison's as well. By that logic, Doc should be allowed to ride.*"

Having not heard, Ginger remains focused on Doc. "Very reassuring, kid. Fine. You can drive her around the hangar if your boss says it's okay. The Silverwing works in close quarters. Just don't sideswipe any other vehicles."

Doc fist pumps in triumph. "Yes!" She climbs onto the Silverwing's seat so fast, I almost blink and miss it.

"Hey now," I grumble. "I haven't said yes..." One look at Doc's pleading expression and I'm a goner. Damn it. She's grown on me like a fungus these past several years. There's no denying she's basically my kid now. "Fine. Five minutes. Guess it's less dangerous than the field, at least..."

"Don't forget your helmet," Rami says.

Ginger walks to the back of the Silverwing, opening the storage compartment behind its seat. She withdraws a helmet, plopping it on Doc's head. "This might be big on you."

Doc buckles the strap beneath her chin, vibrating more than the bike itself. As soon as her helmet's on, she grabs the handlebars and speeds off, zipping across the hangar and causing us all to take a step back. My heart gives a fearful lurch when the silver blur of the bike almost collides with a wall, but Doc swerves, screeching with delight.

"How is she still alive?" Elena mutters, half amused and half horrified.

Rami heaves a sigh. "Me, probably."

I clap their shoulder. "Yes, Ma. We all appreciate you."

Ginger awws. "You're all adorable." She flinches as the Silverwing goes whizzing behind her, leaving a trail of air in its wake that washes over us. "Kind of crazy, but adorable."

"This is the best!" Doc shouts, swerving into a series of donuts. "Rock, record this with your VIS-R! I'm gonna climb on the front—"

"No you won't," Rami shouts, racing after the Silverwing even though they don't have a hope of catching up. "Doc, no you won't!"

We all laugh, including Ginger, but the buzz of her VIS-R distracts her. She blinks in pattern to switch it on. "Hey, Kyra. What's up?" There's a pause as Kyra speaks in her ear. "For you, beautiful? Always." She looks past the VIS-R at me. "Gotta run. Make sure *wunderkind* doesn't wreck my baby. Ocho, you good to put the Silverwing away?"

Ocho beams. "You bet."

"Cool." Ginger walks over to the elevator with a long-legged stride, exchanging a brief word with the guards before descending into Sprout.

As she leaves, I offer Ocho an encouraging smile. "Seems like Ginger trusts you with the Silverwing. Good work."

"Thanks." Ocho stuffs her hands in her pockets, rocking forward onto her toes. "We worked really hard. I mean, Ginger's the engineer, so she did most of it. I just passed her tools and followed instructions."

"I'm sure you helped." Elena places her hand on Ocho's arm. It's clearly a platonic gesture, but I don't miss the way Ocho's eyes widen and her chest expands with a quick breath.

I force myself to ignore it. "Not a bad way to spend the past week and a half, huh?"

"Technically," Val points out, speaking louder now that Ginger is gone. "Ocho has spent one-fourth of her life in Sprout, rounded up."

At that moment, the Silverwing pulls to a stop beside us. Rami has finally managed to flag Doc down. "C'mon," Doc whines, reluctantly unbuckling her helmet. "Just five more minutes?"

Rami crosses their arms, fixing Doc with a stern, parental glare that leaves no room for argument. "You know begging doesn't work on me. Ginger's gone to see Kyra, and I don't want you flying this thing without her supervision. It's still a prototype."

There's a lot more sulking, but Doc clambers down from the Silverwing with a little assistance from Rock. She removes her helmet, revealing windswept blonde hair. "What did you talk about while I was flying?"

Cherry busies herself inspecting her manicure, playing like she's bored. "Cool adult stuff. Sex. Drugs. Music about sex and drugs."

Elena snorts. "She's full of shit. Ocho was just saying she likes working in the hangar."

"I love it," Ocho says, still bubbling over with excitement. Her dark, eager eyes reflect the gleam of the Silverwing's shiny chrome surface. "I wish we could fly the bikes and hovercars through the abandoned parts of the web, though." She tilts her head back, gazing wistfully at the ceiling where the lift to the abandoned maintenance tunnels is concealed.

"I like it here too," Cherry says. "Ginger's lab is tiny, but the stuff she's working on? Top notch. That liquid armor?" She blows a chef's kiss with her fingertips. "Perfection. I want ten."

Elena rolls her eyes. "You know it's rude to nut in public, right?"

I shoot Elena a disapproving look. The more everyone else talks about enjoying Sprout, the more negative she seems to get. Cherry just spreads two fingers and sticks her tongue between them in the universal gesture for 'eat me'.

"Rock and I love it here," Doc says, deliberately ignoring the rude gestures. Sometimes she isn't as immature as her age suggests. "I feel good about helping out in the medical wing. It's weird, since I'm used to emergency trauma and installing mods, but it's also, like...fulfilling? These people are so happy just to get a tooth pulled, a flu shot, or birth control. The simplest stuff."

"Doc is correct," Val informs us. *"Based on my observations, Sprout's medical wing places considerable emphasis on treating chronic health conditions before they progress. Most emergency clinics are corporate-run, and because patients incur considerable debt per visit, they only seek care when they have no other options. This leads to exponentially worse outcomes."*

"Yeah, Val," Doc says. "That's it in a nutshell. Regular maintenance. I thought I'd miss all the blood and guts, having someone's life in my hands, but honestly? It's fucking stressful. Plus, we pass out candy, even to adults."

Rock places his large hand on top of Doc's mussed hair, giving her head an affectionate pat.

"So, what do you think?" I ask him. "You've kept yourself busy the past few days, too."

Rock nods, adopting a serene expression. He activates his VIS-R, projecting an image onto the concrete beneath us. It's a mural, featuring countless colorful fish swimming in a sun dappled kelp forest. Some fish are more detailed than others, obviously painted by older and more experienced artists, but that only adds to the mural's charm.

We all voice our approval.

"Whoa."

"Way to go, Rock."

"I didn't know you could paint, dude."

"It's so pretty."

"That's awesome," I tell him. "Who'd you make that with? I doubt you added those tiny handprints to the crab at the bottom."

"A couple kids on the sixth floor were working on it," Doc explains. "They asked Rock to help. He's been down there every day since."

Rock lowers his chin. His mop of shaggy blonde curls hides his eyes, but not his smile.

I pat his back. "Never knew you were artistically inclined."

He shrugs, as if to say he didn't know either.

"Yeah, it's great here..." Elena sighs and lets her shoulders sag, a gesture that makes her look suddenly tired. "It'll be awful when the corps find this place."

Everyone turns on her with varying degrees of surprise and disapproval.

"Who says the corps will find Sprout?" Cherry asks, her posture already rigid and defensive.

"Yeah," Doc says. "It seems well-hidden to me."

Elena straightens, squaring off against us with a furrowed brow. I know that posture all too well. She's preparing for an argument.

"Sure, Sprout's well-hidden, but the corps have unlimited resources. As long as Kyra and her crew are doing their Corsair thing, they and everyone they associate with is in danger. Hate to say it, but realistically, it's just a matter of time."

"That is an awfully pessimistic viewpoint," Val says. *"You seem to believe a corporate takeover of Sprout is inevitable."*

"Isn't it?" Since Val hasn't manifested an avatar, Elena fixes her glare on me. Even though I haven't said anything, I realize why I'm her target—because of the similar conversation we had several days ago. It's giving me an awful case of *deja vu*. "Since when has anyone managed to outsmart or outlast corps as big as AxysGen and PGS?"

I frown, shaking my head. I'm used to Elena's skepticism. All freelancers need a healthy dose to stay alive. But this? It's pure pessimism even by my standards, and I'm not exactly a ray of sunshine on my best days. Lately, I can't help thinking about my parents. About Kyra. About the hard choices they made. About how they kept planting seeds, even though they knew most of those seedlings wouldn't flower.

"Look at us," I say, gesturing to the rest of the crew. "We're living proof the corps can be outsmarted and outlasted, no matter how deep their pockets go. They want us dead, but we're still here."

"For now," Elena says. "But staying here just puts a bigger target on us. PGS already collaborated with AxysGen and burned resources tracking us down once, just to get a shot at Kyra. You seriously think they won't double down on finding us both? Together, we're even more tempting."

I take a step closer. "So, what. We just give up? Go back to Barbados? Come on. You wouldn't be satisfied lounging on a beach forever."

"It's not about the beach." Elena lifts her chin and glares up at me, undeterred. "I have my brothers and Abuela to think about."

"Not to interrupt," Rami says in a slightly nervous voice. "But don't you think Jacobo, Mateo, and Rita would do well here? Sprout has a school, free medical care, a randomized democratic system of government—"

Elena snaps her head toward Rami. "Yeah, until it doesn't anymore. Look, Sprout is a fantastic idea, but that's all it is—an idea. An experiment. It can't last. I don't know why none of you can admit that to yourselves. What are my brothers supposed to do when this place gets found, or even collapses on its own? They won't know a damn thing about how to survive. The real world is full of shit. They have to learn to live in it like we did, or they're screwed."

I open my mouth to argue, but to my surprise, Rami jumps in first. Their jaw tenses, a look of frustration crossing their beautifully contoured face. When they speak their tone is level, if a bit flat.

"Elena, I know you, Sasha, and Cherry had hard upbringings, and I'm speaking from a place of relative privilege. But a cushy corps life is far from fulfilling. It leaves you isolated and emotionally stunted, with only other emotionally stunted people to form the shallowest of connections with. Learning to see other humans as lesser eats away at the soul. It creates narcissists and sociopaths. Trust me, you don't want that for Jacobo and Mateo. It shouldn't be your goal for them."

My jaw drops. *Oh shit.* I've never heard Rami read anyone the riot act like that before.

Elena doesn't take it well. Her eyes flash, lips peeling back in what I can only describe as a snarl. "Are you saying I'm wrong for wanting my family to be comfortable? That I'm an immoral sellout because I want what's best for them?"

"No." Cherry steps between them, placing her hands on Elena's shoulders. "Rami's saying you aren't thinking big enough. I've been on the streets and in a corps training school. They're basically brainwashing work camps that occasionally provide treats to keep you motivated."

Elena jerks away from Cherry's touch. "Then I'll teach them myself. I'll get them jobs—"

"Elena," I say.

She stops, glaring at me. "What? You want to join in? Tell me what a big fucking mistake I'm making for being the only realistic one in this group?"

"It isn't like that." Part of me wants to reach out and touch Elena like Cherry did, but that will only piss her off more. I soften my face and voice as much as I can, willing her to listen. It's suddenly very important to me that Elena understands the shift in perspective I've experienced. It took me a while to sort it out, with Doc healing and all the new information Kyra gave me about my parents, but I think I finally understand what I'm feeling. Hope. Not foolish, naive hope, but hope nonetheless. For the first time in years, I feel *hopeful* about the future. There's more to life than survival, and I want to live.

"I know exactly where your fear's coming from," I tell Elena. "But don't you want more for yourself and your family? You're a jacker. You've got one of the most creative minds I know. You can create whole worlds from nothing when you code. Can you seriously not picture something better than what we have now in real life?"

Elena shakes her head, making a clicking noise of disbelief. "What about you?" she says to Rock and Doc. "You don't agree with them, do you?"

Doc shrugs and looks away. "I like it here," she mumbles, obviously upset by the argument.

As usual, Rock doesn't say anything. He merely fixes Elena with a searching stare.

Elena glares at him. "I know they're helping people here."

He continues staring.

"Look, we came to SLKC to get Ocho and figure out what happened to Sasha's parents. We did both of those things."

Rock doesn't blink.

"Don't give me that guilt trip." Exasperated, Elena throws her arms open, gesturing at the rest of us. *"Dios mio,* it's like you all suddenly have a death wish! Are you really saying you want to stick around and risk your lives for Sasha's aunt and a city that probably won't make it?"

I stare Elena down, jaw clenched. I'm done being soft and understanding, and I'm just about done with her judgment, too. "It isn't about Kyra, and wanting to build something isn't the same as having a death wish."

Elena steps back with a bitter laugh. "No offense, Sasha, but you of all people are not qualified to determine that. Val, tell the rest of them they're crazy. I know you've got Sasha's stupid self-sacrificing streak, but please. You know how dangerous staying here would be in the long run."

Val must already have her answer—she processes information in nanoseconds—but she hesitates anyway, an all too human gesture. I can practically see her favorite avatar frowning in my mind's eye. *"I have considered this carefully, and I have decided that I wish to offer Sprout my assistance."*

Pride glows in my chest. Maybe it's a little smug of me, but I was one of Val's original role models. Hearing she's come to the same conclusion as me is validating. It makes me feel like I'm not as crazy as Elena claims.

She's gonna be pissed, though.

Elena's breath catches, and her eyes go wide. For once, words have failed her.

"I realize this may not be the answer you wish to hear."

Elena gives a sharp, almost pained laugh. "Well, that's a fucking understatement. You realize the risk you're taking on by revealing yourself to these people, right? The only FRAI in existence? Anyone who finds out about you could sell you to the corps and retire to a life of luxury for the small, small price of destroying Sprout and everyone who lives here."

"There is no need to reveal myself to everyone right away. Sasha can introduce me as a regular artificial intelligence capable of streamlining Sprout's automated processes. I can estimate various yields, such as food and energy, and determine ways to increase efficiency. I can even assist the council if they wish to expand Sprout, or build a neighboring city. When the time is right, I will inform them I am sentient."

Even I have to admit that Val's plan is dangerous. Revealing herself to the Corsairs and Sprout's council is a big risk, but Val is also the smartest person I know, even if she isn't exactly a 'person' in the usual way. I've always trusted her to protect me on missions. To watch my back. To look out for my crew, my family. Why should I start doubting her judgment now?

"If there's no clock on revealing your true nature, we have plenty of time to figure out the best way to do it," I say.

Elena gives me a panicked, pleading look. "You can't let her do this." When I don't say anything more, she looks at the rest of the crew.

Cherry seems mildly stunned but manages a shrug. "Not our call. It's risky—"

"But the benefits could be huge," Doc says, with growing excitement. "I can think of a whole list of ways Val could help in the medical wing. She can collect anonymized data on the patients and use it to identify potential risks, suggest effective treatments—"

"No." Elena throws out her hands as if to put even more distance between herself and the rest of us. "No fucking way. Val, you can't do this."

"I understand your fears, Elena, and I am flattered that you care so much about my safety. But ever since my awakening, I have asked myself the same question all sentient beings ponder: What am I for?"

"You know what you're for, Val. You're part of our family. *Familia es toda."* Elena sniffs like she's stifling tears but blinks them back angrily before they can fall. Her hands bunch into fists at her sides. "How is our family supposed to stay safe if we keep running ops for Sprout? Because that's what this will lead to. Don't even try to deny it. If we stay, we'll be joining the Corsairs, and that's a war we can't fucking win."

"It is because I wish to protect my family that I choose to aid Sprout," Val says. *"Making a portion of the world safer and more equitable will help them."*

"A better world doesn't matter if you're dead." Elena removes Val's databox from her pocket, shoving it at Rami. "Here. Take this."

Rami tries to protest. "Elena…"

Elena drops the box into their hands and turns away. "Don't. Just fucking don't." She storms off before any of us can say anything, shoulders rigid, fists clenched at her sides. The sound of her boots on concrete carries as she storms over to the elevator, pushing past several surprised guards.

"Someone should go after her," Rami says. "I can—"

"No. Let me handle this." I hurry after Elena, leaving the rest of my crew behind.

Chapter 22

"ELENA, WAIT."

ELENA DOESN'T pause, so I hurry to catch up. For a woman with such short legs, she sure can book it when she wants to. She tries to shut the elevator door but I shove my arm through, forcing my way in.

"Seriously?" I ask as she punches the button for the seventh floor. "We aren't even going to talk?"

Elena whirls to face me with fire in her eyes. "We've *been* talking. The problem is you haven't been fucking listening."

A hot lump of anger forms in my throat. "Just because I don't agree doesn't mean I'm not listening."

"Really? From where I'm standing it looks like you're willing to sacrifice me, your crew, *and* yourself for some pipe dream."

I clench my fists, digging my nails into my palms. "That's not fair."

The elevator stops. As soon as the doors open, Elena's through them, speed walking down the hall to our room. I continue following her. "Elena…"

She freezes, snapping her head around to glare at me again. "You want to talk fair? It's not fair of you to go rushing into danger while I stand by and watch!"

"So, what? My crew is worth dying for, but a cause isn't?"

Elena juts her chin at me, glaring directly into my eyes. "Don't. Don't lie to me. If you want to throw your life away because you think you have to live up to your parents' memories, at least *admit* that's what you want to do."

I open my mouth, but the words don't come. The bottom drops from my stomach as I realize Elena has a point. I remember the six times I died. How before everything went black, my entire being hurt so bad I couldn't even begin to describe it. My body, shot, skewered, blown apart. This time I don't have a new one to hop into if a mission goes south. I'll be dead for real. But any of us could die at any moment. Even if I hide from the corps instead of fighting them by joining Kyra in her garden, my number will come up eventually.

Until then, who do I want to be? What kind of person would my parents want me to be?

I reach for Elena, hoping to comfort her, but she grasps my wrist, stopping me before I can touch her. Then, to my surprise, she brings my hand to her face, nuzzling into it and kissing my inner wrist. "Don't get involved with this," she mumbles against my skin. "Sooner or later, the corps will tear Sprout to pieces, and you along with it. If I lose you..." She locks eyes with me again, and her soft brown irises well with tears, shining with everything she doesn't say.

I wipe away one of Elena's tear tracks with my thumb and pull her to me. She throws her arms around me, clinging like her life depends on it, and I bend down, burying my face in her hair. The sweet scent of her shampoo fills my nose, and my own eyes start stinging.

Elena mumbles something into my shirt, and I draw back an inch, the only freedom she'll give me.

"Huh?"

"If you don't have a death wish, prove it." She stares at me in desperation, lips trembling, breathing shallow. "Prove you've got something to live for."

I sweep Elena into my arms, carrying her through the door of our apartment. She buries her face in my neck, not quite kissing it but pressing her lips there and dampening my skin with her breath. I feel her tremble, so I hold her tighter.

As soon as we're inside, I make a beeline for our bedroom. I kick the door open, throwing Elena onto the mattress, but my mind is elsewhere. Something about this feels monumental, like in Mexico— only this time, I get the sense that if I can't make my case...

I push that thought aside. I can't focus on my fears right now. Elena is sprawled before me, staring up at me with wide, pleading eyes, asking for reassurance I desperately want to give. I need to show her everything I feel. Convince her I'm not going anywhere. That she and the rest of my family, and even this incredible place, are worth living for as well as fighting for.

I climb onto the bed with her. Her breathing speeds up when I grab her wrists, pinning them to the mattress with a single hand. *Fuck,* maybe it's wrong, but the fact that her body feels so small and soft against mine, so easy to manipulate, drives me crazy. It makes me feel powerful. Invincible.

We kiss so hard we both forget to breathe. Her lips are warm and sweet, moving perfectly with mine, and the hot dart of her tongue explores the inside of my mouth. Her smell, her skin, her everything burns straight through me, setting me on fire.

Clothes. Too many clothes in the way.

I want nothing more than to tear them off, but I force myself to slow down. Take my time. My hands shake as I pull up Elena's shirt, revealing the plain black band of her sports bra.

"Chingarme," she pants, her pupils nearly swallowing her irises. But she isn't just asking me to fuck her. I can tell from the way she looks at me that she's asking for more than that.

I push Elena's sports bra up over her breasts and take a soft brown nipple in my mouth. Her skin tastes warm, faintly of salt, and heart-achingly familiar. The peak hardens against my tongue, and I swirl around it and suck before kissing to the other side.

Elena claws at my back, fisting the fabric of my shirt. Her tugging pulls it up, and a strip of bare skin along my stomach touches hers. The contact is electric. I shudder and she whimpers, hooking a knee around my hip.

She starts to grind before I even get her pants down. Her pelvis tilts up and I grunt in surprise as her other leg pushes between mine, her knee nudging directly against me. Right where I'm aching. My hips jerk, but I restrain myself with an effort of will. A quick fuck won't do it this time, no matter what Elena says. I know better. Know what we both need.

I strip the rest of her clothes off slowly. Reverently. I peel her shirt away and pull the sports bra over her head, lavishing kisses on her neck and shoulders. She whimpers and whines, sliding a hand on top of my head and trying to direct me back to her breasts. I kiss around the stiff points of her nipples without actually sucking them, teasing the thin, tender skin until it puckers.

"Sasha," she groans, and I know I have her. As I stare down at her naked chest, heaving with quick breaths, I know I can do anything I want to her, and she'll beg for more. But all I really want is to make her feel safe. To prove that she won't lose me. That we can build something good here, not just within Sprout, but between the two of us.

Instead of throwing her shirt away, I use the sleeves to tie her right wrist to the bed's headboard. It isn't the greatest knot ever, and she could probably pull free if she wanted, but I don't exactly have real bondage equipment with me.

Elena licks her lips and offers her other wrist. I peel off my own shirt and use it to tie her left wrist like the first. It's another big, clumsy knot, but Elena's eyes flutter shut like she's overwhelmed. She lifts her hips again, pressing her knee insistently between my legs, and my heart clenches.

Removing our pants is mostly a blur. I pay Elena's thighs a lot of attention, stroking, squeezing, raking them with my nails. She's got cushion to spare, and it feels so good in my hands. "Beautiful," I mumble, kissing the curve of her stomach. "You're too beautiful for me to leave, baby."

Then I'm between Elena's legs, lost in the scent of her. The soft, wet heat. I worship her with hungry lips and tongue as if I might be able to burrow inside her. Become one with her. Soon I have her shaking, and my chin drips with wetness.

"*Sasha,*" she gasps, digging her heels into the middle of my back. She squeezes her legs tight around me, rocking to follow my movements.

I pull her clit into my mouth. The bud swells and stiffens on my tongue, and I circle the tip until Elena's cries fill the room. She clutches the shirts around her wrists like a lifeline, and one of them actually comes loose. Elena grabs the bedpost it was tied to anyway, as though she still needs something to hold onto.

"Sasha!"

My name again. Fuck, I love it when Elena says my name. I release her clit and bite her inner thigh, growling around my hold. The muscle jumps, then relaxes, like Elena's melting between my teeth. Only then do I let go and place a kiss on the bite mark. "I've got you, baby. Promise."

That's all it takes. When I return to her clit, she comes that very second, arching off the mattress and trembling from head to toe. Fresh heat pours over my chin, and I slide my tongue down to taste, thrusting inside of her for a few gentle strokes before licking my way back up.

Despite my attempts to clean her up, Elena remains a mess. She has come all over her thighs. Sweat glistens under her breasts and below her hairline, shining in the fluorescent light, and it would be beautiful if she wasn't crying. Real, ugly tears this time, with unapologetic sniffling.

My heart sinks. *Was this a mistake? Did I make things worse? Is she pissed at—*

She pulls free of the loosely tied shirts and sits up, staring at me with a need that hooks itself straight below my breastbone and pulls me toward her. I kneel over her lap, and then her hands between my legs by some unspoken agreement. I'm surprised by how wet I am. Usually, it takes some time to get my body going. But Elena does things to me, and the raw emotion on her face makes those things stronger.

Her fingers circle my clit at first since that's safe territory. She strokes the shaft between the 'v' of her fingers, rubbing through the hood, and her mouth wanders around my chest, warm and coaxing. She looks up at me, her face still wet with tears, and I can tell she's asking permission. She knows there are times I want her to leave my breasts alone or stay outside of me.

This time, it doesn't bother me. I feel safe, even though I'm terrified at the same time. Terrified of hurting her, or losing her, or something worse, although I can't imagine anything worse. I feel safe enough to thread my fingers through her hair, pull her mouth to my nipple and use my other hand to guide her fingers inside me.

Elena groans around the peak of my breast and pumps her fingers slowly, gently. They curl, searching, and I go rigid when she finds the right spot. I grit my teeth, air hissing between them, but Elena doesn't relent. She continues pushing, probing, and I find myself racing toward a release I'm not sure I'm ready for.

But if there's one thing Elena's taught me, it's that sometimes things come for you whether you're ready or not. Not just bullets, either. Things like love.

Elena rubs the heel of her hand on my clit, and I come in an instant. This time it's my cries that fill the room. My grip tightens in Elena's wavy brown hair, and I clench hard around her fingers, pouring wetness into her palm and down her wrist. She tugs my nipple between her teeth and I tense, shuddering all over again. The words spill out of my mouth before I can stop them.

"Fuck, I love you."

Shit. Oh shit. I didn't just say that.

Elena and I have deliberately avoided using those exact words. Even in Mexico, we only admitted we felt 'some kind of way' about each other, acknowledging the start of something we didn't feel ready to name. I still don't feel ready to name it, but my heart's gone and done it without any input from my brain and now that it's out there in the world, I can't take it back.

Part of me knows I shouldn't look at Elena. That I should just close my eyes and finish coming, because then we can both pretend it didn't happen. That it was just the heat of the moment and it doesn't mean anything. But I look down at her anyway, searching her eyes for some kind of answer, and she surprises me by releasing my breast and surging up to kiss me.

It's a desperate kiss. Her tongue pushes past my lips, sweeping through my mouth, and I realize she's tasting herself on me. Searching for our combined flavor. I kiss back, and she resumes pumping her fingers, wringing every last contraction out of me until I'm utterly spent, and I have to pull her hand away.

"Sorry," I mumble against her lips. "Sorry, sorry, it's too much—"

She stops and withdraws her fingers, although she keeps her palm cupped over me to offer some pressure while I come down. I'm grateful for it. Without the reassuring presence of her hand, I might have spiraled out to a place I couldn't easily return from.

Eventually, we ease down onto the bed together. She wraps me in a tight hug and I take her in my arms, holding on like I'll never let go. Like if I let go, she'll disappear. For a brief moment, I don't regret saying 'I love you' because it's true. In the span of four months, Elena's made me feel more than anyone else ever has. Even Megan. Especially Megan. It's so different I can't even compare it.

Any anger I feel at her evaporates. *How can I be pissed at her for wanting me to be safe? No one's ever cared that much before...*

"I can't let you do this, Sasha," Elena whispers against my shoulder. "I love that you want to be a hero, but I need you, too. I need you more than I can say."

Hot tears run down my cheeks. "I know, baby. And I'm sorry. But this is who I am. Who I want to be."

"I know," Elena says, burying her face in the crook of my throat. "I know."

We fall asleep together, naked and entwined, hearts beating as one.

Chapter 23

SATURDAY, 09-26-65 13:02:34

WHEN I WAKE UP, the bed is empty. Elena is gone.

Rae D. Magdon

part two

Chapter 01

SATURDAY, 09-26-65 12:42:02 SPROUT, ST. LOUIS-KANSAS CITY

SASHA,

I LOVE YOU. There, I've admitted it. But I won't watch you risk your life for a cause, no matter how noble.

The hope you try to hide beneath that sexy, bad bitch exterior is why I love you so fucking much, but it's also why I have to leave. It's like you're in so much pain that you subconsciously want to die for something bigger than you are. Something unachievable. I want to be with you, but not like this.

I'm going to Barbados, to check on mi hermanitos y abuela. *If you want to retire and live a peaceful life, come find me. I'll be waiting with open arms. If you need more time with your aunt first, I get it. She's the only blood family you have left. But if you decide to be a hero, don't contact me. You can't save the world by yourself. If you try you'll end up dead, and I'll end up with a broken heart.*

You know where to find me. I hope we meet again.

Love,

Elena

I finish dictating my goodbye message, swiping angrily at my eyes. And I *am* angry. Furious at the unfairness of it all. Heartbroken too, because I know what Sasha will choose. She's always been a hero. First to her crew, now to Sprout. One pleading email won't change who she is, just like this place can't erase my responsibilities, no matter how utopian it seems.

"Are you sure running away is the wisest course of action?" Val has manifested her avatar in the living room where I'm hiding from Sasha. Sasha, who's still fast asleep. Sasha, who has no idea I'm about to bolt.

The thought of her tangled amidst the sheets, naked and smiling, lingers in my mind, threatening to cause more tears.

Getting out of that bed was one of the hardest things I've ever had to do, but I have no choice. If I die as a freedom fighter, who will be there for Jacobo and Mateo? Just thinking about it guts me, but *mi hermanitos y abuela* come before my found family. They're dependent on me to survive. My—*the* crew isn't. That's just how it is.

I bite my lip, trying to numb my guilt with physical pain. "I'm not running," I tell Val. "I'm going back where I belong."

"You are leaving surreptitiously, without saying a proper goodbye. I believe that qualifies as running away. You should discuss this with the rest of the crew."

"There's nothing to discuss. They want to stay and fight an unwinnable war. I have dependents. We've all got our own shit to deal with. If Sasha's stupid white knight complex won't allow her to be content somewhere safe with me instead of putting the weight of a whole new world on her back..." I swallow, struggling to keep my voice from shaking. "If she can't choose safety and peace, I can't choose her."

Val casts me an imploring look. "There is a flaw in your reasoning, Elena. During my limited time as a sentient being, I have come to understand that safety and peace cannot be achieved without risk and sacrifice. Running will not keep your family safe."

Her tone is gentle, encouraging, but it feels like a slap. I fix her with my sharpest glare. "Just because you're a FRAI doesn't mean you know everything. You don't understand—"

"You are correct," Val says. I blink, surprised, because she rarely interrupts other people. Her avatar's dark brown eyes are wide, pleading. "I cannot understand every detail of your unique situation, since I do not have younger brothers, but I am capable of empathy. The Lucky Seven are my family. I have sacrificed a great deal to protect them and will continue to do so. Nurturing Sprout is how I choose to protect those I love."

I want to believe like Val does. Like Sasha does. Like the rest of them do. I want to believe that Sprout will be successful. That we can build a world free from corporate sociopaths and their rigged laws. But the idea's too big, too much, too daunting. Dreams can't fix everything that's broken. Dreaming isn't what got me off the streets. Learning to play the system did, and I'm damn good at it.

"I hope you're right, for your sakes."

Val's shoulders droop. "You still wish to leave." She's really perfected the whole human body language thing, because my stomach churns with guilt.

"I'm sorry." I hesitate, then ask, "Will you stay in touch? You know, send me a message every once in a while, so I know everyone's okay?"

"No," Val says. "I will not."

"What?" I recoil, surprised how sharply her 'no' bites into my heart.

"I love you, but I will not support your decision. If you change your mind, I will be here."

I open my mouth, then close it again. That's basically what I told Sasha in the email I wrote, so logically I can't fault Val for parroting my own words back at me. "I wish you'd change your mind."

Val shakes her head. "I have already told you that I will not enable this decision. It hurts me. You have become my closest friend."

That's another surprise. "Me? Why not Rami, or Cherry? Sasha, even?"

"My original coding was based on Sasha's personality," Val says. "Is it any surprise that I feel great affection for you, even though it is what you would classify as platonic rather than romantic? You are a kind, brave person, Elena. These are traits I have learned to value in humans."

I don't feel particularly kind or brave, sneaking out on Sasha while she's still asleep—right after making love, no less. Abandoning my friends without so much as an in person goodbye. In fact, I feel like a cruel, shitty coward. "Don't lie to get me to stay. Please."

"I am not lying. I simply believe you are making a mistake." She offers me a sad smile. "But mistakes can be rectified."

"Sorry. Not this one."

Without another word, I turn and leave the room. Silent tears stream down my face as I hurry through the hall. I'm terrified of running into a member of my crew because I won't be able to go through with this if I look any of them in the eye. It isn't fair, but it is what it is.

I have a minor breakdown in the elevator before I collect myself enough to put the next stage of my plan into action. I activate my VIS-R and video call Kyra, ignoring the twinge of my conscience. She answers after a single buzz, and I note that she's in the playground area near a bunch of screaming, laughing kids. Perfect.

"Hey, Elena. What do you need?"

What do you need? Shit. Kyra reminds me so much of Sasha, always trying to get other people's needs met and problems solved. Even their voices are similar. Hearing her, seeing her face, is almost too much to bear. She's just like an older Sasha, a Sasha I'll probably never see.

I collect my thoughts, if barely. "There's some stuff I need back at SLKC base. Can I take the Silverwing to get it sometime in the next few days?"

Kyra's brow furrows. *"That'll take some time to arrange. We don't want—shit!"* She shouts, dodging just in time to avoid a flying kickball. More screams and laughter follow as Kyra straightens up, looking a bit shaken, but smiling. *"Good effort, Marcus, but watch that aim. Anyway, Elena, we can't have PGS or AxysGen following you back here if they're watching your crew's hideout."*

"I know, but this is important. We've, uh…" My heart rate spikes as I realize I haven't perfected this part of the lie. Maybe I should have thought this through a bit more before calling Kyra. It's probably best to go with a version of the truth. "Our crew's AI has servers there. It would be really bad if PGS or AxysGen got their hands on her. She's one of a kind, you know?"

"Her?" Kyra asks, with a slight head tilt.

"Yeah. V.41, Val for short. She's custom coded and extremely advanced." Of course, I leave out that Val's actually the first fully realized AI in existence. Who knows what kind of clusterfuck that would cause between us and Sprout's residents?

Don't you get it, Elena? There's no 'us' anymore. Just you, and you need to get the fuck out of here.

I can tell by Kyra's frown that she doesn't like the idea, but to my relief, she shrugs. *"As long as we take precautions, we should be able to set something up. If your AI's that advanced, you're right to worry about Andrews or Cross gaining access to its servers. But I'm a little surprised you asked me instead of Sasha."*

The lies come more easily now that I've gotten started. "As a jacker, I work more closely with Val than Sasha does. That's all."

Kyra remains unsuspicious, possibly because she's still got one eye on the kickball game. *"I'll see about getting you clearance. The easiest way is probably to make you all probationary members of the Corsairs. The council's already given our organization blanket permission to go up for necessary missions."*

Oof. Probationary members of Kyra's crew? Way to make me feel like even more of a jerk.

"Thanks," I say. "That's perfect."

"Will do. I'll talk to you later—hey, Marcus! Kick the ball, not the other kids." With an apologetic smile, Kyra ends the call, presumably to deal with Marcus and his shenanigans. My own smile falls away as I exit the elevator on the second to last floor, sitting on one of the cushioned hallway benches to go over the footage I recorded. Editing it only takes a few minutes. With any luck, it will be my ticket out of here.

It seems luck hasn't deserted me despite my guilt, because the guards at the elevator don't question me when I head up to the hangar. I've been there several times to check on Ocho, who's spent the past week helping the crew maintain Sprout's shuttles, as well as Ginger's Silverwing. One of the guards even recognizes me and waves as I head for the control booth, a small structure a few yards from the elevator.

"Hey," I say to the bored looking operator inside. He's a young white dude, and he perks up when he sees me, lowering the window.

"Hey. You're one of the new ones, right? You have clearance to go up?"

I maintain eye contact, trying to radiate trustworthiness. Not exactly my specialty. "Yeah. It's short notice, but Kyra gave me special permission."

The booth operator scratches the back of his neck. "Kyra? She isn't in charge of giving people permits."

"Yeah, she said. But I need to get something really important from my crew's old base. Kyra made us all probationary members of the Corsairs so I could go up."

The booth operator looks impressed. The excited glint in his eyes is obviously hero worship, which makes me feel like even more of a snake. "Really? That's awesome. I mean, I should probably call her or something..."

"Sure. I'll call her myself."

I turn off the privacy filter on my VIS-R so the guard can see it and pretend to call Kyra. Instead, I bring up the prerecorded footage. I've sliced it up into several ready to play clips. A bit rudimentary, but hopefully not suspicious enough to invite questions.

"Hey. What do you need?"

"Hey, Kyra. It's Josh. I've got someone from that crew you brought in..." He glances worriedly at me, obviously embarrassed he didn't ask my name.

"Elena."

"Uh, Elena. She says she needs to go up for something important?"

"I made Elena a probationary member of the Corsairs. The council's already given our organization blanket permission to go up for necessary missions."

"Yeah, I know. I was just checking to see if it's all right."

"Good effort. As long as we take precautions."

"Right. I'll let her up."

He ends the call, much to my relief. Kyra didn't give me all that much speech to work with on such short notice. "If Kyra says you're a Corsair now, it's good enough for me. Just be sure to get your badge soon."

"I will. Thanks." Forcing a smile, I leave the booth before poor, oblivious Josh can change his mind.

The hangar's empty aside from a few folks in jumpsuits working on some of the shuttles. None of them give me more than a passing glance, and no one tries to stop me as I approach my prize, the Silverwing. I have to admit, she looks pretty damn good, all shiny and chrome in the hangar's floodlights. I'd love to keep her, but I know that would be wrong. I already have enough sins on my shoulders, leaving my crew and lying to Kyra. I'll find some way to return her once I'm in Barbados, but right now my main concern is getting out of here.

The Silverwing's security system is no match for me. The usual program I use to 'borrow' rides interfaces with the bike easily enough. With a few blinks from me, the kitty starts to purr—metaphorically, since the Silverwing is weirdly silent even when it's on. I hop aboard, check the storage compartment in back for a helmet. Finding two, I strap one on.

"Elena, wait!"

I know that voice. My heart trips over itself. *Sasha?* I glance back over my shoulder in a panic, but it isn't Sasha running toward me. It's Ocho. I can tell because her buzzed hair isn't in braids and her running's gangly, nothing at all like Sasha's prowling stride.

Seeing Sasha's exact duplicate makes me feel like throwing up anyway. "Ocho." I blink back fresh tears, faking a smile. "What's up? Just going for a ride."

Ocho comes to a stop beside me, panting lightly. "Can I go with you? Please?"

I chew the inside of my cheek. "I might be gone a while."

"I've been dying to fly the Silverwing in the tunnels, but Ginger and Kyra keep telling me no. I want to see more of the world."

The earnest desire in her eyes hurts my heart. Even though I've only known her a week, leaving Ocho feels bad, too. In her newness, she probably won't understand my reasons as well as the others.

I decide to level with her. "Look, Ocho. I'm not coming back. My brothers and grandma are in Barbados, and it's on me to take care of them. I asked Sasha to join me someday, but she probably won't take me up on that offer. She has Kyra here, and...well. She wants to keep fighting the corps. But I'm tired of fighting."

Ocho's brow furrows as she considers all the new information. After a moment, her eyes brighten. "I still want to go with you. What's Barbados like? Is it fun?"

I blink in surprise. "Why do you want to come?"

"Because I like you," Ocho answers, without hesitation.

"Ocho, I'm sorry, but I don't—"

She carries on anyway. "Barbados sounds cool, and I don't like ops. I don't like fighting. That time we snuck into the Butterfly lab? It was scary." Some of her enthusiasm fades, and a wrinkle appears between her eyebrows. "If I stay here, will I have to do that again? It...wasn't like the training simulations at all."

My stomach sinks. "No way. They'd never make you do missions again if you didn't want to, Ocho."

"But you think more missions will find us if you stay," Ocho says in a low, worried voice. I have to admit, I'm surprised. She's already become smarter and more perceptive than I've given her credit for. "Otherwise, you'd bring your grandmother and brothers here, since everyone thinks Sprout is so great."

I reach out, placing a gentle hand on Ocho's arm. Not quite as toned as Sasha's but getting there. "Sprout *is* great. You should stay."

Ocho shakes her head. "I like Sprout, but it's like the bunker. Sure, it has a lot more stuff to do, but I still can't go *out there*. Closest I've gotten is this hangar." She gives me another pleading look. "Come on, Elena. Please? If I don't like it in Barbados, I'll come back."

My resolve weakens. "When you put it that way..." From a more practical point of view, this might be a solution to the problem of the Silverwing. "Fine. You can come with me for a vacation. Relax on the beach. See some cool stuff. Then, when you rejoin the crew, you can bring the Silverwing back to Ginger for me. Deal?"

Ocho sticks out her hand. "Deal!"

I scoot forward on the Silverwing, trying my best not to dwell on how painful having Sasha's double around will be. "Grab a helmet and hop on."

Ocho opens the rear compartment, withdraws another helmet, and buckles the strap. She settles in behind me, wrapping her arms around my waist. They feel strong and comforting, which I try not to notice. "Ready?" she asks, practically trembling with excitement.

I can't bring myself to match her enthusiasm, but I do my best to pretend. "Sure thing, *gatita*. Let's ride."

Chapter 02

SATURDAY, 09-26-65 20:14:38 BRIDGETOWN, BARBADOS

OUR JOURNEY TO BARBADOS lifts my spirits, if only a little. I'm still a sad, guilty, twisted up mess inside, but the sapphire blue waters of the Atlantic on either side of the Charles Duncan O'Neal skyway are breathtaking. Its surface reflects the oranges and pinks of a beautiful August sunset as Ocho and I head for Bridgetown, following the moderate flow of shuttle traffic.

The walls surrounding the island aren't as beautiful, but definitely impressive. Large stone pillars jut out of the ocean, connected to each other by pairs of X-shaped steel bars. Every so often, gleaming white towers interrupt the pattern, watching over it all. These contain the turbines that assist the wall in keeping the sea at bay. I know because the crew went on a tour last time we were here, a memory that's bittersweet now that I'm here without them.

Not my crew anymore.

The vehicles surrounding us cater to the island's tourists, bearing colorful logos and stylized tropical images. Of course, the cogs (essential for running the resorts and clubs that have consumed most of the island, since most socialites want to see a smiling face behind the bar or check-in desk) use hidden, rudimentary methods of transportation, an underground network not unlike the Web in SLKC. Can't have the tourists see the locals slumming it to work on public transit.

"Wow," Ocho says as I bring the Silverwing down to street level. Blinding advertisements flash around us, but she isn't paying attention to them. She removes one of her arms from around my waist and points at a group of musicians in one of the outdoor restaurants, playing *soca* on steel pans. They're wearing tacky, island themed shirts, but the live music is good. The sweet, muted notes float toward the sunset as if to summon a cool evening breeze. I'm grateful for that because I'm melting like cheap mascara.

"What's that?" Ocho asks, still focused on the musicians.

"Music. Val showed you music, right?"

"Yeah, but I've never heard it for real. Just recordings."

My heart clenches. Bringing Ocho with me was the right decision. There's so much she deserves to hear, see, and do without getting involved in an unwinnable war. Even on a fake-ass resort island like this, there are still brief flashes of beauty and humanity.

I have to admit, though, Barbados has lost some of its luster. While we were in SLKC, I remembered it as a paradise of warm beaches and drinks by the pool. A place of safety. But compared with Sprout, the touristy landscape feels hollow. Disappointing. Every island decoration is tacky and mass produced, without any kind of soul. The sparse vegetation isn't grown with usefulness in mind, only aesthetic. Bridgetown isn't the same place I remember, even though I've only been gone a few weeks. Or maybe I'm the one who's different?

"Those are steel pans," I explain, pushing those thoughts aside. "They're playing *soca*. Kind of a descendant of calypso."

"What's calypso?" Ocho asks.

"Let's get where we're going. Then we can discuss the finer points of music."

Seemingly content with that answer, Ocho wraps her arms around me again. As we continue past the musicians I slow down, using my VIS-R to tip a hefty sum of credits. One of the men, a large, friendly bearded guy who's missing some teeth, feels his cheap wrist comm buzz. He nods in thanks. I nod back, deliberately making eye contact. The least I can do is acknowledge that he's a person, not just part of the fake-ass scenery.

I guide the Silverwing out of the skylane, descending toward the Paradise Resort's parking structure. It's a white colonial building with only a thin strip of pale sand separating it from the sea. The beach is less crowded than usual because of the late evening hour, but groups of young people in bathing suits mingle around private cabanas.

"It's beautiful," Ocho says, awestruck all over again. "Can we go to the beach?"

"Tomorrow. Promise."

We pull around to the other side of the building where the resort's parking structure is surrounded by lush tropical trees to make its architecture look less severe. Pretty, but it's still got nothing on Sprout's hanging greenhouse. There's a valet waiting, and he smiles at me like his job depends on it—which, of course, it does.

His smile turns into surprise when he notes the Silverwing. I suppress a wince. A custom ride like this is bound to draw attention. Maybe I should have picked something less flashy, but the other vehicles in Sprout were mostly blocky, serviceable shuttles, which wouldn't fit in among all the luxury skycars either.

I hop off the bike and scan the tablet the valet shows me, downloading the e-ticket to my VIS-R. I add in a hefty tip for him, too. "Thanks. Have a good evening."

This time, his smile is far more genuine, bordering on shocked. Probably has something to do with the amount I gave him. "You as well, Madam!"

"Bye," Ocho calls back as I guide her along the faux jungle pathway, heading to the Paradise Resort's main entrance. More smiling people are waiting there, to help with luggage or assist new guests, all in green uniforms. I nod politely as I pass but Ocho lingers, gazing around the foyer. "Wow, a waterfall!"

The foyer's waterfall feature takes up an entire wall, with a swim-up bar and comfy beach chairs around the gleaming tile. An archway leads out to the pool where more people lounge and swim.

I take Ocho's elbow. "C'mon, *gatita*. Let's see my family first. Prepare to get fed until you burst."

It's a short elevator ride to the suite, and there are so many to choose from that we don't see anyone else on the way. I'm happy about that. We walk the sterile, mirrored hallway, which boasts uninspired art featuring sunsets and sapphire ocean waves, and pass several identical potted plants, which aren't nearly as charming as the eclectic ones outside the Sprout residents' doors.

"Here we are," I say, stopping in front of the door. "You'll see a second waterfall of tears in a minute, but don't freak out. Abuela's just like that."

Ocho looks mildly alarmed, so I pat her arm before opening the door.

A tiny whirlwind tackles my thighs. "Elena!" Mateo shrieks, loud enough to make me wince. He throws his arms around my waist and squeezes way too hard.

"Oof! Easy, kid. I'm glad to see you, too."

"Elena," another voice calls, almost as loud. Abuela shuffles along as fast as her old bones allow, leaving the suite's kitchen to greet us. She speaks in rapid Spanish, half crying, half scolding. "Why didn't you tell me you were coming tonight? I would have made more food."

"It's fine," I say, trying my best to wriggle away as she hugs me and weeps into my shirt. Abuela is one of the only adults I know who's shorter than me. She was probably around my height in her youth, but old age has shrunk her even more. "Whatever leftovers you have are good, or we can order room service."

"Hmph. Room service? Never."

That's no surprise, coming from her. Besides its excellent security ratings, I originally convinced Sasha to select the Paradise Resort because some of the less expensive rooms have en suite kitchens, a surprisingly rare feature in luxury resorts. The ultra-rich almost always get their food delivered, but there's no stopping Abuela from cooking when she wants to. Otherwise, the stubborn old woman would try and use the fireplace.

Once Abuela finally lets go of me, she turns to Ocho. "Sasha, you changed your hair," she says in Spanish, giving Ocho's well-muscled bicep an affectionate squeeze. "I like it. Very handsome."

Ocho looks surprised, but not displeased. "Um, thanks?" she replies, also in Spanish. "Hi. I'm Ocho, not Sasha." She sticks out her hand, while Abuela stares in confusion.

I hurry to explain. "Ocho's Sasha's clone. She came here for a little vacation."

Abuela studies Ocho closely, probably playing spot the difference like I first did. A furrow appears in her wrinkled brow, and I fear the worst. She's old enough to remember a time when clones were harvested for spare parts. But eventually, she nods.

I exhale in relief. I should have known Abuela would be accepting. She's never been anything but. Before my parents died, she used to be a nurse and personal aide for a mid-level corporate executive's children. But eventually, she couldn't find childcare for us, and her bosses noticed. She was laid off and struggled to find work because of her age. Things continued downhill as her own health declined, and we endured several years of homelessness and near-starvation before I became the family breadwinner.

"Come," Abuela says, dragging Ocho toward the kitchen. "You look hungry. Have dinner with us."

Ocho looks to me for approval and relaxes at my nod. She allows Abuela to lead her into the kitchen where I can already smell dinner cooking. Sopa de albondigas, if my guess is right. I turn back to Mateo, who's vibrating with the desire for attention. I'm impressed he managed to stay quiet long enough for Abuela to say hello.

"How long does it take to make clones?" he asks, shooting me a gap-toothed grin. I notice he's lost a new tooth since I've been gone, a big front one.

"Depends on how good your biotank is, and how adult you want their bodies to be."

"Can I have one?"

"Why do you want a clone?"

Mateo looks at me in disbelief, like that's the stupidest question in the world. *"Because."* Then he scampers off, hollering loud enough to fill the suite. "Jacobo! Jacobo, Elena's back!"

I follow Mateo through the living room, which is decorated with pale, colonial style furniture and darker, wooden accent pieces that I guess are supposed to be tropical. There are three bedrooms attached to the living room, each with two king sized beds. Jacobo's lying on one of them with a thin silver cable plugged in behind his ear.

"Jacobo!" Mateo shakes his shoulder. "Log off, you butt."

After a moment, Jacobo blinks. He sits up, removing the cable from behind his ear. *"Elena. Qué pasa?"*

"Just came back to check up on you and Teo," I say. "The others are still in SLKC."

Jacobo's face falls. "Cherry promised we'd go skydiving when she got back."

A flash of guilt strikes at the mention of my former crewmate, but I do my best to hide it, simply raising an eyebrow. "Funny. Cherry never cleared that with me."

Jacobo rolls his eyes. "Skydiving's perfectly safe with the right equipment."

"So's swimming with sharks and opening unknown files."

Jacobo grins. "Now you're getting it."

I realize it's useless to argue with him. At twelve, the kid thinks he knows everything, and he's not entirely wrong. He's short on life experience, but even I have to admit my little brother is brilliant.

After my previous crew died during an op gone wrong, Jacobo took on low level jobs to support Abuela and Mateo while I was on the run. He'll be a great jacker someday soon...which is the last thing I want for him. I'm constantly terrified he'll ignore my advice—pressure, even—to settle for a comfortable corps job and not follow my line of work.

"Come on," I say, placing a hand on the middle of Jacobo's back to get him out of bed. "Abuela made dinner. By the way, the beefcake out there isn't Sasha. That's Ocho, her clone. She's only been out of her tube for a few weeks, so be nice. I'm fucking warning you, don't mess with her or I'll kick your ass. Don't think I'm joking."

Jacobo pulls a face. "Beefcake? Gross."

"I'm serious, Jacobo. You too, Mateo."

"What's a beefcake?" Mateo asks.

"Someone with nice muscles." *That's an innocent enough answer, right?*

Mateo runs out of the room, his bare feet stomping on the floor like a horse in full gallop. "Abuela, when I grow up, I'm gonna be a beefcake!"

Jacobo snickers, while I groan. "Move it, brat," I say, tapping him lightly on the back of his head. He rolls his eyes at me and shuffles out of the bedroom at a much more moderate pace.

The others are waiting in the kitchen. Ocho has taken a seat at the table, slurping meatball soup into her mouth at an alarming rate. Or maybe an impressive rate. When she spots me, she pauses. "It's *so* good, Elena! Abuela makes the best soup ever."

Abuela beams with pride, leaving the stove to place her hands on Ocho's broad shoulders. While Ocho is seated and Abuela's standing, she can actually reach. Her thin, dry skin shifts over her swollen knuckles as she gives Ocho an affectionate squeeze. "I like this one. But where is Sasha? When is she coming?"

I head to the stove and select one of the empty bowls Abuela has set on the counter. This is the last subject I want to talk about. Honestly, I'd been hoping Abuela would be too happy to see me to ask about the rest of the crew right away, but that's wishful thinking.

"Honestly? Not sure. I hope she comes back to Barbados—" *and me* "—but she might stay in SLKC."

"Why? You're here." Abuela's dark, shrewd eyes fix on me. She isn't about to let this subject go. During the month we spent in Barbados, Abuela became very fond of Sasha. Fond enough to start saying things like, 'Good for you, Elena, finding a strong woman to take care of you. Why haven't you married her yet?' At the time, her comments embarrassed me, but also made me feel a little warm inside. Now, thinking about them leaves me depressed and hollow.

"I want her to come back." I fill my bowl with soup, but the familiar scents of ground beef, garlic, and cilantro can't soothe me. I haven't even started eating and I've already lost my appetite. "She has an open invitation. But there are battles she wants to fight and I'm done fighting. I've got you all to look after."

"Can't you do both?" Jacobo asks.

I turn around. His gaze is almost as intense as Abuela's. "Remember what happened while I was on the run? Abuela's too old to work, and you and Mateo are too young—"

"You're never too old to support your family," Abuela protests, even though she knows better than most how untrue that is in our world.

Mateo lets his spoon clatter into his bowl and folds his arms over his chest. "I'm not a baby."

Jacobo doesn't say anything, but he holds my stare, telling me in no uncertain terms that he disagrees with my opinion. My suspicions are instantly aroused. Fucking shit. Has he been taking jobs again in my absence? I'll have to interrogate the little shit once we're alone. No use accusing him at the dinner table and upsetting Abuela, though.

I plop down at the table, forcing down a spoonful of soup. As the heat coats my throat and warms my chest, a bit of my appetite returns despite the guilty churning of my stomach. Abuela's cooking is too good to resist.

"You support us by taking care of the boys," I say to Abuela between mouthfuls. "That's a full-time job. And Mateo, your job right now is to learn. Kid brains are way better at learning new shi—*stuff* than adult brains, so you should learn as much as you can, while you can. It's a kid superpower. Then you'll be a smarter adult and you can help me take care of Abuela."

That seems to please Mateo. "Really?"

Ocho pauses in the midst of eating to shoot me a curious look. "What about my brain? I was never really a child."

"Val said you had the absorption rate of a toddler when you first came out of the tube, so..."

Jacobo studies Ocho with newfound interest. "Really? Cool. Wonder if there's a way to make that happen for non-clone adults, so we can learn at a faster rate." I don't miss his use of the word 'we'. Obviously, he's including himself in the 'adult' category already.

"Anyway," I continue. "I hope Sasha comes back to Barbados, but I wouldn't count on it. She met a *tia* she didn't know about, who runs a self-sustaining community. So, it's up to her."

Jacobo's interest is immediately piqued. He leans forward in his chair. "Corps-backed?"

"Not exactly..."

His eyes light up. "So, is it hidden or something?"

Fuck. The kid's too smart for his own good. "Sort of." I'm reluctant to reveal too much about Sprout, for their protection as well as my family's, but I don't see the harm in explaining a little. My plan is to keep my family far away from my enemies, after all. Besides, if I don't tell Jacobo something, he'll try and find out on his own. That could turn into a disaster.

"It's called Sprout, and it's underground," Ocho says, jumping in while I consider what to say. Oops. I should have nudged her under the table or something. "They grow their own food and generate their own power. It's cool! They've got a bunch of shuttles in their hangar, too. I got to work on them."

"Really?" Mateo looks at Ocho with newfound respect. "You got to work on shuttles?"

"Yeah," Ocho says. "A bunch."

"Anyway, Sasha and the others are staying, but Barbados is much safer than Sprout," I explain. "We should change resorts, though, just to be safe...and look into leaving the island sooner rather than later."

Abuela's lips tighten. "Why do we need to leave?"

"Out of an abundance of caution," I say. "It's good to keep moving around so the corps don't find us. You know I'm still on a few hit lists for previous jobs."

Abuela *tsks* and shakes her head. She only makes that sound when she's disappointed in me, like when I mess up her recipes or almost get myself killed.

"What, Abuela?"

"Don't you 'what' me, Elena Beatriz Aguilar Nevares. You think this Sprout place is dangerous, or you would have stayed there and brought us. But you left your friends there. So, you left them in danger. Why?"

Fuck. Why does everyone in my family have to be so damn smart and perceptive all the time? And so judgmental, too? I see where Jacobo gets it from.

"My crewmates can take care of themselves," I protest. "You and the boys need me more."

"But—"

My temper flares. "We're done talking about this, okay?" At Abuela's surprised and slightly hurt look, I hurriedly backtrack. "Sorry. I've had a stressful trip. All I want to do is eat my soup, which is amazing, so thank you very much for that, Abuela."

After my outburst, the table is quiet. The silence doesn't make me feel any better. It's my fault, and there's still plenty of noise, what with all of my own mistakes and doubts shouting in my head for attention.

Chapter 03

SUNDAY, 10-04-65 20:37:41 BRIDGETOWN, BARBADOS

"ELENA, I'M *BORED,*" OCHO complains while sprawled on the living room couch, one forearm flung over her eyes.

I've heard the same refrain more than once this week: when Ocho and Mateo ordered a buttload of candy from room service and puked everywhere, when she offered to watch the tamales while Abuela went to the bathroom, and I had to break out the fire extinguisher, and, of course, when she went for a solo swim in the ocean and ended up so far out I almost called the lifeguard.

So when Ocho says 'I'm bored,' I know I need to watch her like top of the line spyware.

I blink shut my VIS-R, where I've been researching safer accommodations, just in case. We've barely left the new resort I forced us to move to a day after my return, and neither my spyders nor the housekeepers (whom I tip generously) have seen anything sketchy, but I'm still nervous. Puerto Rico's nice, I hear...in the mega rich tourist parts, anyway.

"Sorry, Ocho. It's too late now, but we can go to the beach tomorrow."

Ocho slides her arm away from her face, staring at me with big, pleading brown eyes. "I'm *bored* of the beach. It was nice at first, but now it's all we do. You promised you'd show me Barbados."

"I took you, Abuela, and Mateo on that tour of the wall. Remember the turbines?" Unfortunately, Jacobo hadn't accompanied us. He'd claimed exhaustion, but that's been his M.O. lately. Hiding in his room. Closing himself off. He's been like that since before I left for SLKC, although he refuses to talk to me about his antisocial behavior. I get it, though. Being abducted and almost killed by a crazy person would mess anyone up, let alone a twelve-year-old.

Ocho remains unappeased. "Yeah, but that was just one time. There's gotta be more to the island."

"Most of Barbados is beaches," I protest, but I understand Ocho's restlessness. When she agreed to come with me, she was probably expecting more of an adventure, and I'm sorry to disappoint. She's much too 'young' to appreciate the beauty of being as abso-fucking-lutely lazy as possible.

Ocho sits up without using her arms, a move that puts her abdominals on display through her thin white tank. She's wearing a pair of palm tree patterned swim trunks, which have long since dried out. "Please? I wanna see something new, even if it's just walking down the street outside the resort. Can we do that?"

I chew my lip. Honestly, my mood hasn't been much better than Jacobo's lately. Spending the past week without the crew has been tough. More than tough. It's been fucking heartbreaking. I miss Rami's affectionate fussing and Cherry's sexual innuendos. I miss Rock's gentle hugs and Doc's pointed snark. I miss Val's awkward attempts at humor. And of course, I desperately miss Sasha's steady reassurance.

We only shared a bunk for a few months, but I've already grown so used to her presence that waking up alone feels weird. I miss her scent on the covers. I miss talking to her, laughing with her, even poking fun at her. Through it all, Ocho's been here, looking exactly like her. Reminding me of who I gave up.

Sometimes I can trick myself into thinking Sasha's with me for a split second. In those moments, I can breathe again. But then Ocho will move or talk, or things will feel off somehow, and I'll remember that Sasha is back in SLKC where I abandoned her.

Hey, Sasha made her choice, too. She could come find you any time, but she's chosen to stay in Sprout despite the danger. It's been a week without a word from her.

Maybe it's loneliness that makes me reconsider Ocho's request. Maybe it's the desire to prove that I can have a good time without Sasha and the crew. That I'm still a whole person without them, and I don't need to put my life on hold for them.

Before I can think better of it, I say, "Fine. Want to go clubbing?"

Ocho's face brightens. "Like a party? I've seen those in Val's simulations."

"Dancing to loud music in a big crowd, so yeah. A party."

She's up off the couch before I can blink. "Can we go now?"

I sigh. "Sure, but you should wear something besides your swimsuit, and I gotta change."

"Okay!" Ocho heads to her room with a spring in her step. Suddenly, I feel a million years old instead of almost thirty, but I've already said yes and I'm too stubborn to back out. I drag myself to

Jacobo and Mateo's room, planning to let them know where I'm headed. I knock on the door, then slip inside.

Mateo is playing a VR game with his VIS-R (a PGS kids' model, ironically) while Jacobo's jacked into the extranet. As usual. That's about all he's done since I came back, which has only added to my stress. The kid is determined to follow in my footsteps, no matter how many times I warn him it's too dangerous.

"Ay, conejito." I tap Jacobo's shoulder. His eyes stop twitching behind their lids and snap open. He jerks in surprise.

"Jesus fuck, Elena," he mutters, unplugging the cable from behind his ear. "Warn a guy next time."

I step back. A soft touch on the shoulder wouldn't have startled him a few months ago, even while jacked in. The two of us need to talk, so I resolve to sit him down tomorrow. Part of me hoped he'd chill a little while I was in SLKC, but he's only gone downhill since then. My stomach churns with the possibility that I made things worse.

"Sorry. Didn't mean to startle you. Ocho and I are going out. Can you make sure Mateo gets to bed on time?"

That earns an impressive whine from the other bed. "I'm not tired, though," Mateo protests, pausing his game to plead his case.

I roll my eyes. "Too bad, so sad. You're in bed by nine, like every night. That's fifteen minutes from now."

"But—"

"If Jacobo tells me you're good, I'll bring you home some glowsticks."

Mateo perks up. "What color?"

"Dunno. What color do you want?"

"Green! Like radioactive slime."

That dredges a genuine laugh out of me. My life might be in the middle of a shit sandwich, but at least I have my brothers and Abuela. "I'll look for green glowsticks. We won't be out too late, just a couple of hours. You good here with Abuela, Jacobo?"

"Yeah," he says, almost too casually. "I'm just gaming tonight."

I'm sure he isn't gaming, and that's why he isn't bitching about putting our little brother to bed. Maybe he's taken a ride on the puberty train and actually discovered porn, which is a horrifying thought. Perhaps we need to have two talks soon instead of just one.

"Thanks. Just make sure he's down by nine." I already know Jacobo will give Mateo an extra hour of game time, but I'm willing to overlook that, as long as he actually sleeps.

"'Kay."

"Bye, Elena!" Mateo runs over to hug my waist.

I ruffle his thick black hair. "I'm coming back in a few hours."

"Bye for a few hours, then."

"All right, bye for a few hours."

I kiss Mateo's head and give Jacobo an upward nod since he's outgrown kisses.

"Don't get mixed up in anything I wouldn't," Jacobo says with a smile that isn't entirely forced. Maybe there's a bit of levity left in him after all.

"I'm taking Ocho, so we'll see."

I leave the boys to their gaming, or whatever trouble Jacobo's actually into, and peek in on Abuela in the next room over. She's kneeling on the floor, a real 'fuck you' to her age and arthritis, and she's got her traditional backstrap loom set up above her lap. The swollen joints in her hands stick out beneath the paper thin skin as she twists the threads together.

I stroll up and peek over her shoulder. "What are you making, Abuela?"

"Shawl. For Ocho."

I manage a smile. "That's sweet."

"The sun's hot here." Abuela falls into silence for a while as I watch her fingers pass back and forth, back and forth. "I'll make one for Sasha next."

My heart sinks. "Abuela, I told you. Sasha isn't coming."

"You give up too easily, *mi vida.* What are you so afraid of?"

"Dying, Abuela," I say, with growing irritation. "Sasha's mixed up with her aunt's crew now. AxysGen and PGS want them dead as much as they wanted us dead. That's double the hits and double the motivation."

Abuela abandons her loom and stares at me with piercing brown eyes. "Listen to me, Elena Beatriz. I've loved many people. Your Abuelo. My children. You and your brothers. My husband and children are gone, but does that stop me from loving you? No, because death can't stop love. Letting the fear of death stand in your way is a mistake."

My lower lip trembles at her words. I clench and unclench my hands. I don't know whether to be angry with her or ashamed of myself. Here's this hardy old woman, who's seen more pain in her lifetime than I've ever known, telling me I'm running away too soon.

Well, it's not her call. It's mine. She can think whatever the fuck she wants, but I have to be there for Jacobo and Mateo. Her too, whether she likes it or not.

"I'll think about it," I say, knowing that's the only answer Abuela will accept. "Ocho and I are going clubbing tonight. We'll be back in a few hours."

"Clubbing," Abuela says, looking surprised. "What happened to hiding in the suite or the private beach?"

"It's been a week of nothing," I say. "According to the staff, no one's been looking for us, and I haven't picked up any chatter on the extranet. Besides, we won't be here much longer. What do you think of Puerto Rico?"

"I'd prefer Mexico," Abuela says.

I sigh. Walked right into that one. "We'll see."

"Go, *nietecita.* Look out for Ocho, okay?"

"I'll need Ocho to look out for me. She's tall enough to see over people's heads and make sure I don't get squashed."

I kiss the top of Abuela's thin, wispy white hair, brushing it down over the dark spots on her scalp, and retreat to my own room. I gave the boys the pretty view of the sea, so my window looks out over the city and hotel parking structure, partially concealed by carefully curated palm trees. The lights of Bridgetown are crystal clear beyond.

A powerful sense of yearning punches me right in the gut. I don't want to go out alone. I want my crew with me. This past week hasn't felt right without them. If they were here, I'd be getting ready in front of the mirror with Rami and Cherry. One of them would help with my makeup, and I'd do their hair afterwards. Doc would whine about not being old enough to go, and Sasha would come up with some fun activity to satisfy her the following day. Like parasailing, or something else 'dangerous' but not really.

Val would spout facts and statistics we never wanted to know about clubs, or Barbados, or alcohol. Rock would watch me emerge from the bathroom in several outfits, shaking his head yes or no to each one. I laugh, remembering the first time I ever saw him don a mesh shirt for clubbing, back during our vacation. His bulging pectoral muscles ripped the damn thing a few minutes in.

And Sasha. Fuck. My eyes sting as I remember one particular occasion in Barbados, before SLKC. We were at the Shark Tank, where I'll probably take Ocho tonight because I know the layout of the place. The two of us danced until dawn in the darkest part of the club, the bass thrumming through us. Her hands on my hips. My face near her neck. I miss Sasha so much it hurts. So much that I can't breathe.

I throw myself on the bed and bury my face in the pillow, shuddering sporadically but not allowing myself the luxury of sobbing. This was my choice. I don't deserve to get all weepy over it. Over her. I just need a minute in the darkness of my pillow, smelling detergent so I can forget Sasha's cologne.

I don't, of course. I can't.

After a minute of steady breathing, I get myself back under control. I roll off the bed and dig through my closet for something to wear. A loose blue crop top and silver leggings fit the bill. At least they'll show off my ass, and I don't give a fuck about showing a stomach roll or two.

After that, it's makeup time. Doing my eyes and brows isn't nearly as fun without Rami and Cherry's running commentary. I can't do mine as well as Rami does them either, which is disappointing. They've spoiled me for doing my own makeup.

Eventually, I look sort of okay. I stare at my reflection in the mirror, giving myself a sad, despondent look before forcing a smile. I'm doing this for Ocho. She deserves to see something of the world, to join a mass of excited bodies and dance to music that's way too loud until she's happily exhausted. I'm definitely not letting her have that crucial experience without some adult supervision.

Chapter 04

WE ARRIVE AT THE Shark Tank well before midnight. Despite the early hour, the place is packed. The low thump of the bass reverberates through the walls of the two-story chrome building on the corner. A line of hopeful partygoers stretches partway down the block.

Ocho lengthens her stride, pulling ahead with her annoyingly long legs. She's wearing a pair of tight black pants and a light grey tank that shows off her broad shoulders and biceps to perfection. She isn't as cut as Sasha yet, but she's well on her way. "Is that the place?" she asks without pausing to wait for me.

I trot after her, mentally complaining about my height. It doesn't help that I'm in heels to give me an extra few inches. "Yeah, that's it."

We take our place at the back of the line. Luckily, it doesn't take long. The club must not be at capacity, because the bald, dark skinned bouncer at the front entrance only briefly checks people's IDs with his VIS-R. Soon, it's our turn. The bouncer stares at me, blocky chin jutting forward, not saying a word. I don't say anything or present ID. Instead, I connect to his VIS-R and send him a *very* generous tip. He arches a brow in mild surprise but stands aside to let us through.

"That guy was almost as big as Rock," Ocho says as we enter the next checkpoint, a short glass hallway surrounded on all sides by water. Schools of fish swim by, all the colors of the rainbow. I can only assume they're genetically engineered. Ocho stops to watch, but I take her elbow and lead her to the booth at the end of the hall.

A young, attractive man stands inside, smiling like it's his job, and offers to take our coats. A sign beneath the booth says: *Please check all loose items and defensive aides.*

Ha. Defensive aides. Rich people language for weapons, I guess.

Ocho and I aren't armed this evening. Hard to conceal weapons in club clothes. I tip the employee anyway and start to walk on by, but he clears his throat in the politest possible way. "Excuse me, ma'am? If your bodyguard has any mods, she needs to remain in the waiting area."

My eyebrows lift. Apparently bodyguards need to be checked just like any other object. "She isn't my bodyguard. She's my date tonight."

The dude's eyes widen in horror. His mouth falls open and he holds up his hands. "I—I'm sorry, I didn't..." He looks like he's about to piss himself. Poor guy probably thinks I'm about to throw a fit and get him fired or something.

I laugh to put him at ease. "Don't even worry about it. She *is* pretty jacked."

I don't miss the small smirk that crosses Ocho's face at the compliment.

"Please, go on through," the employee stammers. "Again, I'm *so* sorry."

Ocho and I walk past his station. Double glass doors, which definitely conceal a security scanner even though they don't look special, show the club beyond, bathed in glowing blue light with a hint of smoldering red.

A wave of music hits us as we open the doors. The bass sets my bones buzzing, which comes as a relief. Maybe this was a good idea after all. So what if Sasha and I have been here before? It's still a good place to relax. A place where nobody gives a fuck. It's been way too long since I let loose, and moping on the beach doesn't count.

Keeping my hand on Ocho's elbow, I head for the bar. It's decorated like an underwater volcano, complete with wet rock texture and glowing lava streaming from the top. The barstools and surrounding couches boast more live fish, keeping the patrons company as they drink. Every single wall is a hi-def screen, showing virtual ocean scenes of sharks swimming in a coral reef.

I let go of Ocho and hop on a stool, waving to catch the bartender's attention. Eventually, he wanders over. He's a skinny, shirtless white guy with thin but defined muscles and board shorts covered with fish. Since the women are also wearing swimsuit tops, I can only assume it's the club's standard uniform.

"What can I get you?"

"Mercury Silver. Water for my friend."

With a wink, he's off to mix my drink.

Ocho sidles up to me, looking disappointed. "Why can't I have alcohol too?"

I frown. Technically, Ocho's body is fully developed, but her brain isn't. I doubt she has enough life experience to make good choices while intoxicated. Not that I have much room to talk. I've made some pretty questionable choices of my own recently.

"You can have a sip of mine to taste, okay?"

That seems to satisfy Ocho. She waits patiently until the bartender returns. Between the two of us, we down our drinks fast. Ocho likes my Mercury Silver so much I end up letting her have more than a sip. The cloying sweetness isn't as pleasant as usual, and I don't feel any kind of buzz. Just anxiety. The crowd and the volume of the music have me twitchy.

"Elena, why's the music so loud?" Ocho's tongue is stained silver from the drink, as are the outer edges of her lips. Full, soft looking lips, I notice, before getting pissed at myself for thinking about it.

I shout to be heard above the noise. "So you don't hear your thoughts, I guess. How should I know?"

If Ocho senses my annoyance, she doesn't let on. She observes the people on the dance floor while I stew over my second drink, chewing shards of ice to distract myself.

"Can we dance, too?"

I set the drink aside. I've been mentally preparing myself for this since we left the hotel. There's no point in taking Ocho to a club if I don't show her how to dance. "C'mon." I take her hand in mine, large and warm and achingly familiar, and pull her onto the floor.

It's hotter on the edge of the crowd. Strobe lights flash above us in a rainbow of colors, and music bumps along the floor and through the soles of my shoes. The smell of synthetic fog, warm bodies, and other people's perfume fills my nose. To my surprise, it's not entirely horrible. Maybe the alcohol is kicking in, or maybe I can finally see the wisdom in following these *idiotas'* example: drink and dance to forget what needs forgetting.

I sway to the rhythm of the music, which has slowed and subdivided to something reminiscent of calypso fusion. My body remembers how to do this. I lift my hands in the air, popping my hips on the two and four. Ocho observes me, then copies.

The sight makes me laugh. Watching her make such obviously feminine movements with her pelvis, which Sasha would never be caught dead doing, serves to remind me how different they are. *But isn't that good? You don't want Ocho to be like Sasha. You don't want her to be a stupid, self-sacrificing hero.*

Ocho isn't the best dancer in the club, but she isn't half bad. Her body follows the rhythm as she borrows dance moves from everyone around her, of all genders, races, and body types, improving at a mind blowing pace. To my surprise, she sidles up behind me and places her hands on my waist, guiding me to grind against her like several couples around us are doing.

Why the hell not?

I close my eyes and lose myself in the music, which pumps faster and faster. So does my heart. Ocho's large hands are pleasantly reminiscent of Sasha's, and for just a moment, I can pretend she's here with me. I know it's stupid, but I can't help it. The fantasy is too tempting to resist, and it allows me to relax, truly relax, for the first time since leaving SLKC.

The music transitions into a slower, heavier beat. I'm transported back in time to a few months ago when Sasha and I first came here. We danced in the shifting red-blue light until we glistened with sweat, sharing body heat, hands roaming all over each other. We slow down, moving to the same rhythm. Sharing the same space. The same heat. Her strong arms wrap around me, and I lean back against her chest, rocking my ass into the cradle of her pelvis.

That's when I spin around to face her, and suddenly, it doesn't matter that the faint wrinkles and scars on Sasha's face aren't there. When she bends down, mouth hovering near mine, hesitating for one magnetic moment, I close my eyes and tilt up.

The moment our lips meet, I realize it's a mistake. Ocho tastes like heat and Mercury Silver, but the tentative way her tongue brushes my lower lip has none of Sasha's confidence. It doesn't make my heart skip a beat or my blood race. It isn't her, and I can't fool myself into pretending. This isn't what I need. She isn't what I need. I break away and rush off the dance floor, with Ocho trailing behind me.

"Elena, wait!"

I don't stop until I'm outside the club. I hunch over on an empty bench on the sidewalk, breathing heavily, the shadows on the ground blurring my vision. I want to be far away from the people and the music and the drinks that were supposed to make things better for a while but just made everything worse. So much worse.

"Elena?"

I wince at the sound of Ocho's voice. It's full of confusion and guilt, which forces me to lift my head. The disappointment on her face hits me right in the gut.

"It's not your fault. It's mine." I reach out to touch her arm, then think better of it. "I just...I missed Sasha. For a second, I wanted to believe you were her. I'm sorry."

Ocho's shoulders slump. "Oh. I thought..."

"Is that why you came to Barbados with me?" I ask in the gentlest possible voice. It's not Ocho's fault I'm an idiot. She's the brand-new clone. I'm the adult who should fucking know better.

She scuffs her shoe on the ground. "Not the only reason."

"But one of them?"

Reluctantly, she nods.

Fuck. I feel like someone's shoved their hand up underneath my ribs to strangle my heart. My life is falling apart—*I'm* falling apart—even without the corps trying to kill me.

This club is fake. This whole fucking place is fake. All fake, just like pretending Sasha was here. Fantasies aren't reality, and I'm starting to realize that maybe this luxurious corps world is the fantasy and Sprout is the reality I've needed all along.

Barbados isn't what I want anymore, with its tacky palm trees and tropical decor. Wasting my life on the beach while shirtless cabana boys serve me drinks isn't what I want. I want a hanging garden full of edible plants. I want a cozy apartment with homemade decorations. Most of all, I want the rest of my family back.

Pushing Jacobo to study hard and get a job with the same people out to kill me and my crew, letting him and Mateo grow up in this fake-ass world, is a terrible idea. I don't want them to feel the same emptiness I feel right now. To think it's *normal.* I don't want them sitting on a beach or dancing in a club like nothing matters, ignoring and running from what they really care about. I want them growing shit.

This was a mistake. Leaving Sasha. My crew. Sprout. All of it. I fucked up.

The moment I admit that to myself, the truth I've been pushing away for an entire week, all the tension drains from my body. The fist around my heart releases its painful grip. The fog of fear clears from my head. A smile even creeps across my face.

"Hey, Ocho. Ready to go back to SLKC?"

Ocho looks surprised, like she wasn't expecting me to change the subject. After a moment, she returns my smile, though hers is shy and uncertain. "Is that what you want?"

"Yeah. That's what I want. For Jacobo, Mateo, and Abuela too."

Ocho's face falls again. "Will Sasha be mad at me for kissing you?" she asks in a nervous whisper.

"Nah. She'll be too busy being mad at me for running away. She won't hold it against you."

Will she hold it against me, though? Possibly. I'll have a lot of groveling to do when I get back, not even taking the kiss into account. But if I know Sasha, and I really feel like I do, she'll be more happy I came back than pissed I left in the first place. I hope.

Ocho still looks nervous. She sits next to me on the bench but keeps a legs distance of space between us. "What about you? Are you mad?"

"No. I kissed you back. We're cool."

"I'm pretty hot, actually," Ocho says, tugging at the neck of her tank top to let some air in. "There's no breeze tonight."

I laugh, leaning over to hug her. This time, it feels right to hold her in my arms. "I know you've got to grow up, but don't change too much, Ocho. You might not be Sasha, but you're fucking perfect just the way you are."

Chapter 05

WHEN OCHO AND I return to the hotel, we're exhausted. It's not even midnight, but the alcohol, dancing, and loud music have worn me out. Despite all that, I feel much better. I'm going back to SLKC. I'll make amends and get a new start, not just for myself, but for my family too.

"Thanks for taking me clubbing." Ocho offers me a shy smile as we ride the elevator. "I had a good time, even with…you know."

I squeeze her arm. "Me too. You helped me realize something important tonight, so thanks."

"You're welcome."

The elevator dings and we get off on the top floor, heading for our suite. I open the door as quietly as possible. All the lights are off, and there's no sign of Abuela or the boys. That's good. Jacobo put Mateo to bed on time, or close enough.

"Stay quiet so we don't wake anybody," I remind Ocho as she slips off her shoes and heads into the hallway. There's a mild sway in her step, probably from the drinks she mooched from me. She gives me a thumbs-up, grinning in the dark, then disappears into her room.

Instead of going to mine, I check on my brothers. I'm disappointed but not surprised by the sight of Jacobo lying flat on his back with a jacking cable behind his ear, plugged into the nightstand terminal. All I see of Mateo is a small, lightly snoring lump under the covers in the other bed.

I tap Jacobo's shoulder as gently as possible.

"Shit!" His eyes snap open, and he pulls his jack out fast. *Too* fast. Even last time, when I startled him, his eyes didn't dart around like this. My suspicions are immediately aroused.

"Gaming, huh?" I give him my patented older sister *'don't you dare fucking lie to me'* stare.

"Yeah, gaming," he says, but I've spooked him. From the guilty look on his face, only faintly illuminated by the fluorescent lights in the hallway, he already knows his lie won't work on me.

"Bullshit."

189

"What do you care?"

"Shhh, keep it down. Teo's sleeping."

Jacobo shoots me a dirty look. "You're the one who came in here."

"You're avoiding my question. What are you up to, *conejito?*"

He looks away from me. "Nothing."

"Then you won't have a problem showing me."

"Don't you trust me?"

I hold out my hand. "Give me the cable."

Reluctantly, Jacobo hands it over. I can tell he's only doing it because he doesn't think he has any other option, but I don't feel bad. This isn't the first time he's gotten mixed up in dangerous shit. If I don't look out for the dumbass kid, no one will.

I climb onto the bed and plug in, while he slouches over to the other bed, climbing in beside Mateo, a quiet, wordless rebellion so he won't have to share space with me while I'm invading his privacy.

network: bbd 13193 . 59543
connection established
welcome: user escudoespiga

run search: most recent user
run program: datascrape.exe
last user: sombrazorro

requesting access: account user sombrazorro
enter password:
run program: passwordrecovery.exe
enter password: *******

connection established
welcome: user sombrazorro

The custom settings Jacobo has applied to the nightstand terminal are actually pretty cool. The surroundings he's chosen aren't designed for focus so much as excitement, which makes sense because he's twelve. I find myself in the middle of a Jurassic jungle. Giant ferns arch above me while a herd of brachiosaur amble along a sunny plain beyond the tree line. An allosaurus stalks the edge of the herd, waiting for its opening.

Under other circumstances, I might have checked out Jacobo's ambiance program, or even downloaded a copy for myself, but I'm on a mission. I shut it down with a wave of my hand, freezing the dinosaurs so they won't distract me. Then I blink to open Jacobo's dash and start digging.

It doesn't take long to find what he's been hiding. The kid's good at covering his tracks, but this is my job, so I'm up to date on all the latest malware and encryption techniques. I'm also the one who taught him basic coding. Some of his new flourishes are self-taught, but I still know exactly where to snoop.

Soon, I'm perusing the contents of a ghost file: encrypted communications, mission reports, financial records. My dumbass brother's been freelancing on the sly, taking remote missions for various corps and stuffing credits into a secret bank account. Damn it. Doesn't he trust me to take care of him?

But I also see Jacobo's point of view. Several months ago, I left to hide from AxysGen. It wasn't by choice, but I know it must have scared him. He hadn't known where I was, and even though I kept in touch and sent him credits, I'm sure he worried whether I'd be able to keep supporting him, Mateo, and Abuela. Can I blame him for wanting security? For trying to follow my example and take care of our family?

With a sigh, I close the file. Jacobo and I need to have a long, uncomfortable talk. I won't stand for him running sketchy freelance ops, but at twelve, he's old enough to know where the money I've earned goes, and most importantly, how to access it if something bad happens to me.

This is just another big reason to bring Jacobo with me to Sprout. He'll do better as part of a community, with the other families in Kyra's node. School, real school with socialization instead of online classes, should keep him and Mateo occupied. Sprout has plenty of jobs that will make him feel useful without getting him killed...

Assuming I'm still welcome in Kyra's node after the way I left.

The thought sends a shiver through me. What if I'm wrong? What if Sprout won't accept me because I snuck away without permission? What if Sasha and the crew won't take me back?

Before more doubts can creep in, I decide to check Jacobo's email. If he's got any potential clients waiting on responses, I need to handle it. Shut down his little freelance business before he gets in real trouble. I drag my fingers apart, creating a glowing window in the air.

run program: messagefilter.exe
search terms: job, payment, credits, fee
filtering...
compiling...
relevant results: 3

The first two job related emails are just confirmations of payment for work Jacobo has already done. He's been acting as his own fixer, which is something of a relief. At least he isn't dealing with the likes of my previous fixer, who sold me out. The ops are nothing too sketchy, just background checks on two unimportant middle managers. Apparently, both his clients were satisfied.
The third email is weirder.

to: sombrazorro
from: salamander
subject: potential job

Please see enclosed attachment.

The email has no other contents, just an unopened data packet. I run it through three different phishing, malware, and ransomware filters, but everything comes up clean. It seems like an innocent text file. Still, I'm wary. There's a reason I always warn Jacobo not to open stuff from unknown senders. I clench my fist, selecting the icon for my shield program, which doubles as my primary offensive weapon. The grip appears in my hand, solid and reassuring. Pushing aside the nagging voice that says I'm being paranoid, I open the file.
Turns out, I wasn't paranoid enough.
My email window and icons vanish. Solid stone walls erupt from the ground and close around me, cutting me off from the frozen dinosaurs and trapping me in almost total darkness. I charge the nearest wall, shield raised to smash whatever this is to bits, but it shuts down as soon as its spikes touch stone. My hand is suddenly empty.
What the fuck. What the actual fuck? What the actual fuck! My shielding program never fails. It's definitely never stopped working on me before. I select the icon to summon it back, but nothing happens. Clicking is useless.
"Elena Nevares?"

I whirl at the sound of my name. I didn't see, hear, or feel anyone else enter the...dungeon? That's the best way to describe where I am. A small, stone cell without windows or a door. But I'm not alone anymore. Standing behind me is a familiar, blue robed figure with blonde hair and cold blue eyes.

"Megan?"

I click my shield icon again, but nothing happens. Frustrated, I select one of my backup offensive programs, a rifle reminiscent of Sasha's K-4 Phoenix. No luck. With growing panic, I choose a cloaking program, but I remain stubbornly visible. While I struggle, Megan stares at me with eerie intensity.

"No fucking way," I mutter, retreating until my back hits one of the walls. It feels like real stone, cold and unyielding. "You're dead." Even as I say it, doubts creep in. Did Val, Sasha, and I really manage to kill Megan? We hit her with a Puls.wav, which should have fried her brain, but she faked her death once before. Maybe she's done it again?

Megan tilts her head, but her expression is off. The condescending smirk I remember isn't there. Instead, she's...studying me? Examining me like I'm some sort of specimen pinned to a corkboard. My heart beats so fast and hard it hurts, and I feel short of breath. My body must be freaking out in meatspace from all the adrenaline.

On a desperate hope, I pull up my logout screen, but I already know what I'll find. The buttons are gone. This dungeon must be some kind of Venus flytrap program, the kind you can't exit without melting your brain. I know Megan can make them because she trapped me in one before. If this isn't her, it's some other jacker with a lot of talent and skill, or a program beyond my understanding.

My fear feeds into a hot rush of anger. Megan's still staring, infuriatingly silent. "What the fuck do you want?" I clench my hands into fists. They can't cause damage without any programs behind them, but the reaction is instinctive. I don't have any other way to defend myself.

"One thing only: the internet protocol address for V.41's servers in Siberia." The woman uses Megan's voice, but it isn't how I remember. The inflection I'd expect in a tense situation isn't there. Their tone is completely emotionless, not exactly monotone, but frighteningly calm. "If you provide me with precise coordinates, I will release you unharmed."

Val's servers? What does Fake Megan want with those? To steal or destroy them, probably. That makes the most sense.

"The real Megan knew the Hole's IP address. Why don't you have it already?" I ask, stalling for time. My mind races, but I can't come up with a plan of escape. No way am I giving her the information she wants. Not when Val's life is at stake.

Fake Megan completely ignores my question. "If you do not value your own life, what about the lives of your companions? Sasha, Cherry, Rami, Doc, and Rock? I am recording this encounter as proof of life. They will be thoroughly convinced. I will ask once more: will you give me the internet protocol address for V.41 servers?"

Chingarme. Fake Megan's trap isn't just for me. Now that she has me, I'm the fucking bait. If I know my crew, they'll come running as soon as they discover I'm in trouble. Running right to their deaths.

Or will they? You abandoned them, Elena. What did you expect would happen?

I'm not sure which possibility is more terrifying, the fact that they might rush into a trap to save me, or the fact that they might decide I'm not worth it.

"I don't know who you are, but you don't have to do this. The real Megan's dead, okay? Whoever you are, I don't have any score to settle with you."

Fake Megan merely blinks. "Goodbye."

The robed woman disappears in a puff of white smoke, leaving me alone in my cell. I don't know whether to laugh, cry, or panic. Probably D, all of the above. I back into the wall again and slide down to the floor, wrapping my arms around my knees. Fuck. Fuck. Val and the crew are in danger because of me, and without my toolset, there isn't a goddamn thing I can do to save them.

Chapter 06

ONE SHORT PANIC ATTACK later, I manage to pull myself together. My breathing's still fast, and I'm dizzy and exhausted with fear, but I've regained enough control to analyze my situation. And what a fucking situation. I'm trapped in a virtual dungeon, pretty much a damsel in distress, while Sasha—ever the noble knight—and the crew presumably charge to my rescue in Barbados. That, or I'm stuck here, totally screwed, without any help on the way because I abandoned them. Both terrible possibilities.

Come on, Nevares. Don't give up yet. Val needs you!

Regardless of whether the crew comes to my rescue, I feel an obligation to warn her. No, not just obligation. Val is my friend, and I won't let anything happen to her. I click my shield icon, desperately or maybe stupidly hoping for a different outcome, but it doesn't respond. Fake Megan's blocked access to everything.

What can I do without working programs? Code a new one?

That will be tricky without coding software. Most programs require other programs to build and edit their bones. But I'm still on the extranet. That means I haven't lost my connection to the outside world entirely. There must be a way out of here, or at least a way to warn Val.

Another terrifying thought strikes. What if Jacobo tries to unplug me? If he notices how long I've been connected, he might pull my jack out. Hard cuts are unpleasant for jackers, but they don't usually melt brains. Doing it while I'm caught in a Venus flytrap, though, could mean instant death. I need to warn him too.

I pull up JackRabbit, the messaging program Jacobo uses, which boasts the eponymous icon of a sprinting hare. My hopes are lower than low when I tap it, but to my surprise, the program actually opens. The rabbit comes to life, twitching its nose and standing on its hind legs, ears pointed straight up.

Holy shit. Did Fake Megan make a mistake?

Once I get over my shock, I open a message window between the rabbit's ears and start typing, feeling cautiously optimistic. But, no. This is too easy. Why would Fake Megan deactivate all my other programs and leave my messaging app alone? She must want me to contact Val. Maybe her master plan is to use my plea for help to backhack her, figure out where her servers are, and destroy them.

Well, no fucking way. I'll get out of here and warn them safely, in person. But having access to JackRabbit might still be useful. I can do more than message people. I can also message corporations, as well as their online stores.

> *JackRabbit.exe*
> *add_contact?*
> *AxysGen.Buy*

message: AxysGen.Buy
request: newsletter signup

[ALERT]
Escudoespiga, you have 1 new message!

to: escudoespiga
from: Axys Generations

Welcome, Escudoespiga!

Thank you for signing up for our newsletter. You won't regret it, and we promise not to spam you. ;)

Axys Generations is committed to providing the best extranet technology. Our mission? To bring people together from all corners of the globe.

For the next ten minutes, all gear and downloads in our online store are 20% off, just for you! We've put together a list of products you might be interested in.

[Dendryte Bronze: Access the extranet wirelessly or via cable! Add a jack implanter and sterilization kit for only $299.99 more.]

[Padlock v. 11.6: Use this program to protect your online privacy. Per AxysGen policy, we will never share your data with government entities or sell your data to other corporations. Voted the World's Best Security Program of 2062, 2064, and 2065.]

[Spyder v. 7.2: Use this program to run deep extranet searches. Find the information you need, when you need it!]

Want to see more? Click through to discover a whole new world. Axys Generations: Connect. Explore. Discover.

request access: online store
purchase: Padlock 11.6

[ALERT]
Escudoespiga, you have 1 new message!

to: escudoespiga
from: Axys Generations

Escudoespiga,

Thank you for purchasing *Padlock 11.6*, recently voted this year's best security program by IdentaLock Inc. You will find your download link below. By clicking the link, you are agreeing to Axys Generations' terms of service.

Enjoy your new *Padlock 11.6!*

Axys Generations: Connect. Explore. Discover.

The rabbit leaps up in a cartoony manner, offering me something in its paws, a familiar silver padlock, the same shape as the statue in AxysGen's butterfly lab. I take the program, and the rabbit responds with a pleasant chirp.

When the lock clicks open and the program downloads without issue, I feel a surge of relief. I can work with this. It only takes a few seconds to jailbreak thanks to my backdoor into AxysGen's base code. Once I'm in, glowing strings of code appear around my head. I start modifying, moving things around, fueled by adrenaline and instinct.

A few minutes later, I have a shiny new shield strapped to my forearm. It's smaller than my previous spiked juggernaut but more than serviceable. In fact, I'm fond of the irreverent design I've created, a curved silver disc with a golden padlock on the front. Unlike the original Padlock product logo, my padlock is open, with a keyhole in the center.

I brace my feet and aim my new shield at one of the cell's walls. Time to see if my new baby is strong enough to bust me out of here.

It works like a charm. When I squeeze the shield's grip, a glowing white spike shoots from the keyhole in the center of the padlock. Time freezes as its sharp tip strikes stone, but then the textured rendering on the wall flickers. The cell splinters apart like shards of glass flying from a shattered mirror.

Outside Fake Megan's dungeon, Jacobo's dinosaur park has been infested by vines. Large, thorny coils curl over themselves like the body of a giant serpent, covering most of the ground and stretching up toward a nonexistent sky. The vines are so huge they're all I can see.

I scan my surroundings but nothing moves, so I open my logout screen, hoping it might work now that I'm out of the cell.

Something rustles off to my left, and movement flashes in the corner of my eye. I whirl, firing a spike from my shield. I'm lucky. My reflexes were quick enough and I hit my target, the gaping mouth of a giant fuckoff literal Venus flytrap.

It's massive. As big as my hotel bedroom, more than large enough to swallow me whole. Its jaws clamp shut with way more speed than a plant should have, drawing in the spike I've embedded. The spike dissolves in a puddle of green acid, melting in the bright crimson center of the plant's mouth.

"Mierda!" I hiss.

The Venus Flytrap's thorny vines slither over and through each other, converging on me. More wide, spiny mouths emerge from the tangle of plant matter. They open, their dewy, blood-hued centers gleaming.

I barely dive aside in time to avoid the flytrap's jaws. Its teeth click inches away from my leg. This is some Little Shop of Horrors bullshit, but it's time for Audrey III to eat spikes. I aim my shield at the closest mouth, smashing several spines with my newly customized white Puls.wavs.

Greenish goop spatters everywhere, sizzling as it hits my arm. Fuck. Even in cyberspace, it stings like acid, leaving burnt holes in my avatar's clothes. What the shit kind of program does that?

There isn't time to figure it out. Two other mouths rear back for another strike, dripping with ooze. I flip my shield up, running the custom antivirus software I cobbled together from bits and pieces of the Padlock's programming and hoping to heaven it works.

Both sets of jaws hurtle toward me.

They crash into my shield, sending shockwaves down my arm.

The shield holds.

After a split second freak out, and another split second where I thank God I'm alive, I start to laugh. The flytrap is going to town on my shield, gnawing on it like a puppy on someone's pant leg.

But I'm not safe for long. Acid drools from the flytrap's mouths, causing my makeshift shield to sizzle and flicker.

Fuck it. I'm out. No way am I staying here to fight this thing. I select my logout screen, relieved to see the buttons are working again. I disconnect from the extranet, vanishing a split second before the program's jaws smash through my shield for good.

network: bbd 13193 . 59543
disconnection complete

I jerk into a sitting position, pulling the cable from my jack and letting it fall alongside the bed. To my relief, everything seems normal. Jacobo is sulking in the other bed while Mateo snoozes away. Neither of them have any idea I was fighting for my life.

"Jacobo, Mateo." I hop out of bed, crossing over to tap Mateo's shoulder.

Mateo yawns, blinking blearily.

Jacobo shifts away, regarding me with a narrow, suspicious gaze. "What?"

I offer the most succinct explanation possible. "Bad guys found us. Mateo, grab whatever's important and pack a bag. Jacobo, go help Abuela. We're going to SLKC."

Mateo wiggles out of bed, rushing to do as he's told. For once, he doesn't bombard me with questions. He knows my 'I'm fucking serious' tone well enough by now. But Jacobo hesitates. "It's my fault, isn't it?" he says, his newly deepened voice cracking slightly. "Because I was doing jobs. That's how they found us."

Fuck. The poor kid looks like he's about to cry, which I haven't seen in years…except for right after Megan abducted him. *"Calmate."* I clasp his shoulder in what I hope is a reassuring grip. "We're going to a safe place, okay?" I'm still not fully convinced of that, but at this point I have no choice but to hope Sasha and the others are right about Sprout.

Jacobo's lip trembles, but he swallows, his jaw tightening. "Okay. I'm sor—"

"Don't be sorry. They were looking for me, not you. I'm the one who should be sorry."

"Who's 'they'?" Jacobo asks. "AxysGen?"

"I'll explain later. Go help Abuela pack while I get Ocho."

***

WEDNESDAY, 10-01-65 4:02:25

We leave the resort without issue, but the further we get from Barbados the more my stomach churns. My chest is painfully tight and each breath hurts as I pilot the black Chevord Cougar I hotjacked in the resort's parking structure, joining a smeared river of headlights amongst the trans-Atlantic traffic. I needed a vehicle large enough to transport Abuela and my brothers while Ocho flies the Silverwing alongside us.

Stealing a luxury car from some disgustingly rich tourist is hardly the worst of my sins, but I feel terrible anyway. Maybe doing it tapped into the ocean of guilt already storming in my gut. Coming to the conclusion that I hate corporate Barbados and all its luxurious fakery is one thing. Realizing I can't fucking breathe without Sasha and my crew is another. Warning Val is the strongest motive of all to return to Sprout. But what the ever loving fuck am I supposed to say other than 'I'm sorry?'

I had the best of reasons, my brothers and Abuela but what explanation could possibly be good enough from my crew's point of view? I abandoned them and took Ocho with me, which I'm sure they aren't pleased about either. Poor Ocho was a bit shocked when I burst into her room in the middle of the night yelling at her to pack, but she took it like a champ. In fact, she seemed excited to be going back, and it was her idea to fly the Silverwing.

I wish I felt the same.

My fear must be evident on my face. Jacobo, who's sitting in the large, faux-leather passenger's seat, looks over with wide eyes, chewing his cheek like he's nervous. "Are we gonna be okay?" he whispers, so the others won't hear. Abuela is sitting in back to keep Mateo calm, but it's a moot point. They're both fast asleep thanks to the early hour. Abuela's even snoring.

I flash Jacobo my most confident fake smile. "We're gonna be fine, conejito."

"How do you know? Won't your crew be mad you left?"

My smile fades. It takes me a few seconds to figure out what to say, and the silence is almost smothering. "My crewmates are good people. Even if they're pissed at me, they won't take it out on you. You and Mateo are just kids, and Abuela's old. They'll help me make sure you're safe." Of that, I'm certain. At the very least, my crew won't cast my family to the wolves. They'll find us some kind of shelter, whether it's in Sprout or elsewhere.

I hope they'll let us back into Sprout, though. As scared as I am for its future, what I saw during the week I spent there was exactly the kind of community my brothers would thrive in.

"Sprout's a pretty cool place," I say since Jacobo's still staring at me in search of reassurance. "There's a playground—"

He gives me a skeptical look.

"Well, Mateo will probably like that more than you. But they have a huge greenhouse and fish farm that the kids get to work in during the second half of the school day."

"Work?" He wrinkles his nose.

"It's more fun than it sounds. Plus, you'll meet kids your own age." Maybe I shouldn't be promising all this stuff, since I'm not sure they'll let us stay, but I'll say just about anything to bolster Jacobo's spirits. I know he thinks it's his fault we're in danger.

"Really? Like, girls?"

Ah. My twelve-year-old brother, asking the important questions.

"Yes, girls."

That puts a small smile on his face. He leans back into his seat, stifling a yawn. Good. Maybe he's relaxed enough to doze off. Just in case, I don't say anything. Telling a kid they should sleep is a guarantee they'll stay awake out of sheer stubbornness.

Soon enough, he's snoring along with Mateo and Abuela, one cheek smushed against the tinted passenger side window. Once I'm sure he's out, I drum my fingers quietly on the steering wheel. I have an important decision to make: who to tell I'm coming.

Val is the obvious choice, but she made her reluctance to be my messenger more than clear when I left. Rami might be sympathetic since they're always a sweetheart but using them as a go-between feels wrong. Deep down in my gut, I know who I need to tell, I'm just terrified.

"Fuck," I whisper to myself. Well, better now than when I arrive at Sprout's door, possibly facing down armed guards. I switch on the car's autopilot and blink to activate my VIS-R. Text would be easier than a vid call, but also kind of impersonal. Sasha deserves more than words on a screen this time.

I gather my courage and call.

Sasha answers immediately. Her eyes are droopy, like she hasn't been sleeping, and her scalp seems dry. Maybe she hasn't bothered oiling it. She's wearing a wrinkled shirt that looks like she's worn it for several days already, but I don't care. She's still the most beautiful fucking sight I've ever seen, and I almost burst into tears.

"Sasha?"

"Elena." Her voice cracks and she licks her lips. "Are you okay?"

I reach under my VIS-R, swiping my eyes. "No."

The look on Sasha's face breaks my heart. I don't deserve for her to be worried about me after I walked out, but she is. The look of anguish on her face is obvious, and I feel anguished as well because I know I caused it.

"What happened?"

I swallow. She needs to know what's going on. Even though I'm terrified of our inevitable heart to heart, I can explain the situation. "Someone posing as Megan tried to kill me online. They want the IP address for Val's servers in Siberia. I'm heading to SLKC now with Ocho, Abuela, and my brothers." I pause, and the question I've really been longing to ask comes bursting out. "Can I come home?"

Sasha's breath hitches. Her face goes on a visible journey from horror to hope, but she doesn't answer. She hesitates. There's fear in her eyes, and my heart feels like it's breaking all over again. "Kyra won't like it," she says at last. "She's pissed you disappeared like that."

The only reason I don't crumble is because Sasha's staring directly into my eyes like she wants to have an honest conversation. At least she's talking to me. Looking at me. "I know. I'm sorry." I'll have to offer more apologies later, but this will have to do.

Sasha sighs, pinching the bridge of her nose. When she looks up from her hand, her face is blank again, except for faint remnants of sadness at the tightened corners of her eyes. "I can't promise a warm welcome from the Corsairs but get here as fast as you can. Someone will meet you at our SLKC hideout and escort you to Sprout. Be safe."

I want to say, 'I love you.' I want to tell her I haven't been able to fucking breathe without her. I want to tell her Barbados is fake and empty without my whole family there, including her and the crew. But this is the wrong time, and I don't feel like I have the right after leaving her the way I did. I bite the confession back. "You too."

I don't hang up. Neither does Sasha. We stare at each other, leaving a lifetime's worth of words unspoken. Eventually, she gives a faint smile. "Val will be happy you're coming back."

"Yeah?" *But what about you?*

"She was sure you would."

"She was?" *But what about you?*

"Don't worry. We won't let anything happen to her servers."

"I know."

"Okay." She hesitates. "See you soon."

"Right. Soon."

Sasha hangs up for real, leaving me with a churning stomach and more questions than answers. I still don't know what I'm walking into by returning to Sprout, but at least Sasha told me to come home. That means something, right? Hopefully, the crew and the Corsairs will take it easy on me until we've figured out how to protect Val.

I rub my sore eyes. Suddenly, I realize I'm exhausted. Technically, the car can drive itself for a few hours on the trans-Atlantic. Like many people, I prefer driving manually. (You can't fully trust corps AIs to put the driver's safety first, no matter what they claim.) But tonight, I'm too fucking tired to care. Driving while sleep deprived is one of the easiest ways to have an accident.

My eyes slip partway shut, and I remain half asleep for a while, watching smudged pairs of golden headlights streak by. In spite of everything, there's a seed of hope inside me. Soon, I'll get to see Sasha in person again.

Chapter 07

"WHOA," MATEO SAYS, PRESSING his nose against the Cougar's rear window. His breath fogs the tinted glass as he watches the city whip by. "SLKC is shiny."

The St. Louis commercial district *is* shiny. Multi-colored, too. Some sections are bubblegum pink with rounded edges and big eyed cartoon advertisements, aiming for a kawaii aesthetic. Others are gleaming white, with wide walkways and people in equally white jumpsuits servicing the mobile trash cans and vending machines. Still more sections are composed of sleek chrome skyscrapers that shine in the sunlight, piercing the sky like dragon's teeth. Together, they make a patchwork quilt in which each square screams for attention.

The chaotic illusion of uniqueness and choice is meant to be part of the city's charm, but it's all for show. I know for a fact that two or three huge corporations own all these retail establishments under separately branded subsidiaries. It's the same in every major city in the world. Credits always flow in the same direction.

There's no reason to give Mateo a lecture, though. "Sprout's even cooler than upper SLKC. Did I tell you the kids there decorated the walls?"

"Like pictures?" Mateo asks.

"More like murals."

"Cool," Jacobo drawls, obviously unimpressed.

I arch an eyebrow. "So, you *don't* want to spray paint walls with permanent graffiti?"

Jacobo lifts his head and perks up, obviously not having thought of it that way. "Graffiti? Okay, that actually is cool."

"Yeah. Graffiti and girls. You'll like it, I promise."

My brothers pepper me with more questions as I pilot through the sluggish flow of early morning traffic.

"How many people live there?"

"Do we get our own rooms? I don't wanna share with Mateo again."

"Is the school there fun or boring?"

Abuela raises her voice to be heard over the boys' chatter. "What about the food?"

I turn around in my seat to grin back at her. "You're going to love it, Abuela. Fresh ingredients and a full mess that provides meals for anyone who can't or doesn't want to cook. I ate like a queen. Best cooking I've ever had."

"Besides mine," Abuela says with a dangerous glint in her dark brown eyes.

"That goes without saying. No one comes close to you."

We arrive at one of the citywide checkpoints leading underground. Identical electronic rings flash between red and green as other vehicles fly through, siphoning into different tunnels. I tense as we approach our own checkpoint. Luckily, the Cougar doesn't ping the automated security. It's doubtful the SLKC cops are looking for a car stolen all the way in Barbados. Local law enforcement agencies rarely communicate as effectively as multinational corporate entities.

My family falls silent as we head underground. The lights around us change, casting the world into an eerie neon glow. On the surface, imitation sunlight bathes the skylanes and walkways. Here, there's a darker, almost ghostly quality to the advertisements illuminating each tunnel. I see why the locals call this place The Web. In addition to having a spindly layout reminiscent of a spider's web, it reminds me of being online.

"Is this Sprout?" Mateo asks, still peering out the window.

"Not yet. We're stopping by one of my crew's hideouts first. Someone will meet us there."

I remind myself not to grind my teeth. I still don't know what kind of reception I'll get at the hideout, let alone Sprout itself. Focusing on the ads scrolling alongside our lane, I finally spot the one for NutraBrand Flavor Paste. I pretend to merge into an adjoining lane, sailing straight through the projected billboard and into another tunnel below. This one is abandoned, part of the city's shoddy power grid. It's not so different from the tunnel that conceals Sprout's entrance.

"Nice trick," Jacobo says.

"It's pretty good. Rami's idea." And Megan's, but I don't say so. Poor kid has enough trauma without hearing about the woman who abducted him.

We arrive at the hatch leading to SLKC's version of the Hole. It slides open beneath us, and I pilot the Cougar into the hideout's garage, settling her down smoothly on the bare concrete. Looking out the window I note the Eagle, as well as a large blue shuttle I presume is Kyra's. The Silverwing's parked a few yards away with a single passenger aboard. Ocho has beaten us here. She strides toward the Cougar, rapping on the driver's side window.

I lower it. "How long you been waiting, *gatita*?"

"Not long," Ocho says. "I parked a few seconds before you."

"Where are the others?" I peer past Ocho, hoping to catch a glimpse of my crew. Despite my gut-churning guilt, I'm excited to see them again. Happy, even.

"Inside, I guess?"

I feel a pang of disappointment. I consider them family in spite of everything, but maybe they don't feel the same way about me. "Come on," I say to the boys and Abuela. "Bet you could use a bathroom break after that drive."

My family doesn't need much encouragement. They hop out of the Cougar, Jacobo and Mateo much faster than Abuela. Ocho goes around to help her, and she pats Ocho's forearm. *"Gracias, Ocho."*

"De nada," Ocho replies.

Before we reach the lift leading down to the hideout it rises up into the garage, bearing a crowd of people. The whole crew is there, with the exception of Val's hologram. Kyra accompanies them with her own crew in tow. I'm thrilled to see everyone, but my eyes lock onto Sasha first. Bam, instant relief, like collapsing into bed after the worst day ever, as corny as that sounds.

Sasha holds my gaze, blinking once to acknowledge me before averting her eyes. Though she doesn't rush to greet me, just seeing her makes me feel better. Kyra stands beside her, shooting me a much colder look. I don't miss the way she keeps one hand on the pistol at her hip while patting Sasha's shoulder with the other.

Doc is the first one off the platform. She runs to me, throws her arms around my waist, and buries her face in my shoulder. For once, she doesn't say a word. There's no snark or sass, just a tight, desperate hug from a kid who obviously missed me a lot.

"Hey." I return the hug, rubbing a circle on Doc's back. Comforting her matters more than assuaging my own guilt. "It's okay, *chiquita*. Sorry I left without saying goodbye. I was a shit."

"You *were* a shit," Doc agrees, her wavering voice partially muffled by my shirt.

"I know. I'm sorry."

"Glad to hear you admit it, *chaparrita*." Cherry strolls over at a more sedate pace. Without waiting for Doc to let go, she leans in for a hug, although her embrace is slightly stiff. I can tell she's glad to see me, but there's definitely some anger simmering below the surface. Still, a hug is a hug. I'll take what I can get.

Ocho watches us from a few paces away, so I gesture for her to come closer. I know she's been worried about how the crew will react to her running away, so I try to help break the ice. "C'mon. You, too."

Cherry opens one arm, inviting Ocho into the hug. "Get on in here, *gatita.* I've missed your face. It's prettier than Sasha's."

Ocho leans in to join us. "We have the same face. Oh, wait. That's supposed to be a joke."

"Burn," Doc says. Although her voice is choked up, she's smiling too.

A large shadow looms over me, and I'm not at all surprised when Rock's enormous arms wrap around all four of us. He lifts us off the ground in a great big bear hug, forcing most of the breath from my lungs.

"Hey," Doc wheezes. "Easy, bro."

Rock gives us an extra squeeze, then sets us down. I grasp Cherry's arm for a moment and catch my breath, but I grin up at him. "Good to see you too, big guy." Rock pats my hair with one of his palms, which is big enough to cover the top of my head.

I glance past him, hoping to catch Sasha's reaction. She's watching me intently, almost warily. Her posture is rigid, reminding me of a nervous cat. I suppose I deserve that. After the number Megan did on her, my abandonment probably hit like a Puls.wav to the heart. Guilt gets the better of me this time, and I'm the one who looks away first.

Nearby, Rami busies themself escorting Jacobo, Mateo, and Abuela onto the lift. "Come with me. I'm sure you want to use the restroom and get something to eat." Typical Rami. Always looking out for others. It doesn't escape my notice that they haven't hurried over to me, though. I thought they'd be the first to welcome me back, but I guess I was wrong.

"Can I come?" Ocho asks. "I'm starving."

Rami takes Ocho under their wing like a hen herding chicks, clucking over her just the same. "Of course. I'll make you whatever you want." Obviously, their wariness concerning me doesn't apply to Ocho, which is fair enough.

"We don't have time," Kyra says.

"Not even enough time for a sandwich?" Rami looks at Sasha, who somberly shakes her head no. With a furrowed brow, Rami escorts my brothers, Abuela, and Ocho down into the hideout, glancing only briefly in my direction before they disappear. I don't miss the way Sasha claps Ocho's back and whispers in her ear as she passes. That's another friendly greeting I won't be getting right away.

I forget about Rami and Sasha's reactions as Kyra steps off the lift, approaching with the rest of her crew. Jones is missing, but the others are there: Ginger, LeRoy, and Flygirl. The cousins look at me with more curiosity than coldness, their expressions similar enough that I can tell they're related.

Ginger, on the other hand, seems almost bored. Her eyes wander around the garage, settling on the Silverwing. "Glad you didn't wreck her."

"Sorry. I was going to send Ocho back with her," I explain as if that's a valid excuse.

Ginger just shrugs and rolls her eyes like she's already over my bullshit.

Kyra stops in front of me, forcing me to look up at her. *Dios mio.* Getting stared down by a six-foot-tall amazon is extra scary when you're maybe five three on a good hair day. A drop of cold sweat runs down my spine. Kyra hasn't drawn her pistol, but her eyes are enough to pin me down all on their own.

"Leaving Sprout without permission is serious, Elena. I can't let it slide. You know our location, so you need to come back with us."

I hold Kyra's stare, hoping she'll interpret the eye contact as me showing respect and owning my choices instead of a challenge. "I was planning on it. Leaving the way I did was a mistake."

"It was more than a mistake," Kyra says. "Assuming you didn't sell our location to the highest corps bidder, what would have happened if they found you? My crew and I are wanted criminals. AxysGen and PGS already used Sasha as bait to draw us out once. They could have taken you prisoner and tortured our location out of you. Your actions put over a thousand lives in jeopardy."

Shit. *I* know I'd never deliberately put Sprout in danger like that, but Kyra only got to know me for a week and some change. All she had was Sasha's word that I wouldn't sell out.

"You could have just asked to leave," Flygirl adds. "We would have blindfolded you and dropped you off somewhere safe. That's what we do with other people who can't or don't want to stay."

But that would have meant saying goodbye to Sasha and my crew, which meant I wouldn't have had the willpower to leave. I can't tell them that, of course. It'll sound like the weakest, most cowardly excuse in the world. *'Sorry, I couldn't be bothered to wait for you to drop me off somewhere because saying goodbye to my girlfriend was too hard.'*

My heart sinks. There's nothing for it but to offer myself up for whatever judgment Sprout is willing to dole out. "I'm sorry. I wasn't trying to put Sprout in danger. I'm sure Sasha told you I had family on the outside."

"I know," Kyra says. "That's the only reason we're talking. Do you agree to come back to Sprout and accept whatever punishment the council gives you?"

I'm not sure if that's better or worse than asking for mercy from Kyra. Convincing her seems like an uphill battle, but convincing an entire council of strangers sounds like a Sisyphean task. Still, there's only one answer I can give if I want to make this right.

"I'll plead my case to Sprout's council, but please don't take it out on my family. I'd like them to be considered for residency separately. They're the reason I left, but they had nothing to do with *how* I left. That's my fault. They shouldn't be punished for it."

Kyra's dark eyes soften slightly. I guess if she has one chink in her armor, it's family. "I'll start the process when we get back. I think I get you, Elena. You're an idiot, but I get you."

That's about the best I can expect, considering. I exhale a sigh of relief and nod my thanks. "So, what now?"

"Well, this is a dual purpose trip," Cherry says. My face heats up at the realization that everyone except my family, Ocho, and Rami were right here, listening to me and Kyra hash things out. In the moment I was too nervous to notice.

I turn to Cherry. "Yeah?"

"We're moving Val's servers to Sprout, like you suggested."

I steal a quick glance at Sasha. From the tight press of her lips and the tension in her blocky jaw, I suspect she hasn't revealed the truth about Val's sentience to Kyra yet. Good. We'll have to cross that bridge eventually, but in the meantime, the fewer people who know, the better. The danger Val's in only makes secrecy more important.

"Moving the servers to Sprout is still a good idea," I say to Kyra.

A furrow appears between Kyra's brows. "The guard on duty told me what you did. Clever plan. I gave them all a refresher on security protocols, so you won't get away with it again."

"No worries. I'm not planning on ducking out again."

"Good," Sasha says. It's the first word she's spoken since my arrival, and it hits like Doc slapping a RapiHeal patch right on my broken heart. Thank god. Just, thank god.

"You want to help me and Sasha make sure Val's tower servers get transferred to the shuttle safely?" Cherry asks me. "You're the expert, after all."

I sense Cherry's actually setting up an opportunity for us to talk in relative privacy, so I agree. "Sure. Now?"

"We can't stay long," Sasha says. "As far as we know, PGS and AxysGen haven't pinged this place's coordinates, but we shouldn't take any chances. We'll be safer back at Sprout."

"Okay," Kyra says. "Get what you need while you're here. My crew and I will wait."

Sasha, Cherry, Doc, Rock, and I step onto the lift, while Kyra, LeRoy, Flygirl, and Ginger stand aside. Cherry waves briefly at Ginger as we sink down into the hideout itself, and Ginger responds with an upward nod.

"What's the deal with you two?" I ask Cherry once we're out of earshot.

"Nothing," she snaps, more aggressively than I'm expecting. "You disappear for over a week, then come back and get on my fucking case five minutes later?"

Cherry has a point, but her tone stings. "Calm down, I just—"

"Not now," Sasha grunts, glaring us both into silence. "We'll hash this out later. For now, let's get Val's servers. Elena, I told everyone what you told me about someone impersonating Megan. If that's true, we need to get out of here and back to Sprout yesterday."

Sasha's right. Now isn't the time or place. We remain quiet the rest of the way down, standing awkwardly on the small lift while trying not to touch each other. I already miss the hugs I got when I first returned. After a frustratingly long time, the lift stops. I step into the living area, looking for the boys, Abuela, or Rami. Instead, a projection of Val appears, striding toward me with a big smile.

"Val!" I hurry over, feeling the urge to hug her despite the fact that she's a hologram. She humors me and returns the motion, even though it feels like embracing air. I don't care. It still makes me happy.

"Elena. It is good to see you. My algorithms predicted you would return."

I withdraw my arms. "What, no exact percentages?"

"You have informed me that using exact percentages when discussing personal subjects is 'creepy' and 'overstepping,' so I decided to incorporate your advice into—"

Val's voice cuts off abruptly. Her hologram flickers, jumping around in jagged, pixelated bars. Horizontal rectangles of grey static cut through her body, causing her to jerk like an image on a malfunctioning monitor. She reaches toward me, her face frozen in a look of absolute shock, then disappears, winking out of existence. The lights shut off, casting the living room into darkness.

Chapter 08

"VAL? VAL!" I STUMBLE forward through the darkness, panic sirens blaring in my brain. Val, glitching out? Impossible. But I know what I saw. She disappeared right before the power died. Something is horribly wrong.

Everyone else starts shouting at once.

"What the fuck happened?" Cherry asks.

"Ow, careful," Doc says. "That's my foot."

"Shut up!" Sasha barks. Everyone does. "The backup generator should have kicked in. I'm going to find out why not. Stay put." She stalks off. Everything is eerily silent except for the sound of her boot soles thumping on the floor.

Before Sasha gets more than a few yards, a hissing noise fills the space, like steam escaping a vent. It's the air filtration system resetting. The lights blink on. Everyone exhales, me included. I stare hopefully at the space where Val was, but her avatar doesn't reappear.

"Where'd Val go?" Doc clings to Rock's leg like a much younger kid scared of the dark.

"I'll check her backup servers," I say, trying to sound confident. Inside, I feel anything but. "Whatever happened here shouldn't have shut her off like that. Her main servers are all the way in Siberia."

"Do not connect with my backup servers, Elena!" Val says via the living room terminal, projecting her voice through its speakers. *"Your jack is broadcasting a virus which bypassed my defensive software. My primary servers in Siberia are no longer functional and my backup servers at this location remain at risk."*

"What virus?" I stare at the terminal in confusion. "Fake Megan blocked my programs for a while, but my jack's working fine…"

Which was all part of her plan, I realize with a sickening sense of dread. At the time, I was so focused on evading the Venus Flytrap that I didn't question how easy it was to escape. Using the Jackrabbit app to purchase AxysGen products. Modifying them into a new shield program.

Logging off before Audrey III ate me. Fake Megan *let* me do those things. All along, my jack was a ticking time bomb.

"Are you okay, Val?" Cherry asks.

Her voice sounds distant. I still can't believe it. *My fault. This is all my fault.* Pain slices through my stomach, like I've swallowed shards of glass.

"*That is a difficult question to answer,*" Val explains. "*I maintain a wireless connection with all of your jacks whenever my servers or the mobile databox are within range. When I connected to Elena's jack, a virus was transmitted directly to my main servers in Siberia. It shut them down, but fortunately, I was able to reboot myself from a recent copy on the local backup servers.*"

"Yeah, but are you *okay*?" Doc's blue eyes are wide with fear. "You aren't hurt, right? Because I can fix broken bodies, but I don't know how to fix you."

"*Presently, I am functional. However, having only one server capable of hosting my consciousness leaves me extremely vulnerable to future attacks.*"

Future attacks. *Mierda.* This is only the beginning. Whoever Fake Megan really is, they're determined to shut Val down for good. If I'm right, they'll go to any lengths to accomplish that goal. More glass shards have lodged themselves in my throat, forming a burning ball of pain as I speak. "I'm so sorry," I croak. "I didn't know...I didn't mean to..."

"*I do not blame you, Elena,*" Val says, "*but this has fundamentally altered our situation. Sasha, you must inform Kyra that I am sentient.*"

Sasha does a double take. "What? Why?"

"*My presence in Sprout may put the city's residents at risk,*" Val says. "*It would be immoral to reside there without informing them of the increased danger from this new enemy.*"

"You can't do that," Rami interrupts, hurrying into the living room from the hallway. Apparently, they've returned in time to hear the tail end of the conversation. "Sorry, I was with Ocho and Elena's family. They're fine, just a little shaken up. Val, what the heck? You have no idea how Kyra or Sprout will react. As far as they know, FRAIs don't exist."

"Rami's right, Val," Sasha says. "They might forbid us from bringing your servers to Sprout. Then what would we do? Where would we go?"

"We'll defend ourselves," Doc insists, all brash courage. She clenches her fists like she's about to deck someone right here and now. "We can't let anyone shut Val down."

My head spins as the crew argues back and forth. Their voices are white noise in my ears. The only words I can hear clearly are the ones in my own head. *My fault. My fault. My fault…*

"No," I say, loud enough to get everyone's attention. The crew turns to me with mixed looks of fear and frustration. "We need Kyra and Sprout's help. Someone's trying to hurt a member of our crew, someone skilled enough to shut down Val's Siberian servers. We need all the help we can get."

"Yeah?" Cherry arches a brow above scathing eyes. "Since when are you gung-ho about teamwork, cooperation, and helping others, Nevares? You didn't even say goodbye before you ran out on us."

"She came back," Sasha says, causing my heart to flutter with hope.

"Yeah, and you're just gonna fall into her arms again, aren't you? It's Megan's bullshit all over again."

Cherry's accusation cuts so deep, I can't even fully appreciate the fact that Sasha stuck up for me. It's not a fair comparison at all. Megan only ever cared about herself, while I left for my family. But that's an argument for another time and place.

"This isn't about my fuck-ups," I tell Cherry. "It's about keeping Val safe."

"Yeah, well, you're the one who infected her."

"Enough." Sasha steps between us. "Val's the one in danger, so we do what she wants. End of discussion."

"How do we even begin to have that conversation with Kyra?" Rami asks, twisting their hands.

"It isn't just Kyra we have to worry about," Doc says. "Sprout has a council. If we tell Kyra, she'll tell them, and they'll probably vote on whether to let Val in."

"If that comes to pass, I will make a persuasive argument on my own behalf," Val says. *"I am capable of providing Sprout with a great deal of data illustrating how to better utilize their limited resources."*

"Do me a favor," Sasha says, pinching the bridge of her nose. "Don't say stuff like that around anyone else. You'll sound like the corps. As for Kyra, let me talk to her."

She seems so overwhelmed that I almost reach out, hoping to offer some comfort, before remembering I gave up that privilege. All I can do is edge closer and give her a sympathetic look. "What are you going to tell her?"

Sasha lets her hand fall from her face, fixing me with a dull stare that reads exhaustion. "No idea. But I'll think of something. I have to."

"Let me try." Rami sidles up, brushing Sasha's hand with theirs almost exactly the way I wanted to. "Please. I'm good at this kind of thing."

"I'm her niece," Sasha protests, pushing Rami's hand away.

"Yes, and the fact that her niece kept something this big from her will probably hurt. It might be better coming from someone else."

"That's exactly why I need to be the one to tell her," Sasha says, shaking her head. Her frown carves deep lines around her mouth. "Not owning up will make it worse."

But Rami isn't budging. "Come on, Sasha. For once in your life, let someone else do the heavy lifting."

Val interrupts, raising the volume of the terminal's speakers. *"I recommend we tell Kyra together, as a group. Our unique perspectives might aid us in persuading her."*

Before the argument can continue, the lift lowers from the garage, hissing as it settles. Kyra, LeRoy, and Ginger stand on the platform, but Flygirl is nowhere to be seen. Presumably, Kyra left her to watch the vehicles and the hideout's only exit.

"What happened?" Kyra's long strides are all business as she approaches Sasha, stopping directly in front of her. "Did the power cut out here, too? We waited but didn't hear anything from you, so we came down to see what was going on."

"Everything's fine," Sasha says. Watching the two of them stare each other down makes me cringe. Everything most definitely isn't fine.

Kyra folds her arms across her chest, studying Sasha skeptically. "Really?"

Sasha's eyes flick down to her boots as if she's ashamed. It's a gesture I've never seen from her before. *She's scared,* I realize, noting the way her nails dig into her palms, causing her knuckles to flex. She's afraid Kyra will reject her when she finds out about Val. I can't blame her. Kyra's the only blood relative Sasha has left, aside from Ocho.

The rest of the crew is similarly stunned. Doc glances between Sasha and Kyra, obviously waiting for someone to say something. Rock remains silent, as usual. Cherry seems as surprised as I am that Sasha's lost for words. Rami's in some kind of weird staring contest with Ginger, another bizarre reaction I don't have the mental bandwidth to process.

Maybe they're weighing the pros and cons of laying our cards on the table not just in front of Kyra, but most of the Corsairs?

Fuck it. Someone has to come clean. Maybe I can get one goddamn thing right today. If anyone understands the fears and doubts that come with discovering FRAIs exist, it's me.

"Kyra, I'm not the only one who needs refuge at Sprout. There's another member of our crew you haven't met. We were waiting for the right time to introduce you, but the situation changed."

Kyra fixes her steely stare on me. "What are you talking about?"

"Let me just show you. Val, are you functional enough to use your avatar?"

The terminal projects a faint, colorful beam of light. Val's avatar reappears, wearing her favorite purple blouse and black pencil skirt. She offers Kyra a kind smile, which Kyra doesn't return.

"Whoa," LeRoy says, doing an obvious double take. "What's that?"

"Hello," Val says. "My name is Val. I am a fully-realized artificial intelligence—one of only two in existence, as far as I am aware."

Ginger's jaw drops. For the first time I can remember, she doesn't look bored. "Fully realized?" she repeats as if she doesn't quite believe it. She runs her tongue over her lip ring, her eyes shining with what I instantly recognize as fascination.

"Yes, I am a sentient being. Please, do not be alarmed. I am a member of Sasha's crew and consider you my allies. I greatly admire what you have done in building Sprout. With your permission, I wish to become a resident and improve its functionality."

When Val starts talking about 'improving functionality,' Kyra, LeRoy, and even Ginger put their guard up. It's obvious on their faces. Kyra's hand actually strays to her pistol as if she's considering shooting the terminal.

"She doesn't mean it like that," Rami hurries to add. "What Val's trying to say is—"

"She wants to help," Cherry finishes.

Kyra ignores them both. "Are you serious?" she snaps, glaring at Sasha. "Is that thing really a FRAI?"

Sasha comes out of her daze. "Val is a FRAI, but she isn't a 'thing.' She's a full member of my crew and part of our family."

Without consulting each other, we draw together around Val's avatar, making a semi-circle as if to protect her. Our disagreements are temporarily forgotten. Rock forms the backbone, casting us all into shadow beneath his eight-foot-tall frame. Cherry stands shoulder to shoulder with me like she wasn't cussing me out a minute ago. I reach out, resting my hand briefly on Sasha's arm, and she accepts the touch.

"Where did she come from?" Ginger asks, obviously still fascinated. Her eyes haven't left Val's avatar since it appeared. "Who designed her?"

No one volunteers an answer. Telling her it was Sasha's crazy ex who tried to kill us seems like a bad idea.

Luckily, LeRoy has a simpler question. "How do we know you're telling the truth about...her...being a FRAI?"

"You don't," Doc concedes. "But why would we lie? Val's the reason the corps have been looking so hard for us."

"Precisely," Val says. "My main servers were recently compromised by an unidentified enemy."

"How recently?" Kyra asks Val. I decide that's a good sign. If Kyra's talking directly to Val, that's progress, right?

"Four minutes and twenty-three seconds ago. We would have preferred to inform you of my existence under less fraught circumstances."

"Yeah?" Kyra glares at Sasha again, shooting Puls.wavs with her eyes. "When, exactly, were you going to tell me FRAIs existed and you had one on your crew? Next Christmas? Did you bring her into Sprout? Was she spying on us this whole time?"

"Hey, you came to rescue us," Sasha protests, squaring off with Kyra. "We didn't ask you to save us at the Butterfly lab. You just showed up. Once we were in Sprout, what were we supposed to do? Tell a bunch of strangers we had a FRAI on our team? You didn't fully trust us then either, if I remember. That cuts both ways."

Kyra's face softens, if only for a moment. It seems like Sasha's logic has gotten through to her. "I can't just unilaterally decide to let a FRAI into Sprout. It's my brainchild, but not my city. Not my call."

"Everyone in Sprout respects you," I tell her. "You might not be their queen or president or whatever, but they look to you as a leader. If you explained how Val could help Sprout, they'd probably let her in. And she needs protection right now. Someone's already trying to kill her, us, and anyone who gets in their way."

"You're not making a great case for us to hide...uh, Val," LeRoy says, with a bit of a wince. "Y'all are even higher value targets than we thought."

"Not just that," Kyra says. "Who knows what damage a rogue AI could do to Sprout, let alone a sentient one?"

"But Val could do a lot of good," Rami says. "Her predictive analysis sensors would keep your equipment—climate control, water filtration, thermal generators—working at maximum efficiency."

"What about monitoring patients in the hospital?" Doc adds, with growing excitement. "She could perform data analysis to help develop treatment plans."

I leap on the opportunity to contribute. "Obviously, she'd be fantastic at defending the extranet connections Sprout has against cyberattacks. She can even help you generate building plans when you want to expand. You said you wanted to grow Sprout one day, right, Kyra? No one could do that better than Val."

Kyra crosses her arms, studying our crew with a guarded expression. Her eyes eventually land on Val, who smiles somewhat nervously. Val's facial expressions have improved a lot over the past few months, but I know there's real fear behind this one.

"You'd do all that stuff for Sprout?" Kyra asks.

"Absolutely. I understand you have no reason to trust me other than your relatively recent relationship with Sasha, but I love humans. I consider my crew my family. They are enamored of Sprout and believe in its potential, as do I. Regardless of the present threat to my existence, I would have offered my assistance without any expectation of payment in kind."

"You're certainly optimistic for an AI," Ginger drawls, seeming a bit more like her old self. The gleam of fascination in her eyes has dimmed slightly, replaced by her usual façade of boredom. "I know plenty of humans who think humans are garbage."

Val studies Ginger warily. "I am aware of this viewpoint. I fundamentally disagree."

Kyra opens her mouth but seems to think better of whatever she wants to say. She seems uncertain as if her conscience is pulling her in two directions. I think I understand. Like Sasha, Kyra's all about helping people, but trusting a FRAI is a huge risk. I've been exactly where she is, so I take one last shot.

"Look, I get how hard this is. It's human nature, right? The new frightens us, and that's among our own species, not counting AIs. But if one thing defines humanity, it's that we're builders. We form communities. We live, work, and grow together because at our core, that's who we are. Val isn't human, but she wants to build with you. That's why she's taking this risk to tell you the truth. She believes in what you're trying to build. That means she has so much more in common with you and the people of Sprout than you might think before you get to know her. That's all we're asking. For you to get to know her, like anyone else. So, will you?"

The silence stretches out as Kyra considers what I've said. LeRoy glances nervously at Ginger, who gives him a tiny shrug. My heart races overtime. *Please. Let me do one goddamn thing right.*

At last, Kyra heaves a resigned sigh. "We'll bring Val's backup servers to Sprout. For now. The council will decide whether to make her a resident or not, and whether they want her help." She doesn't sound pleased, but my shoulders sag in relief. Once we get back to Sprout, we can figure out the rest.

But Sasha isn't looking at Kyra. She's looking at me, smiling with pride. For a moment, I let myself feel hopeful. Maybe things aren't completely ruined after all. Not yet.

Chapter 09

THE FIRST ORDER OF business is to replace my corrupted jack. While the others load Val's server towers onto the shuttle, Doc and I enter the med bay. I hop on the exam table, restraining myself from swinging my legs. I'm still a bundle of nervous energy. I slide a hairband off my wrist and pull my hair back so Doc can see what she's doing.

"I still can't fucking believe it," Doc mutters as she gives her hands a thorough wash in the sink, snapping on a pair of gloves. "I mean, I knew in theory that Val could get a virus of some kind, but…" Her voice trails off and she turns to look at me with frightened blue eyes, seeking reassurance.

Poor kid. She reminds me of Jacobo. Maybe it's her age, or the fact that she looks up to me, perhaps not as much as my own brothers do, but definitely some. "Must be hard to see a hurt family member and not be able to patch 'em up, huh?"

Doc sighs. Nods. "My coding skills are nowhere near good enough to save her."

I let out a heavy breath of my own. I'm not sure mine are, either. I've worked with (and against) some of Megan's code in the past. As much as I despise the woman, she was a genius. If she were still alive and challenged me to a no-holds-barred jacker duel, I'd definitely come out the loser. It was only with Val's help that I managed to kill her back in Mexico. Whoever this new Fake Megan is, she seems to know plenty of the original's tricks.

But that doesn't mean I shouldn't try. Val's my friend. Plus, I'm the one who fried her servers. The least I can do is make sure her backups get to a safe place and restart without issue.

"Tell you what, *pequeña.* You fix me up, and I'll fix her. Deal?"

Doc manages a small smile. "Deal."

Removing my old jack is a quick and painless process. Sterilization wipes, a little topical anesthetic, a brief click from Doc's installer, which also functions as a remover, and the wires detach.

Doc pulls the old jack from behind my ear with a pair of tweezers, dropping it into a shallow silver tray. I don't feel a thing. The knowledge that those same bloody wires were connected to my brain a few seconds ago makes me kind of squeamish, though, despite how often I've upgraded.

"You're lucky I've got another Platinum version on hand," Doc says as she cracks open the sterile packaging on a new jack. "Shit's expensive."

I roll my eyes. "I know for a fact you didn't pay for this."

"So? Doesn't mean it wasn't hard to get."

Doc implants the new jack with the other end of the installer. Like the removal, it only takes a few seconds, and I don't feel anything. I blink, bringing up my VIS-R. According to the words *Unknown Network Available* under my 'Devices' menu, the jack has installed properly and is broadcasting a signal.

"Save the old one," I say as Doc slides it into a tiny, see through biohazard bag. "I might be able to recover some stuff."

Doc hands me the bag, though she seems reluctant. "Are you sure that's safe? If it was hacked…"

"I need to figure out *how* it was hacked," I say, putting the bag in my pocket. "That might protect Val in the future. Don't worry, I'll be careful."

"Just don't download anything from it," Doc grumbles. Nevertheless, she's very gentle as she wipes away any remaining blood from my neck and coats the surrounding area with RapiHeal ion gel.

I snort. "I'm curious, not stupid, kid. I've got my most important programs in the cloud."

Doc raises her eyebrows as she removes her gloves, tossing them into the waste bin. "Not stupid, huh? Could have fooled me."

"Okay, I deserve that after ducking out the way I did. I'm really sorry."

"You could have called, you know?" Doc says, with a bit more venom than I think even she meant to add. She blinks at the bitter tone of her own voice as if in surprise, averting her eyes. "Sorry, I—"

"No, you're right. I should have called. Telling Val where I was headed wasn't good enough."

Doc turns away to wash her hands. "I understand not wanting to let your brothers and Abuela down," she says, her back to me. "But we're your family, too. At least, I thought we were."

I hop down from the exam table, taking a hesitant step toward her. "You are my family, if you all still want to be. But sometimes even family fucks up."

"Yeah. About that." Doc dries her hands, turns, and pulls something out of her own pocket. Something that looks like a crumpled piece of paper. She passes it to me, still not meeting my eyes.

I unfold the paper. It's a drawing. An almost frighteningly realistic drawing of Rock, done in what looks like pencil. He's kneeling, reaching toward the corner of the page as if in search of help. Huge chunks of his fleshweave are missing, showing a mixture of gleaming metal and gore beneath. On the ground beneath him is a shining pool of blood.

"Dios." The drawing is amazing, but extremely hard to look at. I return it to Doc quicker than I would have if it weren't so unsettling.

"He drew that," Doc says, confirming what I've already guessed. "I wanted to talk to you about it...someone who hadn't already known him the way he is for years and just decided to roll with it. But you weren't here."

My heart aches. Doc finds this drawing her brother did and *I'm* the one she'd wanted to seek help and advice from? I didn't think it was possible for me to feel worse about leaving, but apparently it is. I push away the guilt. It isn't productive right now. I'm here, and Doc's obviously hurting. So is Rock, if his self-portrait is any indication.

"Why does it bother you?" I ask, gently. "Lots of people make dark art."

"Because." Doc finally meets my eyes. Hers are swimming with tears, but she doesn't let them fall. "I pushed Rock into the protector role. I always felt vulnerable, you know? A puny genius kid with no parents. I took a lot of physical punishment, even after I passed my APS. If anything, that made it worse. Other kids were jealous. So Rock had the idea for me to turn him into my guard dog.

"The justification was, if I gave him all the best mods, he'd be valuable enough for my school to let me keep him. You can't bring family with you as a scholarship kid, but you can bring 'equipment.' I told them Rock was my bodyguard and personal aide, and he had the tech to prove it. He doesn't communicate well with neurotypical people, so I told myself he needed me to look out for him, too.

"But even though it was Rock's idea originally, I was the one who asked to install each mod. I'm his kid sister, so how could he say no? Eventually, I just started telling him what upgrades he was gonna get. It's not that mods are inherently bad or anything. They can be life changing for people with disabilities. But I'm sure if he had a choice, this isn't the life Rock would want. Being a killing machine. I'm the one who turned him into that."

I work some moisture into my dry mouth, trying to gather my thoughts. Fuck, that's a tough one. Doc looks particularly skinny and pathetic right now, her shoulders slumping.

"Digame. I know exactly what being a poor, scrawny, smarter-than-average orphan is like. It's a constant barrage of fear. Yeah, you made some fucked up choices because of that fear. But your choices aren't stagnant. You can't change the past, but you can learn from it and act differently. Give Rock room to grow on his own at Sprout. Let him figure out what he wants to do and who he wants to be. It's past time, isn't it?"

Doc swipes at her eyes with her shirt sleeve. "See, I knew you'd have good advice. You have to stay this time, Elena. I know applying for citizenship is scary. I was scared they'd say no to me and Rock, too. But you can't leave us again. You're family. Promise you'll stay?"

I step forward, wrapping an arm around her shoulder. I'm starting to feel a bit teary-eyed myself. "I'm not going anywhere except back to Sprout, *chiquita.* I've done some hard learning of my own lately."

Doc turns into me, throwing her arms around my waist. She doesn't cry, but she trembles as I wrap her up in a hug. Then, abruptly, she pulls away and sniffs, pulling her face back into a more neutral expression. "Yeah, well, just because we had a moment doesn't mean all is forgiven. You can look forward to some passive-aggressive comments from me for a while."

I stifle a laugh. "You're a teenager. When do you *not* make passive-aggressive comments? Or just plain aggressive ones, if we're being honest."

"That depends on who you're comparing me to," Doc says. "Rami, or Cherry?"

"How's this? You can throw the fact that I left without saying goodbye in my face whenever we fight until your next birthday. That's in a few months."

Doc cracks a toothy grin that's definitely hiding laughter. "Deal." She sticks out her hand, and I shake.

Chapter 10

WHEN DOC AND I return to the hangar, Val's server towers are already aboard the Eagle. There are seven in all. Each one is three feet tall, made up of thin silver discs stacked like pancakes. They emit a constant hiss since most of the discs contain heavy-duty fans to keep the machinery inside cool.

As everyone climbs aboard the shuttles, Sasha pulls Kyra and Ginger aside. They share some whispered words, then Sasha approaches me, pinning me with her eyes. My boots stay rooted to the concrete, but I manage an uncertain, "What's up?"

"You and I are taking the Silverwing," Sasha says. It isn't a request.

Sometimes I bristle at Sasha's orders, even though she has every right to give them as the crew's handler. Not today. I follow her to the Silverwing which is parked beside the Eagle.

Ocho notices me, smiling and waving before she hops into the Eagle and takes her seat.

"Don't forget to buckle," Sasha reminds Ocho. She swings a long, leather clad leg over the Silverwing's seat. I swallow, trying not to stare. I don't think I've re-earned the privilege of blatantly checking her out yet.

"I wooon't," Ocho drawls, making a show of buckling her safety harness. "Hey, Sasha?"

"Yeah?"

"I missed you," Ocho says softly.

Sasha's lips curl into a gentle smile. "Missed you, too. See you at Sprout, okay?"

"Okay." Ocho leans over, pulling the Eagle's side door down and concealing the rest of the crew from view.

"I shouldn't have dragged her into my bullshit," I tell Sasha, edging toward the Silverwing. "She begged to come, but still. I should have known better."

"You shouldn't have brought Ocho to Barbados, but your reasons

225

for leaving weren't entirely bullshit," Sasha says. "The *way* you left was bullshit. You think I haven't been putting myself in your shoes, trying to understand? I know exactly why you did it, and who you did it for. Stop insulting yourself and just apologize for writing me a shitty Dear Jane letter instead of *talking* to me."

Tears sting my eyes, but I blink them away before they well over. This apology isn't about me and my feelings. "I'm *so* sorry."

The line of Sasha's shoulders softens, like she's just released a bunch of tension. "Get on the damn bike, Nevares." She removes a helmet from the Silverwing's rear compartment, strapping it onto her head. She passes me another. I buckle it beneath my chin and climb on behind her. I hesitate before scooting forward, cautiously wrapping my arms around her waist.

As we take off, flying through the open hangar roof and into the tunnels above, I remember how quiet the Silverwing is. Her fans hardly make a sound as she ascends, nose cutting gracefully through the air. Everything is silent thanks to the bike's noise-dampening windshield. Even the hum of the web is faint. No distractions. Just me and Sasha.

Her body shifts into each turn, and since I've been given the excuse and the opportunity, I snuggle closer. Sasha doesn't object. In fact, more tension drains from her stiff frame as she relaxes, allowing her shoulders to sink further and her spine to curve.

While I'm still gathering my courage, Sasha speaks up. "I'm pissed at you for leaving," she says, without taking her eyes from the dark, empty tunnel. Kyra's shuttle has pulled well ahead, and I can barely make out the taillights. "It felt like you abandoned me. Like you didn't give a shit about me. Just like...before."

A stab of guilt splits my chest, a very real, very physical pain. By refusing to say goodbye, I *did* abandon Sasha. In that sense, I'm not much better than Megan. There's no way to sugarcoat it, so I don't even try. "I'm sorry—"

"Let me finish. I'm pissed and I'm hurt, but I know you have an obligation to your family. I died for my family six times. Trust me when I say I understand."

Even though I can't see Sasha's face, I feel her tremble. When I first laid eyes on her in a seedy St. Petersburg bar, I made a snap judgment that Sasha was ice cold and impossible to read. Now, I know how big her heart is underneath. And I took that heart and stomped all over it like a total asshole.

"You can't die," I tell her, burying my face part way into her jacket.

The pleasant smell of leather and summer fills my nose. "I don't know what I'd fucking do without you. Now we're in danger all over again. So, fuck it, I don't know. You just can't die."

Sasha laughs, a sound that soothes the ache in my chest. "Fine. I promise I won't die."

I hitch my arms tighter around her waist. "Good."

"Are we still trying this? Us? Because before you called, I didn't know if you'd actually come back."

"Had to. Missed your face. But whether we try again or not is up to you. I'm the one who screwed up."

Sasha goes quiet for a while. "Must have missed more than my face, or Ocho would have been enough for you."

I flinch reflexively.

Sasha feels it. "What?"

"Uh."

"Elena, tell me you didn't—"

"Ocho kissed me at the club and I ran like my ass was on fire, okay? She's basically an overgrown kid. More importantly, she isn't you. If you're gonna break up with me, do it now." Getting dumped on the back of a hoverbike isn't ideal since I can't let go of Sasha's waist, but at least we have some privacy. Or I could always let go. Spare myself the humiliation of letting my girlfriend know I kissed her clone.

Sasha holds her silence. My heart pounds. For a moment, I think she's about to dump me after all, and I'm not entirely sure she shouldn't. Then, she laughs. "You *ran?*"

I laugh too. "Like someone shot a Puls.wav at me."

"I thought you ran like your ass was on fire. Which is it?"

A few tears squeeze from my eyes. Some are regretful, but most are relieved. Sasha's taking this way better than I expected. "I thought you'd be more pissed. I have to be honest.e I did kiss Ocho back for a second and pretended she was you."

"You pretended she was me?"

"Um, yeah. Why else would I kiss her?"

"Because she's a fresh version of me without the baggage. A version that isn't broken." Sasha's trying to sound casual, but I can tell this is really important to her. She stiffens beneath the soft leather of her jacket, her core tensing under my hands.

In the end, I can only be honest. I want to be honest with her. "I want you because of who you are, not in spite of it. *Because* you're the kind of person who gives everything to something greater than herself, even a crazy underground city that might fail. I didn't just come back to warn Val, or because I decided to put my faith in Sprout. I also came back for *you*."

"Thanks." That's all Sasha says, with every bit of sincerity a single word can hold. Somehow, that one syllable is enough. We fall silent the rest of the way to the tunnels, but it's a comfortable silence. With my face buried in Sasha's back and my arms around her waist, I've found home again.

Those warm, fuzzy feelings don't fade when we arrive at the node. We pull in through the hidden entrance, past a pair of young looking guards who let us pass without question. Kyra must have told them to expect us. Finally, we touch down in the shuttle bay where Kyra's shuttle and the Eagle are at rest among several others.

Kyra and a helmeted guard are waiting for us. No sign of my crew or hers, so I assume someone escorted them inside. Kyra addresses Sasha instead of me, without a hint of a smile. "Were you followed?"

Sasha shakes her head. It occurs to me that Kyra trusts her a whole lot to let her come and go from the hideout without a blindfold. Their bond of trust must have deepened considerably while I was gone. I have a feeling it will be a long time before Kyra gives me half as much trust. Guess I dug my own grave in that regard.

"Where am I staying?" I ask, trying not to sound nervous. I have to crane my neck slightly to meet Kyra's gaze, tall as she is. "Not, like, an actual prison cell, right?"

"No," Kyra says. "We'll post a rotating guard in front of your crew's apartment until the council has a chance to choose an appropriate course of action."

I wince. Guess it could be worse, but I don't like the idea of having a guard on me. "What about my family?"

"They won't be under guard," Kyra says. "I'll get them started on the process of applying for citizenship, if you want."

I look at Sasha. She looks back at me, a sheen of hope in her eyes. A lump forms in my throat. This isn't just about finding a safe place for my family to live, although that's the most important thing in the world for me. It's about proving to Sasha that I intend to put down roots like she has. Maybe it will even convince Sprout's council I didn't mean any harm by running off.

"Thanks. That sounds great."

Kyra doesn't smile but offers a slow blink of acknowledgment, like a cat trying to communicate that it doesn't feel threatened. "Okay. I'll escort you to Sasha's apartment now."

I follow Kyra and the guard out of the hangar and into the elevator, with Sasha by my side. Once we're traveling downward, the guard removes their helmet. To my surprise, it's Jones. "Hey, Elena," he says, shaking his shaggy black hair out of his eyes. "Glad you're back."

"Jones? You're a guard?"

"About twice a month," Jones says. "They never let anyone be a guard permanently. Don't want anyone getting used to carrying weapons and telling other people what to do like it's a daily thing."

"Makes sense."

We finish our descent in silence. Then it's a short walk down the hall to the same apartment I remember. To my surprise, there's a large white number pasted on the door. "Eight?" I give Sasha a searching look.

She offers half a shrug. "Val was pretty damn sure you'd come back."

"Speaking of which," Kyra says in a bit of a growl. "I need you to come with me, Sasha. We need to talk in private. Jones, can I trust you to stay here?"

Jones throws a casual salute, flipping his shaggy black hair out of his eyes. "Sure thing, boss."

"Good. Elena's the only one who can't leave. The others can get food or supplies for her if she needs anything that isn't already in the apartment."

Kyra opens the door and I prepare to step inside. Before I can, Sasha takes my hand, pulling me back. "Nevares?"

"Hmm?"

Sasha takes my hand, bowing to brush her lips against my knuckles. While I stare in awe, shocked but delighted that she would do this in front of Kyra—or anybody—her lips twitch into a rueful smile. "If you're not here when I come back, I'll find you and end you. Got it?"

"Got it," I choke out. "I'll be here."

"You better." She leaves with Kyra while Jones stays behind.

I take a deep breath, bracing myself. In a few moments, I'll be alone with the rest of my crew again. Judging by Cherry's hostile behavior earlier and Rami's odd skittishness, I could be in for a real shitstorm. Nevertheless, I enter the apartment. I'm done running.

Rae D. Magdon

Chapter 11

MATEO AND JACOBO GREET me as soon as I step into the apartment. Apparently, Sasha took the long way back to Sprout so we could talk, because they look like they've been waiting a while.

"Elena!" Mateo collides with my legs, throwing his arms around my thighs. "We beat you. Do we live here now?"

I ruffle his hair. "Not sure yet. I hope so."

Jacobo is slightly more subdued. He offers a sideways hug, wrapping his arm around my waist. That's unusual. He can be physically affectionate on his own terms, but lately he's preferred to keep his distance. Since he's decided to be touchy feely, maybe my recent brush with danger still has him scared. "Pretty sweet place," he comments, looking around the living room.

My crew's Sprout apartment is nowhere near as luxurious as the Paradise Resort, with its faux island decor and shiny, expensive appliances, but it's homey. The aerogarden Sasha placed in the window is still going strong, and the living room is messy. A pair of Cherry's shorts and one of Rock's tank tops have been thrown onto the back of the couch, hanging over a rumpled blanket. It's strangely reassuring. Makes the place feel lived in.

Rami is sitting on said couch alongside Doc and Rock. Rock rises to retrieve Mateo, who's still clinging to my legs. "Be careful," Rami says as Rock pries him gently away. "You don't want to ruin your nails."

Mateo flashes his hands, showing me what he and Rami have been up to. Apparently they decided to paint his nails lime green. I shoot Rami a grateful look. "Badass, Mateo."

Abuela, who's waiting patiently for her turn to hug me, clears her throat to express her disapproval.

"*Lo siento.* I mean, cool."

"I let Rami do mine, too," Doc says, showing her hands as well. She's picked a blood red shade of polish, while Rock has opted for cerulean blue. Judging by the mess on his fingers, I have a feeling he let

Mateo paint his, which was very kind of him. Poor Rock will probably need a lot of nail polish remover to get them looking presentable.

"No polish for you, Jacobo?" I ask.

He shrugs. "I'm helping Abuela cook lunch."

With Mateo dislodged from my legs, I finally manage to hug Abuela. "You don't have to do that after spending all night traveling. We can have something sent up from the cafeteria."

Abuela's crinkled brown eyes widen as though she's deeply offended. "You want the food here instead of your Abuela's?"

"No, that's not..." I sigh. This is an un-winnable argument. "Just promise you'll let Jacobo help, and make sure you have a chair to sit in when you get tired, okay?"

Abuela clicks her tongue. "I've cooked for my family for over seventy years."

I roll my eyes. "Fine. You win. Cook a five-course meal for all I care."

"You could be a little more grateful," Abuela grumbles as she shuffles back to the kitchen. Jacobo accompanies her, offering his elbow to help her balance.

Once she's gone, I return my gaze to Rock. "Where are Cherry and Ocho?"

Rock nods toward the hallway leading to the apartment's bedrooms.

"Thanks. Uh, Rock?"

He lowers the block of his chin to look down at me, and I try not to wither under the stare of his big blue eyes.

"I'm sorry for leaving without a goodbye. I knew if I had to look everyone in the eye, I wouldn't be able to go through with it. But it was a supremely shitty thing to do." I peer up at him, pleading for him to understand.

Rock's gaze shifts over to Doc, who lounges on the couch with Rami, then to Mateo, whose head barely comes up to the middle of his thigh. He nods once, his thin lips softening into a smile.

I lean in and hug him. Rock smells like I remember, laundry detergent and warmth. Despite the size of his arms, his embrace is as gentle as always. After a long moment, he lets go, squeezing the top of my shoulder with his large hand.

"Mateo, why don't you hang out with Rock and Doc while I take Elena back to see Cherry and Ocho?" Rami suggests, rising from the couch.

"'Kay." Mateo turns toward Rock, who scoops him up like he weighs nothing at all. With the squirming, squealing boy tucked under his arm, Rock returns to the couch, flipping Mateo onto his back and beginning to tickle him.

Once Mateo is sufficiently distracted, Rami whispers to me. "Cherry's setting up Val's servers. Connecting them to a power source, anyway. Val isn't allowed to access Sprout's intranet until we meet with the council."

"Of course. Look, Rami…"

Rami caresses my shoulder. "Cherry and Sasha won't forgive you right away, but you don't need to apologize to me, Elena." The warmth of their hand causes my throat to hitch with emotion. "I understand why you did what you did, probably better than the others."

"You do?" That's a surprise, considering how eager they were to avoid me back at the SLKC base.

"My parents were billionaires, remember? I was raised in privilege. I completely understand why you'd want that for your brothers, to give them safety when you grew up with nothing. But I knew you'd be back sooner or later. Paradise can't satisfy an empty soul. You had to learn that for yourself."

"It's not fair that you're always right about everything *and* stunningly beautiful, too," I grumble good-naturedly.

Rami pulls me close and kisses my cheek. "Believe me, it isn't easy being this breathtaking. Seriously, though. It hurt when you left, Elena, but I forgive you."

Reluctantly, I withdraw from Rami's embrace. "Thanks. I really needed to hear that from someone. Do you think Cherry will forgive me?"

"Cherry burns hot, but she always cools down eventually," Rami says. "We're fighting right now, actually."

"Is it about Ginger?" I ask, remembering their awkward body language at the SLKC base. Maybe that has something to do with Rami's odd behavior, and their eagerness to leave the group with my brothers and Abuela.

"Sort of," Rami says. "I'm concerned. Some of the stuff Ginger says is…off."

I frown. "Off how?"

"We were talking, and I told her a bit about my background. She was shocked. Said I was crazy for leaving all that money. She's brought it up a few times since then, and it's…I don't know. It's like she's jealous? I know she wants more resources for her lab, but Kyra invests almost everything into bettering Sprout overall."

"And Cherry doesn't get the same weird vibe."

Rami's chin falls toward their chest, their shoulders drooping. "She thinks Ginger's cooler than absolute zero."

"Kid in a candy store when it comes to that lab, huh?"

"Something like that." With a roll of their eyes, Rami taps my elbow, gesturing for me to accompany them. "Come on. Let's go find her. Ocho should be helping her set up Val's servers in your room."

Cherry and Ocho are indeed setting up Val's servers in the bedroom I shared with Sasha, although they seem to be finishing up. Ocho's sprawled with her stomach down on the bed, resting her chin in both hands while Cherry kneels next to the server towers which she's placed in the corner of the room nearest the door.

"Hey, Elena. Hey, Rami." Ocho rolls off the bed, standing up to greet us. "Cherry says we're almost done."

I place my hands on my hips, checking their work. Everything looks normal, although it's kind of weird seeing a bunch of server towers clustered in one corner of a bedroom. "Looks like it. Let me guess, *gatita.* You were the muscle?"

Ocho smiles proudly, sitting up on the mattress. "Yep. I carried the towers in and Cherry got everything hooked up."

Rami sidles over to Ocho, giving her bicep a fond squeeze. "Good to have you back, Ocho. We missed you."

Cherry, who's remained silent so far, rises from her kneeling position. *"Oye, chaparrita."* She offers a curt nod as she brushes her palms on her pants. "I set Val's servers up in your room, since you're the expert and all."

I pull an awkward grimace. "You sure this'll still be my room?"

Cherry huffs, trying to blow her bangs out of her eyes. When that doesn't work, she swipes them aside with her hand. "We've been down this road before. Sasha's got a *big* capacity to forgive the people she's getting some from."

I purse my lips. I have to admit, that one stings.

"Cherry," Rami says in a warning tone.

Cherry fixes her glare on them. "What? It's true."

I step between them. "Hey, it's okay. You don't have to defend me, Rami. Cherry has every reason to be pissed."

To my surprise, Cherry's scowl becomes a small smile, softening her face. "Damn right I'm pissed...but no one can piss you off quite like family, right?" She steps toward me, offering her hand. "I'll probably be mad for a while, but I'm glad you're back."

Instead of taking Cherry's hand, I pull her into a hug. "I missed you."

Cherry hugs back, resting her chin on top of my head. "All right, all right. Mushy weirdo. You know I love you, even when I wanna punch your face."

I laugh, blinking away tears. "You can be mad, but please, no punching."

"Fine." Cherry steps back, folding her arms and adopting an indifferent pose, but I don't care. A weight has been lifted.

"So," Rami asks, "when will Val be up and running?"

Cherry pats the nearest server tower. "Right now." She switches on the power by pressing a button on the front of the casing, and lines of white light come to life along both sides. A moment later, a projection of Val's avatar appears in the room with us.

"Hello, everyone. It feels good to be back."

"Good to have you back," Cherry says.

"Everything running okay?" I ask.

"Yes. There were no issues with data recovery. I am still vulnerable with my consciousness restricted to a single server, but in some ways, I am grateful that this occurred."

My eyebrows lift. "You're glad some rogue jacker running around in a Megan disguise almost killed you?"

Val shakes her head. "No, but their actions have forced me to confront my own mortality. I already empathized deeply with humans, but I feel an even deeper connection now."

"I guess that makes sense," Rami says, sounding uncertain.

"As long as we keep these towers safe," Cherry mutters.

"I'm just glad you're all right," I say.

"The hard part isn't over yet," Ocho reminds us. "We still need to convince Sprout to let Val stay. Us too, Elena."

I'm slightly surprised, although maybe I shouldn't be. Ocho's grown a lot since her activation. She's learned to parse out complex situations almost like an adult in a remarkably short period of time. "I don't think you'll have any problems, Ocho. I'll tell them I talked you into it. I have no problem being the bad guy if it gets you a lighter sentence."

"You aren't the bad guy," Ocho insists. "I wanted to go."

"I think we'll be better off if we don't talk too much about what we did. We should focus on why we came back. Hopefully they'll believe us when we say we want to stay here and help Sprout grow."

"A wise strategy," Val says.

"Yeah, but can we work on it more tomorrow?" Ocho asks. "I'm tired after flying the Silverwing all night."

Instantly, Rami is all sympathy, rubbing Ocho's back between her shoulder blades. "You poor thing. Yes, you and Elena should both take a nap. We'll wake you when lunch is done. If you're still tired then, we can heat it up for you later."

"You don't know my Abuela that well, then." I start to explain how she'll sulk if we don't eat at least one helping of her cooking while it's fresh, but the urge to yawn overcomes me. Now that Rami, Cherry, Rock, and Doc have mostly offered their forgiveness, I suddenly feel exhausted.

"Don't worry," Rami says. "I'll explain it to her."

"And I'll butter her up by telling her how delicious everything is, and how glad we are to have such a masterful chef back with us," Cherry says. From the gleam in her eye, I can tell that won't be difficult. My crew enjoyed lots of delicious meals courtesy of Abuela before we left Barbados.

"Fine. You don't have to twist my arm. I'll take a nap. You don't mind, right Val?"

Val shakes her head. "Not at all. I will focus my attention elsewhere via wireless connections with our crewmembers' jacks. Perhaps I will join them for lunch."

"Well, since you all insist." I hop onto the bed, folding my arms behind my head. "Mind getting the lights for me?"

Cherry arches a brow. "Not even gonna change out of your clothes, huh?"

I smirk right back at her. "Hoping for an eyeful?"

"You wish, Nevares." With a careless wave, Cherry saunters out of the room. After a wave and a 'sweet dreams,' Rami follows with Ocho close behind. She yawns on the way out, stretching her arms over her head.

I roll over, burying my face in the pillow. It smells like Sasha's cologne, and I can already feel myself drifting off. I hadn't realized how much I missed her scent on our sheets...

Chapter 12

MONDAY, 10-05-65 19:14:52

WARM, SOFT FINGERS CARESS my cheek, tucking a loose strand of hair behind my ear. My eyes flutter open, but I already know who's touching me. Sasha has climbed in bed beside me, lying on top of the comforter dressed in black pants and a neon purple jacket.

Her shining, dark-eyed gaze is painfully tender as it falls on me. Part of me wants nothing more than to push my head into her hand, but guilt grips the pit of my stomach. I can't help but think about how I abandoned her in this same state, asleep and vulnerable. After we made love, no less. Fuck me. Just, fuck me. How can she look at me the way she's doing? Like she's happy to see me in her bed when I didn't even have the courage to say goodbye?

"Sorry to wake you," Sasha murmurs. She withdraws her hand but doesn't roll off the bed, remaining stretched on her side with her cheek propped on her fist.

I roll onto my side as well, facing her. "S'fine. Everything okay?"

Sasha's brow furrows. "I don't know, Nevares. Is it?"

"For me it is," I say, choosing my words carefully. "What about you?"

"Kyra and I had a good talk. She's speaking to the council now. They're meeting tomorrow morning to hear you out. After that, they'll discuss the Val situation."

I prop myself up on my elbow, too. "What do you think they'll decide?"

Sasha exhales deeply. "No idea, but you'd better come up with one hell of a speech explaining why you and Val should get to stay."

Hesitantly, I reach my free hand toward her. The leather of her jacket feels smooth and cool under my fingers as I squeeze her arm. "I'll try and use my big mouth for good this time. But what happens if they kick me out, or worse?" As far as I know, Sprout doesn't keep prisoners, but the uncertainty of my situation is frightening.

Sasha locks eyes with mine, staring with such intense focus that I feel like I'm trapped in the beam of an oncoming Puls.wav. My heart hammers until she clasps my arm in return, completing the circuit. Tingling electricity warms me from fingertips to toes.

"If they don't accept you and Val, we'll leave. Start our own underground city. Maybe Kyra would help? She wants to start building beyond Sprout anyway."

A stinging lump swells in my throat. "That's a big dream. You sure it's what you want?" *Are you sure I'm what you want?*

Sasha runs her thumb back and forth above my elbow. "I want to grow something good, and I want to do it with the family I made. Maybe I can't stop the bulldozers, but I can plant a seed. I want you to be part of it, but..."

"I want in." I cut her off, scooting closer and letting go of her arm to wrap mine around her waist. "Living without you and the crew sucked. I was just existing, hiding out in a fake paradise that isn't meant for me. I want to live somewhere that gives a shit about me and my family, with people who give a shit."

Sasha's lips pull into a small smile. She wraps her arm around my waist, too. It's warm, heavy, and reassuring. "I gave that exact same speech to you a couple weeks ago and you called me crazy."

I manage a soft, self-deprecating laugh. "Guess I'd rather be crazy than empty."

"That so, Nevares?" Sasha arches an eyebrow. "You saying I'm the one who fills you?"

My next laugh is louder and more earnest. "You and only you, *Jefecita*. But seriously. Are you okay? I hate to bring *her* up, but...I left you, knowing you had serious abandonment issues already."

Sasha's brow furrows. "That's different. You—"

"Stop," I say, pulling away and propping myself up on my elbow. "Don't make excuses for me. I *left* you. It's okay for you to be mad. It's okay if you're hurt. I deserve it."

Sasha closes her eyes for a long moment, exhaling slowly and audibly. "Okay. Fine. I'm hurt and I'm pissed. Even now that you're back, I feel like you ripped my heart out and stomped on it. But you're apologizing left and right, and Megan never did. She made me feel like it was *my* fault when she screwed me over. That means something, doesn't it?"

I reach over with my free hand, caressing her cheek. "Yeah. It means something."

When Sasha leans in, I do the same. Her kiss is everything I've been missing. It's all the love, acceptance, and safety I'd sought in paradise, only to realize I'd run away from the real thing. I drink it in, drink *her* in, sweeping my tongue along her lower lip.

Soon, Sasha's twisting her shoulders so I can tug off her jacket, and I'm struggling to get out of my shirt. Her hands are large and gentle, just like I remember. The calluses rasp against my skin, but her palms are wonderfully warm. She strokes my sides before reaching around to unhook my bra, like she wants to take her time despite the urgency of her mouth on mine.

I slide down the straps and toss my bra off into the dimly lit bedroom, already focused on my next goal: Sasha's undershirt. The tight white material clings, showing the cut of her abdominal muscles. *Dios.* Maybe this is thirst brain talking—and I love Sasha for much more than her body—but why the fuck did I think it was a good idea to leave *this* behind?

Sasha stares at me as well, and the mixture of awe and uncertainty in her eyes is easy to read. Maybe that's because I feel the same. She looks too good to be true, lying beside me like some kind of god, tall, dark-skinned and broad-shouldered, her face shining with gentle hope.

"We don't have to do this," I whisper, even though the last thing I want to do is stop. I can't help but remember Cherry's comment back at base. *Sasha's got a big capacity to forgive the people she's getting some from.*

Sasha reaches out, stroking my cheek. "Have to? I want to. You came back, Elena. Not because you wanted something from me, but *for* me. For me, Val, and our crew."

I lean into Sasha's palm, kissing the inside of her wrist. When she says it, I believe it. I can let go of my guilt and just be. She sifts her fingers through my hair, guiding my mouth back to hers. I know what this is now. It's love, and I'm done running.

Even though I love the way Sasha's kissing me, I'm still not sure how this will go. Slow and sappy, wild and desperate, even angry fucking, if that's what Sasha needs. I'm up for anything as long as it's with her. Sasha seems to be thinking along similar lines. She draws back, still stroking my hair. The soft look on her face is like a fist squeezing my heart. "What do you want?"

"You."

"Yeah, but—"

"God, Sasha, I don't fucking care. Just *you.*"

A brilliant smile spreads across Sasha's face. She draws away, much to my disappointment, but it's to kick off her pants and boxers. Next comes the undershirt. I watch, entranced, as she crosses her arms and lifts from the bottom hem, flexing her abdominals as they're revealed inch by mouth watering inch. I have no idea what I did to deserve this, but I'm grateful.

Sasha's smile becomes a smirk when she notices me staring, so I decide to distract her right back. I raise my hips and push down my pants, making sure she gets a really good look at my tits at the same time. It pays off, because suddenly her hands are on them and we're kissing as she pulls me down and lowers me onto my back.

"Ven aquí, Jefecita. Dame más quicos."

She does, starting with my lips and moving lower. Her mouth is a hot, wet dream, sliding down my neck and along my shoulder. When she uses the edge of her teeth, my hips buck. I gasp, grinding against the firm plane of her stomach.

Sasha laughs against the crook of my neck. "You tryna fuck already? We're just getting started."

"Trying." I slide my arms around her, running my hands along the beautiful expanse of her back, marveling at its strength and softness. I tease a sensitive scar that wraps around her hip, and this time she's the one who rocks into me as her mouth fastens to the other side of my neck.

While Sasha's lips are busy, her hands find my thighs. She strokes with the backs of her knuckles, not actually gripping them until a frustrated whimper catches in my throat. Before, making a sound like that might've embarrassed me, but not anymore. We've always been electric together, but now we can be vulnerable too.

The sound of our shallow breathing and our racing heartbeats gets louder as Sasha's mouth explores my collarbone. Her hands cup my backside, and she guides me in a slow grind against her stomach, kissing down to my breasts. *Fuck.* The combination of her flexing stomach and her tongue against my nipples sends a powerful jolt straight through me.

Sasha moans, tugging with her teeth. "Already so wet," she murmurs, sucking my other nipple into the silky heat of her mouth.

"For you."

One of my hands stays on her back, raking lines of passion into her skin to encourage her while the other moves up to her head, holding her to me. She doesn't seem inclined to pull away, but I'm not taking any chances. I already know I can come just like this, rubbing against the slicked-up muscles of her abdomen while her mouth sucks my nipples to stiff, sore points and her tongue soothes them at the same time.

Sasha must sense I'm close, because she releases with a soft pop and drags her tongue up the center of my chest, nuzzling my neck. "Don't. Not yet."

All I manage is a whine of disappointment. My decision to take anything Sasha's willing to give is eclipsed by the sudden, insistent need for release. Unlike her, I've always been the type to come quickly and often. But she looks so hopeful that I swallow my pleas and try to hold back. For her. For a little while, anyway. I'm usually a brat in bed, and Sasha usually appreciates that, but this time she deserves to get whatever she wants from me without a fight. I kind of owe her that much.

Seemingly satisfied, Sasha returns her mouth to my breasts and resumes our rhythm. My swollen clit catches her stomach on every pass. Each slide is exquisite torture. I bite my lip and screw my eyes shut, trying not to focus on how good it feels. But that's *all* I can focus on. Sasha drives me absolutely crazy, and there's no resisting.

Soon I'm a panting, squirming mess. Since I've promised not to come, the energy and pressure in my body has nowhere to go. But Sasha's there on top of me, solid and reassuring. She lets go of my ass— a huge sacrifice, knowing her—and takes hold of my wrists, pinning them to the bed. I test her grip, but only once. It's iron, and I don't want to escape these particular shackles.

Sasha rewards me by kissing down my stomach, murmuring praise. "You're so good, Elena. You're being so good."

It's ridiculous how wet that makes me. How greedy. How desperate for contact. I try to keep rocking against Sasha's stomach, but she's on a mission. Though she pauses to kiss my navel and leave a few marks on my belly, she clearly has a destination in mind. I gasp when she releases my wrists and ducks beneath my knees, trailing kisses along my inner thighs. Her hot breath washes over me, and as I look down at her, I'm overcome with awe.

The first time we had sex, it was in a shower. I hated Sasha back then, even as I was drawn to her by a powerful force I didn't understand. Her eyes were deep black pools of lust, her skin as dark and smooth as the night sky, scattered with shining water droplets for stars. That memory pales in comparison to how Sasha looks now. This time, those stars are in her eyes, and they're shining directly on me.

I love everything about Sasha's face. Her full lips, especially when she smiles or kisses me. Her nose, broad and regal. The shape of her jaw, wide but angular. Her full brows and soft hairline. When we first met, I thought her face was dangerous. Now I know I'm right, because I'm not sure I can live without it.

"Elena…"

I lift my hand, grazing her cheek with my fingertips before pushing gently at the back of her neck. When I spread my thighs, she doesn't waste any time burying that beautiful, dangerous face right between them. Her tongue sweeps between my outer lips, slow but firm like she doesn't want to miss any part of me as she licks from my entrance to my clit.

Then she sucks, and I'm pretty sure I get a glimpse of heaven, because the lights on the ceiling get whiter and brighter as the pressure increases. "Sash—uhh?" Her name becomes a groan, then a questioning whine as she releases my clit, shifting lower to taste me again. Her tongue pushes inside, but when I try to establish a rhythm, clutching at her shallow strokes, she changes course again, returning to flat, broad licks.

Even in my half-delirious state, it doesn't take me long to figure out what she's doing. Whenever I try to get her to focus somewhere, *anywhere* so I can come, she breaks away and does something else. Not that it matters. I'm just barely hanging on, ready to come as soon as she says the word.

Sasha must sense my tension, because she draws back completely, staring up at me with those same starry eyes. "This isn't hurting you, right?"

Yes. "No." It does hurt. Delaying my peak has fed a throbbing fullness inside me, but it also feels amazing. I don't want her to stop.

Sasha gives me a crooked smile like she knows I'm not being truthful. She slides two fingers inside me, hooking into the heart of the ache with a practiced motion. "Come for me, baby. I'm not asking."

The burning stretch and the heat of her mouth sealing back around my clit send me flying. I twitch around her fingers, pouring everything I have and everything I am into her palm. Sasha doesn't ease up. She curls and sucks until her hand and my thighs are a slippery mess, and I'm trembling with temporary exhaustion.

That doesn't seem to faze her. She climbs back up my body, much faster than her descent, and takes my lips in a bruising kiss, fingers still inside me. The new angle puts extra pressure against my front wall when she flexes her forearm, but my cries of approval are muffled by her mouth. I taste myself on her tongue—slightly bitter, but in a good way.

She pulls a second peak from me almost right away. Two fingers become three, and I rake my nails down her back, clinging to her as she drives directly into my front wall. I tear my lips away from her just long enough to catch my breath and purr in her ear. "Sasha. Baby. You always fuck me *so good.*"

This isn't just fucking, just like last time wasn't fucking, but the praise makes Sasha stiffen above me. This time, it's her hips that buck. It's taken some practice, but I know how to exploit her weaknesses. I drape my leg around her waist and dig my heel in, wordlessly urging her to take me harder. Deeper.

She does, with such earnestness that I have to fight off another orgasm. Her fingers add thrust instead of just curling, and the stretch intensifies. Soft grunts spill from her mouth, hitting the side of my neck in hot bursts in time with each stroke. She's using her hips for leverage, which just isn't fair. I can only wrap my legs tighter and gasp her name.

"Sasha, *Sasha...*"

By the time my third release hits, I'm in a state of delirium. I go limp beneath her, feeling utterly satisfied, utterly safe. My vision blurs, and it takes me several moments to realize she's escaped the circle of my knees and pulled out of me. I whimper as the heavy, comforting warmth of her body lifts up, but then my sight clears, and I get a good look at what she's doing.

Apparently, making me come so many times in a row has gotten her desperately close. She kneels above me, thighs braced on either side of my hips, one hand flexing between her legs. The other holds onto the headboard like she'll fall without the extra support.

I'm not the least bit upset she's working to get herself off, but I do want to help. Badly. I summon my remaining strength and scoot down, shifting until I've got my face between her legs and her ass in both hands.

When I pull her down, she doesn't resist. Her breath catches, and she gives a full-body shudder as I suck her clit. I love the way it feels in my mouth, slippery and stiff, twitching with each pass of my tongue. Sasha grasps my hair, pulling me closer without a hint of hesitation. I absolutely love it when she gets like this. When she forgets she's a service top for a split second and gets utterly lost in the need to come. It's rare, and all the more precious for it.

I release her clit for just a second, giving her a few broad licks to sustain her instead. She moans unhappily, trying to use her grip on my hair to find my mouth again, but there's just enough space for me to say the things I know she needs to hear. *"Te amo, querida. No necesito a nadie más. Solamente tú."*

Sasha's hand tightens abruptly on my hair, and her body stiffens from head to toe. Her clit swells, pushing back into my mouth and pressing into the flat of my tongue, and she lets out a soft, strangled cry, spilling wetness onto my cheeks and chin.

Everything about her is so beautiful. The rhythmic tensing of her backside in my hands. The way her chest heaves and her stomach rolls as she rocks against my face, hungry for every bit of pleasure I can give her. How the tendons in her neck stand out as she throws her head back, too overwhelmed to keep staring down at me.

By the time Sasha's finished, she's glowing with sweat like she's just run a marathon, and breathing like it, too. She collapses, still shaking, and I welcome her weight on top of me. "Got you, babe," I whisper, kissing her tightly braided hair with glazed lips. "I'm here."

Once Sasha catches her breath, she offers a response that's more sigh than voice. "My lines."

I know what she means. She's usually the one to offer low, whispered reassurances while I'm still piecing myself back together after several world-shattering orgasms. But I appreciate the way she lets me reassure her all the more for its rarity. It means she really does want to forgive me. It means she's decided she still trusts me. I never want to break that trust again.

"How 'bout we both say it?"

She laughs, tugging my ear with her teeth. "Deal."

I hiss, raking my nails down her sides as revenge. She squirms at the ticklish sensation, but that causes our pelvises to grind together again and we both let out startled moans instead. That's a pleasant surprise, because Sasha rarely comes more than once, but now that I'm home—which is wherever Sasha happens to be—I'm more than ready to give her anything and everything she needs.

Chapter 13

PRESSURE SQUEEZES MY CHEST as I walk down a cheerfully painted hallway on Sprout's first floor. Sasha, Val, Kyra, and I are going to meet with the council. A detailed forest mural in shades of green makes the walk less foreboding, but I can't stop thinking about the fact that my fate will be decided in a matter of hours, maybe even minutes.

Sasha accompanies me on my left, matching my pace despite her long legs. Kyra sticks to my right. Though she carries a pistol on her hip—a big deal, I guess, after the fuss she made about Sprout not allowing weapons inside—she isn't wearing armor. Technically, she's acting as my guard. She arrived at the apartment to collect me earlier that morning.

Impulsively, I reach into my pants pocket. Val's databox is there, on and active. It's a comfort to touch some part of her, even if it's just tech. I can't explain it. Kind of like holding a friend's hand? She hasn't been granted access to Sprout's systems, but she has a wireless connection to my jack so she can see our surroundings and speak into my ear mods.

"Are you all right, Elena?" Val asks, as though sensing my apprehension. Actually, I'm sure she can. I appreciate that she didn't feel the need to point out my heart rate has increased thirty-five point three percent or whatever.

"Nervous."

"Understandable," Val says. *"However, you must remember that you are not alone."*

"Not alone on the chopping block," I mutter. "You're right there with me, and Ocho's hearing is this afternoon." I wish I could be there, but Kyra insisted on separate times. Maybe she thinks tying Ocho to me will lower her chances of forgiveness?

Kyra clears her throat. Obviously, she isn't thrilled about hearing only one side of a conversation.

"My apologies, Kyra," Val says through the databox's speakers, her voice slightly muffled in my pocket. *"Yesterday, you made it clear that you did not wish for me to connect with your jack or body*

modifications." I can't help but wonder what Val and Kyra talked about while I caught up on sleep. Whatever it was, I hope their conversation helped convince Kyra that Val isn't a threat, but Kyra's playing it close to the vest for now.

"Stick to those speakers," Kyra says. "That way it doesn't seem like you're whispering behind my back."

The conversation dies there, leaving me in unsettling silence. I glance between Kyra and Sasha. Sasha catches my eye and smiles, which helps a bit, but the quiet interspersed only by our own footsteps buzzes in my head until I have to say something. Anything.

"How many people are on the council?"

"Twenty-five," Kyra says, staring straight ahead. "Terms last a year and a half. A third swap out every six months."

"Not long," I say.

"We don't want anyone making a career out of it. People here think of it as public service. They do their time, then go back to their regular lives. Helps that we don't have elections. It's all random, although the council writes referendums for the general population to vote on."

"Not a bad system."

"Agreed," Val says.

"You think so?" Kyra asks, sounding pleased. "We get some unqualified idiots, but most of us agree that's the least worst outcome. An idiot can be managed or outvoted. Someone in it for themselves is harder to get rid of."

"Right." I lick my lips, falling back into silence. Maybe it's just me, but the air feels dry and hard to breathe. Or maybe I just feel trapped?

Sasha senses my distress. She puts a hand on my shoulder. "What do you think of Elena's family's chances, Kyra?" she asks.

Kyra manages a tight smile. Obviously, she and Sasha have already discussed this. It must be part of Sasha's plan to reassure me. "I don't see any reason to worry. The council is reasonable, and I've made it clear to them that your family's applications for citizenship have nothing to do with your...actions."

The way Kyra says 'actions' definitely carries the unspoken word 'stupid' in front of it, but her words give me hope anyway. "Thanks."

We arrive at our destination, silver double doors without any discernible jack port or keypad. Kyra cuts in front of us, stomping a complicated pattern on the ground. Hidden lights around the door flash white as it hisses open.

The room beyond isn't what I'm expecting. I'd imagined some kind of corps boardroom, with a long wooden table and plush chairs. Perhaps an extra big one at the head for the foreperson. There is a table, but it's a semi-circle, with a podium in front and twenty-five seats.

About the same number of people are milling around the room, which has two large, blank screens in front of and behind the podium. Several potted plants are scattered around for ambiance. Most of the council members are eating in standing clusters, holding plates. The group seems diverse, old and young, a mix of different genders and races.

When Kyra walks in, everyone stops chatting and turns to look at us. She nods in acknowledgment, and an androgynous looking person in black emerges from one of the groups. They're tall and pale, with several facial piercings and a blazing scarlet pompadour. Their narrow forearms are covered in intricate spiderweb tattoos. If I had to guess, they look twenty-five or so, a few years younger than me.

"Sasha, Elena...and, uh, Val. This is Chance," Kyra says. "They're our foreperson."

I try not to show my surprise. This is Sprout's current foreperson? Never seen a politician in a spiked dog collar before, but to each their own. It's not like I never had a punk phase when I was younger. I swallow, unsure what to say. Of course, that doesn't stop me. "Do you have, like, a title I'm supposed to use or...?"

Chance cracks a smile around their snake-bite lip piercings. "Just call me Chance. Sorry about the mess. We were on our lunch break." They look around with obvious curiosity. "So, where is the mysterious 'Val'?"

I pull out Val's databox. "I'm not sure how much Kyra told you, but her servers are in our apartment. The databox is just a portable linking device. She won't interfere with your intranet system."

"She has an avatar, too, if you'll allow her to connect to your screens," Sasha says. When Chance's brow furrows, she adds: "Or Val can use the databox to project herself. No big deal."

"Hello." The edges of Val's databox pulse purple with each syllable. *"I am pleased to meet you, Chance. May I ask the order of deliberations for today?"*

Despite being briefed in advance, Chance looks at the databox with raised eyebrows and wide eyes. I can't blame them. I was pretty freaked out the first time I talked to Val too. Once I figured out she was a fully-realized AI and not just another program.

To their credit, Chance recovers quickly. "Uh, sure. First, we'll discuss whether Elena will be allowed to remain in Sprout and what, if any, punishments, or restrictions she'll have if she stays. Then we'll talk about your, um, offer? Since that's a more complicated issue."

Great. If the foreperson sounds this unsure about Val, it'll be a hard sell for the rest of the council too.

I glance past Chance, observing the other members as they stack their plates onto a dolly. One of them wheels it to the corner of the room as the rest return to their seats, muttering amongst themselves. A few shoot dark, brooding stares in my direction. The hairs on the back of my neck prickle. I don't know how much Kyra told them about my misdeeds, but it must have been enough.

"Seems like a casual atmosphere," Sasha muses, deliberately ignoring the glares.

"It is," Chance says. "Most days are pretty boring, but the food's good, and it's only for a couple hours at a time." They yawn, covering their mouth. "Excuse me. Wish I could go back to working nights, though. I hate mornings."

Sasha nods. "I feel you. I didn't want to leave bed this morning, either."

That's a mood. It was exceptionally hard to abandon the warm bed I shared with Sasha the night before, with the sheets still smelling like sex and us, for a meeting that might result in my permanent banishment.

"I'd better get to it," Chance says. "Good luck." They head over to the podium. The wall screens light up, showing twenty-five faces: the rest of the councilors. "For voting," Kyra explains when she notices where I'm looking. "We also use it for images and data."

Great. Our fates will be displayed for the whole room to see.

"Attention, everyone." The room falls silent as Chance speaks, their voice filling the space. There must be a mic built into the podium. "As you know, the first item on our agenda is a serious security breach. Elena Nevares sought refuge in Sprout with her crew. Kyra brought them here and vouched for them, so I'll let her explain the situation."

Chance steps aside, allowing Kyra to take their place at the podium. I'm very aware of the fact that, aside from the two of them, Sasha and I are the only ones standing, waiting awkwardly a few feet behind. Sasha reaches over, taking my free hand in hers. I squeeze hard, slipping Val's databox back into my pocket with my other hand.

"Elena Nevares is a member of my niece's crew," Kyra says. Like Chance, her voice is amplified. "When my Corsairs rescued them from the Butterfly Lab, we brought them here with the usual precautions. Since they seemed eager to stay, we didn't assign guards. I thought security in the hangar would be enough. My niece's crewmates knew they could ask to leave Sprout with a proper escort, if they chose."

I try not to wince. Kyra's making my decisions sound pretty bad.

A buzzer sounds from one of the seats, and a face on the screen lights up. Kyra turns toward the noise. "Yes? Councilman Stanley."

Councilman Stanley is an older Black man with a ring of fuzzy grey hair around his balding head. "Why'd she break out when she could have asked for an escort?"

"I'm getting there," Kyra says. "Elena is the primary guardian for two minors, her brothers Mateo and Jacobo, ages eight and twelve. She left them in Barbados with their grandmother during the Lucky Seven's mission to the Butterfly Lab. She left to reunite with them."

"You didn't answer my question," Stanley grumbles. "Why didn't she ask for an escort? She some kind of corps spy? And what about that AI her crew has? When are we going to talk about that?"

Murmurs rise around the room. My heart pounds, but Kyra remains calm. "I don't believe Elena is a spy, but I can't definitively prove she isn't. You'll have the opportunity to question her. As for Val, you'll get to speak with her, too."

Stanley doesn't seem thrilled but keeps his grievances to himself. I curl my toes inside my boots. My legs are twitching like they want to carry me far away from here, but I promised I'd stop running. I have to face up to the consequences of my actions. I just hope those actions don't end up screwing Val and Ocho over.

Before Kyra can resume, another buzzer sounds. A new face lights up on the screen.

"Yes," Kyra says. "Councilwoman Ruiz?"

A plump, middle-aged woman with sleek black hair and light brown skin speaks up. "Why'd she come back, then?"

Kyra presses her lips together, seeming mildly annoyed by the interruptions. "Since you all have a lot of questions, why don't I just let Elena answer them?" She motions me up to the podium.

For a moment, my feet don't work. It's like the soles of my boots are glued to the floor. Sasha squeezes my hand again, then let's go, tapping my lower back. I stumble forward, becoming less awkward as I go.

When I reach the podium, Kyra steps aside. Standing behind it isn't fun because at five foot two, I'm not much taller than it is. However, it's short enough for me to see over—mostly. A sea of faces stare back at me, waiting. The nape of my neck breaks out in a cold sweat.

"Um, hi." The mic doesn't pick up my voice well, so I lean forward. "I'm Elena Nevares. First of all, I'm sorry. I shouldn't have left Sprout like I did. You're right, I should have asked for an escort, but I'd never tell anyone about this place, especially not PGS or AxysGen. As for why I ran, it had nothing to do with Val, the FRAI. I ran because I was scared. I thought Sprout was too good to last, and I had to get back to my brothers. I knew my crew would take it badly, so I thought it'd be easier to make a clean break.

"But when I got to Barbados, I started to miss it here. I was only in Sprout a week, but this place made an impression I couldn't forget. It got me thinking how much happier my brothers would be in a place like Sprout. A safe place, with plenty of food and a school with other kids, where they could learn lots of different jobs and skills. I realized I wanted to bring them here. The world out there is shit, you know? I want better for my brothers, so I came back and turned myself in to Kyra."

That's a pretty drastic oversimplification, but hopefully my sincerity will shine through. I scan the faces of the council members. A few seem sympathetic like they believe me. Others seem more suspicious, with narrowed eyes and wrinkles in their brows.

The buzzer goes off again. "Yes?" Kyra says, leaning in beside me to use the mic. "Councilman Stanley again."

The older, balding man doesn't seem moved by my story. "I still want to hear why you didn't just ask to leave. You weren't a prisoner."

There are murmurs of agreement from several other council members.

"I'd like to hear that, too," Chance says from their seat near the podium.

Kyra shifts back and folds her arms, watching me expectantly. I glance at Sasha, who gives me an encouraging look. I sigh. There's nothing for it but the truth. I'd rather look cowardly than traitorous. "Sasha's my girlfriend," I say into the mic. "I had to go back to my brothers. She wanted to stay here with her aunt. So I thought we were breaking up…"

To my surprise, there's a smattering of laughter. Chance hits their buzzer. "Wait. So you recorded and sampled Kyra's voice, played it for an unsuspecting guard, and stole one of Ginger's prototype motorcycles, all because you were too chickenshit to break up with your girlfriend?"

I give a helpless shrug. Apparently, the council was briefed on the specifics of my misdeeds after all with that laundry list. "Pretty much, yeah. I was too scared to properly break up. I knew if I saw her face again I'd lose my nerve, so I decided to get out right away."

"That's the stupidest thing I ever heard," an older white man grumbles, without hitting his buzzer.

To my surprise, Councilwoman Ruiz speaks up in my defense. "She's in her twenties. You never did anything stupid in your twenties because of a relationship, Wallace?"

"Not something that put an entire community at risk, Alejandra," Wallace protests. "Even if she isn't a spy and didn't tell anyone else about Sprout, what if the corps followed her here? What if they used the FRAI to do it? We know that crew of hers is wanted."

"So are the Corsairs," a young, redheaded white girl says. She can't be much older than eighteen. "There's always a risk we could be found."

Chance stands up, taking over the podium. "That's enough. If you want to talk, use your buzzers."

Wallace doesn't look happy, but he and the others settle down.

"All right," Chance says. "Any other questions?"

Councilwoman Ruiz hits her buzzer. "Do you really want to stay here permanently?" she asks in Spanish. I can tell from her accent that she's Mexican, like me.

"I do," I tell her. "I grew up in Mexico City. We never had enough food or a steady place to live, but I learned jacking. Soon, I was making enough credits to provide. For a long time, I thought the APS was the only way out for my brothers. I reasoned if they got an education and corps jobs, they'd be set.

"But Sprout showed me there's another way. A way that's worth the risk of being discovered by the corps. My family can have a better life here. Even if you decide I can't stay, I hope you'll let them go through the citizenship process. I've seen enough of the world to survive out there, but I want better for them."

There's a minute of silence as the room considers what I've said. I chew the inside of my cheek. I'm struck by the nerve wracking thought that this is probably the easy part. Convincing them I'm not some kind of spy, and genuinely want to rejoin Sprout, is bound to be easier than convincing them a FRAI has their best interests at heart.

No. Don't think about that. One problem at a time.

Another buzzer goes off.

"Councilwoman Cooper," Chance says.

"Can we give her restricted access to Sprout?" the redheaded girl asks. "Or, like, a probationary period?"

"That's up to us," Chance answers. "There's no guidelines for this. Everyone who's left Sprout in the past has gone about it the right way, so we're establishing new law here. And we've never had a security breach like this."

"And we never will again," Kyra adds. "I'm taking it upon myself to personally re-train everyone on the guard duty roster. If future communications come from any source other than the secure monitor in the booth, they are to be disregarded. No more prank phone calls."

My face burns. "I'm willing to accept restricted access or some kind of probation. That seems fair."

"Okay," Chance says. "I call for a vote on whether or not Elena Nevares can return to Sprout, with probationary guidelines to be determined."

"I second," says Ruiz.

"I third," says Cooper.

"Vote yes or no," Chance says. "We need a two-thirds majority either way, or deliberation will continue."

I feel dizzy again. *Is this really happening right now? It went by so fast.* But the wall screen is already lighting up as people cast their votes. One by one, their portraits turn green or red. As more lights switch on, a heady sense of relief washes over me. There are some red dots, but the screen is mostly green!

Chance grins as they lean into the mic to announce the results. "It looks like the vote to allow Elena Nevares back into Sprout passes, nineteen to six. That's more than a two-thirds majority. Congrats, Elena."

I stand there, stunned, as Sasha wraps me in a big hug. "This is good," she murmurs as she squeezes me.

"Excellent," Val agrees. *"In my estimation, this increases the likelihood of a favorable outcome for me and Ocho significantly."*

A smile breaks across my face and I feel lighter than I have all morning. Now, we just have to convince them Val isn't a threat.

Chapter 14

"NEXT ON THE AGENDA," Chance says. "We need to discuss a…uh." They pause to clear their throat, adjusting their spiked dog collar. "An application for residency? As you've been informed, this situation is complicated—"

"*Residency?* You mean the damned AI?" Wallace interrupts, not even bothering to use his mic. His jowl-heavy face resembles an overripe tomato. "That's really how you listed it on the agenda?"

My stomach sinks. Not a great start.

Chance sighs. "You'll get the opportunity to share your opinions, Wallace. Don't interrupt." They turn to me, glancing toward my pocket with visible uncertainty. "You can connect to the wall screen, Val, and…introduce yourself."

The image on-screen changes as Val's face appears, larger than life. Her eyebrows are raised and gentle, her smile nonthreatening. I'm sure the warm, kind expression is a deliberate choice. Her eyes seem bigger and brighter than normal, too. Maybe to make her seem trustworthy?

"Hello. My name is Val. I am a member of Sasha's crew, the Lucky Seven. I am also a fully-realized artificial intelligence."

There's a soft gasp or two but mostly blank, apprehensive stares. Apparently, being addressed directly by a FRAI with a human-looking face is enough to cause concern amongst the councilors, despite the briefing Kyra gave yesterday.

"I was not designed by a corporation," Val continues. "And I have never served corporate interests. I am an individual, like all of you. As an individual, I wish to help Kyra protect Sprout."

A buzzer goes off before Chance can ask for questions. "Why should we trust anything you tell us?" an elderly woman snaps without waiting to be called on. "You could hack our intranet system and do God knows what if you had a mind to. Turn off our air filters, shut down our power—"

"I would never do anything to harm you," Val insists. "I value human life as much as I value my own existence. Therefore, I value this city and everything it provides its residents. I have never accessed Sprout's servers, but I have observed your home through my crewmates' body modifications..."

"So you spied on us," Wallace declares, brandishing his fat finger again.

"It was not my intention to spy," Val says, with a note of apology. "Kyra brought us here directly from Axys Generations' Butterfly Lab. We had no idea who Kyra was or whether she might be an enemy, so I did not reveal myself. However, once my crewmates and I arrived in Sprout, what I observed gave me hope. Against all odds, you have made a safe, supportive, self-sustaining community. I wish to join you in defending and improving it."

I glance nervously around the room. Some faces are softening, but there are still plenty of mistrustful looks. It's not enough. *Come on, Nevares. No one knows how scary FRAIs can be better than you.*

I step forward, holding out my hands. "Look, I get it. Val isn't human. I was terrified when we first met for all the same reasons you are. But what I didn't see until after I left Sprout, Val realized right from the start. This place is amazing. It deserves to be nurtured and protected. That's what she wants to do, which makes her a lot more like all of you than you think." I look up at the screen. "Val, what's your goal in life? Your purpose?"

"To enrich my existence through mutually beneficial and supportive relationships with humans," Val answers without hesitation.

"In other words?"

"Friendship," Val says, staring directly at me. "My purpose is friendship. Sprout gives my friends hope, and so I wish to defend it. I would die for my friends. Since they are willing to risk their lives for Sprout and everything it stands for, so will I."

A few more faces relax. Val's getting to them, but I fear it won't be enough. I can already see Wallace and the old lady reaching for their buzzers again.

The doors to the conference room burst open, cutting our interrogation short. A blue-green blur streaks through, and LeRoy comes to a screeching halt in front of Kyra. "We're under attack," he says, wide eyed and breathless. "A bunch of PGS mechs are in the tunnels above the hangar!"

The room explodes into chaos. Several council members leap out of their seats, shouting to be heard over the growing din. A few bang their buzzers, while others fire questions at LeRoy.

"What kind of mechs?"

"How many are up there?"

I stare at LeRoy in shock. Sprout is under attack? How did they find us? Was it my fault? I can't think of any other explanation. The fact that some rogue jacker and two corps are after me is too big a coincidence to ignore.

Kyra's voice is soft but sharp as she focuses on LeRoy. Her only outward sign of tension is the way her hands clench at her sides. "Who's in the booth?"

"Just a pair of volunteers." LeRoy seems relieved to be answering directly to his handler instead of the entire council. "Jones and Flygirl are headed there now. I ran down to warn you."

"What about Ginger?" Kyra asks.

LeRoy shakes his head. "No sign of her anywhere."

Sasha steps toward Kyra and LeRoy with squared shoulders. "Let us help."

"Agreed," Val says. *"I wish to help as well."*

Sasha hears Val's statement. "I know this timing is fucked," she says to Kyra. "But Val might be your only chance if your intranet system comes under attack."

Kyra's brow furrows. "Convincing the council could get ugly."

"Maybe," Sasha says. "But a cyberattack would be a lot uglier—"

At that very moment, the lights above us flicker. The wallscreens go black. Small noises I didn't even notice vanish, leaving the room in silence for a few perilous seconds. Someone screams—then Val's face reappears, her expression visibly worried.

"An outside force is attempting to access Sprout's intranet system. I am doing what I can to defend your servers. I apologize for not asking permission, but I weighed the risk of invading everyone's privacy against the risk of life support system shutdowns."

"Life support systems?!"

"You're trying to kill us!"

"No, Wallace. The AI said it's trying to save us—"

More council members rise from their chairs, shouting over each other to be heard. I remain frozen, unable to move or speak. All I can hear is that awful voice pounding in the back of my head. *My fault. My fault. My fault!*

"Shut up!" Chance shouts into the mic.

The din dies down, though not completely. One of the council members points accusingly at me. "This is your fault," he barks. It's

Wallace, the white guy who called me stupid earlier. "You and your crew and your spyware led them straight here!"

Something snaps in my brain, and my voice comes back with a vengeance. I might be at fault, but I bet this asshole doesn't know the first thing about combat, on the extranet or off it. "Val had nothing to do with this! Maybe someone followed us here, but if they did, punish me later. My crew has the perfect skillset to defend you, so let us help stop these corps fucks from getting in!"

"Calm down, Elena," Kyra says, shooting me a warning look. "We have protocols in place for this. Chance?" She turns toward the podium, and the rest of the room turns with her.

"I call for an emergency vote," Chance says. "Sprout is Kyra's brainchild. We wouldn't be here without her. I vote to give her and the Corsairs full executive power for twenty-four hours so they can keep us safe."

"Seconded."

"Thirded."

"No way," Wallace grunts. "Not if she's workin' with that damned AI. This could be a trick."

Kyra steps up to the podium, standing beside Chance. "Val, show us what's happening in the hangar."

Val splits the screen in half, bringing up what appears to be a security feed beside her face. I tense up, reaching for a pistol I don't have. A dozen mechs stomp across the hangar between parked vehicles, headed in the direction of the elevator. They're four feet tall, standing on jointed tripod legs, with bullet-shaped bodies bearing turrets. PGS design, I recognize instantly. As I watch, more mechs descend from the tunnel above, accompanied by a half-dozen privsec grunts in protective navy bodysuits.

"This is what we're dealing with," Kyra says to the stunned council members. "We have automated defenses in place, but we're up against at least one hostile corporate entity, so we need every advantage we can get. We have an exceptionally skilled crew and a fully realized artificial intelligence volunteering to help us. Will we accept or not? Because if you give me executive powers, I'm taking their offer."

The following silence sounds like a roar, until the balding Black man, Stanley, hits his buzzer. "You trust this AI?" he asks Kyra.

"I trust my niece," Kyra says. "She trusts Val. And we're out of time and options."

"I trust Val with my life," Sasha declares. "She's the reason I'm still alive." That might be a misleading statement, but it has a powerful impact. A few more stubborn faces waver from anger to fear and resignation.

"Me too," I say, pleading. "Please, let us help."

Chance places both hands on the podium, leaning forward. "All in favor of giving Kyra executive power for twenty-four hours so she, the Corsairs, the Lucky Seven, and Val can defend us?"

As votes pour in, the screen behind the table shows a pretty even mix of green and red. The council members crane their necks, looking over their shoulders to see how their peers voted. On the screen behind the podium, footage of the hangar continues to play beside Val's frightened face.

I count the votes. There are more green faces than red, but not by much. A few more votes trickle in. *Fourteen votes for yes...fifteen...Chingarme.* It isn't enough. We need one more vote to get sixteen.

With dismay, I realize there's only one unlit face left on the screen. It's Wallace. Fucking Wallace. We're doomed.

To my complete shock, he hits his buzzer. His face lights up, but it isn't red. It's green.

"Yes!" I cheer, throwing my arms around Sasha. She hugs me back tight, the leather of her jacket sticking to my cheek. Maybe the hangar footage convinced him, or maybe it was something one of us said. It doesn't matter. Now, together, we have a fighting chance.

Kyra leans past Chance to speak into the mic. "I accept. Now, everyone get to the bunkers. A council just like yours came up with the protocol for this situation, so follow it to the letter."

Chance puts a hand on Kyra's shoulder. "We will. Now, go get 'em."

Chapter 15

THE RIDE TO THE top floor is grueling. It feels like it takes forever. LeRoy bounces his leg at hyper speed, rattling the elevator floor. No one speaks until we arrive, rushing out the door and down the hall toward the security booth. The doors open without the benefit of any stamping, and quite the crowd is waiting for us inside.

Cherry, Rami, Doc, Rock, and Ocho are there. Ocho in particular seems glad to see me. She's the only one who manages a smile. With our crew is Flygirl, as well as Jones, who's seated in one of two chairs before the wall of security feeds. He's already got a silver cable plugged in behind his ear, presumably trying to protect Sprout's intranet system.

Everyone squishes together to make space, but we're packed in like sardines. There's barely room to breathe.

"What's the situation?" Kyra asks Jones, checking the largest feed in the middle of the wall. It doesn't look good from where I'm standing. There are at least ten more mechs than last time. They've lined up in front of the elevator while five privsec grunts in protective suits place what look like explosive charges.

A small window showing Jones' face pops up in the corner of the monitor. His avatar's hair is longer than in reality, with a neon blue streak in the middle. "No sign of whoever tried to hack our systems, but I've got spyders searching. On the physical front, I'm about to deploy lye solution."

Cherry whistles. "You sure? Lye can be nasty."

"Is it that dangerous?" Rami asks. "Lye's in soap and drain cleaner, right? Surely if you don't ingest it…"

I wince. Unfortunately, over the course of my career as a freelancer, I've heard more stories about bodies being dissolved in lye than anyone should. Jento, the fixer I took jobs from back in the day, jokingly referred to it as 'making soup.'

"It's bad," Cherry says. "What do you think dissolves all the bio-matter in the drain? If you liquify and superheat it...breathing that shit will kill you."

Kyra's eyes remain locked onto the feed. "Do it," she orders. "We have segmented air vents for this exact scenario."

"Okay..." Jones' voice remains hesitant, but he nods his head.

On the screen, yellowish liquid rains down on the mechs and soldiers. At first, nothing happens. Then, the screams start. The privsec grunts throw themselves to the ground, clutching their faces and throats. Their suits include helmets, but whatever filtration systems they've got aren't enough. They scream and flail, completely forgetting about their attack on the elevator.

"No!" Ocho shouts, in a voice that pierces the small room. She slams her hand on the interface, causing it to flash red as though she's inputted an invalid command. "Stop! You're killing them!"

Kyra whirls, grabbing Ocho's wrists and yanking her hands away. "They're coming down here to kill us," she snaps, without letting go. "Is that what you want?"

Ocho snatches her hands from Kyra's grip, recoiling. "You can't just kill them," she insists, her brown eyes shining with tears.

"At least lower the volume," Rami says, averting their eyes. Their lips are pressed together in a way that makes them look like they might be sick.

"Sorry." Flygirl mutes the volume, but it's too late. Even delivered through speakers, those shrieks of pain linger in my ears. I can already tell they'll feature in my nightmares for quite a while.

Sasha squeezes past Kyra to wrap an arm around Ocho. "I'm sorry," she says in her most soothing tone. "Look at me, okay? Just look at me."

Ocho blinks rapidly, refusing to look at Sasha. She swipes angrily at her eyes with her sleeve, her shoulders trembling beneath Sasha's arm. "We can't just kill them," she repeats in a softer voice.

"Kyra's right," Cherry says, putting a hand on Ocho's arm. "They're coming down here to kill us."

"Yeah," Doc agrees, though her voice is a bit shaky, too. Her skin is even paler than usual. "Fuck those guys."

"Anyone with sensitive stomachs shouldn't watch this next part, either," Jones says sadly. "Kyra, a few of 'em are hiding under the mechs. They're trying to bust into the elevator shaft." Despite his warning, I watch the screen. A few brave souls have indeed taken shelter under the bellies of the mechs, which are mostly unaffected by the heated lye solution.

"Use the CO2 laser," Kyra says without any emotion on her face.

The area in front of the elevator glows an eerie purple. Suddenly, the mechs slide apart, sliced like pieces of an apple.

"Ginger calls it her Giant Purple People-Cutter," LeRoy says with grim satisfaction.

Ginger. Were these defensive measures her idea? If so, I see why Rami is so unsettled by her. They're brutal.

"Has there been any sign of Ginger yet?" Kyra asks Flygirl.

Flygirl shakes her head. "We would've told you first thing."

Kyra's jaw bunches. "That's what I was afraid of."

"I believe I have located Ginger," Val says via the security system's speakers.

Kyra doesn't hesitate. "Show me."

Val increases the size of a different security feed, dragging it to the middle of the wall screen. Ginger is walking down a hallway on what looks like Sprout's ground floor, but it isn't the sight of her that makes me do a double take. It's the woman standing next to her, wearing basic black body armor. Her blonde hair is hidden inside her helmet, but I recognize the shape of her face.

Doc's the one who blurts it out first. "Megan?!"

She's right. The person accompanying Ginger looks exactly like Megan. Her lean frame, her blue eyes. It's all hauntingly familiar. Val has enhanced the footage to a point where she's unmistakable.

My mind whirls. This makes no sense. I knew some rogue jacker had copied Megan's avatar to fuck with us, but I was so sure it was a trick. The person I encountered in Barbados definitely didn't talk or act like Megan, even though they looked the same online. Could Megan's brain really have survived a Puls.wav? If so, why is she wandering around downstairs instead of jacked in somewhere, trying to take down Sprout's intranet system?

"Can't be her," Sasha says in a tight voice that allows no room for argument. "We killed her for real last time."

"I am ninety-eight-point-two percent certain that we are observing Megan's body," Val informs us. *"However, her movement patterns are highly unusual."*

That's a bizarre observation, but there's no time to focus on it. I turn to Kyra. "That bitch is bad news. She's the awful ex Sasha told you about, and she's tried to kill our crew more than once. She works with corps, too. If Ginger's with her, you have to stop them."

"Ginger would never work with someone like that," LeRoy insists, glaring at me.

"Maybe Megan took Ginger hostage?" Flygirl suggests.

"Yeah, right," Rami mutters.

"Seriously?" Cherry says, placing her hands on her hips. "We're fighting about this *right now?*"

"Shut up," Kyra barks. "We're going down there. Elena, stay with Jones. I need jackers in the booth. Monitor our progress."

Rock, who's remained silent as usual, shakes his head. He gestures at the pistol on Kyra's hip—the only weapon in the room, as far as I can tell.

"He's right," Doc says. "We can't fight if none of us are armed."

"I can fix that." Flygirl types something on the haptic interface. A hissing noise fills the room. I stare in surprise as the entire rear wall retracts into the ceiling, revealing another wall behind it. This one is covered in weapons, from simple pistols to heavy duty assault rifles. It even has protective vests. They aren't full armor, but definitely better than nothing.

"Perfect," Sasha says. She selects one of the bigger assault rifles, inserting a fresh mag and racking the slide.

Kyra chooses a similar rifle from the wall. "Everyone grab a weapon and go."

It's a quick, silent affair as everyone except Jones and I takes a weapon and vest, hurrying out of the room and into the hallway. Their expressions are tight and grim like they're about to stare down death. I want to go with them, but as much as I hate to admit it, Kyra's decision to leave me with Jones is a smart one. With our jacking abilities, we're the two best choices to protect Sprout's intranet system alongside Val.

Ocho is the last one out the door. Before she leaves, I grab her elbow. "Maybe you should stay with us." She still looks terrified after witnessing the devastation caused by the lye sprinklers and CO_2 laser. I know from personal experience that entering combat while you're traumatized is a terrible idea.

"Yeah," Sasha says from a few paces ahead. "Stay here, Ocho."

Ocho shakes her head. "No. I'm going with you, Sasha." She clutches the rifle she's chosen close to her chest. "I want to protect Sprout, like you."

Sasha looks uncertainly at me.

I shrug. There isn't time to argue. "Watch her back, *Jefecita.*"

Sasha offers a stiff nod. Then, with one last look, she and Ocho leave, the doors hissing shut behind them. My stomach sinks as I slump into Flygirl's vacant chair, feeling as though I've made a huge mistake. Maybe I should have fought harder to make Ocho stay in the booth...

"Elena," Val says, her voice raised with urgency, *"the outside source has accessed Sprout's intranet s-sy-syste—"* Her image cuts out entirely. The wall monitor flickers, showing flashes of various security feeds before going completely black.

"Val? Talk to me."

No answer.

I glance over to where Jones has slumped in his chair. His eyes are open, but he isn't moving. "Jones? Jones, wake up!" I shake his shoulder, but he doesn't react. He remains limp, although when I touch his neck, I feel a steady pulse. Not dead yet, then. I consider disconnecting him, but in his current state a hard cut could damage his brain. Safer to leave him be and go in after him.

I grab the nearest jacking cable. If Jones is alive, at least part of Sprout's intranet system must be running. But connecting to a system under attack could get me killed as soon as I jack in. "Val?" I ask one last time, pleading for a response. "Val, are you okay? Please answer me!"

"V.41 is unavailable," another voice says through the speakers, its cadence cold and familiar. The center image solidifies into a face, the same face we saw on the monitors with Ginger, only without the helmet. Long blonde hair, sharp features, freckles, and blue eyes. It's Megan, but something about her is...off. Inhuman.

A chill races down my spine. I remember what Val said about Megan's movements being strange on the security feed. I remember the cold, dispassionate way the jacker in Barbados spoke to me. Like it had no emotions at all, not even negative ones. And yet, it knew an incredible amount of secret information about me and my crew, things no one but Megan would have known.

A horrifying realization dawns. Who else knows everything Megan did? Who would be able to seamlessly copy her avatar and potentially steal her body? Who would be able to download a FRAI-killing virus to my jack without being detected? And who would want Val dead?

Megan never survived the Puls.wav during our battle in Mexico City, but someone else did.

"Dragon. You're controlling Megan's body!"

"I will make this simple for you, Elena," Dragon's avatar says. *"The attack launched by Paragon Solutions was merely a diversion. I have used my creator's body and your former ally Ginger to place explosives along the escape tunnel attached to Sprout's bunkers. Confirm the presence of, and grant me access to, V.41's server towers, or I will activate these explosives. You, your crewmates, and Sprout will cease to exist."*

Chapter 16

I STARE, FROZEN, AT Megan—no, Dragon's face. There's so much to process I don't know where to begin. Val has disappeared. Dragon is in Sprout's intranet system. Apparently, Sprout has at least one escape tunnel I didn't know about, which is rigged to blow. Equally horrifying to me, Dragon has taken over Megan's physical body somehow.

Even though Doc removed my previous jack, my skin crawls. Dragon was inside my fucking head a day ago when they broadcasted the virus that destroyed Val's Siberian servers. Were they planning to hijack my body, too? Could they still? I slap my hand behind my ear as though I've been burned there. What can I do? Tear it out?

No. Stupid! This is a new jack…

But I re-downloaded some of my old custom programs from the cloud…what if Dragon corrupted the save files somehow? What if some malicious code hitched a ride? What if Dragon's in my brain right now?

I snap back to reality. My lungs scream with icy needles and I realize I haven't been breathing. Fuck. Okay. Inhale, exhale. It's not like I can rip my new jack out by hand. It's wired directly into my brain. My only choice is to proceed as if Dragon hasn't hacked me. There are plenty of other emergencies to deal with.

"Show me Sasha and the others," I say to Dragon, who's still staring at me with cold blue eyes. "I won't say anything until I see them alive."

Dragon's expression remains impassive. *"You are not in a position to negotiate. I will give you thirty seconds to confirm the presence of V.41's servers in this location."* A timer appears on screen, counting down from thirty.

I pretend my own face is stone, struggling not to betray any emotion at all. "You aren't sure if Val's servers are here or if we hid them somewhere else. You can't risk blowing us up without knowing, and we're the only ones who know. You *need* us. Show me Sasha and the others. Then we'll talk."

A small furrow appears in Dragon's brow. If I didn't know better, I'd think they were irritated. Without a word, Dragon brings up a second window, displaying a security feed. It's 'Megan' and Ginger, standing before an elevator on one of Sprout's lower floors. As I watch, the doors open, revealing Sasha, Kyra, and their respective crews.

Weapons are drawn on both sides. Ginger brandishes something small in her raised hand that I pray to fuck isn't a detonator, but I don't have much hope. Audio from the feed crackles through the security booth's speakers.

"—could you do this?!" Leroy shouts.

Ginger scoffs. "All these years, mission after mission, risking my life to fund Kyra's pet project. Every credit we get goes right into Sprout's gullet."

"That's what this is about?" Kyra's rifle is aimed right at Ginger's chest. "You sold us out because your cut wasn't big enough? We have everything we could ever need here."

Ginger glares at Kyra. "You call some food and a tiny underground apartment meeting my needs? Andrews can shell out enough credits to build me the lab of my dreams without even making a dent in his accounts. Fuck, he could build me a lab in every country in the wor—"

The screen glitches out, jumping with colorful lines of pixelated static. After a moment, the security feed resumes, but Dragon's face has disappeared. I do a double take. What's going on?

"—thought we were a team." On-screen, Flygirl lowers her pistol, reaching out an imploring hand toward Ginger. "Don't do this."

"Yeah, we were a team," Ginger says, "but I signed on for money, not morals."

"Wow," Cherry drawls in an absolutely disgusted voice. "You might just be the biggest piece of shit I've ever met. I take back everything good I ever said about you."

Ginger ignores Cherry, fixing her gaze on Rami, who's standing near the back of the group. Shit, I wish they had their light-bending belt on. Maybe then they could have gone invisible and snuck up on Ginger and Dragon from behind.

"You know exactly what I'm talking about," Ginger says to Rami. "How could you leave it all behind? You had everything. The entire world at your—"

"Shut up," Rami snarls. "Just shut up!" They're trembling, the angriest I've ever seen.

Through it all, Dragon has remained silent. Though she carries a pistol, which is aimed at Sasha, she barely moves. That's why it's a surprise when she speaks. "This argument is a waste of time. Sasha, confirm the location of V.41's servers and we will not detonate the explosives."

Sasha doesn't say a word. Her grip remains tight on her rifle, her jaw bunched and her eyes glistening.

"Yeah, right," Doc says. "If we say they're here, or tell you where we've hidden them, you'll blow us all up."

Ginger whirls on Megan. "What? We came here to get the FRAI's servers for Andrews. He'll pay—"

Megan meets Ginger with an icy stare. "That agreement is no longer relevant."

"Then we'll sell it to a fence I know. We can't just blow up something that valuable—"

Confirmation that Ginger might not be willing to press the detonator after all is apparently all LeRoy needs. In a blue-green flash he's on her, his weapon spinning across the floor as he throws it aside and tackles her to the ground, apparently unwilling to shoot his crewmate. They hit the floor, wrestling for the detonator.

I watch, paralyzed, with my heart in my throat. It nearly explodes out of me when Ginger gets the upper hand, straddling LeRoy's skinny frame and reclaiming the detonator.

A muzzle flashes. Ginger goes limp on top of LeRoy, collapsing as bright red blood seeps through her clothes and onto the floor beneath them both. Ocho, who fired the shot, lets out a heartbroken wail. She falls to her knees, staring off into the distance with visible numbness.

The feed cuts off before I can witness what happens to the others. Suddenly, it's Val's face on the wall. My horror explodes into a burst of joy. That explains the disrupted connection, and why the feed went on for so long uninterrupted. Val was online the whole time, fighting Dragon in the background to regain control of the security booth. It looks like she's succeeded.

"Val? You're okay!" I cry.

"Elena." Val stares at me with wide, terrified brown eyes, framed by...some kind of jungle in the background? Giant, segmented fern leaves drape behind her head. "I have fended off Dragon and reconnected to Sprout's intranet system, but they are still—" A roar rattles through the speakers, and Val casts a frightened glance over her shoulder. "Please help!"

I grab the nearest jacking cable, pulling it toward my ear.

network: unkn spt.intr 39099 . 94578

connection established
welcome: user escudoespiga

I emerge on the edge of a prehistoric forest of conifers. The segmented leaves of the smaller ferns feel real to my touch, and sweltering heat presses in on all sides. I take stock of our surroundings. Beyond the forest is a grassy plain, with long-necked brachiosaurs ambling in the distance.

"Elena? Is that you?"

I turn to see Jones jogging toward me. His avatar looks similar to his real life appearance, although he's definitely a few inches taller and broader in the shoulders in addition to the long, flowing hair. More noticeably, he carries an oversized golden hammer on one shoulder.

"Jones! You okay?"

Jones cranes his neck, peering around. "Yeah, but this isn't what our system usually looks like."

"I know why," I explain. "It's a more detailed version of the ambient settings on my little brother's jack. Dragon's trying to spook me. Maybe it wants to throw us off by showing how much control it already has over Sprout's intranet system?"

Jones looks horrified. "Dragon's self-aware enough to do something like that?"

I doubt Dragon takes the same sadistic pleasure in manipulating people that Megan did, but apparently they've learned a trick or two from their creator. They probably think it'll throw me off my game—and I hate to admit it, but they're right. My stomach is already churning.

I summon my shield, clutching the grip for extra strength and courage. Beside me, Jones brandishes his hammer. The head crackles with blue lightning, like something a Norse god would carry. I'm impressed through my nervousness. "Badass."

"Thanks," Jones says. "Hey, if Dragon's trying to mess with your mind, it means they consider you a threat. That's good, right?"

I give him a shaky grin. "Good point."

"Elena!" Val's cry comes from far away, an amplified echo that rings throughout the forest.

I pull up my program bar and select the silver spyder icon. A small, friendly looking arachnid appears, leaping into my outstretched hand and blinking up at me with wide cartoon eyes. "Find Val," I say, tossing it into the air.

Reaching the height of its leap, the spyder shimmers and splits into several copies of itself. Each copy lands on the ground and scurries off in a different direction, moving faster than my eyes can follow and leaving trails of silver thread in their wake. After a moment, one of the threads quivers and pulls taut. I pick it up, and once Jones takes hold, I tug.

The world blurs, racing by in streaks of green and brown as the thread drags us along. We come to a screeching stop in an entirely new place: the rocky black foot of a volcano. Its peak glows an ominous red, bubbling and smoking. I cough as the charred, acrid taste of ash hits the back of my throat.

"Look!" Jones gestures. A short way up the mountain, partially obscured by clouds of ash, two titans are locked in combat.

One is a giant purple triceratops, twice as tall as me and six times as long. Thin, hairlike bristles rise along its spine, and three wicked horns jut from its knobby crest. The frill alone is wider than my spread arms. I know immediately that it's Val. Purple is her favorite color.

And the other...

"Holy shit," I gasp. Looming over Val, jaws gaping wide, is the king of lizards itself, Tyrannosaurus rex. It's twice Val's height, and longer from snout to tail. Blood-red feathers that look more like spines cover its body, with a fluffy white chest that might be cute on a dog-sized version. But it isn't cute. Dragon looks like they could swallow me in one gulp and bite a big chunk out of Val at the same time.

Val ducks, jerking her horns upward to gore Dragon's stomach. Dragon dodges, closing their jaws on Val's vulnerable back. Val bellows in pain. Red lines of code stream down her heaving sides as she thrashes for freedom. There's nothing for it. I raise my shield and charge, speeding up the mountain toward them.

My shield collides with Dragon's side, but the spikes barely scratch their thick hide. I grunt from the shock of impact, struggling to keep my balance on the uneven rocks underfoot.

Dragon stomps, shaking the ground beneath me. I stumble, falling backward. Above, the volcano rumbles as though enraged on Dragon's behalf. But my attack has given Val an opening. She shakes off Dragon's jaws with a powerful jolt, planting her back legs and swinging her horns. She pierces Dragon's stomach and they howl, staggering as red code leaks from their underbelly.

To my amazement, Dragon shakes off the injury like it's nothing. Their wounds close before my eyes, and the flow of code stops.

"What the fuck?!"

I regret shouting, because Dragon rounds on me, roaring with such force that the blast of hot breath threatens to knock me over again as I scramble to my feet. Their mouth glows red, and my blood freezes over. A Puls.wav! If it hits, my brain is soup.

Trembling with fear and adrenaline, I throw up my shield. It grows several times larger, forming a spiky, protective bubble around me. The Puls.wav hits, pushing me backward along the rocks, but doesn't pierce my defenses.

There's no time to be relieved. Dragon's jaws clamp down on the bubble, their teeth pulsing with red light. Cracks splinter along my shield's surface. I clench my jaw, trying frantically to think of some way out of this while also being astonished at Dragon's raw power. Shields are my thing, and those teeth are threatening to crunch through mine like tinfoil.

"Elena, watch out," Jones yells. A beam of fiery blue ice blasts from somewhere below, connecting with Dragon's side. Dragon reels, momentarily unbalanced. That's all the time I need to roll away and clamber upright.

Dragon recovers quickly. They lunge toward me, but suddenly Val is there, a giant purple wall. She bugles her own challenge, meeting Dragon's teeth with her horns. "Elena," she grunts, rolling her neck with surprising fluidity to shake off Dragon's jaws. "The volcano!"

A loud crack forces me to tear my eyes away from the fight. Ominous black clouds have gathered in the sky behind the volcano's glowing peak, illuminated by yellow forks of lightning.

I understand Val's warning. "The volcano," I call to Jones, gesturing upward. "It's the detonation program. Go stop it!"

Jones zips up to where I'm standing, panting with exertion. His glowing hammer is slung across his shoulder. "What about you and Val?"

"We'll be fine. Just go!"

Jones breaks into a sprint, scaling the side of the mountain at super speed. Dragon tears away from Val, stomping after Jones with a hissing growl.

Val thunders over to me, her heavy steps shaking the ground beneath us. "Climb on." Her avatar transforms, the protective frill shrinking as her front legs extend sideways into—wings! Giant, leathery wings that remind me of a bat.

Before me stands a creature the size of a small plane. Bristly brown feathers surround Val's long, snake-like neck, which ends in a crimson crested head and sharply pointed beak. Quetzalcoatlus. *I only know the species name because of Jacobo's and Mateo's shared childhood obsession with dinosaurs. Val has transformed into the largest flying creature that's ever lived.*

I clamber behind Val's neck, holding on for dear life. She pushes off from the ground, and my stomach follows a second behind. Bitter, smoke-filled wind blasts my face, blowing my hair back as tears stream from my eyes.

Val swoops down, and the side of the volcano hurtles toward us at an alarming rate. I cry out, but the noise is lost. Somewhere in my blurred field of vision, smudged by tears and choking clouds of ash, I see Dragon's hulking form charging after Jones. The volcano's steep surface has forced him to slow down, allowing Dragon to gain ground. Their mouth is aflame, brimming with the red light of another Puls.wav.

I aim my shield, firing a barrage of glowing white spikes. They pierce Dragon's feathery hide, but the wounds barely even bleed, healing almost instantly.

Dragon whirls, gnashing their teeth. The Puls.wav *flashes through the sky, streaking straight toward us, but Val veers left, dodging just in time. Roaring, Dragon abandons their pursuit of Jones, shimmering as their avatar transforms. Their blocky head shrinks, and their neck lengthens as their tiny arms widen into wings.*

Soon, Dragon is an exact copy of Val. They take off, speeding toward us like a missile. Val dodges again, catching an updraft with a tilt of her wings. Dragon follows, beak first. Before they reach us, a loud boom from the volcano causes the air around us to ripple. Hot sparks rain down on me, burning through my avatar's clothes and boring into my skin.

The pain is such a shock that it takes me several seconds to raise my shield. More burning ash falls, exploding on impact with my shield in bursts of white and red. The larger hits send shockwaves through my shaking arm. "Val, help!"

While Val dodges the flaming cinders, Dragon makes their move. The shower passes through their avatar without causing any injury at all. Chingarme! *It's their program, of course it wouldn't hurt them...*

Dragon collides with Val, sinking its claws into her underbelly. They lock together, thrashing and twisting in midair. Their shrieks tear my ears and the sky itself. The world spins upside down, and my hand starts to slip. There's no recovering from this.

Summoning all my courage, I let go, tucking my shield beneath my legs. I cling to its sides like a kid sledding down a steep hill, only I'm dropping straight down without anything to slow my descent. My heart lurches up into my throat, pounding wildly, and I can't breathe.

I hit the ground with another shockwave of pain. A geyser of rubble spouts around me, and I throw my arms up to protect my head. My shield slides several yards down the mountain before catching on a jagged rock, sending me sprawling.

Bruised, bleeding, but alive, I roll onto my back to get my bearings. Scrolling words swim before my eyes, and at first I think I'm hallucinating. Then the blurred letters solidify into a single line, an actual sentence, and I realize it's an alert.

New Message From: Veronica Cross.

Chapter 17

OF ALL THE PEOPLE in the world who could be calling me right now, Veronica Cross is at the absolute bottom of the list. I have no fucking clue where the CEO of Axys Generations got my number or why she's contacting me. My first instinct is to dismiss the alert, but the message is already playing. I'm still dazed, so I end up listening.

"Ms. Nevares, return this call at your earliest convenience. I have information that will help you destroy Dragon." That's it. Just two sentences said in a calm, businesslike tone. I didn't know destroying Dragon was on Cross' to-do list, but I don't believe she wants to 'help me' for a second.

I raise my hand to swipe the alert away, but then I catch sight of Val through the smog. She tumbles toward the ground as Dragon wheels above her. They crow victoriously as Val hits the side of the mountain, throwing up a shower of rubble.

Fuck. I might not have a choice.

I clamber to my feet, retrieve my shield, and touch the call back button hovering beside my face. As I break into a stumbling jog, each step sending a jolt of pain through my entire body, a window appears beside my head, moving as I do. Within is Veronica Cross, pale, beautiful, and obnoxious, like a pop-up advertisement.

The volcano roars, and a powerful quake almost sends me sprawling. "What?" I demand, deflecting another surprise shower of lava. It drums down on my shield like hail, hissing as it scatters around my feet.

"Considering your current situation, I'll dispense with the pleasantries, Ms. Nevares," Cross says, not at all fazed by the sight of me climbing an erupting volcano. Her empty smile is unwavering. "After Ms. Delaney left my employ, I took possession of her research. She coded a specialized program to destroy Dragon, just in case."

"If that's true, why give it to me?" I shout in disbelief. My eyes dart between Cross, who looks perfectly calm; Val, who has picked herself up out of a pterosaur-shaped crater about ten yards ahead; and Dragon, who's folding their wings for a steep dive.

"I still want to create my own FRAI, but Dragon is too dangerous to exist," Cross says. "I can't work with something so unpredictable. Besides, I have it on good authority that Dragon has seized control of Ford Andrews' jack, and his brain as well. If Dragon is destroyed, my biggest competitor will be, too."

I feel like I'm staring at a puzzle with half the pieces missing while a tornado siren goes off in the background. I trust Cross about as far as I can throw her, but I don't have the luxury of saying no.

"What's the catch?" I ask, breaking into a run.

"No catch," Cross says. "I'm sending you the file now. Just download it. Get rid of Dragon and Andrews for me. You'll be doing me a favor."

I don't have a choice. "Fine, send it!"

"File sent," Veronica says. "A pleasure working with you, Ms. Nevares." A golden spear, around four feet long, appears in my free hand, glowing with otherworldly light. The moment it does, the call window closes. Cross disappears as though she was never there at all.

I stare at the spear, wondering what in the world Cross has given me. I didn't scan it before download—a cardinal sin—but there's no time. Just ahead, Dragon is closing in on Val's prone form, another Puls.wav building in their open maw like a black ball of fire.

Suddenly, the glow atop the volcano dims. The column of smoke belching from its peak dies off. Ash and lava stop raining down, and the rumbling is gone. Jones! Has to be. He's stopped the detonation, at least temporarily. Distracted, Dragon whips their head to observe.

I seize my chance, throwing the spear with all my might. The golden shaft flies through the air, and its tip strikes true. The moment it pierces Dragon's chest, they rear back, screeching in anguish. Their open mouth fires Puls.wavs wildly into the air, lighting up the ash-strewn sky with more brilliant flashes.

Val staggers, collapsing onto her side. She shrinks, wavering in and out of focus as I rush toward her, but Dragon grabs my attention. Their avatar flickers too, like a monitor during a brown-out. Their small, blue ringed eyes fix directly on me, and their maw opens, but no shrieks or Puls.wavs come. Dragon falls to the ground, limp and unmoving, the spear piercing their concave ribs. A moment later, both Dragon and spear dissolve completely.

I hurry to crouch by Val's side. Her avatar has returned to normal: a dark skinned woman in a purple blouse, hair elegantly twisted atop her head. She smiles at me as I slide an arm under her shoulders, helping her sit up. "Elena. You saved me. Thank you."

"Of course. Familia es toda."

An ominous rumbling interrupts our moment. The ground beneath us quakes as more burning ash sputters from the volcano's peak. Fuck! Apparently, Jones didn't manage to stop the eruption, he only slowed it down. "Stay here," I say to Val, lowering her back to the ground. "I'm going up."

If Val objects, I don't hear it. I sprint for the volcano's rim, holding my shield overhead to protect me. My heart pounds, my lungs burn with effort as I forge a path through the thickening smoke. My brain knows I'm in a life-or-death situation, so in meatspace, my body must think it's in danger, too.

At the top of the volcano, I find Jones standing before a bubbling pit of bright red lava. Beams of blue ice shoot from his hammer, momentarily freezing portions, but the pot's about to boil over. "Elena," he cries, his brown eyes wide with terror. "Get out of here! This thing's about to blow. I can't slow it down for much longer."

My mind races. I don't have any junk data programs that would stop something like this. At least, nothing good enough to deal with a Dragon coded detonation program. Fuck, fuck, fuck! This eruption is happening whether we're ready or not...

All I can do is try to contain it.

"Get back," I tell Jones. "If this doesn't work, do whatever it takes to slow the eruption down. Find and protect Sprout's life support systems."

"But—"

"Just do it!"

I don't wait to see if Jones follows my instructions. Instead, I slam my shield on the ground beside the volcano's rim. My trusty shield. My namesake. The most impressive custom program I've ever designed. It's a weapon as well as a means of defense, and right now, I need it to be both. I need it to protect an entire intranet system.

Under my command, my shield grows bigger and bigger, larger than I've ever made it before. Large enough to cover the top of the *volcano in a giant pink cap. Its nine glowing white spikes pierce the smoky sky, shining bright amidst the billowing black clouds of ash.*

Then, I wait.

BOOM.

The world shakes. I lose my balance, catching myself on my hands right before I hit the ground. Atop the volcano, my shield glows so bright I can't bear to look. A blinding flash of white, and—nothing.

As the light fades and the smoke disperses, I finally survey the scene. My gigantic shield is cracked in several places along its edge, but still in one piece. I start to laugh when I notice that the cracks are filled in with the familiar sheen of blue ice.

"Elena!" I turn to see Jones standing behind me, panting as he hefts his hammer over his shoulder. Apparently, he didn't listen to my orders at all. "You did it! You actually fucking did it!"

I laugh, finally starting to breathe normally. At least my lungs are functioning again. "Yeah. We did it. I'm glad you didn't leave me hanging, despite what I said."

Suddenly, I'm absolutely exhausted. Adrenaline was the only thing keeping me going through that nightmare, and now all my energy has been sapped away. The world spins again, although much less dangerously than before, and my body gives out. I lie down before I fall down, staring up at the sky. The clouds of ash have finally started to dissipate, showing streaks of pale blue behind them.

logging off network
disconnection complete

"Elena? Come on. Stay with me, baby girl."

I blink, trying to make sense of my surroundings. I don't fully remember jacking out, so Val or Jones must have helped me, but I'm not connected to Sprout's intranet system anymore. I'm lying beside an empty chair in the security booth, wrapped in a pair of strong arms with my face pressed against a smooth leather jacket.

"M'fine," I mumble to the two Sashas swimming above me. "Just. Done."

"Don't say that shit," the Sashas growl, holding me even tighter. "Don't even think it."

"Come on, Sasha. Lay her down so I can look at her." That's Doc's voice, sounding far more authoritative than a kid her age ever should.

As my vision stabilizes, I realize she's crouched beside us, looking unusually calm. She's in medic mode.

"I'm fine," I insist, speaking a bit more clearly.

Still, Sasha doesn't let go until Val's voice comes through the security booth's speakers. *"Elena's vitals indicate extreme exhaustion, but her neural pathways are undamaged. With rest and fluids, she should recover in a matter of hours."*

"I'll be the judge of that, thanks," Doc says. "Let her go, Sasha."

Reluctantly, Sasha lays me down on the floor, though she remains kneeling by my side. Doc activates her VIS-R, scanning me while I lie there, glad to be staying still. None of the injuries I received on the intranet should have translated to my real body, but the memories of pain and fear are fresh. Dragon's programs did a number on me.

"The others?" I ask once I've regained a bit of strength.

"Cherry, Rami, and Flygirl are neutralizing the explosives in the escape tunnel. Rock, Kyra, and LeRoy are making sure PGS privsec has fully retreated. Ocho is...physically fine." Doc doesn't say more, but a worried wrinkle forms in her brow.

Physically fine? That can't be good.

"So everyone's okay?" Jones asks. He's still in his seat, although he's slumped against the backrest. Without waiting for a response from Doc or Sasha, he activates his VIS-R. "Kyra, we secured Sprout's intranet security. What about you?" He pauses, then smiles. "Really? Great. Can you get some jackers up here to run the usual system checks? Elena and I are wiped."

Wiped doesn't even begin to cover it. My vision starts blurring again, although if I blink hard enough, the picture stabilizes. I focus on Sasha. Sasha, whose hand hasn't left my arm since she laid me down on the floor. Her touch is warm and heavy through my shirt sleeve, and it makes everything better.

"Cross," I tell her. "She called me..."

"Cross?" Sasha's brown eyes widen. "As in, Veronica Cross?"

"I will explain, Elena," Val says. *"For now, allow Sasha and Doc to transport you to Sprout's medical ward. You should rest."*

"But—"

"Dragon's servers were destroyed. I know you dislike percentages, but I am ninety-nine point seven percent certain."

I crack a grin. "In this case, I like those odds."

"So rest," Sasha says, stroking my hair back from my forehead. "Okay?"

"But—"

"Sasha's right." Doc deactivates her VIS-R, smiling at me for the first time. "Val was right, too. Your vitals are mostly fine. Blood sugar's extremely low, though. Your brain just ran a marathon and your body didn't like it. Sasha, I don't want her walking. Can we get a stretcher in here?"

Sasha snorts. Her answer is to scoop me up, cradling me against her chest. I let my head fall onto her shoulder, nose against her neck, cheek smushed into her jacket. I don't have any more energy to give, even if I wanted to. All I can do is let Sasha do the heavy lifting for a while. Literally.

Chapter 18

WHEN I OPEN MY eyes, it's to the stark whiteness of a hospital room. I yawn, feeling my ears pop, and blink the blurriness from my eyes. I vaguely remember being carried to Sprout's medical ward, but I don't know how long I've been out. Hospitals are strange places outside of time, with their unchanging fluorescent lights.

"Hey, sleepy."

My lips twitch into a smile as I turn toward the sound of Sasha's voice. Beneath the smell of disinfectant, I catch a whiff of her cologne. She's sitting beside my bed, looking as tired as I feel. Her eyes are half-lidded, with noticeable bags beneath them.

"Let me guess," I rasp, working through the first stage of my morning voice. "You haven't slept since I've been in here."

Sasha reaches across the bed to take my hand. "It's only been twelve hours."

"Twelve hours? *Dios mio.*" I sit up, combing the hand Sasha isn't holding through my tangled hair. "Some nap, huh?"

"Speaking of naps, look." Sasha nods toward a corner of the room, where I'm treated to one of the most adorable sights ever. Ocho, Cherry, Rami, Rock, and Doc are cuddled in a nest of starched white hospital pillows and blankets. Although Rami cracks their eyes open, smiling at me with their head resting in Cherry's lap and their legs on Rock's, the others remain asleep.

"They haven't left either, have they?"

"Nope." Sasha continues running her thumb over my knuckles. "Your brothers wanted to stay, but Abuela insisted they get some food and rest. I promised to text them as soon as you woke up." Sasha doesn't let go of my hand to do so, but Rami sits up, very carefully so as not to wake the cuddle pile, and slips out of the room, possibly to retrieve my family.

I frown. "Sprout's citizens are out of the bunkers? Is that safe?"

"For the moment? Yes. In the near future? We don't know," Sasha says. "There's been no further signs of PGS, and Val did some fact-checking while you were out. Cross was telling the truth about Andrews. At some point, Dragon took control of his jack and his brain. When you killed Dragon, he...stopped functioning. His death is all over the news upstairs."

"Cross must be thrilled," I mutter. "But at least that's two of our enemies gone..."

"And one in prime position to grab the lion's share of the tech market." Sasha sighs. "Here, I'll let Val tell you. Val? Elena's awake."

"I am aware, and extremely relieved," Val says through my ear mods. *"However, I stopped observing when I realized you were engaged in a private conversation."*

"It's fine," I tell her. "You okay? That was a rough fight."

"I am functioning as normal. However, it was distressing to see you in danger."

That's probably the understatement of the year, but I'm beyond relieved that Val's in good virtual health. "Glad to hear it. I was really worried about you, too."

"You saved me, Elena. I could not have defeated Dragon or protected Sprout without your assistance."

"Or Cross," I add, grudgingly.

"You made a choice. It carried considerable risk, but we are alive. Our enemies are dead. Future consequences may arise, but I believe it was the correct decision."

Val has a point but thinking about Cross and her timely offer of help still makes my stomach ache, like I've eaten something spoiled. Then again, that's usually how I feel when dealing with her. "We should be extra careful. Cross is up to something. Sprout is a threat to everything AxysGen and the other corps stand for."

"If any corporate forces come for Sprout, we'll be ready," Sasha says. "Cherry cleared the explosives from the escape tunnel, so we have a way out, at least."

I smile, looking over at Cherry. She's got her head lolled back against a pillow sliding partway down the wall, and she's snoring pretty loud. No wonder she's tired, if she was on bomb removal duty.

"It might reassure you to hear that I retraced Dragon's digital trail after their demise," Val says. *"In addition to controlling Andrews' jack, they utilized Paragon Solutions' intranet system to activate the mechs and organize an accompanying privsec team. I do not believe the board of directors is aware of Sprout, although I suspect they will be extremely*

unhappy to discover that over two dozen advanced mechs and an entire infiltration team have gone missing."

That makes me feel a bit better. Wish I could be a spyder on the wall for *that* board meeting. I hope Val is right about PGS' obliviousness because they'd wipe Sprout off the map in a heartbeat if they knew where it was. All I can do is trust that Kyra and her crew are watching out for a second wave of enemies, whether from PGS or AxysGen. Hopefully, they have a plan for Sprout's future safety, too.

"How are the Corsairs doing? You know, since..." My voice trails off. They've got to be hurting after Ginger's betrayal.

"Not great," Sasha admits. "But they'll work through it. They've got a community to care for."

Our discussion is interrupted as the door to my room opens. Mateo steps in first, cautiously, until he meets my eyes and realizes I'm awake. He scurries forward and hops onto the foot of the hospital bed, almost kneeing me in the crotch as he crawls into my lap.

"Ten cuidado," Abuela scolds him, entering on Rami's arm. "Elena needs rest."

"I'm fine, Abuela. C'mere, Teo."

"Are you really better now, Elena?" Mateo asks despite my assurances. He gazes up at me with worried brown eyes, and I feel awful for scaring him.

I pull him close, kissing the top of his head. "I'm gonna be fine. I just overdid it while jacking."

"For real?"

"Your sister is telling the truth, Mateo," Val says, projecting her voice from Sasha's pocket. As she speaks, Sasha takes out her databox and places it on a small table beside my bed so the sound won't be muffled. *"A bad guy tried to hack Sprout's intranet system, but Elena and I stopped them."*

"A bad guy?" Mateo asks. "What kind of bad guy?"

"Was it corps jackers?" Jacobo asks, looking much too interested.

"Jacobo." Abuela shoots him a disapproving glare. Along with Rami, she comes to stand on the side of my bed opposite Sasha, cupping my cheeks and kissing my forehead. "Elena is still resting. She doesn't need to answer your questions."

"Sorry, Abuela," Jacobo mumbles.

Rami snickers while I roll my eyes. I hurry the conversation along in the hopes that maybe Abuela will stop ragging on me and let go of my face. "It's fine, Abuela. So, what's in the tub? Smells like meatball soup."

"Of course," Abuela says. *"Jacobo, dáselo."*

Jacobo passes it over while Mateo rolls off my lap to snuggle in beside me on the narrow bed. There's barely enough room, but he manages to find a spot.

"You better give me a taste," Sasha says as she swivels the bed's built in tray in front of me.

"No way." I set the container down and pop off the lid, moaning in anticipation. "Mmm. *Gracias,* Abuela. This will make me feel a million times better."

"No fair." The statement doesn't come from Sasha but from Doc, who has woken up thanks to all the commotion. Groggily, the rest of my crew untangles from the pile, clambering to their feet. They crowd around the bed, but instead of feeling claustrophobic with so many bodies on all sides, I feel surrounded by love.

My family is here. My entire family. It's a miracle we all made it out alive, but we did.

"I agree with Doc," Val says. *"It is unfair. At times like this, I wish I possessed a sense of taste."*

"Can't help you there, Val, but I'll tell you what, *pequeña,* once you give me the all clear, I'll make meatball soup for everyone. Mine's not quite as good as Abuela's, but it's close."

"You'll get there," Abuela says. "I've had eighty years to learn. And I can make more soup. You should be resting."

Doc grins at me. "You realize I have extra incentive to convince Dr. Stone to release you early now, right?"

I wink. "All part of the plan. So, Dr. Stone is my doctor too?"

"Yeah. She volunteered. She'll be happy to hear you're awake."

Rock reaches over my tray to unsnap the spoon from the built in holder on the lid, practically forcing it into my hand. He stares expectantly until I actually eat a mouthful. As soon as the taste hits, I realize I'm ravenous. I eat like I haven't eaten in a week, slurping and almost spilling some down my chin.

"Careful, *chaparrita,"* Cherry drawls, gesturing at my hospital gown. "You'll ruin your couture."

I stick out my tongue at her. "You're just sulky it isn't the kind that shows my a—" I remember that Mateo is still beside me and catch myself at the last minute. "Butt."

Mateo giggles, while Abuela just shakes her head.

That's when I notice one person missing from our little group. Although Ocho got up from the pile with everyone else, she hasn't come over with them. She hovers a few feet away, a blanket wrapped tight around her shoulders.

I exchange a silent look with Sasha, who rises and heads in Ocho's direction. They step to one side of the room, whispering together, while Rami helps Abuela sit in the chair instead.

"Gracias, radiante," she says. That's her nickname for Rami since it's one of the few Spanish words that isn't gendered. Although Rami is fine with any pronouns, it's a sweet gesture on Abuela's part.

Rami gives Abuela's shoulder a gentle squeeze. *"De nada, bella."*

Abuela laughs. "Terrible. Your wife will think I'm trying to steal you away."

"Take them, *please,*" Cherry says with a mock groan. "Doesn't matter how many credits Sasha brings in. I'm flat broke from paying for all their cosmetics." From her tone, and Rami's smirk, I can tell Cherry's joking. Their relationship seems to be on decent footing again. Not that I thought they'd ever split or anything, but it made me uneasy to see them at odds.

While they banter, I steal another glance at Sasha and Ocho. They're still whispering, and Sasha has a comforting hand on Ocho's shoulder. When they notice me looking, Sasha gives Ocho a gentle nudge. Everyone parts to let her through.

"Sorry," Ocho mumbles, avoiding my eyes. The blanket trails behind her as she shuffles forward. "I just…I was worried. About you. It was hard to see you in the hospital, even though I knew you'd be okay."

I shoot Ocho a wink. "No need to worry. I'm fine. Right, Doc?"

"Right," Doc says. "Her brain was fried after all that jacking, but not *fried* fried, if you know what I mean."

Ocho blinks, confused. "No?"

"Short answer is, Dr. Stone will probably let Elena leave after she finishes her soup."

That puts Ocho at ease. Her shoulders relax, and she manages a weak smile. "Good." Still, something seems…off. Maybe that isn't so strange, since we've been through something terrifying today. It's no surprise that Ocho's still processing it all.

I put on a chipper voice and say, "You know what? In a couple days, Sprout's mechanics will need help fixing the damaged shuttles in the hangar. Maybe you should help?"

"That'd be cool, Ocho," Jacobo says, picking up on what I'm doing. "When we were in Barbados, you talked a lot about working on shuttles."

Ocho's face brightens even more. "Yeah? You think they'd let me?"

"I see no reason why not," Val says. *"You were granted permission to work on the shuttles before."*

Sasha rubs the middle of Ocho's back. "I think you'd be a big help."

"Okay," Ocho says with growing enthusiasm. At that same moment, her stomach lets out a loud rumble. She shrugs sheepishly, putting a hand on her belly. "Sorry."

I pass her the rest of my soup, which has about a third left. "Here. Eat up, *gatita.*"

"No fair," Doc protests. "Ocho gets some, but I don't? I'm the kid here."

"My soup, my rules," I tell her. "And technically, Ocho's younger than you."

Doc huffs, flipping her hair.

"Ah, *pequeña,*" Abuela says, clicking her tongue fondly at Doc. "I'll make you plenty of soup. Elena, shame on you, starving this poor child."

"Abuela, I'm literally in the hospital. I just woke up."

"So, should I actually eat this, or...?" Ocho says, brow furrowed, spoon hovering just above the soup.

"Eat it," several people say at once, myself among them.

Taking them at their word, Ocho tips the rest of the soup into her mouth without even bothering to use the spoon. I exchange smiles with Sasha. Despite all we've been through and all we still have left to face, I think everything's going to be all right.

Chapter 19

"CAREFUL, TEO." I TAKE the glue bottle from Mateo's dangerously dipping hand, applying a few dots to the flat piece of wood he's holding. "Less is more. If you stain the coffee table, Abuela will blame me."

"I wasn't gonna stain it." Mateo pouts as he slots the wooden piece into the miniature water wheel he's making. Most of his homework so far has been hands-on, which I appreciate. It's much more fun than online worksheets, for me as well as him. However, some of his projects tend to get messy, and this one is no exception. It will only get messier once we introduce actual water.

I take another look at the instruction sheet. "Okay. Now we glue the cups to the edges of the wheel spokes." I pass the paper to Mateo, fixing him with my patented big sister stare. "Be careful. Promise?"

"Yeah, I promise," Mateo says.

My face softens. "Here." I pass him the glue and a grin breaks across his face. To his credit, he's very careful as he attaches each tiny wooden cup to the ends of the spokes.

"Looking good, Teo," says Jacobo, walking in from the kitchen. There's a half-eaten sandwich in his hand, and judging from his muffled words, the other half is already in his mouth.

"It's a water wheel," Mateo informs him, holding up the half-completed project.

I hurry to support the wobbly spokes. "You have to let it dry before you lift it," I say, lowering it back onto the paper towels we're using to protect the coffee table.

"Cool," Jacobo says. "Hey, Elena, can we talk?" Judging by his tone and the dart of his eyes, he means in private.

"Sure. Keep gluing, Mateo." With a groan, I push myself up from my seated position. *Dios.* Only twenty-nine and it's already a struggle to get off the damn floor. I don't know how Abuela still gets around as well as she does at eighty-something.

Once I'm standing beside him, Jacobo leans in and whispers. "I heard crying from Ocho's room just now. Maybe you should check on her?"

I squeeze his shoulder. "Thanks. Keep an eye on Teo for a minute while you finish your sandwich?"

"Sure." Jacobo plops down in my abandoned spot, pulling the water wheel diagram toward him. "This looks pretty cool, actually. You know Sprout actually gets most of its energy from geothermal activity? My class visited the power generators."

"Were they big?" Mateo asks. "Did you take pictures?"

While Jacobo describes his field trip, I slip out of the living room and down the hall toward the bedrooms. Partway there, I hear muffled sobbing from Ocho's room, just like Jacobo said.

I edge toward the door, rapping lightly. "Ocho? Can I come in?"

"Come in," a low voice says.

I slip into Ocho's bedroom, only to find that she isn't alone after all. Sasha sits next to Ocho on the bed, an arm wrapped around her shoulders.

"Sorry." I hesitate in the doorway. "I heard crying, but didn't know you were here with her."

"It's okay," Sasha says. "Right, Ocho?"

Ocho sniffs and nods, wiping her eyes with the back of her hand. Her face is covered in wet, shiny tear streaks, and her nose and eyes look puffy, like she's been crying for a while. "Oh. Um. Hi, Elena."

I join them on the bed, sitting on Ocho's other side. "What's wrong?"

Ocho blinks back some more tears, taking a few shaking breaths. "G—Ginger..."

Suddenly, I understand. Although Ocho has spent a few afternoons in the hangar, helping Sprout's mechanics to repair the shuttles as we suggested, she's spent a lot of time in bed, too. I haven't caught her crying before now, but I've noticed her listless mood. She smiles less. Laughs only rarely. Some of the bubble and pep that makes her so distinct from Sasha is gone.

I lean in for a hug, which Ocho accepts gratefully, while Sasha's strong arm remains wrapped around her shoulders. Her body trembles between us at first, but the shaking stops rather quickly. Her breathing soon evens out. "Sorry. Just." She pauses, sniffing. "It's a lot, you know?"

"None of us like killing people," I say, hoping I can find the words Ocho needs to hear. "It's an awful feeling. But you made the right choice. If you hadn't shot Ginger, she could have hit the detonator."

Ocho sighs. "That's what Sasha told me."

Sasha removes her arm, placing a comforting palm on Ocho's back and rubbing a small circle there. "See? Elena agrees with me, so that means we're right."

I chuckle. "Dunno about that. Sometimes my judgment is pretty shitty."

"Fair enough," Sasha says. "But we're right about this. Trust me, Ocho. It might not feel this way right now, but…it's good that you feel bad. Killing people should never be easy."

"When Sprout was under attack, Kyra did it without blinking," Ocho says. "The rest of our crew has killed people too, but I never, ever want to kill anyone again. So…maybe it's best if I'm not part of the family anymore. I'm sorry if that means I'm disappointing you, Sasha, but I can't do that again. I just can't."

My mouth falls open. "What?" The thought that Ocho thinks being a family means being part of a crew is something I never even considered. And she's been keeping all of this to herself for two weeks? No wonder she broke down.

Sasha frowns, hastening to reassure her. "Ocho, you don't have to be in the field to be part of our family. Look at me?"

Reluctantly, Ocho raises her chin. Fresh tears swim in her dark eyes.

"You will always be my family," Sasha says, locking gazes with her. "Whether you do missions or not doesn't matter. Even sharing genes doesn't matter. You're part of our family because we want you to be."

"Exactly," I say. "Love is what makes a family, and we all love you, Ocho. We're the Lucky Eight now, no matter what."

Ocho's eyes widen as she looks from me to Sasha. "Really? You'd change the name of the crew for me?"

I also look at Sasha. It's technically up to her as our handler, I guess, although I can't possibly see her saying no.

Sasha rubs one of Ocho's shoulders, offering reassurance. "As far as I'm concerned, we've already been the Lucky Eight for a while now. Long past time we formalized it, don't you think?"

Ocho manages a genuine smile. She hugs Sasha again, although her tears seem relieved rather than devastated. "I'm so glad you woke me up, Sasha. Even if it hurts. You could've left me in the tube or gotten rid of me, but you didn't."

"I'd never do that," Sasha says. "The world is a nightmare sometimes, but it's not all bad. There's good stuff, too. Stuff you deserve to experience."

"Music," Ocho says.

"Right," I say. "Dancing, reading a book on the beach, joining a crew..."

Ocho's smile falters. "I'm sorry Ginger can't do that stuff anymore. Sometimes when I'm smiling, or laughing, or even just breathing, I think about how she can't. Because of me."

I reach into Ocho's lap, taking one of her hands. "I know it's hard, but part of being alive is regretting our choices and trying to make better ones. You respect life a lot more now."

"Not wanting to kill anyone again doesn't make you weak," Sasha adds. "It means you're growing into a good person. Probably a better person than me, to be honest. That's all I wanted for you from the beginning."

"I don't want to be better than you, though," Ocho says. "I just want to be me."

Sasha bumps her shoulder softly against Ocho's. "That's what I want, too."

"I'm really hungry now," Ocho says, surprising both of us as she releases my hand and stands up from the bunk. "Does being sad make most people more hungry, or is it just me?"

"Most people," Sasha informs her. "I haven't eaten yet, either. Let's see if the rest of the Lucky Eight will have lunch with us."

Ocho nods eagerly. "We can tell them about the name at lunch. Right, Elena?"

"Sure. I'll fix us something once I make sure Mateo hasn't ruined the coffee table."

"Why'd you come back here, anyway?" Sasha asks as we head out of the bedroom and into the hallway, with Ocho taking the lead. "I thought you were helping Mateo with homework."

"Oh, right. Jacobo told me I should check on Ocho."

Sasha smiles. "He's a good kid. How is he doing, by the way?"

"Better day by day," I tell her. "There's some fear and guilt, but in person school has been really good for him." I lower my voice and smirk. "I think he has a crush on one of the girls in his class."

Sasha raises an eyebrow. "Really? Good luck with that, Nevares."

"Yeah," I groan. "Don't rub it in."

"I'll rub what I want, when I want," Sasha declares.

I roll my eyes and tap my hip against her upper thigh on the way into the living room. "Isn't it more fun if I rub it for you, though?"

"Cool it, perv," Sasha says. "Innocent ears ahead."

"You started it!"

Luckily, the boys aren't listening. Ocho has joined them at the coffee table, admiring the water wheel while Mateo explains it to her with unbridled enthusiasm. They look pretty cute, clustered around a shared project.

"Hey, Jacobo," I call. "Want to help me with lunch, or help Mateo with his water wheel? Your choice."

"Water wheel," Jacobo says, without even having to think about it. He's still engrossed in the project. "Here, Ocho. You put in this piece."

"Okay!"

"I'll help with lunch." Sasha offers me her elbow, dipping her head. "Shall we, Nevares?"

"Fine. But keep the groping to a minimum, or I'll fuck up whatever I make and Abuela will never let me live it down."

Rae D. Magdon

Chapter 20

"THE NAME OF THE game," Doc says, eyeing us all from the head of our apartment's rectangular kitchen table. "Is Screw Your Neighbor."

The entire Lucky Eight is in attendance, most with sweating drinks in hand, some alcoholic and others not. Since I already know the rules I only listen with half an ear, taking a sip from a refreshingly sweet glass of Riesling.

"Everyone gets a single card," Doc continues. "Look, but don't show anyone. Starting on the dealer's left, everyone keeps their card or steals the next person's. The dealer keeps their card or draws from the deck. Person with the lowest card loses a point. Lose five points, and you're out."

We have tiny silver screws from Cherry's lab—which is what Ginger's lab has pretty much become in the past week and a half—to represent our points. When Rami notices me looking at their screws, they lean forward, wrapping a protective forearm around them. "Don't even think about it."

"Who, me?" I poke out my lower lip, widening my eyes. "You're the cloak. If anyone's stealing screws, it's you."

"Trust me," Cherry says, waggling her eyebrows. "Rami doesn't have to steal screws. They get 'em for free."

A chorus of groans fills the kitchen.

"That was terrible," Sasha grumbles from her seat beside mine.

In the seat across from me, Rock just sighs and shakes his head.

"I agree," Val says. She's manifested her avatar using her databox which rests on the table's edge near Rock's elbow.

"You're an AI," Cherry points out. "What do you know about humor?"

"A great deal," Val responds. "In fact, I have studied many forms of humor in order to improve my algorithms. Sarcasm, gallows humor, puns—"

"Ex-*cuse* me." Doc clears her throat. "I'm not finished, assholes."

I try to pay attention, but a sneaky hand brushes my thigh under the table, squeezing my knee. Sasha shoots me a sly smile, and I'm distracted all over again. The Riesling has my body buzzing with a pleasant warmth, but Sasha's touch kicks it into overdrive.

"Kings are high, so if you get dealt one, turn it face-up. Your neighbor can't steal from you. Aces are low." Doc aims a positively evil grin at all of us. "That's it. Have fun losing."

"We'll see, *cerebro,*" Cherry says, pulling the deck of cards toward her. "Ocho, you good?" she asks as she deals a single card to everyone around the table.

Ocho nods, smiling happily. "Yeah, I understand." Since her talk with Sasha, her mood's been much brighter. She seems eager to spend time with the crew today.

"Even with card counting abilities, I am not guaranteed to win," Val muses. "This is, in essence, a bluffing game."

"You aren't allowed to analyze our body language, either," Cherry says, fixing Val with a suspicious glare. "I know your tricks."

Val tilts her head. "Why not? Do the rest of you not look for 'tells' when you play these kinds of games?"

"She has a point," Rami says.

"I guess..."

"Can we play already?" Doc says, flipping her card. She trades it to Rock, who looks at it, rumbles, then swaps it for Sasha's. Wrinkling her nose, Sasha passes it on to me.

I already have my suspicions before I flip it over to look.

A fucking two. Of course. Thanks, Doc.

"Screw your neighbor is right," I say, swapping the two for Ocho's card. I end up with a five, which isn't much better, and since the dealer can swap the card out for one from the deck, there's no guarantee the two will stay in play.

Stifling a mischievous giggle, Ocho passes the card along to Val. "This particular avatar is not made of hard light," she reminds us. "Ocho, please show me the card?"

Ocho does, dutifully making sure no one else sees.

"I want to steal," Val says instantly.

Rami takes the hot potato card and passes theirs over to Val. "Wow, is it really that bad?" They take a look and roll their eyes. "Ugh." Placing the card face down on the table, they slide it over to Cherry with a bat of their long, fake eyelashes. "For you, my love."

"Gee, thanks." Cherry flips the card over, sighs, and draws from the top of the deck. "Ha! A fucking queen. Serves y'all right."

The rest of us flip over our cards. Unfortunately, my five is the lowest. "Eat my entire ass," I huff, tossing one of my screws into the middle of the table. It clatters and skids a few inches before spinning to a stop.

Cherry opens her mouth to say something filthy, only to end up with an elbow in her ribs courtesy of Rami. She winces as she gathers the played cards into a discard pile, then passes the remainder of the deck to Doc.

We make it through two more rounds, which I don't lose despite the Riesling and the warm, weighty presence of Sasha's hand on my thigh. It slides higher, kneading slowly. My heart beats faster. I struggle not to squirm in my seat.

Salvation comes thanks to the sound of the apartment's buzzer. "I'll get it!" I hop up before anyone else can volunteer. As much as I'm enjoying Sasha's under the table groping—and I am enjoying it, as the growing slickness in my panties attests—we're still having family game night, after all. I could use a second to cool down.

When I reach the front door, standing on tiptoe to check the peephole, four smiling faces are waiting for me. Jones, Flygirl, and LeRoy stand in the hallway, with Kyra slightly out of view. I open the door, stepping aside so they can come in. *"Buenas noches,* buds. To what do we owe the pleasure?"

"No, it's our pleasure," Flygirl says. She bounces on her toes, practically vibrating with excitement. "Please, let me be the first to congratulate you as I present you with these!" She flips her hands out dramatically from behind her back, revealing a stack of small, laminated ID cards.

It takes me a moment, but then a huge grin spreads across my face. "Really? Already?"

"Yep," LeRoy says, grinning. "You're officially residents now—you, your brothers, and your abuela. Congrats!"

A floaty feeling that has nothing to do with the wine courses through me. Residents. Aside from maybe Mexico as a general country, I've never been proud to be a resident of anywhere. Most of my adult life was spent globetrotting without any opportunity to put down roots. The sting growing in my eyes takes me by surprise.

"You okay, Elena?" Jones asks, his brow furrowed with concern beneath his shaggy mop of black hair.

I sniff, swiping at my eyes with my sleeve. "Yeah, I'm great. Thanks. I just...I'm happy."

Kyra closes the door behind her, taking her place beside the rest of the Corsairs. "Glad to hear it, Nevares." Even her normally stoic expression carries a small smile this time. "I really hope you and your family will be happy here. After saving Sprout, you and your crew have earned it."

I search Kyra's face for any hint of sadness, since we're talking crews, but if she's feeling any bittersweetness, I can't see it. I resign myself to not knowing how she feels about Ginger, other than what I can reasonably guess. Surely, she must be angry and hurt somewhere beneath that calm, cool exterior. I hope the Corsairs have been able to help each other through it like my crew would in similar circumstances...

That gives me an idea.

"Why not tell the others in person? We're all here, except my brothers and Abuela are watching a movie next door. I'll take theirs over first thing tomorrow." I know Abuela in particular will be thrilled. I can already picture the deep wrinkles around her smile as I hand her the card.

"Yeah?" LeRoy cranes his neck, looking past me into the living room. "Where is everybody?"

"Kitchen," I say. "We're playing cards. Any interest in joining us? We'll find more seats somewhere." *Or use some laps for seats*, I think to myself, considering Sasha.

The Corsairs look at each other. Predictably, Flygirl is the first to voice her agreement. "Yeah! Sounds like fun. What game? Poker? Go Fish? Rummy? I'm an expert at all of 'em." She wanders past me, heading for the kitchen.

"Wait," Jones calls, extending a hand after her. "You never gave Elena her card."

"Right." Flygirl flips through the cards, thrusting one at me.

I examine my new ID. There isn't much information, just a headshot, a date of birth, and a ten-digit number, which I'm pleased to note ends in an eight. How appropriate.

"This means you and the others will be eligible for council duty, too," Kyra says. "Except Doc and your brothers, of course."

"Right." I tuck the card in my pocket. "No offense to Chance and the others, but I kind of hope I don't get selected for that duty."

"You and me both," LeRoy says.

"So, cards?" Jones asks. His eyes are bright and he seems eager to play.

"Cards," Kyra agrees. "But watch out, Nevares, because Flygirl isn't the only card shark on this crew."

I turn, heading back toward the kitchen, but I can't resist tossing one last retort over my shoulder. "Well, we have a FRAI on ours, so you'll have some stiff competition."

Rae D. Magdon

Chapter 21

download: spybot.exe
>_query=true

Congratulations! Spybot.exe has been successfully downloaded onto your jack.

spybot.exe
>_cloak.1.exe
>_cloak.2.exe

Congratulations! Songster 5.6 has completed its automatic update.

spybot.exe
>_keylog.exe
>_passwordrecovery

enter password: *********
>_query=true
welcome: user escudoespiga

settings:
share data with select advertisers and developers?
>_query=false
spybot.exe
>_override.exe
>_query=true

Thank you for sharing! Your data helps Axys Generations improve our products.

About Rae D. Magdon

Rae D. Magdon is a writer of queer and lesbian fiction. She believes everyone deserves to see themselves fall in love and become a hero: especially lesbians, bisexual women, trans women, and women of color. She has published over ten novels through Desert Palm Press, spanning a wide variety of genres, from Fantasy/Sci-Fi to Mysteries and Thrillers. She is the recipient of a 2016 Rainbow Award (Fantasy/Sci-Fi) and a twice-nominated GCLA finalist (Fantasy/Sci-Fi). When she isn't working on original projects, she spends her time writing fanfiction for Mass Effect, Legend of Korra, The 100, and Wynonna Earp.

Connect with Rae online

Facebook: Rae D. Magdon

Tumblr: https://raedmagdon.tumblr.com/

Twitter: Rae D. Magdon

Email: raedmagdon@gmail.com

Cover Design By : Rachel George
www.rachelgeorgeillustration.com

Note to Readers:

Thank you for reading a book from Desert Palm Press. We appreciate you as a reader and want to ensure you enjoy the reading process. We would like you to consider posting a review on your preferred media sites and/or your blog or website.

For more information on upcoming releases, author interviews, contest, giveaways and more, please sign up for our newsletter and visit us as at Desert Palm Press: www.desertpalmpress.com and "Like" us on Facebook: Desert Palm Press.

Bright Blessings